CW01646575

A.V. Pierce

# LOVE SEX & The Narcissist

Published by A.V. Pierce Press




ISBN: 978-3982790602
First edition.

Published and distributed by A.V. Pierce Press
A.V. Pierce
c/o Dein-Impressum
Stettiner Strasse 41
35410 Hungen

For permissions and enquiries: hello@avpierce.com
www.avpierce.com

# Love Sex & The Narcissist

A.V. Pierce

DISCLAIMER

This is a work of fiction. While parts of the story may have been inspired by real events, the characters, names, places, and incidents are products of my imagination or are used fictitiously. Any resemblance to actual persons, living or dead, or to real events is purely coincidental.

AUTHOR'S NOTE

Contemporary romantic fiction about emotionally complex love (not formula romance).

CONTENT WARNING

This story contains themes of psychological manipulation and emotional abuse (no physical abuse).

Cover design: Sarah Schaefer
Typeset: Sharlyne Schütter
Editing: Sarah Karwisch

*An ode to living a life true to yourself,*
*even when the world tries to hold you back.*

# Content

CHALLENGE 1

# Bold Move Moment

"Are you finally ready, Sophie girl?" Rani called through the closed sliding door between my bedroom and the living room. I heard Eliyah giggling.

"Just a moment," I said.

I stared at the mirror. At her. The new Sophie—dressed in colorful clothes, skin bare, lips bold. Someone meant to be seen.

Just three months ago, at a business event, shortly after my thirty-seventh birthday, I had caught the image of another version of me in the mirror and froze. Minutes later, I had broken down in the bathroom and resigned from my job.

It had all started an hour earlier that day, in the middle of a design science conference, with the announcement of my promotion.

*

I stood at a high table tucked in the corner of the corridor, flipping through my notes.

The buzz of the conference hall filtered in—doors opening and closing, soft conversations, the occasional burst of laughter from the main room.

My—back then—boss Kathrin approached, heels clicking. "Your panel starts in ten, Sophie," she said, glancing at her phone. "Do you have a minute for me?"

"Sure, what's up?"

"So, Sophie. This isn't official yet, but the board has decided." She leaned in slightly. "You got it."

"What—really? How did that happen so fast?" My lips lifted, but it felt mechanical.

"It was a pretty easy decision," she smiled. "They interviewed people from around the globe and didn't find anyone who even comes close. You've done an outstanding job over the years, and moving from Local to Global Design Director is a big step. Congrats. You've earned it."

She hugged me briefly—my arms barely moved—and rushed off. "I'm heading back in. See you in a bit."

*Something feels odd.*

I pick up my notes, hands moving without direction, and step into a hidden corner near the fire exit. People pass by without a glance.

I plant my hands on my hips.

Inhale.

Exhale.

Again.

My heart races—sharp and too fast.

I'd known this might happen eventually.

But not today.

Not like this.

I hadn't said yes.

Not to any of it.

*I'm the one who decides*, I remind myself.

*Global Behavioral Design Director for a prestigious flagship initiative, combating urban loneliness.* It sounds impressive.

It's everything I worked for. A dream, technically.

But it doesn't feel like it. Not right now. Not after those ten years of chasing, pushing, proving. Of working twice as hard as anyone else just to be seen, make it as a woman, surrounded by men.

Years of trying to become someone

—and somehow ending up further from myself than ever.

The air is thick, and my blazer scratches at the back of my neck. I press my hands to my hips again, trying to anchor myself.

"Ladies and gentlemen, the panel is about to start in five minutes," a voice booms overhead.

*Pull yourself together, Sophie. You can do it.*

I step out from the corner, and my eyes fall on Ben. He stands by the window, on the other side of the room, across from me. Laughing. My colleague Rebecca touches his hand, light and familiar, clearly intimate. Her thumb brushes along his knuckles.

***Of course**, he's with someone like her.*

Floating dress. Shiny hair. That effortless smile. She's the kind of woman who could wear a trash bag and still make people turn their heads.

I'm not even into Ben like that, though he's a catch. But if I were? No chance. Not as the Sophie I am right now, at least.

*Why do you think about Ben and Rebecca right now, Sophie? Focus.*

My legs feel slightly numb. I'm not sure if I'm cold or just floating.

Then I see it—My reflection in the mirror behind them.

—and freeze.

That dark, sad, professionally dressed version of me.

Drawn face. Dry, lifeless hair. An oversized black outfit swallowing my body.

The blazer's sharp. A designer piece. A power look.

But today, it doesn't work.

It hangs off me like armor I no longer believe in.

I don't look strong.

I look like I'm hiding—from the world, and myself.

For a moment, it feels like I'm looking at someone else entirely.

*Who is this?*

*Who the fuck am I?*

My mind scrambles. My chest tightens.

Thoughts scatter in every direction and land nowhere.

I begin to sweat, and my vision narrows.

*What is happening? Am I collapsing?*

"The panel is about to start," the voice echoes again, louder now, cutting through the noise in my head.

*Sophie, you have to go in.*

***Now.***

*You can do it.*

*Just give your usual performance.*

*Let the audience see the unshakable, flawless, witty version of you that got the promotion.*

I take a breath—deep, shaky—and walk into the hall.

I feel like a robot.

Rows of chairs. Dozens of faces. Eyes shifting toward the stage.

The moderator calls my name.

I step forward, legs shaking.

My heels feel too tight. Too loud.

I climb the steps, smile, and sit beside four other guests—top experts in their fields, like me.

The entire panel is a blur.

I'm on complete autopilot.

My lips move and words come out, but I don't hear any of them.

*I hope I'm not doing anything weird.*

*I hope no one notices I'm not really here.*

I glance around. Everything seems in check.

I spot my best friend Rani in the third row. Smiling at me.

And after what must be thirty minutes, based on the program, everyone starts clapping.

It's over.

*Thank god.*

The other guests get up, and so do I.

I step down from the stage, pass by people who want to shake my hand, ask questions, and chat. I don't stop.

Without a word, I slip into the bathroom and close the door behind me. My breath goes heavy. Fast.

*What on earth is this?*

My chest tightens, like a fist curling inward, and I can't get enough air.

The room tilts slightly—just enough to make me question if the floor is still solid.

My hands are shaking, fingers stiff and useless, like they belong to someone else.

*A panic attack.*

I press my back against the wall and try to breathe more slowly.

*In. Out.*

But it's too late.

My throat tightens, shrinking until each breath feels like pulling air through a pinhole.

My heart slams against my ribs—fast and loud, as if it's trying to claw its way out.

I grip the edge of the desk to ground myself, but everything feels distant. Muted. I can't hear the clapping anymore. I can't hear anything except the rush of blood in my ears and the voice in my head screaming

***—Get out. Get out. Get out.***

My knees buckle. I slide to the floor, arms wrapped around myself like that might hold me together. I don't know how long I sit like that—eyes wide, unblinking—just trying not to disappear completely.

A knock at the door. "Sophie?"

It's Rani. Her voice is low, careful. "Are you okay? You looked really pale."

I don't say anything.

"Sophie?"

I force myself up and open the door. "Rani, can you get me out of here? Just make sure no one talks to me. Just get me into a cab."

"Oh my god, girl. What's happening? Of course," she says. She takes my hand and walks me outside, stops a cab, and opens the front door next to the driver.

She slips the driver some money. "We are going to stay in Manhattan. Meatpacking District. Wait a few minutes, please—I need to grab her things."

"You get in the front, Sophie. I'll be back soon."

*

We stop at my favorite ice cream shop.

Rani guides me inside, her hand gently on my back like I'm something fragile, and steers me toward a corner booth. She gives me a playful nudge into the seat. "Okay, girl. What's it gonna be?"

"The magic cup."

Her mouth curves. "The magic **kids** cup?"

I nod, a small smile tugging at my lips. "With extra sprinkles and gummy bears."

"You got it, love," she says softly, then heads toward the counter.

I sink into the red leather bench, its cushion folding around me. The little shop hums around me—soft chatter, the churn of the ice cream machine, the occasional ding of the door.

I watch Rani at the counter, pointing and chatting with the woman behind the glass. Cupboards open, metal scoops clang. She's moving quickly and efficiently. Like she knows I don't have much energy left.

A few minutes later, she's back—juggling two massive cups of colorful ice cream, a tall glass of water, and a napkin rolled up with a cool compress.

She places it all in front of me like a small feast, then presses the damp cloth to the back of my neck.

I blink up at her.

"Now, what happened, Sophie?"

"I'm not sure. Maybe that's what they call a midlife crisis?" I laugh. I pause, then add, "I got the promotion..."

Her face lifts, eyes bright. "You did? Wow. That's incredible. You've wanted that for so long."

"Yeah... right. I did." I pick up the spoon, the metal cool against my fingers. "But when I actually got it, all I wanted was to get out of there. I'm exhausted."

Rani sits down across from me and takes my hand. "Well, you've always been working like crazy," she says with a soft smile.

"I don't think I saw you take a single free weekend in the last two years—for god's sake. But I thought you were happy."

I nod, dragging a spoonful of ice cream through the sprinkles before it melts.

"I know... so did I," I say, with a slight shrug. "I actually think I **was** for a long time. I **loved** my job and I **loved** working hard."

I pause, taking a bite of ice cream, cold and sweet, and let it melt in my mouth before I speak again. "You know what was the weirdest part?"

"What?"

"I was about to go on stage. And then I saw Ben, standing close to Rebecca—you know, the human magnet one I once told you about—and next to them was this mirror. I caught my reflection, and it suddenly felt like I couldn't breathe anymore."

I pause, the image still fresh.

Rani's spoon pauses midair. "Wait—are you into Ben?"

I shake my head. "No. That's the thing. I'm not. It wasn't about him. It was... for a second, it felt like I was looking into the future. Like a sneak preview of what my life might look like if I kept going the way I've been going; If I'd keep on being Business Sophie and nothing else: Tough. Polished. Successful. But not really living my life. Just... watching others living it, like a movie I'm not part of."

Rani doesn't say anything. Just looks at me, eyes softening.

I keep going. "I don't know... It was like there was this whole other world happening right in front of me—and I'd somehow locked myself out of it." I press my spoon into the ice cream, then set the tub down. The colors blur together in my cup, the gummy bears disappearing in it.

Rani reaches over and places a hand lightly on my arm. "Oh, Sophie girl. You can get back in there any time, you know."

I feel my energy return. My hands are steadier now.

I get up, grab my empty glass, and walk to the little sink in the back of the shop. Refill it with cold water. Then, I return to the table, still standing.

"Yes, I can." My voice lifts. "And you know what? I think this might actually be a really good thing." I take a sip and lean against the chair.

"Not the breakdown itself, obviously," I laugh. "But at least now I know my career isn't making me happy anymore. Not if it's **all** I do. People spend **a lot** of time and money in therapy to figure out stuff like this."

"Of course, you're already spinning this into a win. God, sometimes I wish the whole world had your optimism," Rani says with a smile, walking over.

"You go, girl." She looks at me with warmth in her eyes, her dark curls falling softly around her face. "If anyone knows how to flip the script and reinvent themselves, it's you."

She's right.

If there's one thing I know how to do, it's go all in. When I need or want something, I pour everything into it until it becomes real. I push, build, make it happen—it's what I've always done. It's the one thing I **could** do to get through the chaos of my childhood. Maybe it's drive. Maybe it's survival instinct. Probably both.

"Wait—is this one of our **bold move moments**?" Rani asks.

My face softens into a smile.

*Bold move moment.* It was our code—always had been—for those cliff-edge choices. The ones that felt terrifying, uncertain, but also somehow necessary.

Over the years, we'd pushed each other into them—jobs, breakups, cross-country moves, hard conversations. We never used the phrase lightly.

"Maybe," I say.

Rani glances at her phone. "Oh, shoot. I need to head home and make dinner for Rhea. She's probably back from school by now. Can I leave you alone, girl?"

"Of course you can."

"Okay. Let me know if you need anything," she says, grabbing her bag.

Then she pauses, smiles, and reaches into her coat pocket. "Almost forgot—here's your kids' cup surprise." She drops something small into my hand and pulls me into a warm hug. "Love you, Sophie."

"Love you too, Rani. Thanks for being there for me."

She leaves, the door closing softly behind her.

I look down.

Nestled in my palm is a tiny green smiley face with ridiculous, wobbly ears. I can't help but smile back.

I call a cab home, and when I finally hear the click of my apartment door behind me, something inside me shifts.

It's only 7 p.m., but my whole body caves in. I barely make it to the bedroom before collapsing into sleep.

*

I opened my eyes the next morning, and before the stress could kick in—before the mental to-do lists, the pressure, the noise of a life I'd just left behind—there it was.

A feeling I hadn't touched in far too long.

**Excitement.**

Not the kind fueled by deadlines, adrenaline, or too much coffee—something quieter. Lighter. Like I was taking a first breath after holding it for too long.

Still in bed, I reached for my phone and scrolled to my favorite bright mood playlist. The opening chords spilled into the room: a little old soul, a little indie sunshine.

I threw off the blanket and got up, bare feet hitting the wooden floor. My body still felt heavy from everything that had happened yesterday—but my mind? Crystal clear.

I walked over and opened a window. It was a slow Tuesday in March—surprisingly bright sunlight piercing through the clouds, the air crisp and refreshing.

I stood there for a moment, letting it hit my skin.

*You're free, Sophie. You can do whatever you want.*

I knew exactly what I had to do.

I crawled back into bed, covers pulled around me, and reached for my laptop.

No hesitation. No second-guessing.

**Bold move moment.**

I opened a blank email and started typing:

> **Subject:** Promotion
>
> Dear Kathrin,
>
> Thank you so much for offering me this incredible opportunity. I'm honored and truly flattered.
>
> But this new role would require an eighty-hour workweek at the very least. And while I thrived in that rhythm for a long time, I'm at a point in my life where I need to explore what else there is beyond work.
>
> Since my former project contract just ended, I'll be resigning effective immediately. I hope you'll find someone incredible to take this role forward—and continue the mission of combating loneliness globally.
>
> With deep respect and gratitude,
> Sophie

I hit send.

*Oh, my god, you really did it, Sophie.* A squeaky, delighted sound escaped my mouth.

And for the first time in a long time, I felt like I could breathe. I didn't know what was coming next. But it was mine to shape. And honestly? I couldn't wait to get started.

CHALLENGE 2

# Meeting Men Worth My Time

*Three months later*

"Are you finally finished, Sophie girl?" Rani called through the closed sliding door between my bedroom and the living room.

"Just a moment," I said.

I stared at the mirror. At her. The new Sophie—dressed in color, skin bare, lips bold. Someone meant to be seen.

*Three months ago, I wouldn't have imagined any of this. But* here I was—about to move into a new apartment, exploring new career possibilities, and more than anything, becoming a version of myself I actually wanted to be. One I'd pushed aside for too long, too busy toughening up in every part of my life. One that made space for fun. For exploration. For simply being me. And maybe—finally—one that could get me what I truly wanted.

For ten years, I told myself independence was everything. That work should come first. That everything else didn't really matter to me.

Now, as I redirected my life, I was finally honest with myself: putting work first **didn't** make me happy anymore. And the other parts of my life? They mattered more than I'd realized.

It felt strange and exciting to build a brand-new life.

To become a version of myself I hadn't dared to be in so long. One I wasn't entirely confident in yet.

But I was doing it—step by step, one challenge at a time. And today was one of those challenges.

Because if I were being radically honest these days, I had to admit: I'd never really experienced love. Not the kind that felt healthy, safe, and real. I'd never truly felt like I belonged—except maybe to myself, and to my work. And no matter how much I'd tried to pretend I didn't need anyone or anything... deep down, I wanted all of it.

It was time to stop pretending—and start doing something about it.

*Starting now.*

"Alright, friends. Ready?"

My two best friends, Eliyah and Rani—waiting on the couch—stopped giggling, straightened, and turned toward the closed sliding door.

Eliyah leaned toward Rani in a quick, eager motion, nearly spilling his Prosecco.

"Haha, easy there, love," Rani chuckled, setting her glass down on the side table. "Maybe opening two bottles on an empty stomach at 6 p.m. wasn't the best idea."

"Let's count down," Eliyah said. His legs bounced impatiently, heels tapping in a fast rhythm, like the door couldn't open fast enough. He exchanged a quick glance with Rani. "Start now? You count, I'll back you up."

"Whatever that means," Rani laughed, her black curls falling into her face as she pushed them back with a quick swipe. She started counting loudly, deliberately taking her time, "One... two..."

Eliyah snapped his fingers dramatically, adding a "Dum, da daaa!" like some grand cinematic moment was unfolding.

Rani rolled her eyes, laughing. Then they both shouted, "... Threeeee!"

I opened the door and stepped outside.

"Oh my god, **who** is this?" Eliyah jumped off the couch and gave me a once-over, eyes wide. Without saying a word, he marched straight into my bedroom, like he was searching for the old me under the bed.

A moment later, he came back, lifted my arm like he was examining a mannequin. Turning to Rani with mock seriousness, he said, "Rani, I'm afraid we lost our girl. She's gone. Vanished.

Replaced by this... **stunning** impostor."

"Haha—silly much?" I laughed.

Eliyah blinked. "It's like I'm seeing you for the first time. So much color—I can barely look."

He took a step back. "Where's all-black Sophie?"

"When she goes for it, she goes for it," Rani said, still sprawled on the couch. "But really: Wow, Sophie. Just... wow. You look incredible."

Eliyah lifted my other arm, spun me around, skirt flaring, then pulled me close and started to sway, humming, "Buckle up, New York gents, here cooomes Sophie..."

"Okay, stop it now, you goof," I laughed, shoving him off. "How much did you guys have to drink?"

"Well, obviously, we need even more Prosecco," Rani announced, floating to the fridge. She poured generously into all three glasses, eyes flicking to me. "I swear, Sophie, this feels like a damn time-lapse. Like—boom—the return of Sophie. I still remember when you ditched color completely, ten years ago, thanks to that idiot business coach."

"Wait, what?" Eliyah cut in, eyebrows shooting up. "Why don't I know this story? Huh? Is this one of those 'we've known each other longer than you' things?" He pulled a wounded expression.

"Ohhh, darling, you know how much we love you," Rani cooed. With Prosecco in hand, she rushed towards him, planting a kiss on his cheek.

"Okay, okay, I believe you," he laughed, wiping his face. "Now spill the story."

We sank into the couch, Rani tucking her legs under herself, Eliyah sprawling out, one arm draped over the backrest. I curled up, pulling a cushion onto my lap.

I swirled my drink, watching the bubbles fizz and rise. "Not much to tell. I wanted to be successful doing what I love, so I took advice from a business coach. He told me dressing too feminine would be a problem."

Eliyah's face twisted. "Excuse me?"

"He said tight jeans, frilly blouses—anything too 'girly'—would distract men and make me seem less credible." I exhaled. "So, if I wanted to be taken seriously, I should make sure no one's focus 'strayed.'"

"And you actually followed this prehistoric nonsense?" Eliyah asked.

I shrugged. "At the time, it made sense. The problem was, I ended up splitting myself in two—one wardrobe for work, another for real life. Eventually, it blurred. It was easier to streamline. Dark, oversized, neutral. Gender-neutral professional."

Eliyah's mouth fell open. "That is actually depressing. I mean... Sophie. No."

"I know," I said. "It sounds ridiculous now, but it still happens all the time, in so many subtle ways—expectations, unspoken rules, and pressure."

Rani nodded. "Be independent, but still soft. Smart, but not too opinionated. Ambitious, but not intimidating. And god forbid you're not pleasant 24/7—then you're 'difficult.'"

Eliyah let out a sigh. "So basically—exist, but in the most palatable, non-threatening way possible?"

"Exactly." I took a sip. "It's exhausting."

"I'm so sorry, Sophie, love. I mean, gender-fluid people like me get crap like that too," Eliyah said, shaking his head. "Such nonsense."

"Well, the important thing is, you're done with that now, Sophie. At least the fashion police aren't running your closet anymore," Rani said with a laugh.

Eliyah turned to me. "Sooo, let's get to the important stuff. How's tonight going to happen, Sophie?" Eliyah wiggled his brows.

I shrugged. "I don't know, let's see where it goes."

Rani snorted. "Oh, come on. You're amazing at bluffing. Sometimes I think you should work as a secret agent."

"Why? It's true," I defended.

I was obviously lying.

Rani shot me a look. "What? Come on... You didn't spend days getting ready just to 'see where it goes.' I think you know **exactly** what you're looking for tonight. And you better—"

Her eyes lit with mischief. "There'll be a lot of really great catches there."

I smirked. "Maybe."

"Now I feel like the third wheel again," Eliyah said, pressing his lips into an exaggerated pout. "I don't even know what's happening tonight. I just rushed over because Rani said, 'Prosecco and surprise.' Fill me in. Now!"

"Oh, it's a party for 'Changemakers.' Basically, a celebration for people who do impactful work. I'm going because my last project received great press, and my former boss, Kathrin, insisted I should go. It's the last event I'll do for them. My grand finale. I mean, in my mind at least. No one else cares about that—I'm just one of 150 guests there."

"And you're dressed up like this because... ?" Eliyah smiled.

"Because... if this is the grand finale, why not celebrate it as the **new** Sophie? I want actually to enjoy one of these events for once. There are usually a lot of really cute guys, and in the past, I've always kept it strictly professional. But guess what? I don't have to do that anymore. In fact, tonight I'm doing the opposite."

"What's the opposite?" Eliyah laughed, shooting Rani a curious look. She just shrugged.

"That's my secret for now..." I said and glanced at my watch. "And on that note—I need to head out immediately or I'll be too late. Feel free to stay, you've got my keys, Rani."

I kissed them each on the cheek, grabbed my bag, and made my way to the door. "Enjoy the rest of the evening," I called out as I stepped into the corridor.

"Have fun!" Rani and Eliyah's voices echoed through the door.

*

I paced down the stairs and onto the streets of the Meatpacking District, the click of my heels echoing against the pavement as I slipped into the downtown crowd.

The venue was just ten minutes from home.

I hadn't told anyone I was on a secret mission tonight: to meet high-quality men worth my time. And this time, not as a smitten girl caught in a daze, but as a clear-eyed woman with intent.

My dating history was... not great. Over the past ten years, whatever personal life I managed was mostly a tangle of poor choices. Emotionally unavailable types, charming narcissists, shallow flirts—often selfish in bed, always wrong in the long run.

But not anymore.

The new goal was clear: no more getting dazzled by the wrong men. No more hiding behind "Business Sophie." I wanted a life that reflected all of me—the full, best, vibrant version. And yes, I wanted love. The real kind. A relationship rooted in honesty, depth, and actual alignment—not because of chemistry, but because the person standing in front of me had earned it.

And if a relationship didn't appear right away, maybe I'd enjoy flings first. Not my usual game—I'd never liked random hookups that treated me like a body instead of a person. But if it felt right, because it was intentional and exciting—why not?

I was finally ready to explore my sexuality—ready to do everything I'd never dared to do before, or had held back to make others comfortable. And if that meant starting with something casual, I was open to it.

... As long as it felt true to what I really wanted. Because most important of all: I was done settling for less. I wanted what I deserved. To feel chosen, seen, respected—and I wasn't letting anyone into my life who didn't meet my standards anymore.

I'd spent weeks getting ready for this moment—hired a coach, got clear on what I wanted, and rebooted my dating mindset.

Then the first challenge hit me: how do I even begin? How do I get back out there in a way that feels fun—and actually healthy?

I'd always avoided online dating. I'd watched too many friends spin their wheels on an endless carousel of creepy dates, only to burn out. I needed something different. Something grounded. So I decided I'd go old-school: meet people in real life.

From now on, I'd show up to work events as the new me—less pitching, more playful. I'd start saying yes to the invitations I usually brushed off—the ones that weren't about networking but about connection. And I'd say no to the rest. No more shouting in loud clubs, no more fake small talk. I wanted warmth. Depth. Real potential.

Then it arrived: an invite to a global changemaker gathering in June. Likely full of smart, driven guys who actually cared about things that really mattered—exactly the kind of people I wanted to meet.

**Bzzz.** My phone buzzed. I was nearly there.

As I turned the last corner and spotted the venue, a flicker of nerves ran through me.

This wasn't just another night out. It was the beginning of something new—where I'd stop performing roles assigned by others, start choosing wisely, and enjoy life.

I'd almost forgotten what it felt like to just have fun. To be free.

It was finally time to play—**on my terms.**

*

I walked up to the entrance and glanced around.

The place was buzzing—stylish crowd, lots of cute guys lingering outside this chic downtown spot, all fresh and polished. Laughter floated through the air, mixed with the soft clink of wine glasses and celebratory toasts.

I checked my watch and smiled. Perfect timing. Not too early to seem overeager, not too late to miss any opportunities.

*Confidence, Sophie.*

I straightened my posture and walked into the venue.

The space spanned two levels, with high ceilings and expansive windows that filled the room with natural light. Sleek lines and rich tones gave the modern decor a mix of warmth and sophistication.

The first floor featured low tables and comfortable seating, along with access to an outdoor area, while the second floor housed the bar. Guests moved easily between the two levels —the ideal setting for what I had in mind. About fifty people had already arrived.

I grabbed a glass of white wine from a passing server and headed upstairs. The second floor was still quiet, and I made my way to the bathroom for one last moment of solitude before the night unfolded. The soft hum of the overhead light filled the room as I stared at my reflection.

I took a deep breath, inhaling a surge of self-assurance. *Sophie, you've got this.*

When I left the bathroom, I spotted a handsome man about to head downstairs. He turned, and our eyes met.

He looked to be in his early thirties, dressed in tailored suit pants and a high-quality, luxurious-looking shirt. I walked toward him.

"Sophie," I said, extending my hand for a firm handshake while maintaining eye contact. I studied his face, eager to uncover the layers concealed behind those dark eyes. His cologne—a mix of woody scents and fresh garden notes floated through the air.

"Lars from Germany," he introduced himself, clearly trying to match my confidence, though the slight hesitation in his eyes suggested otherwise.

*Cute.*

"What brings you here tonight?" I asked, brushing my hair back.

"I flew in from Berlin a few days ago," he replied. "I help organizations around the world make climate-friendly business decisions."

His shoulders squared slightly, like the weight of his work carried pride. "What about you?"

"I'm here for an organization that tackles urban loneliness."

"Interesting..." he smiled.

Our eyes met, and there was a moment of tension between us.

Then he added casually, "It's worth mentioning that my girlfriend lives in New York—that definitely nudged me to come," like he was trying to ease the charge between us.

*Disappointing.*

*But also—congrats, Sophie. Apparently, your nonverbal cues are working. If he feels the need to mention his girlfriend, that means the message is getting through.*

"Sounds like the perfect mix of business and fun," I said.

"Well... I've just arrived and still need to check out the rest of the venue. It was great meeting you—see you around."

*Well done.*

I'd set some rules for tonight, and I was sticking to them: 1. put myself out there, 2. quickly assess if a man was truly worth my time, and 3. leave if he wasn't—simple as that.

I rushed down the stairs, feeling powerful and confident—like I was in on a secret no one else knew.

The room opened up before me, full of possibilities.

I paused at the edge of the crowd, scanning the scene with quiet focus—almost like I was stalking prey.

Pride sparked in my chest. What used to feel intimidating now felt empowering.

I wasn't ignoring my love life or leaving it up to fate anymore.

I was finally in the driver's seat.

*

It was 9 p.m., and I'd already mingled with about twenty men.

A lot of the conversations were naturally business-related, but something in me had shifted.

I wasn't just networking anymore—I was giving off a different energy: flirtatious, open, and trying to steer small talk into something personal. And once we were in that space, I stuck to my straightforward strategy for uncovering their relationship status.

To my surprise, it was easier than I'd expected. A few pointed questions—Where do you live? Who do you live with? Do you have kids or a partner?—were enough to peel back the layers and get the answers I needed, fast.

I stepped into the courtyard and paused at the door for a second when my eyes landed on a man whose gaze was fixed on me.

It hit me—this wasn't the first time. He'd been watching me all night.

His brown, wavy hair framed a youthful face, no older than thirty, like the two men beside him. He was dressed in a simple black T-shirt, dark blazer, and trousers, paired with boots—keeping his style understated yet refined, leaving a quiet air of mystery around him.

I felt an undeniable pull towards this boldly staring stranger, who was clearly sending me an invitation to engage.

*Why not give them all a chance?*

I made my way over to the group, flashing a warm smile. "Hi, I'm Sophie," I said, stepping into their circle as if we were old friends.

For a second, all three men froze, eyes wide with surprise. I couldn't help but chuckle. "What's with the looks?" I teased.

"It's great to meet you," they all said in unison.

We shared a laugh as I shook hands with each of them: Gabriel, the owner of a political media consulting agency in France; Nick, a passionate US climate lawyer; and Adrian, a New York finance expert, whose intense gaze had drawn me in.

"So, are you here with an organization tonight?" Nick asked.

"Sort of. I led an international initiative on urban loneliness, backed by a consortium of city governments, NGOs, and private funders."

"Wait—I think I read about your project in an article about the most game-changing impact projects last year. Didn't you get a huge investment to scale nationwide?" Gabriel wondered

"Yes, we did," I smiled.

"Uh—impressive. What was your approach?" Nick wanted to know.

"Thanks—it was a big team effort. I'm a behavioral designer, and we focused on reducing isolation in cities with that project. Basically, we worked on systems, spaces, and little everyday rituals that make connection easier—whether it's how public spaces are set up, simple social prompts, or subtle digital nudges. Just small things that help people feel a bit more connected and happy in daily life."

"That sounds incredible," Nick said. "And very much needed in our current times."

"True. And I loved working in that space. It's been a heartfelt mission of mine. I just resigned from my job, though. This is my last business event for them."

"How come?" Gabriel asked.

"I just needed a change, I guess. I'm taking time off right now to explore what's next.

"Congrats, it takes courage to leave a position like that," Gabriel said.

"Thanks. What's your work about?" I asked.

He looked at my empty glass. "Let me get you another drink first. Wine okay?"

"Yes, that sounds perfect."

I watched him stride inside with Nick, leaving me alone with Mr. Gaze-Eye, who hadn't said a word since introducing himself —just watched me, like he was trying to figure out how I worked.

Adrian's sparkling eyes were witty, charming, unmistakably alive. Their color was impossible to pin down: hazel, blue, green, gray—all at once.

His hair was just long enough to fall into his face. He kept brushing it aside whenever a strand tumbled across his forehead. His lips were full, soft, and red.

"So, you're making New York a less lonely place... not exactly a small mission," he said, voice low and smooth.

"I'm impressed."

"Because of the project or all the attention we got?" I asked, holding his gaze.

"The project," he said, letting out a short laugh.

"Attention comes and goes. The press, the recognition, the hype—it's all noise. What should matter is whether it means something after the buzz dies down. Obviously, those things help push you forward—it's part of the game. But that's all it is."

He tilted his head, studying me. "I can't stand that elitist bullshit. It's one of the worst things about New York. Everyone's competing all the time. We're all just human, aren't we?"

And then—he paused. Just stood there, leaning casually against the wall, piercing me with his eyes. Letting the silence stretch... long enough to feel like a challenge.

"Is someone who makes others feel less lonely... ever lonely themselves?" he asked, finally.

His voice—low, serious, intimate—lands somewhere deep inside me. A place strangers don't usually reach.

For a moment, the world fades.

The noise, the crowd—gone.

***It's just him and me.***

I hold my breath. Lift my chin. Meet him where he is. "I think everyone is sometimes."

He flashes a slow, knowing smile. "Maybe," he says—just as Nick and Gabriel reappear.

Gabriel handed me my glass of wine with a grin, cutting through our moment. "Alright, Sophie. Since you wanted to hear about our work, here it is. I'm diving deep into gender equality and fluidity—and we were just having a little debate inside," he said. “Do you think people are born with a fixed sexual orientation, or can it shift and evolve over time?”

“Wow, okay,” I laughed. “I think it can shift—definitely. What’s your take?”

“To me, the answer’s obvious,” Adrian cut in smoothly, before Nick or Gabriel could respond. “Honestly? I think everyone has at least a little queerness in them. Whether they realize it or not. I’d say I’m probably... 20 percent.”

“20 percent?” I raised an eyebrow, grinning. “That is a very precise number.”

He smirked. “I’ve done the math.”

“Okay then,” I said, lifting my glass. “Cheers. To queerness, and to the freedom to be whoever the hell we want.”

“What about you?” Nick leaned in.

“I’ve had some fun experiences with women,” I shared openly. “Nothing long-lasting yet—just a few times driven by curiosity. I’ve only ever truly fallen for men so far, but who knows what the future holds.”

“I’m heading in for a drink,” Adrian declared, sliding past me.

Then—out of the blue, with Nick and Gabriel just a few feet behind him—Adrian pauses right in front of me.

My heart stops beating for a moment.

Our sudden proximity knocks the air from my lungs.

Our eyes lock.

My pulse jumps.

*I feel incredibly alive.*

Then he leans in, close. His voice brushes my ear—low and deliberate:

“How about you, Gabriel, Nick, and me tonight?”

He tosses the invitation into the air like a dare.

***What?***

But before I can speak—before my mind even catches up with my body—he’s already walking away, disappearing inside.

Gone. Just like that.

A jolt shoots down my spine.

*Wow, this guy is* ***bold****.*

He was clearly trying to provoke.

And oh, does he succeed.

*Breathe, Sophie.*

The thought of an adventurous night with three undeniably attractive, intelligent, and charming men is—although not what I came here for tonight—**incredibly** tempting.

For just a second, I'm swept up in a rush of possibilities. The wildest images fill my mind, making my head spin. *Is this just a flirtatious game on his part? Or is he serious?*

*Does Adrian genuinely think the others would go along with it?*

Part of me thinks it's too wild to be real.

But another part is triggered by the thrill of it all.

*What if tonight could turn into something unforgettable?*

*Would I actually be open to something like that?*

*I mean... I'm generally open to exploration if it feels right.*

*But does it?*

***No,*** *Sophie.*

I shake off the fantasy.

On another day? Maybe. Probably.

But there are too many great potential relationship opportunities to get swept into an adventure right now—*not my first priority for tonight.*

*

I took a deep breath to center myself as a young woman's voice echoed slightly across the marble floor. "Everyone: the Newcomer Talent Award ceremony starts now. Please join us in the back hall."

Conversations quieted, and like a tide shifting, people began to move. I followed, joining the slow current of bodies weaving toward the hall.

We stepped into the space—dimly lit, slightly cooler—and found ourselves among roughly 150 others, all gathering in front of a low stage framed by soft amber lighting and minimalist banners.

"Can someone remind me what this is actually being awarded for?" I asked Nick and Gabriel, who were still next to me.

"Well," Nick said, leaning closer so I could hear, "it's part of *The Global Economy* magazine's '30 Under 30' list—emerging talents to watch. Now they're choosing one person to honor for their outstanding global impact."

The lights in the room dimmed a little more. A hush fell. The moderator walked onto the stage, holding a sleek, steel award that caught the light like a blade. Applause rippled across the crowd.

"Thank you all for joining us tonight," he began, his voice polished but warm. "We hope you've enjoyed the evening so far. We're beyond excited to finally announce which of our 30 Under 30 talented nominees achieved the most significant global impact with their work last year."

He paused just long enough to stretch the moment. "And the prize goes to..."

**Music thrummed.**

"Adrian De Luca, for his global project *Global Seeds – Support to Self-Support,* helping disadvantaged groups—low-income families, single women, and children—build sustainable livelihoods through smart micro-investments."

A beat. Then cheers. **Applause.**

*Right.* ***Of course*** *it's him. He's hot, smart,* ***and*** *doing something that actually matters—****not*** *impressed at all.*

Adrian stepped onto the stage, tall and composed, yet slightly flushed under the lights. He straightened the lapels of his dark blazer, ran a hand through his thick hair, and flashed a smile that could've powered the room.

He looked hot as fuck, and he knew it—but without arrogance. *Okay, maybe a little bit of arrogance.*

The moderator handed him the award and shook his hand. Adrian gripped it with both hands, nodding slightly, then turned to face the crowd.

His posture relaxed just enough to show he wasn't performing—he meant what he was about to say.

*This guy is infuriatingly grounded.*

He seems like the type who casually gets whatever he wants, no matter what he does. The one who never gets nervous, never chases press—the press just shows up. He walks into panels in beat-up boots, owns the stage like it's nothing, and somehow that only makes people find him more real. He turns down investor meetings if their ethics don't sit right with him. And he makes his own rules—but instead of feeling offended, people end up admiring him for it.

*Who **wouldn't** be attracted to all of that?*

"Good evening, everyone." His voice rang out clear and calm. "First of all, thank you for being here—and thank you for choosing my project. "And to the organizations I work with: thank you for trusting me. It means the world."

**Applause.**

"I also want to thank my team, my organization, and especially my boss for giving me the freedom and responsibility to carry this project forward the way I believed it needed to be done, though I'm only twenty-eight years old.

"Taking a risk on an untested, unconventional idea isn't easy, and I'm deeply grateful for that opportunity." Adrian shifted slightly and glanced toward the back of the room—maybe searching for someone. Then he looked back out, his expression and voice steady.

"Not everyone starts life with the same opportunities. And not everyone has the resources to change their path on their own.

"When I chose a career in finance, it wasn't because I love money, but because I love people."

His eyes scanned the audience with quiet intensity, landing on each face as if every one of them mattered.

"I never wanted to help the rich get richer. I wanted people who don't have much to get a seat at the table.

"My daily work is about carving out those investment opportunities with a global network of organizations and convincing investors to get on board—creating innovative, win-win solutions for everyone.

"There's **nothing** more rewarding than seeing a family with nothing rise above their struggles and build something of their own.

"We're already the most successful global impact investment project of our kind. But I **won't stop** until we're active in every country that needs us—until we've created the biggest impact possible." He planted his feet firmly and smiled as he looked out at the audience, leaning into the podium.

"This world belongs to everyone. And with Global Seeds, we're not just **wishing** for a just future—we're **building** it.

"Thank you."

Applause roared. People stood. A few in the front row reached out to shake Adrian's hand as he stepped down. Someone clapped him on the back.

Adrian smiled graciously, made eye contact, and nodded—fully present.

The moderator returned to the mic. "That was our final highlight on stage. Now we move into the more informal part of the evening—gather, chat, enjoy the open bar, and have a great night."

Music thrummed back into the space, dissolving the moment like steam.

I caught myself watching Adrian a second too long, his silhouette slipping back into the crowd.

Glasses clinked. Laughter returned. The room began to move again—and then someone next to me turned a little too enthusiastically.

My wine glass jerked in my hand, sloshing its contents straight down the front of my blouse. *Oh no.*

I looked down. The fabric clung to my skin—completely transparent. *Perfect. Great time to flash the entire room your bra, Sophie. At least it's white wine.*

I crossed my arms over my chest and started weaving through the crowd, head down, scanning for the nearest bathroom. Suddenly—a warm hand on my back.

I turned. It was Adrian.

"Hey—I saw what happened. Come with me."

"Don't you have more important things to do right now?"

"I've been business-chitchatting all evening. Time for a break," he said, already unbuttoning his jacket. "Besides, I'd feel like a fraud accepting an impact award and then ignoring someone standing right in front of me who clearly needs a little help."

He draped his blazer over my shoulders, carefully adjusting it so it closed across my chest, then nodded toward a dark door tucked near the stage. "There's a room backstage—where the speakers got ready earlier."

I looked up at him, touched. "Your work is incredible," I said softly. "I'm genuinely impressed. Congratulations."

"Because of what I do, or the award?" he asked with a crooked smile, guiding me toward the door. Then he paused, hand on the handle.

"Probably both, if I'm honest."

"That's okay," he teased. "I won't tell anyone you're into my one minute of fame."

"Heyyy, who said I was **into** anything?" I laughed and gave him a light punch in the chest.

We stepped into the room. It looked like a backstage theater prep area—lined with mirrors, scattered cosmetics, deep sinks, and heavy curtains draped across one wall. The lighting was dim and warm, casting soft reflections across the space. The air carried the scent of powder, steamed fabric, and something old, musty, and heavy—like velvet.

Adrian closed the door behind us.

I tugged at the damp fabric clinging to my chest. "Well. Now, it's completely see-through."

"You could take it off," he said, flashing a smile. "We can put it on the heater—it'll be dry in ten minutes or so."

"That's probably the best idea. Aren't people going to come in here?"

"I don't think so. Everyone's out by now. No one else needs to get stage-ready."

"Okay."

"Should I leave you alone?"

"No, it's fine. You can stay if you want." I tried to undo the back of my top. "Actually, you have to. I need help getting this off without messing up my hair or makeup."

"More than happy to assist," he grinned.

"I bet you are," I laughed. I turned around to face him. "It's okay. You can look. I don't mind."

But he doesn't look down, just steps closer.

*So, he's a gentleman, too?*

*Don't be ridiculous, Sophie. He's a bad boy with manners, at best.*

Now he's just inches away.

I can feel the warmth of his body radiating toward me.

"Okay, stand still," he says, his voice low and deliberate. He slides his arms around me, fingers moving with care as he unties the ribbons at the back.

The fabric loosens. I feel it shift—gliding slightly.

*Those eyes drive me crazy.*

"It's still closed at the front," I whisper. "The ribbons are just for show. You'll have to pull it over my head. Carefully, please."

He nods, then lifts the fabric—slowly, deliberately—making sure it doesn't brush my face or disturb a single strand of hair.

It's only the fabric that's moving across my skin—but it feels like his hand is sliding across my body.

Now I'm standing in front of him.

Topless.

*Thank god I'm wearing a sexy bra.*

"Done," he says. He sets the top on the heater, his eyes never leaving mine. "Anything else you'd like to get rid of while we're at it?"

I smile. "No," I say lightly—though my shaky voice gives me away.

My gaze drops to his lips, then back up.

My pulse goes faster.

He leans in, close enough that I can feel his breath on my ear. "What do you **want**, Sophie?"

*Good question.*

The old Sophie probably would've fallen for this.

But the old Sophie also would've ended up drained or in some kind of mess—like always.

Sure, this could be fun—a new experience.

But no matter whether this was only casual or more, flirtation gets better when you hold out long enough to get to the good part—the right moment.

It has to feel aligned. Earned.

I know that now.

I've learned.

*Don't let sheer momentary excitement take away what you **really** want, Sophie.*

*You can feel it in your gut: giving in right now won't get you to the most fun **or** meaningful part.*

*Not yet.*

"I'm not up for a foursome tonight, if that's what you mean," I say at last, finally answering the question he'd tossed out earlier—even though his presence alone keeps challenging my stance.

Adrian pulls back just enough to study my face. "Really? Not even a little intrigued?" His voice is warm with amusement, his eyes sparkling.

He steps closer, not backing down. "Our minds and desires—they don't always want the same. I get it. Women are judged.

Men get a pass. But that's not me. I believe in freedom. Real freedom. He, she, they—it doesn't matter. Everyone deserves to live how they want.
Love how they want.
Explore how they want.
Life's too short for anything else."

*This is just his game, Sophie. Don't fall for it.*

But damn, it doesn't **feel** like a game.

There's something more refined about him—raw energy paired with self-awareness. Sophistication mixed with passion. A rare blend.

His eyes don't demand.
They invite.

For a second, I feel completely seen.
Not just desired—accepted.
With all my deepest desires and instincts.
And that's what really messes with me.

*Ugh. Are you really going to let a guy you just met throw you off like this?*

Apparently yes.
My body keeps getting warmer by the second.

I say nothing.

"I **see**," he murmurs.

"What?"

"You don't want to lose control. Maybe you like being in control or... you're just uptight?"

"What? I'm not uptight!"

"Yeah, I actually don't think so either—you've just got a plan."

I try to keep my eyes steady.

"That's it. You have a plan, and you're not ready to let go of it. I saw it in your eyes earlier—out there. The way you looked at me. The way you walked over. That wasn't casual. You made a **choice**."

He pauses, voice lower. "So tell me—what are you hunting for, Sophie?"

*Damn it, he's good.*

"You know what?" I step back and reach for my top. It's still damp. I toss it back onto the heater. "I don't need a lecture—or a personality reading. Especially not from some twenty-something I just met."

"I'm twenty-eight," he smiles, unbothered. "And why not? I like being challenged. Challenge me."

I pause, then walk toward the window.

Outside, the courtyard is bathed in a soft, golden light. A small fountain bubbles in the center, topped by a statue of a woman holding a sun above her head. Lily pads drift at the base.

No one's out there. The event is on the other side of the building, with all the noise, glasses, and people. The backside space feels like it doesn't belong to any of that.

I hear him step closer behind me. He doesn't say anything at first. Doesn't touch me. Just stands there, close enough that I can feel him.

Then his voice, low, near my ear. "We've got ten, maybe fifteen minutes until your top is dry."

A pause.

"Challenge me. Ask me anything."

I watch the fountain.

The shape of the statue.

The way the water moves around her feet.

I've always loved fountains.

Always wanted to climb one.

Sit at the top like I owned the place—Queen of the World.

*Let's have some fun, Sophie.*

*Get you what you want, right now.*

"I dare you instead," I say. "Any way we can get down there?" I nod toward the courtyard.

I don't wait for him to answer. Instead, I cross the room and sweep aside the heavy curtain. Behind it: a door.

I press the handle. It opens with a soft click. "Are you coming?" I call, already halfway down the stairs.

I hear his footsteps behind me, quick and light.

My heart pounds as I run.

*This is so much fun.*

We step into the courtyard. The air is cooler here, brushing against my bare arms. The sound of the water is louder—steady, calming. The lights catch on the surface of the fountain, on the curve of the statue. Around us, the windows of the building are mostly dark. It's quiet.

None of this feels like part of the event anymore. It feels like something cut loose from it—just ours.

"Let's go up," I say.

Adrian glances at me. "What, up the fountain?"

I shrug, eyes still on the statue. "I mean, I'm already half naked. And you just told me you like challenges."

His eyebrows rise. He hesitates just half a second—then smiles.

I slip off my sandals, unbutton my skirt, and let it fall to the grass. Weirdly, it feels like the most natural thing in the world. Like we've known each other for a long time.

"Okay, you know what—let's do it," he says, undoing his belt and kicking off his shoes. His shirt comes next, then his trousers, all in smooth, confident movements.

Now we're standing across from each other in nothing but underwear.

He's not a cover model—though pretty damn close. But he's not one of those perfectly sculpted types with a razor-sharp six-pack, and thank god for that. I can't help but admire his shoulders, though—broad and solid, all muscle. He looks strong in that quietly obvious way. The kind of strong that doesn't need showing off.

There's power in his build, but it's lived-in, not posed. He works hard, clearly, but he also enjoys himself. He looks like someone who knows his body and trusts it. And something about that makes him feel real.

I don't look like a perfect cover model either. Who does—but I'm good with myself. Comfortable enough to stand here like this, barefoot in the dark, under the open sky.

And none of that matters right now anyway. I don't feel exposed. It just feels like an adventure.

I turn away and step onto the low edge of the fountain, the stone cool and a little slippery under my feet. "Can you help me up?" I say, glancing back at him. "The top of the fountain looks dry."

He moves in behind me. His hands are firm and warm on my waist as he lifts me, holding me steady as I climb up and find a place to stand where I can balance.

I reach down to help pull him up. He catches my hand, hoisting himself onto the base, water splashing lightly around us.

We slowly climb the wide tiers together, laughing, slipping a little, catching each other's hands, until we're sitting side by side on the top ledge beneath the statue—like two kids who snuck out after curfew and ended up in someone else's dream.

I lean back on my hands, legs dangling.

*I'm so happy right now.*

"This feels like we are the King and Queen of the world," he says.

*What the fuck. Is this guy in my head?*

I glance over at him and nod. "Right."

I look up to the stars. "So... if you were king of your world and could let go of one of your burdens—one major fear—and turn it into whatever you wanted... what would it be?"

"Easy."

"Easy?" I tilt my head, skeptical.

"Resolve my FOMO. Let me experience everything I want. Everywhere, at all times."

"Fear of missing out?"

"Yeah," he says, leaning back beside me.

"I always want to experience as much as possible in life. Every moment becomes important—new people, new places, new experiences. The idea of missing something freaks me out.

So, if I could change one thing, I'd make sure I always knew I was exactly where I was meant to be. Experiencing exactly what I need to and doing as much as I want, so I don't even need to have this annoying FOMO anymore."

I study his profile for a second.

He turns toward me. "What about you, Queen of the world? What's the burden you want to get rid of?"

I pause.

"I think it's regret."

"Regret about what?" he asks, gentle now.

I look down at the water below us, my toes grazing the surface. "The fear of making the wrong choices. Choices that could shape my whole life. And that I might regret them one day."

"How come?" Adrian asks, surprised. "You seem confident, strong-willed, and pretty decisive to me."

"I can be. But there are so many voices in life—your past, your family, what you want now, what you **think** your future self will want. Sometimes it's hard to tell which voice is actually yours."

I look at my dangling feet.

"Do you know the number one regret of the dying?"

He shakes his head.

"Apparently 70 percent of people wish they'd had the courage to live a life true to themselves—a life that made them happy, not the life others expected of them."

Adrian watches me closely but says nothing.

"I want to be part of the 30 percent. The ones who live boldly, who are true to themselves. But it's hard sometimes. We try to plan. Try to be intentional. But even when something feels right for us at the moment, there's no way to **know** if it's the right path.

Not really.

Life only makes sense in hindsight. And sometimes not even then."

"That's why I believe in hedonism," Adrian says casually.

I laugh. "Of course you do."

He grins, but he's serious. "Not like reckless, no-plan hedonism. I think about my choices. I've got long-term goals. But I believe that the joy we feel in the moment matters. If you genuinely enjoy something, maybe it can't be the wrong choice. That's my theory at least."

He turns to face me, more open now. "For the big things —career, relationships, where I want to live—I follow reason. I plan those, and I'm pretty down-to-earth and rational when it comes to stuff like that.

But then I try to stay present. Live in a way that feels good. Be with people who make me feel good. The rest... it happens whether we obsess over it or not.

Maybe we don't need to meticulously plot out our lives, since —just as you said—life tends to throw us curve balls no matter what."

I look at him.

*This guy is ridiculously sure of himself.*

It's magnetic.

"Maybe we don't have to get every choice right, Sophie." He holds my gaze. "Maybe we **just** need to live."

He makes it sound so damn easy, and for a second, it feels like we are the only two people in the world. New York, the event, the water splashing around us—all of it fades into the background.

**I want to be part of it.** Part of a world that feels easy, simple, and happy in the best way possible. *Again,* ***who wouldn't?***

"Let's move to the middle—it's getting uncomfortable here at the edge," Adrian says.

"Good idea," I reply, standing up and stepping carefully across the stone.

Adrian reaches for my hand, steadying me as I cross. I lean back against the statue, its cool surface pressing into my spine, just as Adrian joins me.

He stands right in front of me, then slowly turns to face me. "You look **so** fucking sexy right now," he whispers, leaning in close—so close I feel the warmth of his breath against my ear, sending a shiver down my spine.

***Heat.***

Now, he shifts. Slowly. Deliberately.

Positioning himself directly in front of me.

His strong arm presses against the statue behind me.

His muscles flex when he leans in, his body not touching mine, but the tension between us is undeniable.

*What is this guy doing to me?*

*And how the hell did he manage to get to me like this, so fast?*

*I need to get closer.*

*Much closer.*

His eyes hold mine.

Firm.

Steady.

Warm.

That familiar dizziness floods back, making my head spin.

"By the way, I'm in an open relationship," he suddenly says.

***What?***

*Wow, I didn't see that one coming. At all.*

Not because of the open relationship—this is New York after all, and many of my friends are in open or polyamorous relationships—but because I genuinely thought he was single. My self-proclaimed detective instincts, which I'd trusted all evening, turned out to be utterly unreliable.

Then there's the timing—he drops the news so casually, **while** he's making a move. It's a bizarre contradiction: pulling me in with one hand and killing the chemistry with the other.

I'm torn—desire on one side, reason on the other. Not that I have any experience getting involved with someone in an open relationship. But even if this were purely physical, I don't think that's my style.

*What would I be then? Some fleeting thrill—someone who adds a spark for a moment, spices up their relationship, while his girlfriend gets all the intimacy and commitment? That might work perfectly for some. But for me, right now, it's a huge turnoff.*

"Okay, good to know," I say, stepping out from under his arm.

Just like that, I turn and start climbing down from the fountain.

"**What?** Sophie, what's going on?"

"I'm going back in," I say over my shoulder.

Adrian follows.

I hop down from the fountain, land on the grass, and start slipping my skirt and sandals back on.

Behind me, I hear him drop down too.

"Hey, why are you leaving like this? Are you mad or something?"

"No, not at all. I'm just not interested."

*Great job keeping it light, Sophie. You wanted fun, you had fun, right?*

"Don't get me wrong," I add gently. "I think it's great you know what you want and live how you want. Everyone should. It's just not what I want. Not tonight."

Adrian looks at me, and for once, he doesn't have anything to say.

"Don't look so disappointed," I tease him, grabbing his trousers off the ground. "Or... I'll take **these** away from you."

Before he can respond, I take off—running barefoot across the grass, his pants in hand.

"Sophie! **What the fuck?**" he calls out, grabbing his shoes and shirt as he runs after me.

Just before we reach the back door, I pause for a second, place his trousers neatly on the grass, and dart back inside.

Up the stairs. Fast.

I reach the heater, grab my top, and throw it on. No caution this time. I'm leaving. Perfect makeup? Hair? Irrelevant.

I tie the ribbon, step into the hallway, and hear his footsteps catching up behind me.

*This is kind of fun, actually.* It feels like a New York version of Cinderella—minus the glass pumps. I'd never leave my shoe behind. They were way too expensive. And I have no plans of seeing him again anyway.

I rush out onto the street and call an Uber. The night's busy, tipsy party crowds spill onto the sidewalks. My car pulls up within a minute, like a well-timed escape.

I slide into the car and, just as I settle in, I see Adrian appear at the front entrance. He spots me and jogs toward the car, motioning for me to roll down the window.

"Can I at least get your number?"

I shake my head. "No," I say, flashing a wide smile, and roll the window back up.

Our eyes lock—one last time. And for a moment, it's like he's sending me a silent message, cutting straight through the window and the wall I'd just built to protect myself.

No matter how hard I'd tried, it was too late.

He had already gotten under my skin.

CHALLENGE 3

# Light or Darkness?

*Two months later*

*Honestly, this space is perfect. Just so beautiful.*

I peeked into the light-flooded room that, unfortunately, wouldn't be my new design studio.

A hard pill to swallow.

I could see it all so clearly—my desk in front of the vast windows overlooking the Brooklyn Bridge, a small sitting corner tucked beside it for guests, maybe a little showroom area for my work, filled with lush plants along the side wall.

The space I was **actually** getting was nothing like that. That space was tucked away in a back corner, with no windows and no daylight. It was ironic, considering the business idea I was working on was about creating light.

I'd always been fascinated by how light could shape emotions and behavior. So, eleven years ago, while working as a behavioral light designer, I came up with an idea: what if light could do more than just illuminate a room?

I envisioned a mood-shifting lamp—something that resembled art but was grounded in cutting-edge science. There were simple light therapy products out there, sure. But I wanted to create something with more impact—something that could genuinely change people's lives. Help them relax, recharge, or focus—whenever they need it most.

Back then, I got an offer from a top-notch global organization, and I pushed my dream aside, telling myself it was the reasonable choice—the right thing to do.

My dream never really disappeared, though. It was just on hold. And now, as I was building my life from scratch, it had found its way back to me.

I started to wonder: *What if I actually did it?* Started my own business. Something that was mine from the ground up. I had the knowledge. I had the network. I had some money saved.

So, I decided it was time to give this a real shot—and see where it would lead. And today, I took the first step—finding a space to work out of at SPARKS, a creative design community that rents studios. It was exactly what I needed: a fresh start, new people, and a better balance between personal and professional life.

Sunbeams hit me as I walked toward the floor-to-ceiling windows at the front of the empty room.

*Alright, Sophie. Let it go now. You'll make the dark little room work somehow. Start looking at what you have and make the best out of it instead of dwelling on what you don't have. Like you always do.*

I rested my fingertips lightly against the warm surface of the glass, letting my eyes soak in the skyline one last time, when a voice cut through the stillness behind me—deep, familiar, unmistakable. "Sophie. I can't believe this. **Finally.**"

I turned sharply. ***Of course****, it was him.*

Adrian leans casually against the doorway, looking just as dangerously good as I remembered.

I can hear my heartbeat.

"**Adrian?** What are you doing here? Are you following me or something?"

He grins, pushing off the frame with an easy shrug. "I wish I'd found you on my own. But no. I'm a member here. Not one of the creatives, obviously. As you know, I'm just a boring finance guy," he laughs. "I help people around here get started—small business owners without a lot of resources."

"Wow, what are the odds?"

"They're actually pretty decent," he replies. "I'm a member at a few entrepreneurial spaces around the city. They usually offer me a spot—makes collaboration smoother. And you?"

I brush a strand of hair behind my ear, trying to stay composed. "I just signed up as a member. I'm working on a business idea. A light design project. This... isn't going to be my studio, though."

"No?"

"I wish... It's perfect. But it's not available, so I'm taking one in the back. It'll do the job, I guess."

I stop for a second.

"Wait," I said, narrowing my eyes at him. "What did you mean by **finally**?"

Adrian doesn't answer right away. Instead, he crosses the room toward me—slow, deliberate steps.

He stops just short of me, both of us leaning against the window front, pretending this was casual.

*This man has a habit of getting really close, really fast.*

He watches me with quiet intensity.

Behind us, the city sprawls out, blurred and distant.

For a second, I forget how to breathe.

"I've been trying to find you," he finally says.

I stare at him. "How?"

"I asked the organizers from the changemakers event, but they wouldn't share names—confidentiality reasons—just a list of the organizations that were involved. I figured out which one you worked for based on the field you mentioned, but when I called, they only confirmed someone named Sophie had been there. No last name."

He grins. "Tell me, Sophie. Are you secretly working for the CIA or something?"

I keep my tone intentionally even. "Not exactly. But I've actually been stalked by a psychopath before. Everyone at my old job was told to keep my information private."

I tilt my head slightly, studying him. "Are you stalking me, Adrian?"

"**No!**" He says it like he knew how bad it sounded. "I promise, I'm not a stalker." He calmly shakes his head. "I wasn't until now, at least."

He pauses and lifts his hands lightly. His fingertip drifts down the glass beside me, tracing nothing, while piercing me with his eyes.

"I only did it because," his voice drops lower, more heartfelt now, "**I couldn't stop thinking about you.** I don't know what it is. But with you... I felt like a version of myself I hadn't been in a **really** long time. If ever. I know it sounds cheesy..." A faint flush creeps up his neck, just visible under the collar of his shirt.

*Cute. Very cute.*

"I've honestly never chased anyone like this before."

He pauses a second. "To be fair, I also never had to in the past," a small smile tugs at his mouth. "Women don't usually run from me like you did."

*Yeah, I bet they don't. That's what made it so much fun in the first place.*

He leans his forehead briefly against the glass, leaving a foggy imprint that fades almost instantly. "You know, that night we met, **I saw you first**."

"What do you mean?" I can't hide my surprise.

"I saw you when you arrived. I watched you strolling in, talking to a lot of different people—mostly men. Moving from one to the next." He pauses, his eyes scanning my face like he's trying to read me.

"I still don't know what you were hunting for that night, Sophie," he says. "Maybe I never will. But I'm glad you chose me, for whatever reason."

He lifts his head again, catches my gaze, and holds it. "Give me one more date, Sophie."

*I don't know... You are still in a relationship.*

My heart pulls in one direction, my head in another.

"There's an exhibition here at SPARKS tomorrow night. Come with me—just this **one** time. If you don't show, I'll leave you alone. I promise." He pulls a card from his wallet and places it on a nearby shelf. "Here's my number. Just in case."

He backs toward the door, his eyes never leaving mine. "Have a great day, Sophie," he smiles.

And with that, he's gone.

For a moment, I just stand there, looking at the glass beside me—right where his hand had been seconds ago. I let out a breath I hadn't even realized I was holding.

*What are you going to do now, Sophie?*

CHALLENGE 4

# Stick to the Plan or Follow Your Gut

It was Friday evening, almost 7 p.m., and I hurried through the bustling streets toward the exhibition at SPARKS when my phone rang. Rani's name flashed on the screen.

"Hey girl, are you on your way?"

"Almost there," I replied, sidestepping a group of tourists. "How's everything going?"

"The exhibit's a total hit. You're gonna love it. I'm sneaking in a five-minute break, then back to the chaos."

I smiled. "Of course it is, Mrs. Brilliant Curator. You're incredible at what you do."

"Well, I love it. But let's not talk about work," Rani teased. "**Spill it**—are you excited for your date?"

"It's your exhibition. I planned to go anyway. And we are both members at SPARKS. It's not a real **date**," I said.

"Riiight," Rani teased. "Because your encounters so far definitely screamed 'friend-zone.' But hey, as long as you can convince yourself of that."

I chuckled, shaking my head. "Look, I'm not denying the... tension. But you know the situation. He's with someone else. A real relationship is off the table."

"I know it's not your first choice to get involved with someone in an open relationship, but if there's such a strong tension —just go for an adventure, girl. You don't need to marry him right away... ," Rani laughed.

"Maybe... but for that to happen, the chemistry would have to be so intense that my body forgets—just for a moment—that he's in an open relationship. Because the second I think about it, it's a turnoff."

"And?" she pressed.

I exhaled, slowing as SPARKS came into view. "I don't expect that to happen."

"Famous last words," Rani teased.

"And here she goes being pushy, like usual," I laughed. "Okay, we'll see each other in a bit."

"Bye, Sophie girl," Rani texted, sending a selfie with her hands forming a heart, the exhibit's vibrant colors splashed behind her.

I looked at the photo and felt a sudden wave of gratitude for having Rani in my life. I loved how passionate and straightforward she was—qualities that had connected us instantly when we first crossed paths as students in a creative studies seminar at university fifteen years ago.

Having someone who always pushes me forward and tells me the truth, no matter what, is gold—and it makes our friendship the most genuine I've ever known.

*

I turned the final corner toward SPARKS and spotted Adrian, waiting on a bench in the middle of the huge, empty courtyard. It felt like an arena set up just for us.

He wore a worn-in leather jacket over a simple white T-shirt and sturdy boots, pulling off an effortless bad-boy vibe.

*Hot.*

As I walked toward him, he got up and grinned. "I **knew** you'd come."

"Careful," I said, giving him a quick hug. "If you gloat like that, I might change my mind."

"No, don't," he said quickly, his voice low near my ear now. "I'll behave... I promise." He pulled back just enough to look at me, his arms still loosely around my waist.

"Unless, of course, you don't want me to," he teased.

"Stop it," I laughed, lightly punching his chest.

The playful hit only seems to pull us closer, the tension tightening between us. For a moment, neither of us moves. We just stand there, arms still around each other, eyes locked.

*He's so fucking charming.*

His hair falls messily over his forehead, and now that he smiles, a small dimple appears on his cheek. His eyes reveal a blend of admiration and nervousness, boldness and boyish excitement. He's only twenty-eight after all.

"Shall we go in?" he asks.

I nod and we walk towards the entrance.

He shrugs off his jacket and casually drapes it over his shoulder, revealing his toned upper body.

"You look like you play a lot of sports," I say, glancing at his chest.

"I actually played on a professional rugby team in school," he replies. "I'm not playing anymore, though. I just go to the gym to stay fit."

"Why aren't you playing anymore?"

"The reason I was into rugby in the first place was the team. It was never about the sport itself. I loved being part of something bigger—having that sense of community. It's how my whole life works, really. I have a huge circle of friends, and most of them know each other. We're like a big gang," he says, laughing.

He looks at me. "What about you? Were you ever part of a team or a community?"

"No. Not really. Not by choice, though... or maybe by choice. I'm not sure," I said. "I guess I've always been more of a one-on-one, best-friend type." I pause.

"That's partly why I joined SPARKS—to know what it's like to actually belong to a community. I've always wanted that... but somehow, I ended up more of a solo fighter." I let out a small laugh. "Wow. That actually sounds kind of sad when I say it out loud."

Adrian stops walking. "No. It doesn't."

He turns toward me, his expression more serious now. "It sounds like you're **self-reliant**. I admire that. I've always been surrounded by people. Always had a tight-knit group around me. And you know what? Sometimes I wonder how strong I'd be without them. Without all the support. But you—you already know."

"I guess that's true," I say. "I never really thought about it like that."

He holds my gaze for a second longer. "I honestly think that kind of strength is really rare." His hand finds my waist, pulling me just slightly closer. "And incredibly sexy."

*He looks at me like I'm the most precious thing in the world.*

*

We entered the crowded hall, instantly surrounded by a sea of colorful paintings and installations.

As we moved through the space, a group of guys passed by, laughing and chatting. "Hey, Adrian!" one of them called out, giving him a high five.

Another guy stopped, turning toward us with a huge grin. "I just saw your email," he said, shaking his head like he couldn't believe it. "How on earth did you pull that one off, Adrian?"

He turned to me with a smile, like I should already know. "That guy's a literal lifesaver," he said. "Alright, gotta run—but see you Monday, yeah? And thanks again. Seriously—you didn't just make my day. You made my next **year**." He jogged off to rejoin his group.

"Wow," I said, raising an eyebrow. "A lot of people seem to value you here."

Adrian smiled. "Well... I hope so. I do a lot of work here," he said casually.

Before I could ask more, a familiar voice called out. "Hey, welcome to our *Flowstream* exhibition!" Eliyah waved excitedly and made his way toward us.

Just like Rani, Eliyah was one of my closest friends—even though we'd only met two years ago. He had this infectious joy about him, a kind of childlike playfulness most people had long outgrown, and I loved that about him. Officially, Eliyah was a dancer and a programmer—a combination he took great pride in—but tonight, he was here to support Rani and her exhibition.

He pulled me into a warm hug, then turned to Adrian, greeting him with French-style kisses on both cheeks. It was typical Eliyah—he loved doing that with guys he barely knew, as if he was gently challenging male stereotypes right from the start.

Adrian embraced it.

"Okay, my loves. I'm your guide today, so I'll give you a quick intro," Eliyah said, clapping his hands together. "Let's jump right in. This is an interactive exhibition designed to pull you into a state of flow—and maybe even challenge the way you move through life."

"Where does it start?" I asked.

"As you can see, there are different pieces scattered around. But the real heart of it all is right in front of you." he pointed to a massive sculpture. "That's the highlight. Let's start there."

The stone sculpture drew me in: curves upon curves, vivid forms entwined, a wild design balanced between chaos and order. I couldn't look away.

"This sculpture's meant to be touched," Eliyah said. "Come explore—you'll be surprised."

Adrian and I stepped closer, our hands instinctively reaching out to connect with the cold stone.

The gentle lines guided us, pulling our fingers along paths that felt almost natural, but as I traced what seemed like the obvious route, I suddenly felt it—an unexpected resistance, subtle yet sharp. Like the sculpture was communicating with us, nudging us in another direction.

Without realizing it, Adrian and I both veered off the original path. Our hands followed different lines as if led by something invisible.

"Wait—how did that happen?" I asked.

"Fascinating, right?" Eliyah smiled. "It's a visual illusion. You think you see the path ahead, but then the artist throws in a subtle twist. More than 90 percent of visitors drift without even realizing it."

"Really? It's 90 percent?" I asked, still tracing the stone.

"Yep," Eliyah said. "It's hard not to. Pushing against that resistance feels unnatural. In real life, it's the opposite. We ignore the resistance—our intuition—because we think we know better. We follow logic, habit, or fear. This sculpture flips that idea."

I paused, letting it sink in. "So... it's about trusting the unexpected?" I said slowly. "Not forcing everything to go the way we planned or wanted it to?"

"Exactly." Eliyah nodded. "And most importantly: letting intuition guide you, even when it doesn't make sense at first. Trusting it."

"Wow. I love it," I said.

"I knew you would," Eliyah smiled. "I'll leave you two to it now—I've got to take care of the incoming guests. Enjoy the exhibit, and I'll see you later!" He rushed back to the entrance.

I turned to Adrian, scanning his face. "Are you okay?" I asked, nudging him lightly with my shoulder. "You're much quieter than last time."

"Maybe," he said, running a hand through his hair, making it stick up in a way that somehow made him look even hotter. "I'm having fun, don't worry," he said, flashing a quick smile.

"I guess I've just never really been the artsy type. I love music, dancing, food, culture... but exhibitions are still new territory for me. And when I'm new to something, I tend to observe more than talk."

"Interesting," I said, tilting my head. "Cute," I added, smiling.

*And weirdly sexy. (I'm keeping that part to myself.)*

"I already figured you were the type that's good at everything," I teased.

His grin widened as he closed the space between us—just enough for me to feel the heat radiating off his body. "No, not even close," he says, his voice lower now, meant only for me.

"**Please**," he murmurs, pulling me slightly in and holding my gaze, "show me your world, Sophie. I'd hate to miss the chance to impress you."

My body starts heating up. *Would anyone else think this sounded sexual right now? Or was it just me?*

***God**, I'm turned on.*

*Let's go, Adrian.*

*Find a dark corner, rip our clothes off, and then please—show me what you've got.*

*Impress me.*

*What are we waiting for?*

Before I could get carried away, Eliyah appeared out of nowhere. "Hey, you two," he said, giving us a playful look. "What did I miss? Are you having fun—made your decision yet?"

*Great timing!*

"What decision?" I asked.

"Ah—you won't leave here without it, my love," Eliyah said. "Turn around."

We turned to find a large, sleek gray machine with two ropes hanging from the ceiling. Above it, glowing in bold green neon, were the words:

*** Thanks for visiting the Flowstream exhibit ***

Now, what's your life going to be like in the future?

Beneath the sign, two choices were displayed:

The right rope:

**Stick to the plan.** (Stay on track, no surprises.)

The left rope:

**Follow your gut.** (Leap when it feels right.)

The floor beneath the ropes was scattered with colorful confetti, like the scene was already celebrating whichever future you chose.

Eliyah grinned, glancing between Adrian and me. "This one's going to be interesting," he said, bouncing lightly on his heels. "Okay. Let's decide together. On three."

Adrian and I exchanged a look. A small, subtle smile passed between us, and we nodded in agreement.

"One... two... three." Without hesitation, we both reached for the left rope, our fingers brushing for the briefest moment before pulling it down in unison.

Instantly, a deep, rhythmic beat vibrated through the floor. And then—**confetti**. A whirlwind of bright colors rained down around us, catching in my hair, dusting Adrian's shoulders like tiny fragments of celebration.

I blinked up at him, laughing in surprise—and found him already looking at me. His smile was wide, unguarded, a flash of pure, boyish joy that made my heart stutter. He ran a hand through his hair, scattering the confetti, and chuckled under his breath.

*I'm loving this.*

"Well," Eliyah said, his voice warm with amusement, "guess that settles it."

Rani appeared. "Hey, kids. What's going on **here**?" she said, a knowing smile tugging at her lips. Then her eyes landed on Adrian—and widened. "Wait a second... are you Sophie's date?"

She looked at me. "Sophie, girl. You didn't tell me it was **Adrian** you were meeting tonight," she said, laughing as she pulled us into a warm hug.

I glanced between them, a little thrown. "Why—do you two know each other?"

Rani grinned. "Yeah. He's the reason we could pull off the exhibit," she said, teasingly bumping Adrian with her shoulder. "He's been working with my art collective for two years now, helping us raise funds and keep the whole thing alive."

"Well, it's a lot of fun working with you guys," Adrian just said, like it wasn't a big deal.

"Anyways. I hope you've had a great night so far. Sorry it took me so long to find you. I had to give our major sponsor a private tour," she said, rolling her eyes. "But I'm finally free. Now —drinks at Lola's? I need some fresh air. I've been stuck inside for days," she pleaded.

*

On our way out, we bumped into another group of Adrian's fans.

"Hey Adrian, glad you're coming to the barbecue next weekend!" one of them called out, clapping him on the shoulder as they passed.

"Wouldn't miss it. See you then, Ryan," Adrian said, flashing a quick smile and wave.

I laughed. "Wow. Okay, I know you work here, but still. Three hundred people in this building, and you seem to know half of them. Are you a VIP or something?"

He shrugged, unfazed. "I help people realize their dreams and make money. People tend to remember you for that."

*So, he's humble too.*

"Fair point," I said.

Rani and Eliyah strolled ahead of us, lost in a bubble of laughter, their arms wrapped around one another. Adrian and I walked a few steps behind.

"Are those two together?" Adrian asked.

"No way," I laughed. "Rani's a single mom. And Eliyah has several relationships—he's polyamorous. But not with Rani. Eliyah, her, and I—we're basically an inseparable friend trio. And now, we are all members at SPARKS. They were already part of it and convinced me to join too."

"You've got great friends, Sophie. I don't know Eliyah yet, but he seems fun. And Rani's just great. I love her," he said.

"I know, right? I love her **so** much."

*... And he likes your friends.*

*Stop being so great all the time, Adrian, or this is definitely going to spiral out of control tonight.*

*Or actually... don't stop.*

*I kind of want it to at this point.*

I see Rani and Eliyah turning around the street corner, heading towards our favorite wine bar.

*Alone. Finally.*

We walk quietly for a moment. Just leaving a subtle trail of confetti behind us.

Adrian's gaze lingers on me.

In a small, unexpected moment, he reaches over—brushes a few stray pieces of confetti from my hair. His fingers skim lightly against my neck, drifting lower along the curve of my back before pulling away.

A tiny shock runs through me, quick and hot.

Then, out of nowhere, he takes my hand and, with one smooth pull, wraps me into a hug. My head lands on his warm chest.

It rests there. Steady, calm, protected by his arms. Moving up and down with his heartbeat. The world around us blurs into nothing.

*This feels* ***right****. So incredibly* ***right****.*

Time doesn't just slow down—it stops.

*So* ***this*** *is what they talk about in all those cheesy romance novels.*

*It's settled. I don't want the night to end yet. I said from the start—I* ***am*** *open to casual adventures, as long as it doesn't feel random. And this? This feels like the opposite of random.*

*Wait—what's the opposite of random? Am I getting myself into trouble?*

*Maybe.*

*Probably.*

*I hope not.*

*Okay, stop overthinking it, Sophie. If you keep analyzing everything, you'll never have any real fun—or great sex—ever again. It's too late anyway. You're already in too deep. Just go with the flow.*

"Do you want to come to my place for a drink?" I ask. "I live in Greenpoint."

"For a **drink**?" he smiles, amused.

"I'm not promising anything. I'm not sure where this is headed at all," I say. "I just don't feel like sitting in a wine bar, surrounded by a hundred other people right now."

"No problem," he grins. "I'd rather have you to myself anyway."

I quickly text Rani and Eliyah goodbye, and a few minutes later, I slip into the backseat of an Uber.

*Let's have a little fun.*

I flash Adrian a mischievous smile and pull the door closed behind me, pretending I'm about to drive off alone.

He shakes his head with a grin, immediately yanks the door open, and slides in next to me, his shoulder brushing against mine. "Forget it, Sophie," he murmurs. "I'm not letting you get away this time."

The door clicks shut, the car pulls into the street, and we race through the night—arm in arm, the city lights blurring past us.

Neither of us says a word.

Talking feels like the wrong language right now—unnecessary, irrelevant. We're far too excited for the part that comes next.

The silence becomes a quiet countdown between now and the moment the apartment door finally closes behind us. We both know that's when the night will actually begin.

CHALLENGE 5

# Shameless

"Wow," Adrian says as he steps into my apartment. "This feels like we just walked into the next art gallery."

"Thanks," I smile. "I finally traded my impersonal box in the Meatpacking District for this place. It's still a work in progress, though. I just moved here a week ago."

The apartment is part of a cozy, historic brownstone building, with the original brick façade still intact. It has a stunning East River view and a spacious, open kitchen that seamlessly flows into the living room.

I want everything here to be intentional but so far, I'd only added a few things: a bed for the enclosed bedroom, and in the living room, oversized botanical plants, a massive sand-colored couch that filled nearly a third of the space, and walls covered with a mix of art pieces Rani had recommended, my own dream-like illustrations, and a pink paper flower by my godchild Rhea—Rani's four-year-old daughter.

We are still in the corridor as I take off my boots and start to unzip my jacket.

"Wait," Adrian says, touching my arm lightly. "The confetti... It's going to get everywhere." He smiles.

I glance down—tiny flashes of color cling to my clothes.

***Fuck it.***

"Well," I raise my eyebrows, "I guess there's only one solution to that." I slide off my jacket and let it fall to the floor.

Then, without hesitation, I pull my top over my head and drop it beside it.

My eyes are piercing his. "It's not like we haven't already seen each other in just our underwear," I say.

*I'm starting to like the new Sophie.*

Adrian grins.

He immediately bends down and kicks off his shoes. In one smooth movement, he peels off his jacket too, then his sweater —standing there in just jeans, with bits of confetti dusted across his bare skin.

I swallow hard. *God, I'm so drawn to him.*

Almost in sync, we both move our hands to the buttons of our jeans, pausing there for a second.

*Sophie, breathe.*

He chuckles slightly.

Then, as if by silent agreement, we shove them down in slow motion.

And just like that, we stand there—in our underwear. Again. Facing each other, eyes locked.

Chests rising and falling.

Hearts pounding.

"So, about my relationship. Kate and I..." Adrian suddenly says.

***Wow.*** *This is already the second time he's destroyed our moment.*

*Maybe this is our new thing: Hang out half-naked, chat, get really turned on by each other... but doing absolutely nothing about it. And then—part ways.*

*I certainly hope not.*

I take a deep breath and break eye contact.

Then I spin around, pace down the corridor toward the kitchen, grab two wine glasses, and pour—fast.

Still silent, I walk into the living room and settle onto the couch.

Adrian has stopped talking by now, confused for a beat, then he joins me on the couch, keeping a careful distance.

"Hey, what's going on—did I do something wrong?" he asks.

*Defend your boundaries, Sophie.*

I take a deep breath. "Look. You told me you're in an open relationship—if that works for you, great. And obviously this

—us—can't be anything beyond physical. I get that. I respect that. I wouldn't want anything more with someone who's taken."

He stays quiet, his hands loosely clasped between his knees.

"The way I see it, it's your job to stick to whatever boundaries you and your girlfriend agreed on—and to let me know if there's a line we shouldn't cross. The rest is between you and her. No need to chat about it. Especially not in a moment like this."

My eyes drift briefly...

*This part has never been easy for you, Sophie.*

*But you've got to be open now—be vulnerable—even if it's uncomfortable.*

*Otherwise, he won't get what's really going on.*

... before locking back on his.

"To be honest, this is all new to me. I've never been involved with someone in an open relationship. But I do know one thing: when I'm with you, I want it to feel like it's just us. Not like a third person is crushing our date."

*It's bizarre that we're having this conversation half-naked and sprinkled with confetti.*

"That sounds totally fair," Adrian says. "All of this is so normal for me that I forget it isn't for everyone."

"It's okay," I say.

"And no, there are no boundaries we shouldn't cross. No limits to what we can or can't do, how often we see each other, or what this is. I'm alone in town for the upcoming months, too."

He pauses. "I'm just wondering... have I told you about my second girlfriend, Jenny?"

I blink. "What?"

"Just **kidding**," he says, flashing a mischievous grin.

*That one was risky.* ***Bold.***

Without thinking, I grab a pillow and launch it at his head.

"What the fuck, Sophie?" he says, laughing as he catches it. "How old are you?"

"If you don't listen to me, I have to make myself heard," I reply, my face perfectly neutral. I hurl another pillow—harder this time.

"**Heyyy**," he protests, laughter bubbling up.

I'm already winding up a third. "Are you just gonna sit there and whine, or are you finally going to defend yourself?" I tease, one eyebrow raised. I lift a fourth pillow, weighing it in my hand like I'm deciding.

Adrian lunges forward, grabs my wrist mid-throw, and tosses the pillow aside.

We burst into laughter.

Now we're standing—chests rising a little faster, inches apart.

Our laughter quiets as he leans in, his lips brushing the shell of my ear. "There's no second girlfriend," he whispers, voice low and rough. "And there are no other dates. You're **the only one** I'm seeing right now. The only one I want to see."

He pulls back just enough to meet my eyes.

The world narrows to just this.

Just him. Just us.

Everything else fades.

Time slows again.

I know I can take the night wherever I want it to go.

It's my choice...

My heart flutters.

"Are you planning to kiss me at some point?" I hear myself say.

Adrian's eyes widen, and a boyish smile flashes across his face. He pauses for a heartbeat, then leans in with rushed intensity. His warm hands slide around my neck, the touch unexpectedly gentle. And then—his lips, full and irresistibly soft, meet mine.

His kiss is meaningful but brief—like he's testing the waters, before his eyes meet mine again.

We are studying each other's faces for a second.

**Silence.**

*I feel this urge.*

*I'm still lit up from our pillow fight energy, and honestly, I kind of want to keep fighting him.*

*I've never done it before, but I really want to right now.*

*Just go for it, Sophie*

*—what are you waiting for?*

*This guy told you within the first minutes you met that he doesn't do rules or shame. No judgment, no holding back.*

*Game's on.*

*Let's play!*

"That was nice. Soft," I say with a cheeky smile. "But you know, if you wanted to go a little bit harder, that would be fine too."

Adrian's entire face flushes.

He doesn't hesitate for a second—like he'd just been waiting for me to say that.

He rises from the couch in one smooth motion, moves behind me, grabs my wrists, and pulls them firmly behind my back. "Harder, huh?" he murmurs against my ear, his voice low. "You could have just said that instead of throwing pillows at me like a little girl."

He still holds my wrists firmly against my back, but I'm not ready to surrender that easily. "I threw the pillows at you because it seems like you don't know when it's time to stop talking," I say as I push back, wriggle free from his grip, and turn the tables, pressing against him.

We wrestle playfully, testing each other, both of us determined to gain the upper hand. Then he pauses, his tone becoming more serious. "Wait. If we're doing this, I need to know you really want it. I need your consent."

"You have my consent," I say immediately.

"Good," he smiles. "Then you'd better do as I say now." His grip softens as he takes my wrists again, then gently turns me so my back is to him. One hand holds both of mine behind me, while the other slides slowly up the length of my back—until it settles at the nape of my neck.

“Lie down,” he says, firmly but gently guiding me with a hand on my neck until I’m on my belly, the soft couch beneath me, and him standing beside me. He lifts my hips and puts some pillows underneath my belly—my hips are slightly raised now.

For a moment, I just lay there in my barely there black thong and revealing sheer see-through bra—Waiting.

His warm hand returns to my neck and slides down until it arrives at my hips.

Then it raises and comes down on my ass with a sharp smack.

*Oh my god, this feels incredible.*

“Is that what you want, you sassy little thing?”

“**Yes**,” I breathe.

Another smack.

Then he pauses for a second. “You can stop this whenever you want. Just say the safety word. In fact, let’s not use stupid code words. Just say ‘**No, I mean it**,’ If I do anything you don’t want, I’ll stop. Now or later. Whenever I do something you don’t like, you say no, and I’ll stop immediately.

It’s very important that you don’t do anything you don’t feel comfortable with.

Got it?”

“Yes.

Harder.”

His hand comes down with another smack.

“Hey,” he whispers, his fingers gently tracing the curve of my hip. “I just hit you pretty hard there. Are you okay?” His touch is warm on my skin.

“Yes, I’m okay.”

He lifts me effortlessly and pulls me toward him as my feet land on the floor.

His hand is on my neck, and then he kisses me.

Slow, deep, passionate.

**Those are the softest lips I’ve ever kissed.**

Now, he wraps his arms around me tightly as he sinks onto

the couch, guiding me into his lap. He pulls me close with steady strength—making me feel small, safe, and completely protected.

Our bodies are close, so close.

I start feeling dizzy. But his skin's scent—earthy, musky, and raw—grounds me, pulling me back to the moment.

"Are you really okay?"

"More than okay," I smile.

"Do you want more?"

"Yes."

He slowly takes my wrists in one hand, guiding them behind my back with a grip that's gentle but firm. His other hand finds my neck, drawing my upper body just slightly away from his, creating a stretch of charged space between us. He moves his hand away from my neck, raises it, and delivers a sharp slap to my right breast.

I gasp.

He gives me just enough time to absorb the sensation before his hand strikes again, this time on the other side.

The sharp sound echoes through the room.

My pulse thrums.

He pauses for a second, his eyes meeting mine.

There's something primal, almost predatory in his gaze.

Then, he kisses me, this time even more intensely.

My head starts spinning.

"Wait a second," he suddenly says.

He walks into the corridor and slips off the belt from the trousers on the floor, then comes back and lifts me effortlessly into his arms. *So strong. So warm. So protected.*

He carries me to the bed and lays me gently on my back.

Now, he kneels above me, the leather sliding through his fingers with quiet authority.

My body starts to shiver.

He pulls me slightly up, ties my hands together with his belt behind my back, and lays me down again.

Then, he rises back up in a controlled motion and—bam—another sharp slap landed on my right breast.

Now faster, another—bam—on the left.

My gasps fill the room.

***Dizzy. So dizzy.***

He stops for a moment—his eyes hold mine—and slowly moves his hands lower onto my legs, tracing a path that makes me ache with anticipation.

He pauses again, teasing, holding back just enough to make me plead. "Say it," he commands. "Do you want me to continue?"

"**Please**," I breathe.

His fingers continue their slow descent, parting my legs with a deliberate, measured confidence.

Then, he leans forward to kiss my neck—warm, so warm—while his fingers slide into me in one slow motion, deep and unrelenting.

"Oh my god, Adrian, what are you doing—how can you make me feel so fucking good?"

His fingers continue to explore, and pleasure surges through me so intensely I can hardly contain it.

"Oh **god, oh god,**" my body trembles.

He stops for a second, just pierces me with his eyes.

"**Please**," I beg. "**Please don't stop.**"

His fingers slide inside me one more time, slowly yet determined, moving deeply with a rhythm that sends waves of heat through my body.

Now, his left hand rises and lands on my left breast again—my skin burns—while his right hand continues to move inside of me.

He pauses—just a second—then lets his hand fall on my right breast, with the same controlled intensity.

A thrill shoots through me, and before I can recover, the fingers of his other hand continue their deliberate rhythm, pushing deep inside of me.

The switch of sensations is almost too much to bear.

The line between pain and pleasure blurs.

It consumes me.

**All of me.**

His left hand moves away from my breast onto my face, slipping past my lips.

I instinctively open my mouth, taking his hand in.

*What the fuck are we doing here?*

*And why does it feel like this is how it should've always been?*

*My whole life—just him and me.*

*Fucking.*

*Fucking like nothing else matters.*

*Like there are no rules, no right or wrong.*

*Just instincts.*

*Just us, following them wherever they lead.*

Slowly, Adrian withdraws. "Wait, I'll get a condom," he says, abruptly breaking the flow.

"No!" I blurt out, my voice firm and resolute. "I'm not going to sleep with you today."

"Did I do something wrong?"

*Maybe it's because he's taken.*

*Or it's because we've just met and it's been a while...*

*Either way, I'm not ready. And honestly?*

*I don't owe sex to anyone.*

I fight hard to return to my senses and string a sentence together. "No. I guess I just went with the moment, not thinking ahead. It's just how I feel right now. If that's a deal-breaker for you, I understand. It's okay."

He smiles, leans forward, and meets my eyes. "On the contrary," he says, his voice low and steady. "Let me make it very easy for you—I'll make sure you keep all your boundaries in check. I'll take care of you and nothing else."

He kisses my neck and whispers into my ear, "There's nothing hotter than a woman who's not afraid to say no."

Then he pauses and leans back, his gaze burning into mine. "And for the record—I haven't been this turned on by anyone since I was sixteen. I'm having **the** best time.

So... do me a favor, beautiful Sophie. Lean back. Relax. And just enjoy."

He pushes me gently down, kisses me with an intensity that makes my head spin again, and continues to fuck me with his hand.

I finally let go—completely—and break free.

My body arches.

I tremble uncontrollably.

A scream rips from my lips.

And I come.

Harder than I ever had in my life.

*

The next morning, Adrian had to leave early for a weekend work event.

I curled up in bed alone.

The fresh air drifted in through the open window, and a profound sense of calm set in—a feeling I hadn't experienced in a long time, if ever, after spending a night with a man.

I liked Adrian—we had a great time together, no doubt about it. But strangely, I wasn't obsessing over what it meant or what might come next.

Not like I usually would.

*Okay, this is new. How did **that** happen?*

I thought back to past moments that now felt like they belonged to another life—times when sex with someone new had left me caught up in messy emotional loops, probably driven, at least partly, by a potent hormonal cocktail.

I knew the science of it: women release oxytocin almost instantly during intimacy, creating a deeper bond with their partner, even when having casual sex. Men, on the other hand, often appear able to connect physically without that same emotional gravity. *Who knew biology could be so impractical for women?*

But despite the science, this time felt different.

Perhaps I didn't feel as unhealthily entangled because I knew he was taken. No matter what my heart wanted, I wasn't **expecting** this to lead anywhere—and strangely, that realization was liberating.

Or perhaps it was because I'd discovered that intimacy didn't have to mean surrendering myself completely. In the past, my interactions with guys during sex had often felt one-sided—like I was just being pulled along, a passenger in someone else's story.

But not last night. Last night, I dared to be a raw, unapologetic, shameless version of myself. The version I'd always craved to be—but never fully admitted. Not even to myself.

And for the first time, the night had been just about **me**. It hadn't revolved around **pleasuring some guy**.

Adrian's dick was never inside me. He didn't cross the line since I had not allowed him to.

Maybe that was the key. He wasn't taking; he wasn't claiming. He served me, was devoted to my pleasure, and focused entirely on making me feel seen, heard, and satisfied. It was like he existed solely to honor me.

I didn't know whether that changed the biochemistry of it all or whether it was just my attitude—the fact that I had truly owned my choices, was clear with what I wanted and didn't want, and set boundaries accordingly.

But for the first time after casual sex, I didn't feel the slightest bit used. I didn't feel like an object that had to obey to satisfy some man, something to be consumed and discarded. I didn't feel empty or hollow when it was over. I didn't feel an instant craving, a desperate longing for something more.

Instead, I felt whole.

I felt calm.

I felt as if everything that had just happened was exactly as it was meant to be.

There was no ache for what wasn't there, no sense of incompletion—just the quiet, profound satisfaction of being held, cherished, cared for, and free.

It was a longing I didn't even know I had. And the realization that I had crafted this new reality myself felt nothing short of magical.

**Ring.**

My alarm went off.

*Time to get up and ready for your journey, Sophie!*

CHALLENGE 6

# Be My Own Boss

I jumped into my Uber to the airport when I saw Adrian's message.

**Adrian:** Thank you for last night, Sophie. I had so much fun with you! :)

**Me:** Me too! Are you still at your work event?

**Adrian:** Yes. For another hour. We'll wrap up at 2 p.m. I just sneaked out for a minute. Hard to focus anyway. Too many fresh images in my mind...

**Adrian:** What are you up to for the next few days?

**Me:** Do you miss me already?

**Adrian:** Honestly? Yes...

**Me:** Wow—it's been only a couple of hours you know?;) I'm heading to LA for work. On my way to the airport right now

**Adrian:** For your lighting project?

**Me:** Yes! I'm meeting with someone at a potential production site.

**Adrian:** Sounds great. Exciting! When are you back?

**Me:** Next week Thursday late at night

**Adrian:** Will I see you next weekend?

**Me:** Maybe... Let's keep in touch okay?

**Adrian:** Definitely. Safe travels

**Me:** Thanks—enjoy the rest of your event

**Adrian:** Thanks :)

When I arrived in LA, I saw a new message had already arrived.

**Adrian:** Heading to bed now. Hope you made it safely. Sleep tight—fingers crossed for your project. Is the production site visit tomorrow?

**Me:** Thanks :) I got in safely. The first meeting is just an informal coffee with a designer tomorrow afternoon. The actual site visit is on Monday. Sleep well!

My next day started with a good morning text from Adrian—and another one followed that evening.

**Adrian:** How did your coffee date go?

**Me:** Really great. I think he might be able to build some prototypes for me.

**Adrian:** That's incredible. I'm so happy for you! Will you send me some pics of the production site tomorrow?

**Me:** Not sure I'm allowed to, but if I can, I will. How was your day?

**Adrian:** Had a great time barbecuing with friends—Ryan, the guy who invited me when we left SPARKS, remember?

**Me:** Right... sounds fun! Enjoy the rest of your evening—gotta dive into some production planning now

**Adrian:** Alright. Sweet dreams

**Me:** You too :)

*The next morning...*

**Adrian:** Good luck today, Sophie. You've got this. Honestly, they'd be crazy not to want to work with you. If you want to talk anything through or need support, I'm here

**Me:** Thanks, that's very sweet of you. Have a great day, too!

*A few hours later...*

**Me:** The production visit was incredible (pics). They're on board. I'll be spending the week with them building out the first prototypes. Need to stay focused for a few days—so might not be super responsive—but I'll be back in NY Friday to set up my new studio

**Adrian:** That's amazing news. I'll be Upstate on Friday but let's meet over the weekend?

**Me:** I'm not sure yet—will text you on Friday, okay? :)

**Adrian:** Perfect. Have a great week!

*

**Adrian:** Good morning :) Back in the city?

**Me:** Good morning :) Yes—back in the city and just about to head into SPARKS now. In a hurry—need to pick up the key in time... will text you later in the afternoon.

**Adrian:** Okay. Enjoy your first day at the studio!

I raced through the doors toward the reception desk, slightly out of breath. "Hi, I'm here to get the keys for my new studio. It's for the lighting project."

"I know. Sophie, right?"

I nodded. "The contract was supposed to start on Monday, September 1st, but we'd informally agreed I could get in early to start setting up today."

"Just give me one second..." The woman reached under the counter and pulled out a set of keys. "Here it is. Come with me. I'm Jayne, by the way."

We headed up the broad staircase, our steps echoing faintly off the polished concrete. The walls were dotted with bold, oversized art prints and handwritten notes pinned to corkboards. A mix of paintbrushes, camera cases, and fabric swatches peeked out from open doors as we passed.

Jayne turned left.

I hesitated. "Jayne?"

She glanced back. "Yes?"

"My studio's on the right side in the back," I said.

"Just come with me for a second," she replied with a small, knowing smile.

*Okay... what's going on?*

We stopped in front of the door to the space that I had so desperately wanted to rent in the first place. Jayne unlocked the door and pushed it open with a quiet click, then stepped aside and gestured for me to go in.

"This one just became available. I understand you had your eye on it?"

I stepped inside slowly, letting the warmth of the sunlight hit my face. "Yes," I breathed. "I tried everything, but I was told it wasn't possible."

"Well, things changed," she said lightly. "If you still want it, it's yours. Take a moment, let it sink in. I'll be downstairs if you need anything." She placed the keys in my palm, gave me a little wink, and walked off.

The door closed behind me with a soft thud.

I was alone. And I was standing in my **dream studio**.

The entire room was bathed in late-morning light. Through the large glass windows, the skyline came into view—and for a moment, it took my breath away.

I took a few slow steps into the room, letting my fingers brush the cool edge of the window frame. I could picture where I'd set the lamp prototypes, where the sketches would go. This place already felt like mine.

Then I noticed a small table near the entrance—one that definitely hadn't been there during my first tour.

On it: a chilled bottle of champagne, three crystal glasses, a furniture design magazine opened to a spread of curved wood and warm brass... and a white card, propped neatly beside it.

My heartbeat quickened as I reached for the card.

> Sophie,
>
> Someone who creates life-changing light doesn't belong in a tiny dark room... I hope you like your new studio. It's yours if you want it.
>
> There's a furniture start-up in the building—I thought it could be a good start for you and great exposure for them. So, I told them about your incredible idea, and they'd be happy to offer you some pieces for free. Totally your decision, of course, but now you've got options.
>
> I would have loved to celebrate with you today, but maybe Rani and Eliyah will raise a glass with you.
>
> I have a feeling your idea is really going to take off and help people around the world become happier, healthier versions of themselves. We've only just met, and you've just started your business... but somehow, I feel really proud of you. Strange, isn't it?
>
> Enjoy your first day in the studio.
> —Adrian

I didn't even realize the tears had started falling until one splashed against the corner of the card.

I bit down on my lip, hard.

My throat tightened.

*I can't believe this.*

I sank onto the floor, the card still in my hand, my gaze drifting toward the wall of windows. The skyline stretched wide in front of me, calm and golden in the morning light.

*Adrian had no idea.*

He didn't know I was only **just** becoming this version of myself. He didn't know what it had taken to get here, or what I'd left behind—how new this present, this future, still felt: raw, fragile, full of hope... and sometimes, doubt.

To me, this wasn't just a kind gesture. It was something else entirely. It was belief.

Belief in a vision, I was only just beginning to believe in myself. Encouragement not just in words, but in action. In trust. In showing up.

I was used to handling everything on my own—self-reliant and independent. Always the one taking care of myself. Carrying myself, because no one else would.

**No one** had ever done something like this for me.

Especially not someone I had **just** met.

*Should I call him? No, you're too emotional right now, Sophie... text!*

I reached for my phone, took a deep breath, and started typing.

**Me:** Oh my god, Adrian. I've just arrived at my studio space (pic). I can't believe you did this for me. It's incredible. **You** are. Thank you so much

**Adrian:** Will you take it?

**Me:** Of course I will. I can't even begin to tell you how happy I am right now

**Adrian:** Well, nothing makes me happier than to hear that. Glad I could support you and your idea :)

**Me:** How did you do it? Are you a magician or something? I'd tried everything

And I'm usually known for being very persuasive...

**Adrian:** I offered them a consultancy deal—but what really convinced them was your idea itself. The heart behind it, the potential impact. They're currently trying to highlight meaningful projects at SPARKS, and yours fits perfectly. They instantly got it. So, making your work more visible in one of the best spaces in the front building was the obvious choice—to them, and honestly, to me too

**Me:** I'm impressed

**Adrian:** Impressed enough to say yes to another date with me this weekend?

**Me:** Definitely :) I have to finish some files for the production site tomorrow, but I'll be free for a bit. Pick me up at 10 a.m. for a walk?

**Adrian:** Sounds great. Can't wait to finally see you again. Enjoy your new studio, Sophie

**Me:** I sure will. Have a great day Upstate! I'll see you tomorrow :)

CHALLENGE 7

# The Kind of Trouble I Swore I'd Never Walk Into Again

It was 10 a.m. sharp.

I slipped on my favorite camel-colored wool coat, headed downstairs, and spotted Adrian waiting in the courtyard. Tall, handsome, flashing a warm smile.

My pulse quickens dangerously the second I see him.

*He's in a relationship, Sophie. Be careful.*

Adrian walks up and wraps me in a deliberate hug—like we'd known each other forever and had just spent too long apart.

Then, slowly, he pulls back.

His hand brushes a strand of hair behind my ear.

His eyes meet mine.

And then he kisses me.

***Dizziness.***

"Shall we just go for a stroll and then to Transmitter Park?"

I nod.

As we start walking, I'm all over the place—jittery, jumpy, bursting out in random directions like a kid at the edge of a new adventure.

*What's happening?*

*Why am I* ***this*** *excited?*

Adrian glances at me, clearly amused by my energy. "I suggest we walk side by side," he says with a warm smile, gently taking my hand and guiding me closer.

"Okay," I say—way too squeaky and enthusiastic—and practically bounce into his arm.

He laughs. "You're awfully playful today. I really like this side of you."

My cheeks flush. "Of course I am!" I shoot back. I'm like this all the time."

*The new (old) Sophie is, at least.*

*But right—that's the only version he knows.*

*And honestly? I like that—a lot.*

We stroll hand in hand through the vibrant Greenpoint streets. The sidewalks filled with cafés and people sipping matcha lattes, the early autumn sun casting golden stripes through the trees.

A group of very design-y looking guys walk past us—one in a wild patterned beanie, another in oversized plaid, all of them effortlessly mismatched and yet on point.

I glance at them out of habit, scanning their colorful outfits.

Adrian notices.

"Are you into those kinds of guys?" he asks casually.

I tilt my head, amused. "What do you mean by **those kinds of guys**?"

"You know... creative, artsy types who dress to stand out."

I stop walking and turn to him, eyebrows raised. "Why do you ask that?"

He pauses mid-step, then shoves his hands into his coat pockets, suddenly looking quite boyish. "It's like... the guy wearing those outfits is always the trendsetter—the designer type or the artsy dude. Like all the people at SPARKS. I guess you're part of that crowd."

I squint at him. "Okay, and? What's going on here? I'm not following."

"Alright. I have to admit something. I don't know how to dress." He gives me a look. "Like. **Not at all.**"

I blink. "You what? You literally always wear black and white. Minimalist. You look well put together."

"That's because my sister helped me create a wardrobe I couldn't mess up. You don't want to see what I'd pick out otherwise."

"Oh, I **really** do now. What would it be?"

He looks down, cringing. "Think... smiley socks. Corduroy pants."

"Nooo." I burst out laughing, almost doubling over. "Sorry —I'm not trying to make fun of you. I just... I cannot picture you in that at all."

"Well," he says, grinning, "believe it."

We start walking again, our arms brushing now as we move closer together.

"That's hilarious," I say. "You've got this sexy minimalist thing going on. No one would ever guess you're secretly a corduroy guy."

He chuckles, bumping my arm with his. "Alright, want to know what else no one would ever guess about me?"

I nod.

"I've got impostor syndrome."

I stop mid-step and looked at him. "What? **You?**"

"It's not that I'm not confident," he says. "I am. But nothing ever felt that difficult professionally. Things kind of just... fell into place. I'm good with people, I know how to work a room, and sometimes it all feels a bit too easy. Like, I didn't really earn it."

"Wow." I squeeze his hand. "Again: would never have guessed that."

"I know. No one outside my family knows. But once a year or so, I spiral—just for a few minutes, hours, or maybe a day—thinking someone's going to figure out I'm not who they think I am. It always passes, but when it hits... I'm a total mess. The opposite of the usual calm, steady, rational me."

He grins. "Want to hear another one? Last one though. Then it's your turn."

"Always. And deal."

"I'm addicted to pasta. I can't be trusted around it."

"Pasta?"

"Yeah. My grandparents are Italian, and I guess it just stuck. I actually had a weight problem in kindergarten—no joke. I still have to watch myself. But on bad days? I totally cave. I'll eat a plate of pasta... then come back twenty minutes later for two more. I love making it, eating it, even just thinking about it."

"Oh my god, Adrian," I say, laughing again. "You look amazing. You have nothing to worry about."

"Thanks," he says with a half-smile. "But I think once you've been mocked for your weight as a child, that somehow sticks in the back of your mind forever."

"Okay." He nudges me gently. "Now you. What's your secret?"

"Fine," I say. "When I like something, I overdo it."

"That doesn't count," he replies. "That's what people say in job interviews. Like: I care too much about delivering excellent work."

"No, no. This is different. Like... obsessively. With food, for example. One dish? If I like it a lot, I eat it every day for a month. One podcast or Netflix series? I binge the entire thing right away, and I can't stop. Until it almost feels like that TV show is my life. I get lost in things. Really lost... to an insane degree. To the point where I have to avoid things I love—because I know I'll overdo it otherwise and get off track."

He raises an eyebrow, amused. "So, if I ever see you eat the same meal a couple of days in a row, I should be concerned?"

"Yes," I laugh. "Be very concerned."

He lets out a deep laugh. "Okay, we should **definitely** avoid sharing food obsessions then. That could get dangerous."

I grin. "Oh god, yes. It totally could."

"What else?" Adrian wants to know.

"I hate being strategic. I look like I've got it all together—but that's just because I work so hard at it. I have to keep things together. Even more than most people, because I'm naturally a head-in-the-clouds, dreamworld type. Emotional. Sensitive. It's exhausting sometimes, pretending to be so grounded, making rational decisions to keep everything on track."

"Stay up there in the clouds as much as you can. It's boring down here," Adrian jokes. "I mean, that's what I love about you.

You do seem like you've got your life organized and sorted out—but I can tell you've got this wild, playful drive. Like you want to escape reality half the time."

He pulls me even closer. "Alright, last one," he says. "One more quirk?"

"I carry a lint roller. Always."

He stops walking and looks at me. "You what? Even right now?"

I nod, dead serious, open my bag, and show him. "I even want to lint-roll other people when I see fuzz on them. It's a problem."

He burst out laughing. "No way. I almost can't believe this one. It's one of the weirdest things I've ever heard."

I smirked, looping my arm through his and pulling him closer. "I can see in your eyes that you like it, though."

"Oh yes, I really do," I laugh.

We kept walking for a while, our hands clasped, matching each other's rhythm now—effortlessly, like we'd been doing it forever.

When the wind picked up, Adrian shifted his coat to block it from hitting me directly.

And there it suddenly was: An irresistible urge to follow him wherever he might lead.

As we reached the park, he pointed to the empty jetty floating in the water, about 150 feet away from land, with the skyline in the background.

"Let's walk out there," Adrian suggested.

No one was on the platform but us; there were just a couple of faraway people passing by the waterfront here and there. The sun still peeked out from behind the clouds, casting a golden hue over the city.

We walked up to the railing.

As soon as we arrived on the edge, Adrian took both of my hands and pulled me toward him.

He brushed a strand of hair from my face, holding my cheeks gently in his hands.

Then, he leaned in and kissed me softly before wrapping me in the warmest hug imaginable. "I just want to be so close to you," he says, as if surprised by his own feelings. "Just my body against yours."

The warmth of his chest and the sun's rays made me feel as if everything around us was spinning, and at one point, I thought my feet had left the ground.

My thoughts drifted, and in my mind, I turned into one of my favorite icons, Audrey Hepburn in *Roman Holiday*—timeless, elegant, slightly mischievous—a black-and-white daydream with a great gentleman by my side. I felt the pull to step into the moment as if it were a scene from an old movie.

"What do you think you're doing?" I ask, my tone light but edged with mock scandal. "Waltzing up to an innocent woman like this... doing whatever you want, taking whatever you want?"

Adrian searches my eyes, catching the cheeky glint in them. A smirk tugs at the corner of his lips as he understands where I'm leading him.

Without a word, he turns, leans casually back against the railing, and pulls me in, facing me. "So, you're **that** innocent?" he asks, raising an eyebrow.

"Yes, I am!" I replied with an exaggerated pout. "I really didn't intend this to happen today. I didn't want to do anything with you at all, only strolling through the park. I thought you were a gentleman."

His body shields mine from view, though there's only water in front of me anyway.

My back, just about fifteen meters from the park, is covered by my long cashmere coat, like it's all part of the plan.

To anyone walking by, we're just two people standing close —nothing to see here. But under the fabric, something entirely different is unfolding.

His hand moves slowly, starting at my neck,
gliding down over my chest and stomach,

slipping beneath my sweater.
He unbuttons my jeans, then pulls the zipper.
His movements are deliberate and slow.

"So, innocent girl," he murmurs, his voice teasing, mocking, "maybe you still want me to keep going?"

"No," I say, maintaining the pretense. "We shouldn't. Really, we shouldn't." My tone mimicked an old-fashioned movie heroine, full of feigned innocence.

"You can say stop whenever you want," he reminds me. "You know, the code word is 'no, I mean it,'—say that, and I'll stop right away. Understood?" His voice is gentle but firm.

I nod.

His hand slides beneath my pink silk thong, and his fingers stroke me, up and down, teasing, with a deliberate softness as if handling something fragile.

I hear passersby engaged in light conversation, oblivious to the intimate moment hidden by my long coat.

Adrian's hand ventures further, each motion drawing me closer to the edge. I feel myself becoming hotter, the sensation building with every passing second.

Without warning, he drops to his knees, pulling my jeans down.

"Adrian," I say, my voice barely above a whisper. "People will see us."

"They won't," he says with quiet confidence. "You're well covered with your coat. I'll protect you. I'm paying attention—nothing will happen to you. I promise. Trust me. Will you?"

I nod.

He leans forward, pressing his lips to my leg,
then moving upward with an unhurried intensity.
His tongue and lips reach for me,
his kisses deepening as his fingers join, sliding in and out.

*It's warm, so warm.*
*This is the first time, I like the feeling of a man's tongue inside me.*
My past partners didn't seem to like it—an experience many of

my girlfriends share—and I could never surrender to something that felt obligatory.

But Adrian is different.

The way he **consumes** me isn't just an act—it's devotion.

He wants me. All of me.

He doesn't stop; his movements are relentless but controlled. My breaths come faster, shallow and uneven, as I struggle to keep from crying out.

The tension builds, rising higher and higher until I can barely hold on.

"Come up," I finally manage. My voice shakes.

Adrian stands, pulling me against him, his fingers still working their magic inside me.

He kisses me deeply, his grip firm as he holds me close, his fingers continuing their rhythm until I come

—intensely, completely.

My body melts into his, trembling.

The world around us disappears.

Adrian carefully pulls up my jeans, zips them up, and fastens the button with a practiced ease.

"Wait—what about you?" I ask.

"No. You keep your boundaries in check. We go further when it's the right time for you. Until then, I'll take care of you and you only," he says.

He draws me close. "Would you like to come home with me and eat something? We could be food addicted together," he offers, his eyes lighting up.

I still feel shaky, as if I might collapse at any moment. "That sounds amazing," I say with a warm smile. "But I think I'll head home. Maybe next time?"

"Let me take you back home at least," he insists, guiding me down the hill.

Once we arrive at the boardwalk, he casually shifts to the other side. His hand slides into mine.

“Why switch sides?” I ask, glancing up at him.

He flashes a grin. “I can’t tell you that.”

“What? No way, now you **have** to.” I punch him lightly in the chest, feeling the heat of his body through his jacket.

“Ouch,” he winces, a dramatic hand clutching his chest, his shoulders lifting slightly in mock defense.

“Okay, okay. Before you get violent... It’s a habit I picked up from my grandmother. She taught me how to treat women. It’s to protect you from the street.”

I raise an eyebrow, scanning his face for any sign of a joke, but his expression is serious. “What? Are you for real? I mean, it’s sweet... I guess, but—what are you protecting me from... cars?”

He shrugs. “I know, it’s old-fashioned. But it’s automatic now. Doesn’t even cross my mind.”

I stare at him for a beat, then let out a soft laugh. “Okay, this is officially becoming the **getting to know each other’s secrets’ day**. What else did you learn from your grandmother?”

Adrian turns to me, his gaze softening. “Making sure a girl gets home safe,” he says.

He leans in, his lips brushing mine, slow and careful. My heart beats faster and for a moment, it’s like I’m in some old black-and-white film again—feeling elegant, cherished.

“Looks like I’ve done my job,” Adrian says, pointing at my building. “Enjoy the rest of your day,” he smiles and walks away, his coat swaying behind him.

I stay there for a couple of seconds, watching him walk away.

Feeling Happy. Alive. Emotional.

Something is different this time—different from after our first night.

And then it hits me—sharp and clear.

I’m starting to **really** like him.

Not in that old, messy way—where I’d fall for someone toxic, way too fast, and get addicted to the chaos.

This feels different. Grounded. Real. Healthy.

Because the more I get to know him, the more it turns out... he's genuinely a great guy. One who respects my boundaries, owns his flaws, embraces mine, and roots for my business vision like it's his own.

*If I let this go any further, I'm not just flirting anymore.*

*I'm free-falling.*

And that... could get me into serious trouble.

The kind of trouble I swore I wouldn't walk into again.

The scary, uncomfortable truth is:

I need to end this.

Now.

CHALLENGE 8

# New Life Scripts

It'd been almost a week since Adrian and I had last seen each other.

I'd avoided SPARKS and worked from home, wanting to keep my head down. And though Adrian had texted nonstop, my replies had been infrequent, short, and almost clinical.

I needed space—time to gather the strength to end it. Without a long emotional back-and-forth and without second-guessing.

Clean. Immediate.

A healthy choice that would protect me from future pain—and keep me from spiraling into another messy entanglement, like I had too many times before.

But just as I stepped out the door—hair tied up, hoodie on, for a quick walk at 9 p.m.—I practically collided with him.

**Adrian.**

Standing right there in front of my building, like some new scene from a movie I didn't know I'd been cast in.

"Sophie!"

I froze.

"Wow, is this a coincidence?" I asked.

*It can't be.*

"Well, it is, and it isn't," he said. "I promise I haven't been pacing back and forth in front of your building, if that's what you're thinking." He smiled—half charm, half disarming honesty.

"I'm still not a stalker. But... I admit I decided to walk instead of taking the train, hoping to run into you. My organization's headquarters is nearby, remember?" His gaze lingered, searching my eyes for a reaction.

"Well, I have a mountain of work waiting for me, but I wanted to get some fresh air," I said. "Want to join?"

As we quietly walked towards the East River, in the dark, I was instantly pulled back to my teenage years—those thrilling late-night visits from boys, sneaking out to hidden corners, whispered secrets, and soft kisses.

"Do you think your parents will see us coming back?" Adrian asked as we settled onto one of the benches. "It's late at night, after all, and you're out with a stranger," he teased, clearly picking up on the vibe.

I couldn't help but laugh.

"If we're going to do this, we should do it right," he joked. "Do you want to come a little closer? Wait—maybe you should sit more comfortably," he said, pulling my legs toward him, his hands resting on them. Then, he pulled his coat around me, the fabric settling over my shoulders.

His eyes meet mine. **Quiet.**

For a moment, we just sit there, gazing at each other.

His thumb traces slow, lazy circles on my leg, like he doesn't even notice he's doing it.

I can feel myself slipping, inching closer to forgetting the thing I promised myself I'd do. The thing I **need** to do.

I'm dangerously close to letting it all just... continue.

But I won't.

My chest tightens.

The breeze rolls in off the river, cool against my skin—but it does nothing to steady me.

"Adrian..." I finally find my voice. "What is this—**us**?"

He exhales, eyes flicking to mine.

"Honestly? It all feels too intense for someone who's already in a relationship. You get me my dream office, take care of me, and you message me nonstop. I mean, how often do you actually think about me?"

He doesn't flinch. "Within an hour?"

"Wrong answer," I say, laughing.

"Okay. A lot," he grins, but there seems to be tension underneath. "And you're right. Too much, probably."

I glance away. "Well, you have a girlfriend, and I don't want to keep going down this road just to crash at the end."

**Silence.**

His eyes find mine. "I've actually been thinking about ending things with Kate."

*What?* My heart skips a beat.

"When we lived in New York together for the first two years, it all seemed so promising. But we've been long-distance for over a year now, and it feels like we live completely separate lives. We don't even want the same future anymore." He pauses.

"I thought time might help, but now? It just feels like I'm delaying the inevitable."

"Wow," I say. My heart is beating incredibly fast right now, but I somehow manage to force calm into my voice. "That's surprising... what do you want to do now?"

He runs a hand through his hair. "I'll make a decision within the next few days. No dragging it out."

"That's fast," I say.

"Yeah," he nods. "But not impulsive. I've been thinking about this for a while now."

A part of me wants to ask so many questions

—*Why now? Does it have to do with me? Are you sure?*

But a voice inside me holds me back.

*Don't get too involved,* it says. *This isn't your moment to take up space. And you don't want to get entangled in this.* This is between him and Kate. Their history. Their decision.

*Stay out of it.*

He pauses, then looks straight into my eyes. "Do you want kids?"

I blink. "Okay. That's... direct." A laugh escapes me—part surprise, part deflection. I shift slightly, my legs still draped across his lap.

"You really want to know that? Like, **now?**" I say, not quite meeting his eyes.

"Yeah," Adrian says, seemingly unbothered. "It's come up a lot between me and my girlfriend lately, so I'm curious where you stand."

I can feel the pulse in my neck, blood thrumming steady and loud.

I take a breath. "Honestly, I'm not sure," I manage. "A part of me wants it all, I guess—but only with the right person. If I meet someone I can truly imagine having a family with, I'm open to the idea. But if not, that's okay, I think..."

The warmth of his hands resting on my legs suddenly feels more noticeable. Intimate.

"You?"

"I **definitely** want kids," Adrian replies immediately. "Family means a lot to me, and I want to start my own. The sooner, the better."

"Oh, really? Do you picture having more than one?"

"Yeah," he says with a grin. "I come from a pretty big family—four kids."

"Let me guess—your parents are still married."

He nods. "Yeah. Happily."

"One of those families..." I joke. "No, honestly, you're so lucky."

"I mean, of course, they had their struggles too. My mom's an art teacher and always busy. My dad runs a chain of fitness studios and works very hard. But despite the craziness of a big family, limited finances, and never enough time, we had an amazing life."

His face lights up. "I still remember our low-budget holiday trips. We'd buy the cheapest food—feeding four hungry kids meant we couldn't afford all organic products. We'd pack everything into our camper van: games, sleeping bags, and pillows. For weeks, we'd eat pasta and have the best time together.

This was all before we inherited some money and a family house in Italy from our extended family—part of my distant family is Italian. Nowadays, my parents are well off, and my siblings and I are doing fairly well too."

He looked at me, his voice softening. "But yeah, my childhood was filled with fun family adventures."

He pulls out his phone, scrolls through photos, then shows me one: His family gathered around a large table by the ocean, the green camper van parked nearby, showing signs of age. "Look, this is one of my favorite memories. One of the vacations we went on. Our van had just broken down, so we decided to sleep by the ocean for the night."

He pauses, his voice softening. "That's what I want for my future—a family just like that."

I can feel Adrian's warmth and enthusiasm radiating from his body as I look into his family's smiling faces.

They look **so** bright, happy, and close—eating together and hugging each other.

***I never had a family like this. And I never dared to dream of one.***

I'm suddenly short on air.

***Breathe, Sophie.***

My heart aches.

Then it feels like it expands...

... as if something—Adrian—had reached it and cracked it open.

My mind gets flooded with images...

... I see a sunlit garden, my kids laughing as they run barefoot across the grass, their energy all over the place.

The scent of freshly baked cake drifts through the open windows, mingling with the earthy smell of rain on warm soil.

A loving, supportive partner by my side.

Someone to share the small things with—the beautiful, the messy, and the funny.

I love. And I feel loved.

There's belonging. And happiness.

Pure, quiet happiness.

It feels like a new door swinging wide open...

*Wait, Sophie. Where is this coming from? Garden, kids, cake? You don't even want that. Do you?*

Adrian places his hand gently underneath my thighs, pulling me a little closer. "Are you alright, Sophie? You look like you're somewhere else entirely."

I nod slowly, shifting my legs and arms—subtle movements, like I'm trying to shake myself back into the moment. And just like that, it clicks back into place: reality. "But, you know," I say, "I'm thirty-seven, and I'm not sure if time plays in my favor. Even if I do meet the right guy."

"You've probably still got a couple of years, right?" he reassures me. "And there's always adoption if you're open to it."

"That's true, I guess."

A cool breeze cuts through the quiet, and I shiver slightly.

Adrian tightens the coat he'd draped over my shoulders earlier, then wraps an arm around me. His other hand finds mine, warm and steady. "Do you want to get married?"

My breath catches, stuck somewhere between my chest and throat. *Deflect, Sophie.*

"Now? This kind of feels like you're proposing," I joke.

He chuckles, those cute dimples showing as he leans back just slightly to read my face.

"Do you want me to propose to you right now, Sophie? I can get on my knee, if that's what you want to see."

"God, no. Please don't," I say, laughing.

He grins, eyes locked on mine. "So?"

"You're asking quite a bold set of third-date questions, my friend."

"I'll take that as a compliment," he grins.

"Honestly... I don't even know. I wouldn't rule it out with the right guy, I guess."

"What makes the right guy?"

"Okay, this is going to be very unromantic," I laugh.

"Spill it!"

"Well... aside from the obvious things, I need someone who's securely attached and stable. I recently found out I have a partially anxious attachment style—total revelation by the way—and I want a peaceful relationship. If I'm with someone who isn't capable of secure attachment, the relationship will just be a lot of pushing and pulling forever, and that's exhausting."

"That actually sounds really smart," he says. "And just for the record," Adrian adds with a wink, "I'm definitely a secure type."

We pause for a few seconds, then he takes my hand. His eyes are piercing mine.

"What is this for you, Sophie?"

A pause.

I can feel my chest rise and sink.

"Just fun or do you really like me?"

A quiet charge moves through me—like my whole body is suddenly waking up.

"I **do** like you," I reply, keeping my tone deliberately vague. I'm still figuring out if this is something I can really open my heart to.

"Have you told anyone about me?" Adrian asks.

"No," I say, looking him straight in the eye. "I mean, Rani and Eliyah obviously know we've been dating. But I haven't spoken to them about us recently."

"I've told literally **everyone** about you." A broad smile spreads across his face.

"You did?" I laugh.

"I did."

"What did you tell them?"

"That I met a really special person.

Someone who makes me feel in ways I've never felt before.
That I can't get you out of my head.
And that I'm texting you like an obsessive addict,
hoping you don't think I'm crazy."

Time freezes as I look into his eyes.
For a second, it feels like I might dissolve in them.

"What was it like growing up in **your** family?" Adrian asks, his question cutting through the moment. "You seemed quite emotional before."

My entire body starts to feel tense, and my gaze drops, fixed on his hand in mine.

"You don't have to talk about it if you don't want to, of course," he adds, his thumb brushing over my skin, warming my hand.

"No, it's okay," I reply, focusing on my breath to steady myself.

"Growing up with my mom was... difficult." The words feel heavy as they leave my mouth.

"Only child?" he asks, his eyes searching mine.

I nod.

"Did your relationship improve over time?"

I shake my head. "On the contrary. I had to cut off contact for good—fifteen years ago. But I don't want to talk about it."

"I'm so sorry, Sophie. Come here." He presses a warm kiss to my cheek, his lips lingering for a moment.

"Don't be sorry. I'm fine. It's been a long time."

"What about your father? If you don't mind me asking, are you getting along with him?"

I let out a slow breath. "I guess... I don't really know, to be honest...

I haven't seen him since I was eight, when he decided he no longer wanted to be part of our family. My mom packed our things, and we left. After that, he just completely disappeared from our lives.

But before that? I loved him more than anything in the world."

Adrian's eyes soften.

"I'm okay now. Don't worry," I say quickly. "I just don't want to drag it all back up. I usually never talk about this with anyone. I want the past to stay in the past." I finally lift my gaze to meet his.

Without a word, Adrian pulls me closer. Then, with an effortless motion, he tucks me into the warmest hug imaginable. "Well, it's clearly their loss," he whispers, his words warm against my ear.

*Don't cry, Sophie.*

"Let's go back to my place, it's getting late."

He walked me home in silence, but it wasn't awkward—just peaceful.

We both needed to get up early the next day, so Adrian left.

Later in bed, I couldn't shake the emptiness that lingered. For the first time since we'd met, I felt the absence of him beside me.

*

That night, I tossed and turned in bed, unable to sleep as images kept flooding my mind.

Instinctively, I walked over to my desk and pulled open the drawer. There it was—the small, white-gray shell I'd kept since I was thirteen.

I picked it up and ran my fingers along its rough, uneven edges. That little piece of shell had once sparked something in me—in a way, it had been the seed of everything that came after. My drive. My escape. My career success.

My aunt had given it to me during a moment I would later realize was life-changing. I could still remember it vividly...

... The two of us in our tiny gray kitchen, sitting on those creaky, rusted chairs. I was small, feet barely brushing the floor.

"Sophie," my aunt said, her voice more serious than usual, "your mother and I never chased our dreams. We just chased the wrong men. Always thought something better would eventually happen or someone better would come along for us.

Time flies. One day, it'll be too late, and you'll end up old, stuck here, wondering where it all went—just like your mom and me."

She glanced toward the kitchen ledge, at the neat row of shells—my mother's collection—other people's souvenirs from beaches she'd never seen. Places she talked about visiting someday, but never did.

"Your mom's battling her own demons. She won't be of any help. But you are a clever girl. If I can give you one piece of advice—take your life into your own hands."

Then she picked one of the shells—a random one. Not special at all. Just kind of lost and lifeless in between all the other ones—and took my hand. "Here," she said. "Keep it to remember and get out of here." ...

It was literally the first—and only—life lesson anyone in my family ever gave me. And it etched itself into my mind.

First: no one was coming to save me. If I wanted to survive—let alone thrive—I'd have to do it on my own. Second: letting men distract, derail, or define my path could cost me everything.

Back then, I made a promise to myself: my parents' choices would **not** become my inheritance. I would not end up like my mom—stuck, mentally troubled, addicted to alcohol, and dependent on men.

Instead, I'd become everything she wasn't: stable, strong, in control. I'd succeed on my own terms. And I would never need rescuing.

That promise was why I never focused on relationships.

Why I threw myself into school.

Why I studied hard, worked harder, and built my life brick by brick with discipline and precision—until the panic attack five months ago, when I realized I'd built myself a different kind of trap.

But now that I'd chosen to build a new life, I was finally opening the door to everything I'd muted before. And Adrian was walking right through it, letting in future worlds I never knew were possible for me.

They didn't even feel like a distant dream—right now, they felt strikingly real. That, in itself, was a miracle.

After all, I'd never truly dared to fantasize about having a family before.

And apparently, we hardly ever get to imagine what we haven't experienced yet. It's just how our brains are wired—something I knew from behavioral design. Science says **it's almost impossible to picture and believe in a life you've never seen**. That's partly why generational patterns repeat. Why we follow the same scripts, even when we ache for something different.

But somehow, Adrian had managed the impossible. He'd brought me here.

When he shared his memories and future vision of family, his words slipped past the walls I'd built over the years. And for the first time, I could believe it

—believe that love, belonging, and a family might actually be within reach.

Not necessarily with Adrian.

Just that it was an option at all.

A sharp edge of the shell pressed into my palm, anchoring me back into the moment.

I placed it back in the drawer, walked to bed, curled up beneath the covers—and finally, peacefully, drifted off to sleep.

*

The next morning, I woke up tired, my phone buzzing with a message:

> **Adrian:** I just booked a flight to see my girlfriend in Canada. I'm going to end the relationship. My flight is in two days

*What on earth?*

Until yesterday, he'd given me no indication that his relationship wasn't solid. And now, he was suddenly leaving someone he'd been with for years? Was this really happening?

My heart sank.

A cold-hot wave of fear and excitement rushed over me and for a moment, I felt like the ground had disappeared beneath my feet.

CHALLENGE 9

# Crossroads

**Adrian:** I'm heading to the airport now. I could briefly stop by your apartment around 8:30 a.m. before you head out to SPARKS

**Me:** Okay :)

**Me:** Don't come up. I'll come down

For a second, I stared out the window, suspended—like I wasn't quite in my body, just hovering slightly above it, watching everything unfold. *He's really doing it.*

I pulled on my coat and stepped outside.

The sharp October air hit my face, waking me up just enough to realize how surreal it all felt.

At the corner where the taxi would turn in, I waited.

A subtle weight settled in my chest. Everything about this moment felt delicate—exhilarating and terrifying at the same time.

Deep down, I knew it was all too sudden to be just about his relationship with Kate. But I wasn't going to push now or ever. The decision whether or not to end things with her was his to make, and I didn't want any part in it.

He'd been unraveling in that relationship long before I showed up. He never said this was about me, and I never asked it to be. I didn't promise anything either. Until now, we'd just let the unspoken hang between us. It felt easier this way.

A yellow cab slows at the corner.

My breath catches.

Adrian steps out.

His face looks different—softer, exposed.

Vulnerable in a way I haven't seen before.

"Hey, you."

A wave of his warm, clean skin scent hits me. We hug tightly.

His voice brushes my ear. "I'm glad we got to see each other to say goodbye."

"Me too."

I feel his chest rise and fall beneath mine, solid and warm. Just when I start to lean into it, he pulls back slightly, eyes on mine.

"It's going to be **really** hard not seeing you for ten days," he says, his brows drawing together, a flicker of something raw passing over his face. His hand lingers at my waist, like he doesn't want to let go just yet.

"Ten days?"

"I booked a bit extra. In case I need time. I'll also visit some friends while I'm there."

I nod, my throat dry.

"I don't think we should be in touch while you're with her. It doesn't feel right. Just... text me when you're back?"

He nods. "I'm afraid that'll give me serious withdrawal symptoms though," he murmurs, voice low.

Then he leans in, his mouth grazing the edge of my ear, breath warm against my skin. "I guess I'm addicted after all," he whispers.

A pause.

"I want you so damn much, Sophie. You know that, don't you?" I feel my skin tighten where his voice touched it, heat spreading just beneath the surface.

He leans back slightly. "But you're probably right. It's the best thing to do." His gaze holds mine—quiet, steady—as his hand brushes lightly down my arm. Then he kisses me. Soft, warm, sure. "Take care, Sophie. I'll text you."

He squeezes my hand once before letting go, then climbs into the cab.

I stand there, watching the taillights disappear down the street.

My chest starts to hurt. A tear slides down my cheek before I even notice I'm crying. A deep, unbearable ache forms in my stomach, making it hard to breathe.

Adrian seems confident about his decision, but who really knows what would happen once he sees her again?

*What if he changes his mind?*

*Or doesn't?*

This was a crossroads, and we both knew it. If he left her? I had no idea what that meant for us. We hadn't gone there. We'd just started dating, and the weight of that conversation was too much for where we were.

But if he stayed with her, I wouldn't see him again. Of that, I was sure.

Up until now, I'd played it cool. Held it together.

But now, with him gone, it was obvious—whatever this was, it had already gone far beyond just fun.

I wasn't **just starting** to like him.

I already **really** liked him.

Funny, isn't it?

How our bodies reveal the truth even when our minds aren't ready to.

*

Then, ten torturingly silent days later, finally a message:

**Adrian:** I broke up with my girlfriend

I reread it again and again, grappling with disbelief.

*No way this is real.*

But it was.

He'd ended things.

And he was already on his way back to New York.

CHALLENGE 10

# All Eyes on Us

**Me:** When are you back in town?

**Adrian:** I'm landing around midnight. I wish I could see you right away. But it's late, and I'm slammed catching up on work tomorrow

**Me:** How are you?

**Me:** Do you want to talk? You can call me if you want

**Adrian:** Not right now. I'm exhausted

**Adrian:** But would you like to come to a party at my place tomorrow evening? Sorry about the late notice, I totally forgot this was happening. Not the best timing...

**Adrian:** I'd prefer to see you alone, but I invited guests and can't cancel right now. The night will end at some point, though... It's set up to be an after-work thing and will only go until midnight or so

**Me:** Who's coming?

**Adrian:** It's a house party—everyone in the building invited friends and colleagues

**Adrian:** Probably around 100 people total

**Me:** Are you sure it's a good idea? Aren't some of them also Kate's friends from when you lived together in New York?

**Adrian:** Yes. We have common friends and colleagues

**Adrian:** But let's keep it low-key, and it'll be fine

**Adrian:** Just one thing: I'll need to host a bit, so I won't be able to be with you the whole time... even though I'd love to

**Adrian:** You're welcome to bring a friend or two

**Me:** I'd have to—already made plans with Eliyah and Rani. I'll check in with them and message you tomorrow, okay?

**Adrian:** I can't wait to see you, Sophie!

*

*Next day*

I pulled my coat tighter as I crossed the street on my way to Adrian's house party.

The October wind had teeth today, but Williamsburg glowed in that golden, late-afternoon light that made even cracked sidewalks look poetic. Everything felt slightly heightened—the scent of roasted espresso drifting out of cafés, bits of music spilling from upstairs windows, the quiet rhythm of my boots on the pavement.

Part of me was incredibly excited to see him again and be invited into his world so quickly.

Another part was nervous. We hadn't even talked since he got back and ended things with Kate. And now I was supposed to just walk into his building and meet everyone?

I had so many questions. But the timing never felt right.

Before, they would've been out of bounds—he was still in a relationship.

*And now?*

He'd barely returned and was already pulling me into his life.

Everything was moving so quickly. It felt a bit rushed.

Yet I was already walking toward him.

After all, life isn't a perfect script. It's messy. Chaotic, sometimes. Perhaps we just need to jump in and figure things out as we go.

**Me:** Almost there. Let's meet outside first? Rani and Eliyah are coming a little later

**Adrian:** Sure. I'll come down

My heart beat just a little faster with each block I passed, each street corner closer to his.

*There he is.* Leaning casually outside his building—a typical modernized, industrial Brooklyn loft—looking as handsome as ever, hands tucked into the pockets of his coat. He smiles when he sees me, but there's a flicker of distance in his eyes.

*Don't expect too much joy from someone who just left a long-term relationship, Sophie.* Still... part of me craves exactly that.

I stop in front of him.

Without a word, he steps forward and pulls me into a hug. His arms wrap around me tightly—like he doesn't want to let go—but there's no kiss. Just the weight of his body against mine, the press of his coat collar brushing my cheek.

My stomach sinks a little. "How are you feeling?" I ask gently.

"I'm okay," he says, his voice steady. Then he leans back, keeping his hands on my waist, eyes locked on mine. "And I'm so happy to see you. You have no idea."

His gaze drops for a beat, and when it returns, it's softer. Vulnerable. Like something's caught behind his eyes, he hasn't figured out how to say it.

"Are you sure you're okay?" I ask.

He shifts his weight slightly, rubbing the back of his neck with one hand. "I just spoke to a couple of Kate's friends," he says. "They were quite emotional."

He pauses.

"I hope I did the right thing in inviting you. I want you here more than anything, and not inviting you would've felt wrong —but yeah... I know this is a bit much."

He lifts a hand and strokes my hair back, his fingers lingering at the side of my face. "I just hate that I won't be able to take care of you the way I want to tonight. And the way you deserve. I'll be pulled in all directions. I want to make sure you'll be okay... Eliyah and Rani are coming later?"

"Yes, they're on their way. And if it gets too intense, I'll just slip out. No drama." I take his hands in mine. "Anything you want to get off your chest before we head upstairs?" I ask. "It feels weird we haven't talked about how it all went."

"I know," he says. "But honestly... I prefer it that way. Let's not talk about what's in the past. There's not much to say anyway. It was emotional. She was heartbroken. But I'm sure it was the right thing. And I told her it's final." His fingers tighten slightly around mine. "I'm just really glad you're here. I've missed you so much, Sophie."

Then, without another word, he glances around and pulls me gently toward a quiet corner in the courtyard.

We slip out of view.

He backs me against the cool wall, his eyes locked on mine, breath shallow.

My pulse surges.

One hand slides behind my head, threading through my hair.

His body leans into mine, warm and steady.

His mouth finds mine—slow at first, searching, then deeper, hungrier. Like he's trying to make up for every second of the ten days we've been apart.

Then, he leans back slightly. "It will be so hard not to touch you in front of everybody..." he murmurs, brushing his thumb along my cheek. "But it's probably best to keep it under wraps once we're upstairs. It might be... sensitive, with so many of the guests being mutual friends of Kate and me."

"Sure," I nod.

He takes a small step back, then tilts his head toward the far side of the courtyard. "There it is," he says.

He lets go of my hand, and we walk in silence—My nervousness is building with every step.

*

"Here's my apartment—let's take off your coat first," Adrian said, opening a large door just in front of us. I stepped inside.

"So... the party isn't in your apartment?" I asked.

"No, this is a co-living building, mostly young entrepreneurs. Everyone has their own apartment, but we also have additional shared spaces upstairs, including kitchens, lounges, and areas for hosting events. That's where the party is. Just one floor up."

I glanced around the living room.

Dark, rich wood with industrial metal accents and a black leather couch created a space that felt both grounded and aspirational. One of the walls was decorated with a world map and framed photos.

The biggest of them caught my eye. Adrian and a woman —clearly Kate—on a sunlit terrace by the ocean. They were holding hands, barefoot, wind sweeping through her long black hair. She wore loose gray trousers and a white shirt, no makeup.

They both looked tired. And happy.

Something twisted in my chest.

She was at home right now, grieving the end of her relationship. Meanwhile, I was here. One day after he'd ended it.

I hadn't done anything wrong—we'd met while he was still in an open relationship, in line with their agreement, and he'd made his own decisions. Still, it dawned on me—this evening was a minefield of emotions, and I had to navigate through them wisely.

I spotted a heavy wooden table in the corner of the room, scattered with tools. "What's this?" I asked, trailing a finger along the edge of a plank.

"I've been learning to build furniture with my uncle," he said, stepping beside me. "He's a craftsman. Every summer, when we meet at our house in Italy, we build something together," he smiled.

"Oh, I love that."

Adrian gestured toward the back. "There's the bedroom and attached bathroom." He slipped my coat from my shoulders. His hand brushed down my arm as he placed it neatly on his desk. "Okay, let's do this," he said as if trying to summon his courage, gently ushering me toward the open space on the second floor.

The party was already in full swing. About fifty guests filled the large living room, chatting, mingling, and laughing.

The crowd was somewhat mixed, making it difficult to understand the group's vibe and distinguish between Adrian's friends and the other guests. Some looked chic and professional, while others resembled typical Williamsburg hipsters, and the rest blended in quite unremarkably.

We bumped into Gabriel, Adrian's friend from the changemakers' event. "Sophie! So great to finally see you again," he said, pulling me into a warm hug and brushing a quick kiss against my cheek like we were old friends.

"I'll go make sure everyone's good. Take good care of her, Gabriel," Adrian said, scanning the room with a quick glance.

Then he turned back to me, his hand brushing mine for a beat. "Sophie—if you need anything, just text or come find me, okay?" A soft smile tugged at the corner of his mouth. "See you in a bit."

I watched him disappear into the mix.

Gabriel chuckled. "Now he's in his element. Born host. Social butterfly. The man thrives on making sure everyone has a drink and a good story. People love him for it. Honestly, he could be out at a different event every night—he's always invited somewhere."

I smiled. "Yeah, I kind of guessed that about him."

Gabriel raised an eyebrow, teasing. "And you, Sophie? Big night, huh? I was hoping he'd bring you."

"You were?"

"Oh yeah. He's been talking about you nonstop. Like, actual monologues. It's been intense."

I laughed. "Really?"

He nodded, grinning. "Honestly, I've never seen him like this. Adrian's usually the calm one—composed, and emotionally waterproof. With his ex, things were... balanced. A bit more toned down from the start. But since he met you? He's a mess—in the best way. Emotionally vulnerable, kind of lit up. What did you do to him, Sophie?"

Before I could answer, a familiar voice cut in from behind. "Hey, stranger." I turned to see Eliyah and Rani approaching, drinks in hand, both already halfway into party mode.

We hugged like it had been a year, not an hour. "It's so good to see you both, you have no idea."

"Gabriel, meet Eliyah and Rani—my best people," I said.

Gabriel smiled warmly. "Pleasure."

"I hope you don't mind me asking: are you one of Kate's friends?" Eliyah asked, casually.

Gabriel shook his head. "Not really. I only met her a couple of times." He paused, then added with a shrug, "So no bias or lingering loyalties, if that's what you're wondering. I'm team Adrian's happiness—whoever that ends up being with."

Eliyah stepped forward with zero hesitation. "Well, in that case, let's not waste time pretending. Obviously, we want to know who's been spending all this time with our Sophie—and whether Adrian meets the potential boyfriend bar."

I groaned. "Eliyah, you know I love you... But if you **have** to pull this tonight—which, let's be honest, isn't exactly ideal timing—could you at least **try** subtlety? Just once?"

He grinned, raising his drink. "Not really my brand."

I turned to Gabriel with a helpless smile. "For the record, I had nothing to do with this."

Gabriel laughed, clearly entertained. "No complaints here. Fierce friendship like that deserves some answers. And lucky for you, there's nothing shady to find. Not that I know of, at least."

He glanced between the two of them. "Just to clarify—I've never dated Adrian, so I can't speak to his boyfriend skills directly."

He raised his brows playfully, then continued, "But we go way back. We've worked together, traveled, partied, and seen each other in good times and absolute chaos. And I mean it when I say, he's exactly who he seems to be. Kind, grounded, steady. Weirdly fun and generous for someone who never sleeps."

"Okay, okay," I said, waving a hand. "Let's not build him a shrine just yet."

"Too late, girl," Rani said, deadpan. "I already lit a candle."

We all laughed, and for a moment, the whole night felt light and easy. Like things were actually going to be okay.

"I'll go grab a drink," I said, already weaving through the crowd.

The kitchen was alive with noise—ice clinking in glasses. I slipped behind the counter, scanning for a drink.

"Are you okay?" Adrian's voice came from just behind me, low and warm. I turned just slightly, catching his eye. "I'm having a great time. Don't worry."

He stepped in closer, so close I could feel the warmth of his breath against my ear. "It's torture seeing you across the room all night. You look so fucking hot in that tight skirt," he murmured, the edge of his lips nearly grazing my skin. "All I want to do is rip your clothes off, but instead I'm stuck topping up people's Prosecco."

A rush of heat surged through me, and I tried to keep my face neutral as I poured myself a glass of champagne.

"Adrian!" someone called from the hallway.

He squeezed my fingers subtly as he stepped back. "See you later."

I barely had time to catch my breath when I felt someone staring. I looked up—and froze.

A woman stood across the counter, arms crossed, gaze cool as marble.

"God, you scared me," I said, startled.

"I'm Sarah," she introduced herself, reaching out stiffly. Her handshake was limp, pointedly uninviting.

"Sophie," I said, offering a polite smile.

"How do you know Adrian?" Her eyes didn't soften.

"We met a few months ago. At a work event." I kept my tone neutral. "And you?"

"I'm one of Kate's best friends."

My stomach dropped.

She took a slow sip from her wine, eyes still on me. "What is it that you do for a living?"

"I'm a behavioral designer."

"Sounds... fancy." Her mouth curled slightly, but not into a smile.

"There've been a lot of rumors flying around lately," Sarah added, tilting her head. "I saw Adrian whispering to you earlier.

Don't you think it's a little tacky to show up here the day after he left Kate?"

I glanced over my shoulder toward the living room. "Well, I should probably get back to my friends."

"Why so quickly?" she asked, her voice even sharper now. "Feeling uncomfortable? It's just a conversation. Rude to cut it short, don't you think?"

My shoulders tensed, but I met her eyes, calm and clear. "Respectfully, I don't feel this is a conversation I need to stay in."

"Well, I respectfully don't think you should be here at all."

I heard footsteps—quick, purposeful.

"Sarah," Adrian said sharply. "Stop it right now."

She turned, startled.

"I invited Sophie," he said, voice steady but firm. "She's done nothing wrong. Whatever your opinions are, we're all adults here. We're all free to make our own choices.

Whether you like them or not."

He looked her straight in the eyes. "Look, I get that the situation might be difficult for you. But that doesn't give you the right to be rude to Sophie."

Sarah blinked, her lips parting as if to say something—but then she turned and walked away.

Adrian looked at me, his jaw still tense. "I'm so sorry, Sophie. Sarah is... intense. She canceled, then apparently showed up at the last minute. She's Kate's best friend. If I'd known she'd be here, I would've warned you."

He searched my face. "Are you okay?"

I nod.

He steps closer, lowering his voice. "Don't let anyone make you feel like you don't belong here. You do."

Adrian takes my hand and kisses me on my cheek—many eyes on us.

He pulls me closer, his eyes steady on mine. "I've tried to be respectful, given the timing with Kate," he says, voice low but sure. “But I’m not going to hide you. Why should I? I wouldn’t have invited you tonight if I weren’t serious. I want you here. I want you in my life.”

His hand tightens gently at my waist. “And right now, what matters most to me is giving **you** the respect you deserve. You haven’t done anything wrong. Neither have I. Kate and I were in an open relationship from the start—and she knows that we’re dating. So I’m done with the tiptoeing. **Fuck that.**”

He leans in, his breath warm against my ear. “Is everyone staring?”

My cheeks flush. “Yes,” I whisper, my voice barely audible.

“Good,” he says. “They should get a proper show, then. Are you up for it?”

A beat passes. I can feel every nerve in my body tighten from anticipation. “I think so,” I murmur. A flicker of panic mixed with adrenaline shoots through me.

“Yes?”

“Yes!”

Adrian pulls me closer—his hand slipping to the small of my back—and kisses me, deeply. Right there, in front of everyone.

The room doesn’t fall silent, but it doesn’t matter.

All I can feel is him—and the sudden clarity that we aren’t some secret anymore.

*

“Rani and Eliyah are on their way home,” I said. “Rani had to rush—it’s almost midnight and Rhea woke up.”

“I’m glad they came.” Adrian smiled softly, searching my face. “You’re not leaving, too, are you?”

The tension that’d been building all night was almost unbearable. Until now, I’d been the one drawing the line—not letting Adrian fuck me with everything he had while he was still with someone else.

But tonight was different. He was single now—and we both knew exactly where this was headed.

He leans in—his breath warm against my skin. "I still owe you for everything you put up with tonight. And I intend to make it up to you."

He pulls back just enough to catch my eye. "Come on. Let's get out of here." His hand finds mine—firm, unhesitating—and we slip out through the side door.

We take the stairs down to the ground floor, two at a time.

My heart pounds so loud I can barely hear anything else.

The second the door shuts behind us, something breaks loose. Adrian steps toward me, backing me gently into the wall. His eyes lock on mine for a beat—searching—like he's making sure I'm really here.

Then we kiss.

Coats drop. Buttons open.

My fingers pull at the hem of his shirt, and his mouth moves to my neck.

Everything is fast and urgent, but it doesn't feel rushed—it feels like everything we've been holding back is finally released.

He yanks his shirt over his head. I gasp as his hands slip beneath my top, warm and sure, and then he takes it off too.

We're a mess of limbs, laughter, and sharp little inhales between kisses.

He leads me toward the bedroom, and we barely make it without tripping until I finally land on his bed, only wearing underwear.

"Oh my god, look at you," he says. "You're just so beautiful."

Then, he suddenly slows down. "What do you want, Sophie? I told you I'd make it up to you for tonight. Whatever you want... It's yours."

For a moment, I don't answer.

My gaze drifts, unintentionally, past him—toward the large window across from the bed. The streets down in this part of

Williamsburg are quiet at night—only the soft hum of a streetlight outside, and a couple walking by in the distance.

"Let me shut the curtains," Adrian says, already half-turning.

"No," I say quickly. "Don't."

A slow smile tugs at the corner of his mouth. "Okay," he says, simply. He shifts back beside me, then leans in—his face hovering just above mine, his eyes locked on me.

I look at him fiercely. "I'm done hiding. And I'm done pretending."

I can feel my heart beating.

***No shame. Just freedom.***

I pierce him with my eyes. "You know, I might look like a well-behaved businesswoman. And I pretended I'm just that for a very long time. But it's time to be honest.

Underneath it all, I'm just a slutty girl fantasizing about strangers putting their hard cocks inside me, fucking me hard," I say.

The surprise in Adrian's eyes instantly sends my pulse racing. "Tell me what to do. I'll do anything," he says.

"I think you should get on your knees," I command.

His grin widens as he absorbs the power shift. "Really... ?" he smirks and gets down on all fours. "I guess I might need to use our code word tonight. You remember it, right? If I say it at any time, we stop."

"Sure, I do." I deliver a sharp smack to his ass, the sound echoing in the charged silence between us. Then, I burst into laughter. "Okay, now I'm actually just toying with you. I've just always wanted to try it out."

But my laughter doesn't last long. In one fluid motion, Adrian gets up, seizes my arms, and presses me against the window. "Do you think this is funny, Sophie?" he roars, his voice dripping with dominance. "Look at you, what a little slut you are. A little slut, putting herself on display."

My cheeks flush.

I can feel the blood pumping through my veins.

He presses his body against my back, strokes my hair to the side, and kisses my neck. "You don't want to hide anymore? Let's make sure everyone can see you then."

His hands slide slowly down my back. He opens my bra, then slides the straps off my shoulders and lets them fall to the ground.

My breath goes faster.

"Are you happy now, Sophie? Now that everyone can finally see what a slut you are?"

"Yes," I whisper.

"At least you are being honest. Now, finally, everyone can see the real you. Let's take off that little thong of yours so that we can put you on full display. That's what you want, right?"

"Yes."

He slowly pulls it down.

Adrenaline shoots through me.

The street is still quiet, but pedestrians could walk by any second.

"And you want nothing more than to be fucked by strangers' dicks you say? You should get what you deserve then, don't you think?"

"Yes," I say with urgency.

"I can't hear you, Sophie.

What is it that you want?"

"Fuck me," I say, my voice low and needy.

"Fuck me like the little slut I am!"

He spreads my legs, removes his boxer briefs, and slips on a condom he'd hidden in his jeans.

Then he fucks me. "Is this what you wanted?" he growls.

"To be on display while you're fucked by a twenty-eight-year-old you barely know, you little slut? Just to spread your legs like a little whore?"

"Yes," I gasp.

"That's exactly what I want.

That's **all** I want."

His grip tightens on my hips as he pulls me closer, fucking me harder.

It doesn't take long before we both come, our bodies trembling as he presses a hand over my mouth to stifle my cries.

Adrian turns me around and kisses me—slow at first, then deeper, with an intensity that sends a rush through my whole body. Then, without a word, he lifts me effortlessly and carries me to the bed.

He closes the curtain, then slips in beside me—and just like that, we drift off to sleep.

*

The next day, I woke up to the sound of a coffee machine, distant Beatles tunes, and sunlight cutting through the curtain. For a second, I just stared at the ceiling, replaying last night.

Adrian and I had finally slept together.

A grin spread across my face. Not exactly a slow, candlelit "first time"—and thank god for that. I've never cared much for clichés. Rose petals, soft music, the whole delicate, breathy act. Sure, it can be nice sometimes. But it never really felt like me.

What happened last night? **That** was me.

I finally let that version of myself out.

No holding back. No trying to shape some perfect moment.

We both did just what we wanted.

Even when we role-played, it didn't feel like pretending.

It felt like stepping into different sides of ourselves.

And that's what made it real.

Adrian appears in the doorway, two cups of coffee in his hands. "Want some?"

I prop myself up on one elbow, the sheets falling from my shoulder. "Always."

He hands me the cup and comes back into bed beside me, one arm casually thrown behind his head. "I still can't believe how lucky I am, Sophie," he says, eyes on the ceiling. "Being with you... It's like stepping into a new universe every time."

I flash a smile. "That might be the most poetic thing anyone's ever said to me before coffee."

He laughs, brushing his thumb along my knee under the covers. "Heyyy, I'm serious."

"I know."

A kiss.

"Shoot," I mutter, suddenly upright. "What time is it?"

He glances at his phone. "A little after ten."

"I need to get to SPARKS. I'm getting that furniture delivery—the start-up you recommended? They could only make it today. I have to figure out how to Frankenstein two sideboards together."

"I can help you, if you want," he says, sitting up with me.

I raise an eyebrow. "Really?"

"Of course. I fly to Paris tomorrow for a week for a work thing," he added. "So today works perfectly. And I build furniture every summer, remember?"

"I **do** remember... That's **very** hot, you know." A grin spreads across my face. "Will you be wearing a white tank top for me?"

"Everything you want. Let's set up your space, so my wildly talented Sophie can create her genius lights."

"You're the best," I smile.

He leans over and kisses my shoulder. "I know."

Then he pulls back the covers and scoops me up, carrying me out of bed and kissing me, before gently setting me on my feet.

For a second, it all feels like a scene out of a rom-com. Only better. Because this isn't a script, it's us. And it was real.

*

"This looks amazing," I say, stepping back to take it all in.

The sideboards are perfectly aligned, and the muted yellow is just right against the white brick wall. Clean, sharp. Exactly how I pictured it.

I turn around. "It would've taken me forever without you."

Adrian stands with his back to me, phone in hand, unusually still. I step in close and kiss his shoulder. "Thank you."

He doesn't respond, and his thumb is frozen mid-scroll, eyes locked on the screen.

"Hey... what's going on?" I ask.

He doesn't look at me. "I can't believe this," he mutters, almost to himself.

"What?"

He lets out a slow breath, then sinks to the ground, sitting beside the sideboard.

I follow him down, feeling the warmth of the sun on the wooden floor through my jeans as I sit on the floor.

"I need to tell you something."

"What's going on? You're starting to scare me."

"I applied for a job in Paris a while ago."

I blink. "You did?"

"Yeah. I didn't think anything would come of it, but... I just got the offer."

A second passes.

I hear the faint hum of the lights, the heater kicking on.

"Are you going to take it?"

He finally looks at me—eyes a little glassy, a little far away. A mix of everything.

He nods once.

"Yeah. I am. I have to. It starts in March. So... four and a half months from now."

CHALLENGE 11

# Don't Future Trip

For a moment, we just stare at each other.

The sun cuts low across the floor, catching in the corner of his eye. His phone lies beside him now, forgotten.

Then I reach for his hand. "So... what's the job?"

He lets out a small huff of air, like he's been holding it in. "I basically invented my dream job and pitched it to them," he says with a grin.

I feel my eyebrows lift. "The project you talked about on stage at the award ceremony?"

He nods. "Wow, you remember it. Exactly that."

"You were so passionate about it," I say. "And I loved the way you put it: that you want to help people with limited resources build something of their own—get a seat at the table."

"Right," he says. "I'm impressed by your memory. I didn't think anyone would listen that closely," he turns to me.

"Well, also... You looked very sexy on stage. Maybe that helped."

That finally earns a full smile.

I lean in and kiss him, slow and warm.

He rests his forehead lightly against mine. "I came up with a microfinance system to support underprivileged families, women, and vulnerable groups. The network in Paris I pitched to operates globally. I stay linked to my current organization through it. Think of it as a kind of shop-in-shop setup.

I'll have more freedom to scale and build bigger systems of support. That's the vision. That's what matters most to me. It's why I'm motivated to get up every morning. Achieving maximum impact."

"Are you going full-time?"

"I am. I'll be the Director. Salary's insane."

"Oh my god. All of that sounds so incredible, Adrian. I'm so happy for you." I throw my arms around him. "This is huge. And so deserved. Your work is so impressive. They're lucky to have you."

He holds me tight, presses his face into my neck. "Thank you," he whispers, barely audible.

We loosen our grip.

His eyes search mine.

Then his voice breaks slightly. "**Fuck!** This **really** sucks, though." He cradles my face in his palms. "We've just met. I'm not ready to let you go yet... how do you feel about it?" He's so close I can feel his breath.

I rest my hands on his thighs, grounding myself. "I'm not thrilled for **us**, no. But I'm really happy for **you**."

His arms pull me back in, and we wrap around each other on the sun-warmed floor.

"How about we just keep going like we were?" I suggest. "Pretend nothing big has changed—for now."

He leans back just enough to see my face, a crease between his brows.

"I mean it," I say. "It's too soon for big decisions. Let's not have dramatic talks or make promises we're not ready for. We take it one step at a time. If something shifts, we talk then."

He exhales and kisses me. When he pulls away, he smiles. "You're amazing. I'm so relieved. For a second, I was really scared you might want to end things right away."

"No way I'm letting go of you right now." I turn to him. "Maybe after you're done building all my furniture," I tease.

He squints at me. "What... did you really just say that?"

"Why? Did you think I wanted something else from you?" I say, dry as sand.

"You are getting a bit too sassy, lately, Sophie." Without warning, he leans in and gently tackles me to the floor, hovering above me, pinning my hands beside my head.

I break out in laughter, sunlight spilling across my face.

He dips lower, teeth grazing the side of my neck, his voice a whisper against my skin. "You can pretend all you want," he murmurs. "But you're just as hooked as I am. Maybe you just need to be a little... disciplined to admit it."

Then he lifts his head, locking eyes with me.

I stop laughing.

His hand wanders down my body, splitting my legs softly.

He stops for a second. "Seriously, Sophie. I'm really happy we're still in this."

I nod, a quiet smile forming. "Me too."

Footsteps echo down the hallway, then a knock on the door. "Hey, kids," Rani's voice is playful as she steps inside. "I heard noises and wanted to make sure everything was okay. No one's usually around on weekends—I'm used to dead silence. Didn't know you were coming in today."

Adrian stands and gives her a warm hug. "Great to see you, Rani. I actually need to head out—got to pack my bags." He turns to me, pulls me gently to my feet, and kisses me. "I'll message you later."

And just like that, he's gone.

"Okay, okay, I see..." Rani grins as she closes the door behind her, stepping deeper into the room. "You're having a lot of fun together, huh?"

"We are..." I say. "But... he just got offered a job in Paris. It starts in March."

Her expression shifts instantly. "What? Oh no. I'm sorry. How are you feeling?"

I shrug, folding my arms as I lean back against the sideboard. "I'm okay, I think."

"**Wait**—do you think you'll end up going with him?"

"I honestly don't want to even think about it." I glance at her.

She gives me a look.

"Seriously. It's way too soon. We just started dating—We'll see how it unfolds when it's time."

She nods, then smirks. “Well... if you do move to Paris, I’m visiting you all the time. Croissants, art, wine, and my best friend? Come on.”

“Stop it, Rani,” I laugh, swatting her lightly. “I mean it. No thinking ahead. We just started this. I want to enjoy it exactly the way it is.”

She tilts her head, her voice softer now. “You really have an incredible time together, don’t you?”

I nod. “Okay, yes, I admit it. We do. We have **the** best time. And now, finally, everything feels wide open. No girlfriend. No goodbyes. Just focus on... us.”

I pause, letting the words settle in.

“I don’t want to complicate it, make things heavy or messy. I just want to enjoy this for now.”

*

*A month later*

“Bye all, see you tomorrow,” Eliyah called out, waving to the last few people still hunched over their desks at SPARKS.

He turned to me, already zipping up his puffer as we walked outside. “You sure you don’t want to come for a drink, love? It’s November 15th—they’re kicking off that monthly drag show in the back room tonight at the BABES bar. First one of the season—you know how the queens love a theme.”

“Sounds tempting,” I said, looping my scarf. “But I promised Adrian I’d have dinner with him.”

Eliyah grinned. “Wow, you are doing a lot of stuff together lately... concerts, comedy shows, shopping trips...” He makes goofy dance moves. “Adrian and Sophie, sitting in a tree...”

I give him a light punch to the chest, laughing. “You’re insufferable.”

"Probably. But answer the question—are we calling this a relationship yet?"

I shrugged, tugging on my coat. "We agreed to date exclusively. I told him, given the circumstances, that's the only version that works for me right now. And he said he wasn't seeing anyone else anyway."

"Wasn't he in an open thing before?"

"He was."

"Then Sophie shows up, and suddenly he's Mr. Exclusivity?"

I laughed. "Apparently."

"But without labeling," he added.

I paused for a second, adjusting the scarf around my neck. "Honestly, it **feels** kind of like we're in a relationship. But I'm not letting my mind go there. I was the one who said we shouldn't rush things, and I still believe that. If he were staying, maybe it'd be different."

Eliyah nodded, lips pursed. "Do you know how **he** feels about a relationship with you?"

I shook my head. "He hasn't said anything. And I haven't asked. But I gave him my keys..."

Eliyah gave a slow nod, then grinned. "Mmm. Exciting times..."

I kissed him on both cheeks, French style. "Enjoy the drag queens, and don't cause *too* much trouble."

"No promises. Go have your romantic dinner, exclusivity girl."

*

"Hey, you," I called from the kitchen. "Come in—I haven't figured out what to cook yet. We could also just head to the supermarket. What are you in the mood for?" I dried my hands on a towel as I walked to the door.

Adrian stepped inside, movements slower than usual—his shoulders heavy, his usual spark dimmed, and his eyes tired.

"Hey," I say, watching as he shrugs off his coat. "Are you okay?"

"Yeah. All good." He walks into the living room and sinks onto the couch—right into the deepest corner, half-shadowed by one of my oversized plants, like he's trying to disappear into it.

I sit down beside him, just looking at him. Waiting.

He exhales, rubs a hand over his face, then reaches for me. "Come here."

I curl into his side, feeling the steady rhythm of his breath beneath me. "What happened?"

"You know how much family and community mean to me, right?" His voice is quieter than usual.

I nod.

"There was kind of an emergency with a good old friend today. I got up at six to drive Upstate and see him."

"Oh, wow. Is he okay?"

Adrian's fingers trace invisible patterns on my leg. "I don't know..." He hesitates. "John—he's lived next to my family's house forever—basically family. But lately, something's been off. He's been moody, lashing out for no reason. Last week, he lost it. Smashed a glass on the floor and stormed out of a barbecue. My mom checked on him, and he snapped at her—just... completely out of character."

I straighten a little. "That's awful. Is your mom okay?"

"She's fine." He waves it off, but his jaw tightens. "My whole family decided to give him space—to let him be for a while. At first, I agreed with them. But then... I don't know, the idea of just abandoning him felt wrong. He was there for me my whole childhood. So, I went to see him."

"And?"

Adrian stares at the floor. "He's not well."

I take his hand and squeeze it.

"The thing is, I don't think we should just walk away from him. True, he's pushing people away, but... he's only doing it because he's hurting."

"What's going on with him?"

"He lost his job. His wife left. He can't afford the rent. And now that everything fell apart, all kinds of stuff he buried from his childhood are coming up. Seeing our family—how stable we are—just made him feel worse. And when my parents cut him off, it pushed him even further down."

He swallows hard. "He told me about his past today. Like, **really** told me and shared lots of details. It was super intense. His stepdad hit him, and his mom was struggling with her mental health

—he never had a safe place."

Adrian looks at me, something raw in his expression. "You know what I realized in that moment, Sophie?"

"What?"

"How fucking lucky I am.

And how fast we are to judge people when they act out—When really, they're just carrying things we can't even imagine. We hold them to our own standards, but we have no idea where they started from."

His voice thickens. "I think... we need to recognize where people are in their journey, especially when they're trying to make progress. Not everyone had what I had. I mean, I'm far from perfect, but I grew up with love. With stability. That's more than most people can say."

His words hit me like a punch to the gut.

The room goes quiet, just the muffled hum of the city outside.

I lean into him, his warmth steady against mine.

"Right," I whisper.

My throat tightens. Breathing suddenly feels impossible. My chest heaves as something heavy and raw breaks loose inside me.

"Hey, what's wrong?" Adrian cups my face, his thumbs brushing my cheeks. "Hey, my heart, talk to me." He tilts my chin up, searching my face.

But the tears are already rising.

"Come here," he murmurs, pulling me into his arms. His embrace is firm and grounding. His hand moves through my hair.

My face rests against his chest, my shoulders shaking.

"I think I'll go for a quick walk," I say, my voice tight.

Adrian pulls back slightly. "Are you sure? You seem really upset."

"I just need a bit of fresh air."

His eyes flicker with hesitation. "Do you want me to come?"

"No, no, you stay here. Or leave, whatever you want." I force a small smile.

He studies me for a beat, then nods. "I'll cook something while you're out."

"Sure."

I swallow, blinking fast.

"See you in a bit."

I grab my coat and step outside, cool air slapping my face as I hurry down the stairs.

By the time I reach the courtyard, my chest feels like it's caving in. I don't stop walking until I hit the East River, the water stretching vast and endless in front of me.

I sit on a stone by the water, gripping my coat tighter around me.

I take a deep breath, but the memories have already uncoiled...

... My mom is screaming. I hear her heavy footsteps—fast, angry, coming for me. I run. Slam the door. Lock it. The handle rattles. Then the first kick. Then another. The door shudders.

I back away, trembling. It won't hold.

So I grab my sleeping bag, open the window, and climb out. I'm barefoot, the dirt cold beneath me. And I run.

I'm gone for days. Sleep in the woods. My best friend sneaks me sandwiches wrapped in napkins. I shower in the locker room at school, change into clean clothes, and walk into school like I'm just another kid. No one asks...

A shadow appears beside me. I look up.

**Adrian.**

"I thought I might find you here," he says, voice low.

"If you want me to leave, I'll go. I just—," he exhales.

"I didn't like the idea of you out here alone."

His presence is warm, solid.

I nod.

"Can I sit?"

I nod again, my eyes dropping back to the river.

He sits down beside me, shrugs off his coat, and wraps it around my shoulders. It smells like him—warm and steady.

We sit in silence, the water dark and endless.

A few people pass by, their footsteps soft on the path.

"You know I mentioned my childhood was difficult," I say.

Adrian nods. "Yeah."

I swallow. "It was **really** difficult. A lot of the things you just said about John... they felt familiar."

I stop for a second, hesitating.

Adrian reaches for my hand and laces his fingers through mine. "You don't **have** to tell me," he says gently. "But you can, if you want to. Whatever it is, I can take it. I mean it, Sophie."

I nod. "No, I want to.

Wow, I can't believe I'm telling you this."

I take a deep breath. "My mom was struggling mentally.

She was an alcoholic. Aggressive.

The house was always full of strange, toxic men.

We had no money.

No one looked out for me.

Home wasn't safe."

I pause. "Sorry, is this too much?" I ask, my voice low. "If it is, please say so. I don't want to dump this on you. I don't even know what's gotten into me—why it's all breaking out of me right now."

He shakes his head. "No. Not at all. I'm here for you, Sophie.

I want to know everything that made you **you**.

I'm not a guy who's only around for the easy parts.

If anything, I'm feeling honored that you trust me enough to share such personal things with me."

He pauses, eyes searching mine. "What are we talking about here? Did anyone ever hit you?"

"The worst part wasn't the physical stuff," I say quietly. "Yes, she slapped me sometimes—screamed, broke things. But the real damage was the fear. Never knowing what might happen next, with her or with her crazy boyfriends. Never feeling safe at home."

I pause, steadying my breath.

"... also the extreme emotional neglect...

it was like I didn't exist—got erased—unless I was doing something for her."

I glance at Adrian. "And the loneliness.

Most kids weren't even allowed to play with me because of my mom. Everyone knew how unstable she was, and I was shamed for it—everyone treated us like social outcasts."

Adrian's gaze softens. He squeezes my hand.

There's no pity in his eyes—just warmth.

"The things you say about recognizing someone's starting point in life?" I continue, "The fact that you can reflect like that—and actually reach out to someone everyone else has written off?

That's so fucking rare, Adrian.

And it means everything to me."

My chest rises and falls, sharp and uneven.

*Breathe, Sophie.*

"You know, people with backgrounds like mine—no money, no support, unstable upbringing—rarely make it into the high-achieving spaces I'm in now. And when we do, the cracks show at some point.

Because you can't grow up like that and come out spotless. You can **pretend**, sure—but the closer people get, the more that stuff surfaces.

Maybe it's how we communicate, or how easily we get overwhelmed with certain things, or the moments that hit harder for us than they do for others.

And the people around us—the friends, the partners—if they don't know how to handle it, they leave."

I laugh once, bitter. "In my twenties, it happened constantly. I hadn't learned how to hide it yet."

His grip tightens slightly.

"So," I say softly, "people tend to look away. It's too much—too messy. But with John... , you didn't. You saw the mess, you went to see him, stayed, and you understood. That's what got to me. That's why all of that is coming up right now.

Maybe I've just met the wrong people in life, but I've literally **never** seen anyone do that before."

He nods. "People who grow up with love—any love—and emotional safety have something to build from," he says. "Maybe the people who left just misjudged you. They didn't grasp that they had psychological privileges you never experienced."

*He understands.*

He takes both of my hands now. "It sounds like you had to build from almost nothing, Sophie. And yes, statistically, you probably shouldn't be where you are in life.

But you made it anyway."

"Exactly." I look at him.

"And sometimes, even now, it feels like I'm still catching up. Like I'm still not quite where I could be."

The words hang between us.

Adrian's breath fogs in the cold. Then, finally, he turns to me.

"I don't know where this is going, Sophie.

But I do know this—right now, you're not alone.

You are the most incredible woman I've ever met.

And I'm here.

You are not too much, and you're not overwhelming me."

He brushes a tear from my cheek.

"I **got** you.
More than ever."

His gaze doesn't waver.

"This... us..." he says softly, "I know it sounds cheesy. But it somehow feels like it was meant to happen."

*

The alarm chimes softly at 9 a.m., cutting through the quiet. I blink awake and turn my head.

Adrian lies beside me, still asleep, one arm curled beneath the pillow, his face peaceful.

*I can't believe how much I shared yesterday.*

*And I really can't believe how easy he made it feel.*

Warmth rises in my chest, slow and quiet at first, then unmistakable.

***Fuck.***

*You've fallen for him, Sophie.*

*There's no backup plan. He's leaving soon, and you've fallen for him—completely, irreversibly, no safety net in sight.*

I exhale, steady and slow.

*Okay. Don't future trip. Stay here. Let it be what it is—for now.*

He stirs, eyes fluttering open. Our bodies naturally gravitate toward each other beneath the sheets. He presses a slow, lingering kiss to my forehead before murmuring against my skin.

"Good morning, my heart," he says, voice husky with sleep.

A smile curves on my lips. "Good morning."

Adrian studies me for a beat, then brushes a stray strand of hair from my face. "How are you feeling?"

"Really good, actually. I slept surprisingly well."

Should we have breakfast?" he asks.

"That depends. Are you offering to make it?"

"I am," he says, sitting up. "It's Saturday morning after all. Stay where you are—I'll take care of it."

I nod, flashing a bright smile. "By the way," I say, "Rhea's coming over at 10:30."

Adrian's brows lift. "Rhea?"

"Rani's four-year-old daughter," I say. "I'm her godmother. Remember? I almost can't believe you haven't met yet."

He props himself up on one elbow, watching me. "Right—I remember. That sounds amazing. What's the plan?"

"She mentioned the zoo. We might do that."

Adrian stretches, running a hand through his hair. "I've got to meet a friend later, but I'm free till eleven. Do you want me to stick around? I'd love to meet her."

I smile. "Sure. You'll love her."

"Perfect." He leans over, presses a quick kiss to my temple, then throws the covers off and stands.

"Alright, let's get moving. French toast sounds good? I checked yesterday and you've got everything I need."

"Perfect," I say, sitting up. "I'm jumping in the shower."

By the time I came out, the smell of bread and coffee filled the air—and music, warm and familiar, drifted from the speakers. "You really like those classic tunes, huh?" I asked, toweling my hair as Leonard Cohen's voice filled the room.

He glanced over his shoulder, flipping a slice of French toast. "What can I say? Sometimes I feel like I was born in the wrong era. I mean, the Beatles, Leonard Cohen, Bowie—those guys had vision, you know? Their music... It's food for the soul."

"It's the same with movies for me," I said, my voice softening. "I'm obsessed with old films—50s and 60s stuff. Audrey Hepburn, Grace Kelly, James Dean. *Breakfast at Tiffany's*, *Roman Holiday...*"

"Weren't movies back then mostly about love stories where women existed only for their kids and husbands?" Adrian asked, smirking.

"Sometimes. But that's obviously not what fascinates me," I replied.

"Oh no. That's disappointing," he joked.

"Haha, of course it is to you... No... There's something timelessly beautiful about those movies. They always cheer me up."

He leans over and kisses me softly. "Well, now you have me to cheer you up."

He turns back to the kitchen and says, "I think the only old movie I ever watched with my grandma was *The Wizard of Oz.*"

"Oh, I love that movie."

He grins as he places a plate in front of me—French toast, arranged so carefully it almost looks too pretty to eat. "Well... I always wanted to be smart, brave, and have a big, loving heart —just like the Scarecrow, the Tin Man, and the Cowardly Lion," he says with a laugh.

I look down at the plate and then back at him, chuckling. "Oh my god, that's adorable."

We ate curled on the couch, the playlist weaving around us like a second blanket.

At exactly 10:30 a.m , the doorbell rang. The door had barely swung open before Rhea launched herself at me, arms tight around my waist, knocking me back a step.

I let out a laugh, squeezing her just as fiercely.

"Sweetheart, don't make her fall," Rani said, amused as she set down Rhea's bag.

Then her eyes landed on Adrian, and she smiled. "Hey, Adrian. Good to see you again."

"You too," he smiled.

Rani turned back to me. "Alright, I gotta run. Are you good?"

"Of course," I said, and with a quick wave, she was gone.

I shut the door, then walked back into the living room—only to find Rhea perched on Adrian's back, her tiny hands gripping his shoulders like reins.

He was on all fours, moving in a slow, exaggerated crawl.

I crossed my arms, raising an eyebrow. "Adrian, are you okay?"

He shot me a grin. "Having the best time."

"He's a tiger," Rhea declared, her voice full of authority.

I laughed, leaning against the doorway. "That might be accurate."

Rhea slid down Adrian's back and landed in a heap on the floor, bursting into giggles. "Whoa!" Adrian laughed, turning to check if she was okay. "All good, little one?"

Rhea nodded enthusiastically and made herself comfortable, sitting cross-legged on the floor, her little eyes narrowing as she studied Adrian with intense concentration. "By the way," she said, crossing her arms over her chest, "tigers don't talk."

Adrian, still on all fours, gasped dramatically. "They don't?" He clamped a hand over his mouth, then widened his eyes in mock horror. "Wait... then what have I been doing this whole time?"

Rhea giggled. "Breaking the tiger rules." She climbed onto the couch beside me, still catching her breath. Then, she snuggled up close, her small hand resting on my arm as she looked up at me with wide, hopeful eyes. "Sophie, can he always be here when I visit?"

I glanced over at Adrian, who was grinning like a kid himself, and felt something warm settle in my chest. "Well," I said, stroking her dark curly hair lightly, "I don't think we can promise that, but we can try."

Rhea gave a satisfied nod, clearly okay with that answer, and let out a contented sigh.

"Now, ready to go to the real zoo?" I asked, trying to shift gears, knowing Rhea would be bouncing off the walls any minute.

"Yeeaahhh," Rhea exclaimed, her eyes lighting up.

I couldn't help but laugh at her enthusiasm. It was impossible not to be drawn into her excitement.

Adrian caught my eye, still looking amused. "Alright," he said, straightening up and turning toward the door, "have fun in the zoo, you two. Don't forget to feed the lions." He shot us one last smile before heading out.

"Wait, Rhea, I'll quickly take Adrian outside, okay?" I said, standing up from the couch.

"Okaaay," Rhea replied, nodding eagerly as she watched me.

I slipped outside into the corridor, pulling Adrian into a quick hug. His arms wrapped around me, warm and steady.

"Oh my god, she **loves** you."

Adrian grinned, his eyes softening. "I like her too. She's a blast."

"You are great with kids. How did you manage that—she's usually very distant with strangers," I smiled.

Adrian shrugged, his smile turning a little cocky. "Yeah, I can't deny it. Kids love me. Sooo, should I try to get you pregnant right away, or do you think we should wait a little while?"

*Did he really just say that?*

His smile faltered for a second, then he laughed. "Damn it, it's too soon, huh?"

I blinked, feeling my heart skip a beat. "Oh wow... you weren't joking."

He kissed me quickly, pulling back with a look that was somehow both playful and serious. "I feel what I feel, Sophie."

I stared at him for a moment, laughing, but still processing his words. "Okay, you're insane."

He chuckled, clearly enjoying the chaos he'd just caused. "I know. But seriously... I can see it."

*Me too...*

... Kids in a sunlit garden. The smell of cookies. Us, happy...

*Oh god, Sophie. No. Stop romanticizing.* ***Stop it now!***

I shook my head, smiling despite myself. "I think you need to slow down."

He gave me a quick kiss on the cheek. "You two enjoy the zoo."

"Thanks. I'll text you later."

He gave me a wink as he turned to leave. "Take care, Sophie, heart. And give Rhea a hug for me."

"Will do," I called after him, still chuckling to myself. I closed the door and leaned against it for a second.

*Get it together, Sophie. Falling is one thing; losing your grip is another. You said you wouldn't do this again—Not like this. Enjoy him. Enjoy this. But keep your feet on the ground. He's wonderful. But this is still the beginning.*

*And beginnings can be deceiving...*

CHALLENGE 12

# Labels

"Hey, my heart," Adrian said, pulling me into a warm hug that lasted just long enough to make my shoulders drop. "Finally. I was buried in work, but one week apart is **way** too much. I already had withdrawal symptoms." He stepped back slightly, still holding onto me. "Come on in, I just submitted my report."

I followed him inside his apartment, only half listening—because what he was wearing immediately hijacked my brain.

*Okay, this is officially the most bizarre combination of patterns I've ever seen. A tropical-print T-shirt in blinding colors... under a beige striped jacket?*

I bit back a grin. The corduroy story flashed through my mind, and I had to actively stop myself from laughing out loud.

He settled onto the couch, draping an arm around me with mock casualness, clearly waiting for a reaction. "You haven't said anything about my outfit yet."

I blinked, feigning innocence. "What do you mean?"

He gave me a wounded look. "Well, since you always look effortlessly amazing, I figured it was time I upped my game. My brother was in town and we went shopping. I picked this out hoping you'd be impressed, but... judging by your silence, I've failed."

The effort in his tone was so fake, I narrowed my eyes immediately. "I think it's adorable you dressed up for me," I said, leaning in and kissing him gently. "But really... You don't have to try so hard. I like you just the way you are."

He gave me a smug smile—then suddenly shifted posture and started striking ridiculous poses. "So which part do you like most—the jacket or the screaming palm trees?"

I froze. "Wait..." I eyed him suspiciously. "You're not serious, are you?"

He burst into laughter. "Not even a little. This is the kind of outfit I used to wear a couple of years ago, before I went minimalist for safety reasons. Thought you'd enjoy the full experience of what I've been warning you about."

I shook my head, laughing. "Oh, I'm enjoying it alright. This is **prime** material."

He winked. "Told you." Then he headed into the kitchen. "Wine?"

I nodded, still recovering from the outfit reveal, and watched him move across the room. *This man could wear absolutely anything and still look super hot.*

My eyes land on his open laptop on the table, the report still pulled up. "Who's the report for?"

He calls back, "My boss. I'm not a director yet, remember? Still twenty-eight. Still have to make other people happy."

"Right..." I murmur.

He comes back with two glasses of wine and hands me one.

I lean back, eyes locked on him, a teasing smile playing at my lips. "You know what... since we clearly haven't agreed on your outfit yet, why don't you just take it off?"

His grin deepens as he sets both glasses on the table. "Don't tempt me. If this is the reward, I might start dressing like a disaster on purpose."

I tilt my head. "You just said it yourself. You're just twenty-eight and still have to make other people happy. Since I'm **your boss** right now... don't question me. Just follow my orders."

He raises an eyebrow. "Oh? We're playing **that** game tonight?"

"We are," I state, sipping my wine, eyes not leaving his. "I always wanted to have a male secretary. Someone to help me unwind on those days when work just gets too tense with my start-up. I'm glad I found you," I say, my tone intentionally casual.

"Okay, Sophie. You got it. Should I take all of it off?" he asks.

"All of it," I say, keeping my voice firm.

I watch him undress. "Maybe we should move to the couch. That might be more comfortable," I instruct him.

He follows my lead, and we settle in side by side—me fully dressed, him naked.

I nod toward the laptop. "I see you've pulled together the financial plan I asked for. It looks solid—I'm impressed," I say.

"Happy you're happy," he replies, a hint of a smile on his lips.

I run my fingers through his hair. "You've been working so hard lately. I usually don't do this, but... maybe you've earned a little recognition. What do you think—Do you feel like you deserve it?"

His eyes meet mine. He looks much more boyish than usual, playing his part perfectly. "Yes," he says, almost pleading, his eyes wide.

"Are you sure? Have you truly done a good enough job with that finance strategy to deserve this?" I tease.

He's about to get up and go for the laptop, but I hold him back. "It's okay, you don't need to present it to me now—it's late, after all. Just promise me."

"Yes, I promise it's a really solid investment plan," he says, nodding sincerely.

I lean back slightly, locking eyes with him. "Look, I've noticed how you look at me sometimes at work. It's not okay."

His suddenly very boyish-looking face flushes. "I know."

"I see you staring at my breasts when you think I'm not looking. I see the way your cock gets hard when you're watching me. You've imagined fucking me in the office while you should have been focused on work, haven't you?"

He swallows hard.

"Tell me. Is that what you've been dreaming about?

Me touching you?

Kissing you?"

"Yes, I'm sorry," he murmurs.

"Say it properly," I demand.

"Say, 'I'm sorry, boss.'"

"I'm sorry, boss," he repeats, his voice small but sincere.

"Good," I say, my tone softening slightly but still commanding. "You're a little pervert. But because you've worked so hard, I'm going to give you something special. Just this once.

Do you think you deserve it?"

"Yes, boss," he replies with urgency.

"Would you like to fuck me?" I ask.

"Fuck me with your hard cock, right now?"

"Yes, please," he says, desire in his eyes. His words are barely above a whisper, trembling with anticipation.

I smile, enjoying my power over him. "Alright, but let's be clear. I don't have all day.

Since I'm giving you this gift, you get to choose. Where do you want to fuck me?"

"On the table," he says devotedly.

"And how do you want me?" I ask. "Choose well; this will be the only time," I add.

"Lean forward on the table," he says after a brief pause.

I raise an eyebrow but comply, arching my back and baring myself to him. "Like this?" I ask, looking back at him.

"Yes," he said, his voice heavy with need. "Now spread your legs."

He steps forward, his hands gripping my hips as he pushes into me. Deep.

His movements are raw, desperate, unrestrained.

"Oh my god, Sophie!" His release is loud, almost primal, echoing through the room.

Then, I feel his body relax.

He pulls me up, kisses my neck, and whispers: "You just made me come **so** fucking hard, Sophie."

"Well, I know how desperately you want to get recognized for your good work," I say playfully. I turn around, stroke his hair back, and give him a gentle kiss.

"Come on, let's move this to my bedroom," he says, his hand slipping into mine, guiding me toward the bed.

He lifts the blanket, nodding for me to slip under it, and I do, sinking into its warmth.

He joins me, his body pressing against my back, the heat of him enveloping me. I can feel the steady beat of his heart against my neck.

"It's so liberating that we're both versatile switchers," Adrian says.

"What do you mean?" I turn around, facing him.

"It means we aren't stuck in one role. We can both be dominant or submissive, switching it up whenever we want," he says.

"True," I say. "In the past, I've usually been submissive, and the men I was with were mostly dominant. You?"

"I always end up as the dominant one. But with you, each time is entirely different from the last time. I didn't even know it could be that way. It's absolutely insane."

A mischievous grin flashes across my face. "Let's go to PLAY." I stroke his hair. "You know, that exclusive club for adults? The one where people go to dance and explore, mixing fun with... whatever else happens?"

"Yeah, I know it," he says. "I've been."

"You have?"

"Just once. I'd totally go there again with you. Next weekend, maybe?"

"Sounds good... I've heard so much about that space. Apparently, it's still a secret, hidden away—far too wild for your average New York spot," I say.

"It is. Were you ever interested in going before now?" he asks.

"I thought about it," I say. "But I've never been into the whole hookup-with-strangers thing. I can find them hot and curious. I just usually don't feel safe enough. And I don't like feeling like a random option, just one of many."

"If we went together, you'd be no one else's—just mine. And I'd protect you," Adrian promised, pulling me closer.

"Let's make this **our** experience, Sophie. I'll be all yours. Do you trust me?"

I meet his gaze and nod.

"Yes," I say and pull him into a kiss.

*

*Next weekend*

I opened my coat and turned to Adrian. "Let's do a final check before we go in." He looks me up and down. "You look perfect, Sophie. Hot. So fucking hot."

The preparation for tonight had been fun.

We'd explored a well-known BDSM store in Williamsburg, bursting into laughter as we tried on outfits and found the perfect ones.

I was in fishnet stockings, high leather boots, and a tight leather tube skirt that barely covered my cheeks. Gold sequins glittered across my bra, and a black harness wrapped around my neck. Adrian was wearing black leather shorts and matching boots. Chains glinted along the harness strapped to his chest, and his sleeveless leather vest revealed his muscular chest and arms.

I pulled him close. "You too," I said.

"Let's go." He took my hand and pulled me to the entrance.

The doorman scanned our outfits to ensure we matched the vibe of the place. "Okay, you can go in. Enjoy," he said.

Adrian's grip tightened around my hand as we stepped into the dark entry hall.

We passed by a woman wearing nothing but a barely there thong, her body unapologetically on display. She totally owned it, standing tall under the flickering neon glow, smiling at me.

I raised an eyebrow. "Ok, wow, I said. This place is a bit more naked than I'd expected."

"How do you feel about seeing strangers naked?" Adrian asked me as we moved towards a closed door that appeared to be the entrance to the actual club.

"Oh, I have no issues with that at all. I feel really relaxed about it," I said. "I actually love when people own who they are, whatever that looks like."

We paused before the door.

I turned to Adrian. "I just need to feel like I'm in control of what's **happening to me** tonight—guard my personal space."

We open the heavy door in front of us and step into the dimly lit club. The air is thick with a blend of perfume, heat, and the pulse of music that vibrates through the walls, sinking into my chest. The atmosphere feels alive, electric—like the world outside has disappeared, leaving only this raw, unfiltered space where everything feels possible.

"Don't worry, you **are** in control," he says. "I mean, do I look like someone who'd let anyone near you tonight?" He builds himself up and flexes his muscles. "**Believe me**, I'll protect you."

I raise an eyebrow. "Yeeesss, you are my **hero**," I say, laughing. "Happy?"

"Very," he replies, his gaze locking onto mine as his arms wrap around me, pulling me in closer. "All I want to hear."

He leans in, his voice dropping to a low, seductive tone. "Do you want a drink?"

"A little later?" I suggest glancing over at the long line snaking in front of the bar. "Let's explore this first," I say, tilting my head toward the packed center of the club.

"Really?" he asks, his eyes widening. "You want to go in there right away?"

I nod, a rush of excitement flooding me.

"Yes, I do. I want to see how far I can go."

"Okay, Sophie, you got it." He takes my hand, guiding me effortlessly as we move through the pulsating mix of dancing bodies, in every shape, style, and form. Some wear barely there outfits, strips of fabric clinging to their skin, while others dress in neon costumes or avant-garde-looking designs.

As we walk deeper into the crowd, we pass couples locked in passionate embraces, their hands everywhere, as if the world outside had ceased to exist. Others are lost in the music, their bodies swaying as if nothing matters except the beat. The whole place is alive—a world of possibility.

Near the DJ booth, we find an unexpected pocket of space—a small haven in the midst of the pulsing crowd. People keep their distance, like they are giving the DJ room to breathe.

Adrian squeezes my hand, guiding me into the space, and, with a quick turn around, his eyes land on mine. "Up for a little adventure?" he asks.

The bass pulses through my chest.

I nod.

He takes both of my hands and holds them tight. "Sophie, listen to me. Say 'No, I mean it' if there's anything you don't want. That's really important. I think I know what you are into, but if I do something that makes you uncomfortable, tell me immediately. If you don't say, 'No, I mean it,' I'll keep going.

Do you understand?"

I nod again.

"I trust you."

Adrian positions me so I am facing the DJ, his body close behind mine. The crowd moves around us, lost in their own rhythm, seemingly oblivious to us.

His lips glide across my neck, sending a shiver down my spine as his fingers trace a slow path along my back.

One hand finds my breast, gripping my nipple firmly before delivering a playful smack on my butt cheek, leaving heat across my skin.

The fingers of his other hand tangle in my hair, pulling just enough to make me gasp before his mouth claims mine. "You want more?" he murmurs.

"Yes, please," I whisper."

Then, his warm hand slips from my butt cheek beneath my leather skirt, sliding across my skin.

I look around. By now, many eyes are on us.

*Breathe, Sophie.*

Then, slowly, his fingers glide underneath the front of my thong, slipping inside me.

"Oh god, Adrian."

I melt against him.

"This feels incredible."

"Look how they stare at you, Sophie. You really like putting yourself on display, don't you?"

"Yes."

"You want even more?" he murmurs.

"Yes, please," I whisper.

Adrian slowly turns me around, directing me to face the crowd. He takes his time as if he's putting on a show for everyone.

His hand pulls my breasts free from my bra.

They are on full display now, while his fingers continue their exploration underneath my skirt.

I feel the eyes of strangers land on us, punctuated by flashes of blue and red light moving on the dance floor.

***I've never felt this alive.***

"Come with me," Adrian says. He takes my hand and leads me upstairs to a balcony overlooking the dance floor.

I look down into the sea of bodies moving below us, the music still thrumming with energy in the room.

Adrian pulls up my skirt in one fluid motion and slips off my thong. He presses me against the railing with a firm grip.

I can feel his chest and belly on my back—his breath on my neck.

He pulls me close. "I never wanted **anyone** this much, Sophie. You are driving me absolutely insane," he whispers into my ear.

My hands grip firmly onto the railing, the city of New York watching from beyond the club windows, and the crowd below lost in their own rhythms.

He enters me in one quick movement, and it feels like the whole world is bursting open.

Light—blue, red—flashes across my vision.

People everywhere. Moving. Watching.

He thrust harder and harder, his lips on my neck, driving me to a climax so intense it leaves me trembling.

**Heat** on my skin.

**Adrenaline** in my blood.

**Love.** Desire. Surrender.

**Every feeling, all at once**—flooding through me, too much, but I want more.

**I come.**

Harder and louder than ever before in my life.

**Release...**

I can feel his body sinking on me just as mine lets go too.

Exhausted. Happy.

I can taste the sweat on my upper lip.

He kisses me on my neck, adjusts my skirt and bra.

Then turns me to face him.

It feels like he's still inside of me. **We are one.**

**I see you. And you see me.**

He pulls me close and kisses me.

Deep. Consuming. Filled with passion that feels endless.

*I just want it to stay like this forever.*

*

*A couple of days later*

"Ready? Tadaaa," I said, stepping back to reveal the first prototype of my new lamp.

Adrian, standing a few feet away in the middle of my SPARKS studio, tilted his head, smiling. "Looks clean. Functional. Very you."

"Thank you. But I need you to actually sit and test it. I want to try the different mood settings."

He walked over and lowered himself into the chair at my worktable, surrounded by fabric swatches, tools, and the faint scent of warm wood and solder. The large studio window behind him cast streaks of light onto the polished floor.

"Close your eyes," I said, grabbing the remote.

He grinned. "Bossy again. I like it." But he did as he was told.

I cycled through the three mood modes, each glowing at a different level of brightness. Watching his face shift under each setting—from soft, relaxed light to sharp, focused intensity—made my chest tighten a little. Sharing my early-stage work with him felt weirdly intimate. "This one?" I asked.

He tilted his head. "That one makes me feel like kissing you."

I laughed, stepping closer. "Don't move. This is strictly professional testing."

But he reached for my hand and tugged me gently toward him.

I lost my balance slightly, and we both toppled sideways into the chair, tangled together, laughing so hard my stomach hurt.

"Okay," I said, still breathless. "You are the worst test subject ever."

"Or the best," he said, holding me close.

Just then, Jayne from SPARKS peeked her head in through the open door. "I didn't know you two were a couple," she said, smiling widely. "You look incredible together."

Adrian **freezes**.

His grip loosens. I feel his body tense under me.

"We're not..." he blurts.

"We're not a couple.

We're just friends."

Jayne raises her eyebrows, laughs awkwardly. "Oh... got it. My mistake. Sorry." She disappears as quickly as she showed up.

I sit up slowly, pulling away.

"**Friends?**

Wow. Okay."

I turn toward the window, staring out at the empty courtyard. "I know we aren't in an official relationship, but we **are** exclusive. And we aren't **just friends**." I brush sawdust from my jeans. "Did I get something entirely wrong here, Adrian?"

He doesn't answer right away.

I turn around to face him.

"Is this just a casual thing for you? Is it just about sex? Or is there maybe someone else? If so, just tell me. It's okay. I just need to know."

"No," he says quickly. "Of course, it's not just about sex. And there's no one else. I just... I'm not into labels. I just got out of a relationship. I need time."

"Time is fine. But panic like this isn't," I say.

He looks stricken. "You're right. I screwed that up."

"Honestly? If the idea of being in a relationship with me freaks you out this much, maybe we should hit pause." I grab my keys and head for the door.

"Sophie, wait—" he steps after me. "Please don't go. The question just caught me off guard."

I pause. "Okay," I say calmly. "Then figure it out. I just need some space, okay? We'll talk tomorrow."

He nods, eyes clouded with frustration.

I walk through the quiet hall, take the stairwell down toward the back exit, and rush onto the courtyard.

"Sophie!" I turn.

He's already halfway to me. "Okay," he says, breathless.

"Yes. You're right. We're not just friends.

I care about you.

Deeply."

He hesitates, then looks directly at me. "I've been freaking out because..."

"Because?"

"I've been falling in love with you."

I stare at him. "What?"

"I'm falling in love with you, Sophie," he says again, steadier now. "I don't know what that means yet. I don't think I'm ready for a relationship. But I know what I feel for you."

I smile. "Okay."

His brows lift. "**Okay?** Sophie!"

I breathe out.

Silence stretches.

Then another smile: "Okay. *Maybe*, I'm falling in love with you, too."

He leans in to kiss me, but I place my hand gently on his chest, stopping him. "Also—just to be clear: I actually really like labels sometimes. And the fact is, we **are** dating exclusively. We're **not** just friends."

"Yes," he says, steady this time. "We're dating exclusively. And we are not just friends. You're right."

For a moment, relief washes over me.

And then—just as quickly—comes the fear.

Because even if we **are** falling in love... even if we feel the same way—He's still leaving soon. And it's still too early for big decisions. For a relationship, or even considering crazy things like moving to Paris with him.

*It takes time to really know someone.*

*And as incredible as it all is, my gut tells me I don't know him well enough. Not yet.*

CHALLENGE 13

# Too Good to Be True?

I stand in the bathroom, staring at the calendar on my phone, counting backward.

My chest feels hollow—like the space between heartbeats has stretched just a little too wide.

I didn't pay much attention over Christmas, but now it's clear: my period is late. Much too late.

*No wonder.* Adrian and I have been a little reckless—nothing openly discussed, but we stopped being careful. Not out of passion or heat-of-the-moment impulse, but something quieter. More unconscious.

Neither of us was actively **trying** to make this happen. And yet, we were not really avoiding it either; almost like we're inviting fate to weigh in.

A numb kind of clarity settles in—like my body already knows something my mind hasn't caught up to. No tears. No dramatic thoughts. Just a quiet awareness:

*This could change everything.*

*No panic. No spiraling. Why so calm, Sophie?* I replay the last few weeks in my head. Adrian and I **have** been closer than ever.

We'd spent a lot of time together—even taken a spontaneous trip to the coast for a couple of days. No matter what we were doing, we couldn't seem to get enough of each other. Even the boring, mundane things became meaningful when I did them with him.

And it wasn't just that wild, first-month chemistry—though, let's be honest, we were deep into that too.

This felt more grounded. More real. Our attraction wasn't just magnetic—for once, I actually had good reasons why I liked a guy. He was incredible: empathic, kind, funny, smart, and selfless in bed.

And our interests, our ways of thinking, even how we dealt with discomfort or change—all strangely aligned. We didn't just enjoy the same things; we got **lost** in them, together. I'd never experienced that kind of compatibility before.

Even when we spent Christmas apart—he'd gone to see his family, and I'd stayed in the city with friends—it didn't feel like distance. We stayed close. Silly selfies, voice notes, snapshots of holiday meals. I loved seeing glimpses of his world—his family, his childhood home, his dog—and somehow, even from miles away, it felt like we were still experiencing Christmas together.

It was great—**all** of it. **We** were great.

Yet, I still had uninvited doubts creep in from time to time, wondering *Can it really be **this** good?*

After everything I'd been through in my last relationships—love fading into exhaustion, charm turning into manipulation, and even danger when I dated an actual stalking psychopath—I knew I couldn't afford to be naive anymore.

And yes, there had been a couple of minor things popping up lately. Moments. Nothing huge, yet enough to make me pause and wonder...

But nobody's perfect.

And I decided that I didn't want my past to dictate the story of something new.

So I made a choice: find balance.

Stay open. Stay aware. But let myself trust again.

No spiraling. No overthinking.

Just believing the doubts that feel **reasonable**.

And the ones I had so far?

They didn't.

*So, everything seems fine.*

*Maybe, this time, I don't have to worry...*

*... I just have to figure out how to tell Adrian my period's late...*

CHALLENGE 14

# Grace

Adrian opens the door barefoot, the apartment glowing dimly behind him.

"I might be pregnant," I say, before I even cross the threshold.

He freezes. The color drains from his face. "What?"

"Are you serious?" he asks, as if the ground's shifted beneath him and he's struggling to stay upright. "Oh my god," he murmurs, eyes darting. "What if we really are pregnant?" Panic flashes across his face—quick and sharp, like a pulse. "This could ruin my entire future," he mutters, more to himself than to me. He runs his free hand through his hair, taking a step back, like the air's thinning around him.

"Hold on a second," I snap, stepping inside.

My throat tightens. "This wasn't in the plan, I get that. But you haven't exactly been careful either. And **you've** been the one talking about wanting to be a father. You asked me when we'd have kids—**more than once**. Did you mean any of that?"

"I meant all of it," Adrian says quickly. His eyes flick to mine. "But... I was caught up in the moment. I didn't really think it through. I just said what felt right, but I didn't actually—make the leap into the future."

I blink. "So, you say things you mean in the moment, but not long enough to mean **anything**?" My voice lifts, sharper now. "And now you're shocked that something real might come from it? Do you even hear yourself? How do you think I feel right now?"

He looks stricken. "Shit," he mutters, dragging both hands over his face. "I know... I don't want to be the guy who has a breakdown over this. That's not who I am. I just... didn't expect this. It's a lot."

"Well," I say, stepping back, heat prickling at the edges of my skin, "you might not **want** to be that guy—but that's **exactly** who you're being right now."

This isn't the Adrian I know. Not the grounded, clear-headed man I've been falling for.

I turn away before I unravel in front of him.

I rush outside and walk away. Fast.

*How can he say—over and over—that he wants to be a father... ask me about kids with wide eyes and certainty... and then look completely lost the moment it stops being hypothetical?*

*How did we get here?*

***I** never rushed into the idea of becoming a mother.*

***He** did.*

***He** opened that door.*

The air feels heavier now, filled with questions I don't know how to ask or answer—and the truth is I'm not sure I want to understand.

Something is off. Deeply off.

And I don't know what to do with that.

*

On Saturday night, almost 10:30 p.m., my intercom buzzed. I hesitated for a moment, staring at it, debating whether to answer. Then I pressed the button.

It was two days after the pregnancy incident, and I hadn't really spoken with Adrian yet. Though it was the weekend before New Year's, he'd just texted me to say, "I'm really sorry, Sophie. I know I fucked up. I promise I'll make it up to you, but right now, I need some space."

Adrian's footsteps were quiet on the stairs, and when I opened the door, he didn't say anything at first—just pulled me into a long, slow hug.

His arms wrapped around me like they were trying to erase the past days, but I didn't melt into him. I stood stiffly, my arms eventually moving around him more out of habit than instinct. "I'm sorry, Sophie," he murmured into my hair.

I nodded against his shoulder, but I didn't speak. Not yet.

We ended up on the couch, the living room dim except for the soft yellow glow from the floor lamp in the corner.

I curled into one end, legs tucked under me, while he sat at the other, leaning forward, elbows on his knees, hands rubbing the back of his neck like he was trying to shake something off.

He looked away. His voice was low, almost hoarse. "I panicked, Sophie. It wasn't about you. It was just... too much too sudden."

I gave a quiet, bitter laugh. "You know what, it **was** about me. About **us**. You left me alone to process something huge."

His shoulders dropped. He leaned back, hands resting loosely in his lap.

The silence between us stretched, not angry—just tired and worn.

"I didn't mean to leave you alone," he said finally. "I just... needed air."

I nodded slowly. "You got it."

"I was overwhelmed. With this—us—, and with my big move to Paris soon. It was too much altogether." He looked over, his eyes soft but searching. "And now?"

I pulled the throw blanket tighter around me, not really for warmth, just to feel something solid. "Now I'm not sure where we are."

"You mean so fucking much to me, Sophie. You know that, right?" He reaches his hand across the space between us. His fingers graze the top of my knee under the blanket—light, hesitant, like he's trying to ground the moment without saying too much.

But still—no "How are you?" No "I'm here, no matter what."
Nothing solid.
Nothing steady.

Just more vague affection, more soft touches, trying to fill the space where real support should be.

And it's not enough. Not even close.

We didn't sleep together that night. We barely touched. We just lay side by side in my bed, our bodies close but not quite connected. At one point, I turned my back on him. I needed space of my own.

*

The next morning, after Adrian left, I stood alone in the bathroom, half-dressed.

I glanced down—and there it was: *My period.*

Relief hits first, sharp, and visceral.

My knees soften.

I grip the edge of the sink with both hands, the porcelain cool and grounding beneath my fingers. *Okay. It's over. You're not pregnant.*

I let out a long breath, trying to steady myself.

But then—without warning—tears rise.

They sting as they spill over, hot and fast.

My hand flies up to cover my mouth, trying to hold the sob in. But I can't.

*Where is this coming from?*

*Did some part of me want this? Want us to become parents —silently, secretly, without even knowing?*

The thought feels absurd. Illogical. And yet... My body tells a truth my mind hadn't caught up to.

I wipe my face, still trembling, and pick up my phone. I text Adrian, just plain fact:

**Me:** I got my period

His reply comes almost instantly.

> **Adrian:** Oh my god, thanks for letting me know, Sophie. I'm so relieved

A pause. Then:

> **Adrian:** Not overall—just because of the timing

His words land dull and flat.

I stare at the screen.

Something has shifted.

What once felt magnetic, full of light, aligned—now feels distant and gray.

Something's broken. And it doesn't feel like it can be repaired.

*

"He said **what**?" Rani blinked at me, her eyes wide with disbelief when I told her about Adrian's reaction to my potential pregnancy. "I'm so sorry, Sophie girl. Come here." She pulled me into a tight hug, her hands warm on my back, her perfume faint but familiar.

Eliyah leaned in from across the small table, his voice laced with concern. "I didn't see that coming. Like, at all."

"I know. Neither did I," I said, pulling back from Rani's arms.

The low hum of a disco remix pulsed through the BABES drag bar, the colorful lights flickering across the glittery walls and mirrored surfaces.

"Do you know what kills me most?" I added, sinking into my seat. "In the past, I just didn't put enough effort into my relationships, so I wasn't really surprised when they didn't work out. But this time, I really gave it my all."

"I know you did," Rani said gently, her hand resting over mine.

"I prepared myself for months. I was so careful," I continued. "I mean, some people navigate sex and relationships with ease—sure of their desires, confident in their standards, clear in communication and boundaries."

I gave a dry laugh. "Well... my past hasn't exactly equipped me for that. And let's be honest—I'm clearly not one of those people."

I stared into my wine glass, watching the swirl of red as I tilted it slightly. "Or at least I wasn't. But I've learned a lot these past months. I took it slow, step by step. I made sure he was who he said he was, made sure I didn't get swept up too quickly. I defended my boundaries. Communicated my needs. And he actually met all of them."

"That sounds incredible, Sophie. You can be proud of yourself," Rani said, squeezing my hand.

"Yeah, but somehow I misjudged him anyway, didn't I?" I muttered, dragging a hand through my hair. "God," I added with a bitter laugh. "I promised myself I'd never wear rose-colored glasses again. No more fantasy fog. And look at me—I almost ended up like my mom. Having a child I wasn't ready for, with a man who wasn't really there for me. I swear, I don't even know what I would've done..."

Just then, a drag queen in a full glittery pineapple costume strutted past our table, towering in green platform heels. "Another round of drinks, sweethearts?" they purred, batting gold-sequined lashes.

Eliyah checked our glasses. "Not right now, thanks, darling. But you look fabulous."

The pineapple winked and sauntered off.

We looked at each other—and burst out laughing.

"I'm not sure this venue was built for breakdowns," I chuckled.

"This is **exactly** what it's built for," Eliyah said, grinning. "Drag, wine, and emotional unraveling. It's practically the tagline."

"Of course. I mean... surrounded by sexy fruit and sass, how could you not start healing?" Rani smiled.

"True," I said. "Are they doing a show tonight?"

"Nope," Eliyah answered. "Just bar night. The show's once a month."

Rani leaned in, her voice low. "Sophie, stop punishing yourself. You've been thoughtful. Intentional. You've done your homework—books, podcasts, you've made actual efforts to grow your relationship skills. "

"But I still misread something."

"Were there red flags before?" Eliyah asked gently.

I nodded slowly. "I've been replaying everything in my head. Revisiting things I ignored. Things I minimized because they didn't seem big enough at the time. Maybe they still aren't. Or they are. I'm not sure. Back then, they felt minor.

But now? After how he reacted to the pregnancy scare, everything rushes back—like it's been hiding in the background this whole time."

"Like what?" Rani asked.

I hesitated. "I don't even know if they're worth chatting about..."

"Just say it out loud. It might make things clearer," Eliyah said. "Come on. What are friends for? You've listened to me rant about every guy I've dated for two years now."

"That's true," I laughed.

"So?" Rani prompted gently. "What did you notice?"

I took a slow sip of wine and glanced around the room.

The lights flickered softly on a mirrored pineapple centerpiece at the bar. Somewhere nearby, someone cheered as a RuPaul song came on.

I exhaled. "Okay... here's what I didn't share at the time."

I leaned forward slightly, setting my glass down. "The first thing was this weird feeling I had sometimes after we'd been together—especially after our first night. A heaviness.

I couldn't explain it. It just felt like there was something dark in his energy. But it was subtle. Abstract. And the sex had been incredible.

So I figured it didn't make sense to be bothered by it, and I focused on all the excitement instead.

Honestly, I still don't know where that feeling came from... or if it even meant anything."

"Okay," Eliyah nodded. "What else?"

"There was this friend of his—this Mike guy. He made all kinds of strange comments about Adrian. Joked that he had zero morals, said something like, 'I wouldn't be surprised if he's killed someone,' and mentioned he once threatened to kill some random guy at a bar."

"What?" Rani's brows shot up.

"Wait—hold on," Eliyah said. "What was the context?

Was this, like, a joke? Was it late? At a bar?"

"Yeah. It was at a bar. Mike was clearly drunk, and Adrian brushed it off—said the whole thing was twisted. He framed it as defending a woman who was being harassed, and told me not to believe a drunk guy over the man I'm dating."

"Well... sounds kind of legit," Rani said.

"And it might totally be. But then, Mike also stated Adrian would make the perfect romance scammer."

Eliyah leaned forward. "Excuse me?"

"... He'd be smart, funny, good-looking, charming, know exactly what to do and say so that women fall head over heels for him. And he'd have... urges. He wouldn't be exactly picky and sleep with almost anyone."

"Wow," Eliyah muttered.

"Thanks for that, Mike. What an absolute dick."

"Totally." I paused, pressing my thumb against the rim of my glass.

"And Adrian deflected.

He said that almost all guys would, they just wouldn't admit it. Apparently, in his last relationship, sometimes he had sex with different women on the same day. He and his girlfriend also had sex with mutual friends or people they knew. But he said all of that would be just fun exploration and didn't mean anything. And he emphasized that it'd be different with me.

That **we'd** be different, and just because he's done those things in the past doesn't mean he wants them now."

Rani frowned. "But that checks out, doesn't it?"

"Exactly. That's the thing." I let out a slow breath. "I guess what really shocked me was how the things Mike said felt so wildly out of sync with the Adrian I knew. But if you look at his responses one by one... , they check out. That's why I told myself not to overthink it. Not to read too much into it."

I ran a hand through my hair and sighed. "But then this reaction to the pregnancy scare... It was like a mask slipped. And suddenly I couldn't shake the feeling that maybe—just maybe—there was more truth to Mike's comments than I wanted to believe."

I paused.

"There were a couple of other small things too, mostly about women from his past, but... probably not worth getting into now."

"Why didn't you tell us all of this earlier?" Rani asked.

I hesitated. "Because...

Adrian **is** truly great in so many ways. And I have a complicated past. Wouldn't you have just told me to trust him? To not sabotage something good?"

"Probably," Rani said.

"And I get that. Each moment had its logical explanation. It all **made sense**. And my doubts faded fast—wiped away by his explanations and the fact that everything else between us felt **so** good."

I looked from one to the other. "So, I thought—why bring it up? Why keep wondering and drag you both into it when I didn't have anything concrete—just uneasy feelings I couldn't prove?"

*

I stared at the message, my fingers hovering over the screen.

**Adrian:** Hey. Just wanted to check in. I'll be celebrating New Year's at Gabriel's tonight. I need some space

**Adrian:** Also just wanted to let you know I'll be on a work trip in Asia for four weeks. Leaving in two days

**Me:** Okay

**Adrian:** Okay. Happy New Year, Sophie

**Me:** Happy New Year, Adrian

And with that, I turned my phone off.

No more half-hearted attempts. No more second-guessing. No more heaviness.

I just wanted to be alone.

Despite Rani's best efforts to convince me otherwise, I had already made up my mind: I was staying in tonight. New Year's had never really been **my** event anyways—just another check-point on the calendar, more symbolic than significant.

What I truly needed was a night to myself to slow down. All I'd do was slip into pajamas, binge old movie classics, and let the rest of the world fade away for a little while.

I made it a point to take good care of myself. No cooking, no stress—just ease.

I started the day with a massage, letting the tension melt out of my shoulders.

Later, I ordered sushi from my favorite spot—the same one I used to treat myself to on quiet Friday nights, long before Adrian was in the picture. I added a little extra—three sweet rice desserts I probably wouldn't finish but couldn't resist. A small luxury, just for me.

Then I opened a bottle of champagne I'd bought today at my favorite wine shop. Not for a party, not for a toast—but just because.

I let it fizz and settle while I curled up on the couch and queued up *Breakfast at Tiffany's*.

For a moment, my mind drifted—back to the times when I was thirteen, hiding in old films whenever life got loud or messy. Trying to float up the stairs like Audrey Hepburn, copying that elegance she kept even when her character had nothing.

Poise. Dignity. Style.

I knew it even then: that's what I wanted—to move through the world with grace, whatever it threw at me. A rare quality, maybe—but a good one to reach for.

I hit play, and the moment I saw Audrey, I felt a bit lighter. *Honestly, who can stay sad watching Fred Astaire sing or Audrey Hepburn light up the screen with her smile?*

Not me.

Right now, I was in my own little world, and I intended to stay here for a while. Wrapped in a blanket, a glass of champagne in hand, I let the movie wash over me. Audrey's voice floated through the room—familiar and nostalgic.

It didn't fix everything. But it held me gently.

Sometime before midnight, I drifted off.

The lights still buzzed faintly around me. Outside my window, fireworks burst over the river. I could hear distant laughter, music, cheers—celebration echoing through the city like a party I'd chosen not to attend.

*It's okay, Sophie.*
*It isn't the night you'd imagined.*
*But it's yours.*

*

I woke up on the couch, tangled in blankets, one leg hanging off the side, my neck stiff from the awkward position.

The TV screen had gone quiet—just the looping glow of the home menu, waiting for me to make another choice. On the coffee table sat the half-finished bottle of champagne, next to crumpled sushi cartons and three empty rice dessert wrappers.

I pushed off the blanket and sat up slowly, blinking away the blur of morning. The new year had arrived, but nothing felt new. Just... more real.

In the kitchen, I poured a glass of water and leaned on the counter, letting the coolness hit my throat. I glanced at my phone, sitting beside the fruit bowl.

I already knew what I had to do.

I took a deep breath, scrolled to Adrian's name, and pressed call before I could talk myself out of it. My breath felt too tight.

He picked up after two rings. "Hey," he said, his voice flat, like he already knew. "Happy New Year, Sophie."

"Happy New Year," I replied, my voice hollow.

I didn't let myself hesitate. "Can we talk?" I asked.

"Sure, what's up?"

"Look... to me, this just doesn't make sense anymore. You've got eight weeks left before Paris. Four of those you'll be on a work trip in Asia—not even in New York—and it feels like we have no solid ground to stand on."

Adrian was quiet, but I could hear his breathing on the other end.

I straightened my posture. "You seem overwhelmed, and I get it—you're about to make a huge move across the ocean. But you're not really here with me anymore. Not fully. And I can't settle for something that doesn't feel right. I deserve more than this.

Let's break it off here... and I think we should go no contact for a while, too."

A long pause.

Then, finally, he spoke. "You're probably right," he said softly, his voice lower now—more grounded. "And... thanks. It's impressive how you're taking the lead when I can't. I'm just... really overwhelmed right now."

I closed my eyes. Let the silence settle. "Okay. Enjoy your trip," I said, keeping my tone even.

"Wait—can I call you at some point just to chat? Or on your birthday?" he asked.

"Not on my birthday, please. I need some space. If there's something either of us feels like chatting about, I guess we can do that at some point. But let's go no-contact for at least a month, okay? You'll be in Asia anyway."

"Okay," he says simply. "Take care."

"You too."

Then I hung up.

A flicker of disappointment moved through me

*—That's it? That easy? He's just letting me go like that?*

*Feels almost like he wanted me to do that.*

For a second, I just sat there, staring at the phone in my hand. My chest tightened, like someone had pulled a string around it.

I always knew Adrian would leave. That part was never in question. But now that it was actually happening, the truth was hard to accept—whatever we had was too fragile to last.

Maybe part of me had hoped it wasn't.

Maybe I wanted him to fight harder.

But I also knew better than to hold on to something that didn't work. And this didn't feel like a "breakup for now."

It was a goodbye.

*

During the weeks that followed, I moved through life like a ghost. But I forced myself to focus on my work and health. I went to bed on time, ate clean, tried to stick to the basics—and made it through.

I celebrated my thirty-eighth birthday quietly this year—just a small circle, only the people I truly trusted. Rani and Rhea brought cake, and we spent the afternoon hanging out with Eliyah, crafting paper flowers with Rhea, and keeping things cozy and low-key. It was exactly what I needed.

Though Adrian and I had only agreed to a month of silence, part of me hoped he wouldn't reach out at all—that maybe, somehow, I could gloss over his absence in my life entirely.

But then—four weeks before Adrian's move to Paris—his video message dropped into my life like a stone.

CHALLENGE 15

# Fever Dream

It was a Saturday afternoon, and I was mid-laundry, folding socks, when a video message lit up my phone screen.

It was Adrian—walking through the city like nothing had changed.

His camera jostled as he angled it toward himself, smiling into the lens with that same familiar ease. "Hey, what's up? How are you? Want to meet up—there's a gallery opening around the corner you might like." His tone was casual, light, almost cheerful—a flashback to the early days when his eagerness to see me made every minute feel alive.

But now?

That version of us—of him—felt impossibly far away.

I stared at the message for a while.

*Why?*

Reconnecting didn't make sense. He was leaving for Paris. What was the point of lighting a match in a house that was already burned down?

I took a breath and typed.

> **Me:** Look, I've been doing a lot of thinking over the past few weeks—about my life and where I want it to go. I've realized I've been so focused on us, and right now, I need to put that energy back into myself—my work, my friends, getting things back on track. I'd prefer not to meet up. But if you'd like to say a brief goodbye in a month, shortly before you leave, I'm open to that

A few seconds later, my phone rings.

**Adrian.**

My stomach clenches as I answer.

His voice comes in—startled, sharp: "What's going on? Are we not dating anymore?"

I freeze. My grip tightens around the phone.

Does he really not know?

Or has he somehow convinced himself we're just... on pause?

"Wow. Okay... I can't do this right now," I say, trying to stay calm.

"Sophie. I need to know what's going on," he insists.

I exhale, slow and heavy.

"You should already know what's going on," I say.

"But I don't."

"You really don't?"

"Not really."

A pause.

*Great. Now I need to break up with him* ***again****?*

I can't bear to leave him hanging like this. Now, I feel cornered—trapped between what I want to do and what I can't.

"Okay," I say finally, "but not over the phone. Let's meet briefly tonight. And: this is just to clarify things."

There's a long pause again, and then, I can hear the tension in his voice.

"Yeah. That's fine."

"Let's meet at the East River in an hour," I add, "the bench where we used to sit at 6 p.m.?"

"Okay," he says.

"See you then."

I stare down at the phone in my lap. My heart is racing, and then...

*Oh no.*

I hate the way this feels—not heavy with dread, but lit with excitement, rising fast and uninvited. I don't want to feel that way. But there it is—undeniable.

*Damn it, Sophie.*

*Despite everything, you're really happy to see him.*

I head into the bathroom like I'm on autopilot.

I fix my hair, change my top, and refresh my makeup.

"No matter your feelings for him. This is **not** about getting back together! It's about clarity. Closure," I say out loud, like repeating it will make it more believable.

I pace the room, forcing myself to breathe evenly for a while, to ground myself.

Then, I grab my coat and step outside.

The sky has gone soft and gray, and the air bites at my cheeks.

I keep my hands buried in my pockets, walking fast.

*This is going to be the end, Sophie.*

*You'll keep it short.*

*

When I reach the river, Adrian is already there.

He looks up—half-smile, guarded eyes—and we exchange a brief hug, like we're unsure how to touch each other.

We pass by our usual bench and veer toward a low stone wall. Then, without a word, we climb up and settle in—legs dangling, facing each other.

My body remembers that night in early October, when we sat on the bench we just passed. My legs over his. Same awkward looks at each other. His words tumbling out: *I'm thinking of leaving my girlfriend.*

Now, that feels like ages ago.

I exhale, throat tight. "This is hard for me, Adrian," I say. "I thought we'd clearly broken this off. The last few weeks have been quite emotional for me. We shouldn't keep doing this."

Adrian's face shifts—jaw tense, eyes wet. "So, if I hadn't messaged you..." He swallows. "You were never going to message me again? Just let me leave? No goodbye?"

I don't flinch. "Probably," I nod.

"You leave in a couple of weeks. Dragging it out won't make it hurt less. It'll just lead to even more heartbreak."

He looks away, breathing through his nose.

His hands clench into fists, then open and close again.

"I didn't want this to get messy," he says, quieter now. "I didn't plan for you. Any of this." A gust of wind lifts the edge of his coat, but he doesn't move. Just sits there—spine too straight, like he's trying not to collapse inward.

"I just got out of a relationship. Now I'm moving across the world." He gives a shaky laugh. "And yes, it **was** fucking incredible with you, Sophie. **All** of it. **You** are the most incredible woman I've ever met." He pauses, searching my face.

"But I'm not twenty anymore. I'm in this weird in-between —too old to be reckless, too young to feel settled. I don't know what the hell I'm doing by letting you go. But I do know this—"

He looks me dead-on now. "I **have** to go to Paris alone. I can't just jump from one relationship into another—a really serious one—if I don't have some time for myself first. That part's clear."

"But..." He looks at me. "Don't think **for a second** it means you didn't matter. This—us—it wasn't casual. I meant every minute of it. I'm not going alone because you don't mean anything to me.

You know how I feel about you. You mean **so** much to me. I'm going alone—not because you don't matter, but **despite** how much you do." He pauses. "I didn't want to hurt you, though, Sophie. I'm **really** sorry."

He pauses again, then suddenly buries his head in his hands, making a quiet, sad noise. "Oh no..."

"Hey, what's wrong?" I ask.

"It's just... something crossed my mind," he says, his voice quieter than usual, eyes avoiding mine.

"What?" I ask again, softer now.

He hesitates.

"You don't have to share if you don't want to, but you **can**," I offer.

"I can't believe I'm telling you this right now," Adrian murmurs, clearly struggling with himself.

I gently take his hand.

He looks me square in the eyes. "I already told you that I grew up in a really happy family. One of those rare ones where everyone's there for each other, speaks their mind, and is loved."

I nod.

"But I've never told you about the accident that happened when I was young."

"What accident?"

"Among my three siblings, I was closest to my older brother, Perry. He was creative, artistic, philosophical—he pulled me out of my shell. I've always been emotional, but I sometimes struggle to really access my feelings. I tend to default to logic, stay in my head. But with Perry, I felt free. More capable of being my full, whole self."

He glances at me, something warm flickering behind his eyes. "Actually..." he smiles, "you remind me a lot of him. You have that same energy. And with you, I get that same feeling—like something in me opens. Like you unlock doors I didn't even know were there."

"Anyway," Adrian pauses, takes a breath, then says it all at once—quiet but clear, "When I was seven, and Perry was fifteen, he got into a car accident and died."

"Oh my god... I'm so sorry, Adrian," I whisper, my fingers softly closing around his hand.

"It's okay," he says with a soft smile. "It was a long time ago, and I'm really okay now.

But the months that followed were some of the darkest my family's ever gone through.

They brought us closer in some ways... but ever since, it's like there's been this quiet void—like Perry's spirit left a space no one else could fill.

My parents hold on so tightly to the things that made him special, and sometimes I feel like I've never quite measured up to that... Or been able to fill the space he left behind." His words hang in the air, the weight of them settling between us.

I'm about to respond when Adrian cuts in gently. "Please, don't. I know what you're going to say. I know it's not my job to replace anyone. It's just... something I've carried with me ever since."

"I understand," I say softly. "But where's all of this coming from, all of a sudden?"

He exhales, his gaze drifting past me. "I'm not sure," he murmurs. "I guess my panic about us being in a serious relationship, maybe having a future, having a family... has something to do with it."

He looks at me. "I lost the person who was closest to me, Sophie. And he was in the car that day **because** of me. My parents had asked him to pick up a rugby team shirt

—for me."

I open my mouth to say something.

"And please don't tell me it's not my fault," he adds, cutting in gently. "I know that. But it doesn't change how painful it still feels."

I nod quietly.

His hand grips mine more firmly. "All of that is not an excuse, by the way. I'm really sorry you felt let down by me when you thought you might be pregnant, Sophie."

We look at each other, the silence stretching.

"Let's switch topics," he says after a moment. "It's starting to get to me..."

I nod again.

Adrian gazes off again, eyes distant. "I was supposed to meet a friend tonight—Ben owns a restaurant in Williamsburg," he says, not quite meeting my eyes. "You haven't met him, but this might be the last time I see him before he leaves for Paris. Do you want to come? We could have a drink at the bar."

I pause, the question landing heavier than it should.

Saying yes felt risky. But saying no would end it here—in this strange, quiet place, with all this aching space between us.

*Did our conversation change anything?*

*I **feel** different.*

*But **is** anything truly different?*

I'm not sure. I'm feeling too many things at once to know anything right now.

"Why not," I say finally. "Okay."

We walk to the subway in a silence thick as fog.

His hand hovers once near mine, then drops. Neither of us knows what to do with the closeness anymore.

Half a block from the station, he slows. "Can I touch you?" he asks, barely above a whisper. "Or... hug you?"

My chest tightens. "Of course. But..." I hold his gaze. "Nothing more can happen. I mean it. I just spent four weeks getting over you. You're leaving soon, and I don't want to go through all of that again."

He pulls me in gently, like I might break. His arms wrap around me, and for a moment, everything inside me stills.

No thoughts, no timeline.

Just warmth. Just him.

*

We linger at the restaurant's bar just long enough for a quick drink and a little chitchat with Ben. I barely catch any of it.

Then the door swings open, and an elegantly dressed man steps inside, carrying an armful of colorful bouquets. He moves through the space as he scans the room to catch the eyes of potential customers, then turns as if to leave again.

Adrian glances over his shoulder, then suddenly steps forward. "I'd like to buy all of them," he calls out.

I blink. "What?—Adrian, what are you doing?"

He turns back toward me, eyes lit up. "Giving you what you deserve," he says, grinning.

"You know you can't buy me with flowers," I say, half-smiling despite myself.

"And I'm not trying to," he replies. "I'm just trying to make you smile. Make our last evening as fun as possible."

The man smiles and hands over the bouquets—a wild, unruly mix of lilies, roses, peonies, and sunflowers. Adrian holds them like a ridiculous, oversized prize, then looks around.

"Hey, Ben, do you mind if we put them on the bar counter while no one's sitting here?" he asks, nodding toward the empty stretch beside us.

"Not at all," Ben says from behind the bar.

Adrian gently lays them down, spreading the stems across the glossy wood like some over-the-top centerpiece.

I sit still, taking it in. The heady scent of blooms wraps around me—sweet, floral, almost too much.

My hand rests near the edge of the counter, not quite touching the petals, but close enough to feel their presence.

It's beautiful.

And heartbreaking.

He's making everything harder.

And sweeter.

But I know what I have to do.

*It's time to let go.*

*Or is it?*

*It **is**, Sophie!*

I stand, working hard to keep my voice steady. "I think I'm gonna head out."

Adrian blinks. "Now?"

His chair scrapes on the floor as he shifts toward me, eyes locking on mine with a flicker of panic. "Are you **sure**?" he asks, quieter this time. "Can't we just have one more night?" His voice wavers.

He looks at me like he's hanging on by a thread—and I can see it, the way he's gripping it with everything he's got. Then, his face lights up—a spark, a flash of recklessness in his eyes. "Wait—what if we went to that dance bar?" he says quickly. "The one you love. You always talked about taking me."

Of course, he remembers. And of course it's on my way home.

He smiles. "Let's just go dance, Sophie, just for a little while. **Just us.** To have a proper goodbye. The goodbye we deserve."

His words linger—soft and dangerous.

*Damn it, he's convincing.*

I'd told him about it once—*SPOT ON*. A divey fever dream of a place: neon lights, sweaty bodies, shameless dance moves, and 80s bangers blasting like heartbreak doesn't exist. A place where strangers become backup dancers and tequila fixes almost everything. Not my everyday scene, but on the right night? It's exactly the kind of stupid fun that works like magic.

"Sophie, are you coming?" he asks, leaning in, voice low. He reaches for my hands, wraps them in his.

His eyes hold mine like he's afraid I'll vanish—boyish hope tangled with something heavier—desperation dressed in charm. "Just one drink. **Please.**"

A single rose slips off the bar and lands in my lap, like fate's clumsy attempt at a sign.

*Even the roses want us to go.*

We burst into laughter.

I can already picture it: the disco ball spinning, the music too loud, our limbs finding each other in the dark like it's still safe to pretend.

"What about the flowers?"

"I'll have them delivered to your place tomorrow."

I take a deep breath.

Then nod. Slowly.

Against my better judgment.

Against everything I promised myself on the walk over.

Hoping I won't fall right back into the part of me that never stopped wanting him.

*

"**Hit me baby, one more time**," Britney screams from the speakers.

The second we step inside, it slams into us: the heat, the pulse, the wall of sound. A space where rules don't apply.

It's a blur of dancing bodies under pulsing lights—chaos, glorious and alive—and we fall right into the madness, like it's been waiting for us.

Adrian takes my hand and pulls me onto the dance floor quickly, like he doesn't want to waste a single second.

My pulse starts racing.

Now he's behind me—solid and warm—his breath brushing my neck, his hand around my waist. We move together, instinctively, like our bodies are one.

**One.**

**Just us.**

I sink into his arms and for a moment, I forget about everything.

It's like I'm floating.

Then the unmistakable opening of "(I've Had) The Time of My Life" from the movie *Dirty Dancing* kicks in. Adrian lifts my arm, spins me around, and sings along—loudly, off-key, shameless—grinning like a kid, and I burst out laughing.

Immediately, he grabs my waist. "Ready to fly?" His joy is infectious.

I nod.

Without waiting, he lifts me into the air like we're straight out of the movie.

The crowd cheers.

I yelp, hands on his shoulders, legs kicking in the air.

We're ridiculous. Glorious. Spinning in our own little fever dream.

He sets me down slowly, carefully, arms wrapping tightly around me like he never wants to let go. His lips brush my ear. "You are **the only one**," he sings, voice low, tender. "The only one for me."

***God, this is cheesy.***

It should be too much.

But somehow, he pulls it off.

I feel it hit—straight to the chest.

I look up at him, breath caught somewhere between my ribs. His eyes sparkle with joy—and something more profound.

For a moment, the rest of the world disappears.

We are floating in a parallel universe,

and every warning in my head is muted.

No past. No future. Just this flash of pure, aching joy.

And I let it happen.

Let myself fall.

***Falling.***

Adrian looks into my eyes like he's trying to read me.

*I know he can see it. He can see I've let go.*

He really does. "Can I kiss you?"

I nod instinctively—before I can stop myself.

He leans in slowly, like he's asking again with every inch. When his lips meet mine, it's not urgent. It's soft. Intentional.

Full of all the words we haven't said.

This isn't just a kiss.

It feels like a promise.

Like the revival of everything that feels right.

Adrian takes my hand again and pulls me through the crowd. We slip past sweaty bodies, limbs moving in rhythm, and head up a narrow staircase tucked near the restrooms.

My pulse stumbles, but I don't ask where we're going.

I don't need to.

I'd follow him anywhere in this moment.

He opens the first door he finds, pulls me inside, and shuts it behind us. The noise fades. The space is dim and too big for a bar bathroom.

Adrian's energy shifts instantly—playfulness melting into something heavier. Focused. Intense. Raw.

His hands find my face.

His mouth brushes my cheek, then my lips.

His breath is warm as he leans in close.

Then, softly, right at my ear, he whispers: "Turn around."

I don't.

"Okay..." he tries again. "Here's what you are going to do now. You'll turn around, unzip your pants," he says, his warm breath brushing my ear. "Pull them down and lean against the door."

I hesitate. "No, I won't," I say, my voice unsteady.

"Oh, yes, I think you will."

"No," I insist, shaking my head. "I really don't think I can."

His tone softens, but stays firm. "Then say you don't want it. You know the safe word, Sophie. It's 'No, I mean it.' And I don't hear you saying it. I would never do anything you don't want. And I know you wouldn't let me. Unless you say those exact words, I'll take it to mean you do want this. That you want **me**."

A pause. "Do you?"

"I... I'm not sure... no, I don't think I can do this," I stammer, caught in the tension between fear and desire.

Adrian's gaze doesn't waver. "Yes, you can," he says, his voice steady—calm but certain. "Be honest, Sophie.
Forget the reasoning, the rules.
Isn't this what you truly want?"

I don't say a word.

"Turn around."

Slowly, almost trembling, I turn—my inner conflict waging a brutal war. My mind, my voice of reason, screams at me to stop. To shout: '*No, I mean it.*' But the words refuse to come.

Something deeper—an undeniable craving, my body, my heart—silences my mind's protests.

***I want him. So, so badly.***

I lean forward, breath hitching, and place my hands against the door.

"Now, undo your button. Unzip your trousers," he commands.

I obey, my fingers trembling as I slide them down.

"Take off your underwear," he adds, his voice determined.

I pause and look back at him.

Adrian's eyes hold mine, dark with desire. He steps closer.

His hand moves to my hips as his fingers graze my skin. Without a word, he slides them between my legs.

Warm. Teasing.

**Heat.**

Everywhere.

Washing over my body.

Then, he stops abruptly.

The silence's almost unbearable, broken only by the sound of our breathing.

I feel him move behind me, hear him undressing and opening a condom.

Then he presses himself against me, his fingers replaced by something harder.

He thrusts inside in one swift, powerful motion.

"**Oh my God**," I gasp, my body arching instinctively.

Adrian stops. "Do you want me to continue?"

I don't answer immediately, still wrestling with my own turmoil.

The pause hangs heavy between us.

"**Do you want me to continue?**" he asks again, his voice firm.

"Yes," I finally whisper.

"If you want me to, I need to hear it, and you better be convincing," he says. "Tell me there's nothing you want more right now than this. Than me."

My resistance crumbles. “Please continue,” I murmur, my voice pleading with urgency.

“I want this.

I want you.

Nothing else matters.

Just fuck me.”

“Say it properly,” he urges. “Tell me you’re mine.

Tell me you want to spread your legs in this messy bathroom so I can fuck you the way I want.”

“Yes,” I say. “I’m yours. Just fuck me. **Please.**”

And he does.

His thrusts are relentless, and his hands grip me firmly as I press against the door, unable to hold back the cries escaping from my lips.

The club outside the bathroom ceases to exist.

It’s just us—our bodies, our hunger.

“Sophie”! he gasps as he comes, taking me with him.

We tremble.

**Breathless.**

We sink into each other.

My cheek presses against the door.

I can feel my own breath on my skin.

*Breathe in, breathe out...*

Adrian leans forward and whispers into my ear, “There you go,” he whispers. “Now you know. There’s no point in trying to escape this—escape **us**. You can’t. Not because I’m holding you back. But because you don’t really want to leave.”

His words send a shiver through me—but before I can respond, he turns me toward him, kisses me deeply, then pulls back with a soft smile. “Maybe we can’t just let this end, Sophie,” he says, his voice lighter now. “Maybe we’ll have to find another way to make this work after all.”

“Wow, are you realizing you can’t let me go after all?” I tease.

"Maybe..." he whispers into my ear. "Let me go to Paris first and then we'll see, okay?"

A pause.

His hand slips into mine. "Come on," he says. "Let's get out of here."

I nod.

A minute later, we were in a cab. The door shut with a final sort of thud, sealing us off from the noise, the lights, the heat of the night. Outside, the city blurred past—streaks of color smearing across the windows like brushstrokes.

Neither of us said anything.

The adrenaline had burned off.

I sat back, breathing deep, as it all settled in.

Something had shifted.

I'd crossed a line, and I knew it.

All that time I'd spent second-guessing, trying to stay in control, to act smart—it didn't matter anymore. I wasn't resisting any longer. I couldn't. Whatever this was—we were in it.

*It's only four more weeks, anyway.*

*How bad could it be?*

CHALLENGE 16

# The Right Call

The next morning, I woke up to everything slightly blurred—happiness tinged with question marks, loose ends I was too tired to untangle.

Maybe last night was exactly what was meant to happen. Who knows. With everything Adrian had shared about his past, the lines had gotten messy, and at this point, I couldn't tell anymore what was right or smart—whether sticking to the breakup or diving back in was the better choice. It had all faded into fog, impossible to see through.

It felt like a decision bigger than me. Like something I couldn't reason my way through anymore. As if some invisible force kept pulling me back to him—no matter how hard I tried to let go.

But it was still my choice. And for now, I chose to give in.

So, we made a pact: enjoy the last month together, no drama, all in. And surprisingly, it worked. The moment we stopped resisting, second-guessing, holding back—it was like a switch flipped. Suddenly, we were diving into the other extreme.

And it was incredible.

Texts turned into hours-long conversations.

Days blurred into nights, and nights into soft-lit mornings.

And crazy enough, during those weeks, I was happier than I'd ever been. Floating in an almost artificially worry-free state, as if real life had hit pause.

Adrian came alive beside me—lighter, looser, more unguarded than I'd ever seen him. He smiled more. Laughed louder. And I felt he was just as happy as I was—in my chest, in my bones. A quiet flutter every time he looked at me like I was the only thing that mattered in the world.

We spent so much time together, I struggled to keep up with my own life. My inbox flooded. Laundry piled up. But I met every deadline and made sure my business stayed on track. And late at night, when he wasn't looking—I worked on his goodbye gift. A handmade book. Letters from his closest friends. I poured myself into it, staying up until dawn two nights in a row, hunched over my laptop surrounded by scraps of paper.

At the farewell party, it was handed over to him by his friends. I didn't say a word about it. Not until Gabriel, loud and proud, called me out over the music.

"The gift is from all of us, but Sophie made that whole thing, by the way," he shouted. "Every bit of it. She worked late for days."

Adrian turned immediately.

He crossed the room without hesitation, cupped my face in both hands, and kissed me—long, deep, and in front of everyone.

A few nights later, he surprised me with a belated birthday dinner at the restaurant I'd once mentioned in passing—the one I never let myself go to on ordinary days because it was wildly expensive. He'd reserved an entire section just for us, and when I walked in, I was met with a sea of flowers—just like the ones he'd bought me at his friend's restaurant. Over-the-top. But unforgettable.

For a couple of hours, nothing existed beyond that table. No flights. No boxes. No goodbyes waiting outside the door.

*

Two nights before Adrian was set to leave, I texted him:

**Me:** 6:30 p.m. in front of my building. I have a surprise—no dress code.

When he showed up, he had a half-suspicious, half-curious look on his face. "What kind of surprise?" he asked, hands shoved in his jacket pockets. His smile faltered just a little. We both knew—this was our last adventure.

I pulled two tickets from my back pocket and handed them over. He frowned, then his face lit up. "A movie?" He flipped the stubs in his fingers. "Wait, this is what we're doing on our last afternoon together?"

"Trust me," I said.

He shrugged, a smile tugging at his lips. "Okay. I'm in."

We didn't head straight there. The light was still gold and soft, the kind of afternoon too gentle for goodbyes. So we walked. His hand brushed mine—then held it.

The streets felt unusually vivid, like the city knew we're running out of time. We wandered slowly, taking it all in. Cafés we never entered, doors we never opened, corners we usually rushed past.

I caught Adrian glancing at me when he thought I wasn't looking. Memorizing. And maybe I was doing the same.

An hour later, we arrived. Adrian stopped in his tracks.

"Oh wow. Are we going to the *Cinema Paris*?" His voice is full of wonder. "I've always wanted to, but never made it."

"Well," I said, nudging him, "you're moving to Paris—it's about time."

Inside, the smell of caramel and warm popcorn hits us immediately. Red carpet underfoot, vintage wallpaper on the walls. The kind of place that still holds onto its glamour, even if the seats creak a little. But it's quiet—no crowd, no buzz—just stillness.

A man in a suit steps forward. "Welcome," he says, smiling like he's been expecting us.

"Enjoy your private screening."

Adrian turns to me, eyes wide. "What? You rented the whole place?" His voice drops, almost whispering. "How did you even manage that?"

I shrug my shoulders. "I asked nicely. And I can be convincing, you know..."

He lets out a soft laugh, still stunned. "God, I love how you do these things."

"Popcorn?" I suggest.

He goes right over and orders the biggest tub they have. He doesn't stop at popcorn—and grabs two glasses of Prosecco and a bag of sour fruit gummies, holding them up like he'd struck gold. "I knew you'd want these," he says, shaking the bag with a grin. I laugh, reaching for them immediately.

He was right. I **always** wanted them. Those silly sweets had become a tradition. Since the beginning, on every walk, we'd stop for them. I didn't care how unhealthy they were; when I was a kid, we never had sweets at home, and now that I was an adult, they made me feel like a happy child every time I ate them. Adrian always joked that I looked like a sugar-obsessed five-year-old when I opened the bag.

"You look so fucking cute when you eat these," he says. He shifts the popcorn to one arm and reaches for my hand with the other. "Alright. Where to?"

I guide him through a heavy set of double doors and toward a wide, empty theater glowing with warm sconces and rows of plush velvet seats. "Up there," I whisper, nodding toward a staircase.

We climb to the upper level and slip behind a velvet curtain into a tiny balcony with one oversized, double-seated chair. Intimate. Private. Overlooking everything.

He lets out a breath. "Sophie... this is..." He doesn't even finish the sentence. He just looks at me. "What are we watching?" he asks, his voice suddenly quieter.

"You'll see."

We settle in, setting the snacks between us. His knee presses against mine. He throws an arm over the back of the seat, fingertips brushing my shoulder.

The lights dim. Curtains pull back. And then...

"No way," he breathes. "*The Wizard of Oz*?"

I turn, smiling. "Surprise."

He stares at the screen, then at me. "I can't believe you remembered that."

"Well, it was too cute to forget," I laugh, "that you always wanted to be smart, brave, and have a big, loving heart—like the Scarecrow, the Tin Man, and the Cowardly Lion."

He laughs, burying his face in his hands, groaning. "God, that's embarrassing."

I take his hand, threading my fingers through his. "It's not," I say. "And I know you doubt yourself sometimes. But maybe, now that you're heading to Paris... It's your time to be whoever you want."

He doesn't speak for a long time. The flickering light from the screen dances over his face.

"I can't believe you did all this," he finally whispers. His voice is rough around the edges.

He turns and kisses me—slow and deep, his hand sliding to the back of my neck, thumb brushing my skin like he's memorizing every inch. Like maybe this moment will have to last us both.

And for a little while, it does.

*

Our last night had come.

Adrian wasn't staying over; he'd just come by briefly to say goodbye before he headed to his place and to the airport from there. No airport drama either, we'd agreed—too public, too clinical. We wanted something quieter. Something that still felt like **us**.

When I opened the door, he was already there. Standing in the frame like he didn't want to cross it. Like stepping in would make it real.

Our eyes locked. His were soft, but heavy. Like they already missed me. He didn't say a word, but he didn't have to.

I stepped forward, and he caught me. My face pressed against his chest, the place I'd gone to for comfort so many times. His arms wrapped around me, steady, unshaking.

He smelled warm and comforting, like always, and it suddenly hit me all at once. *This is the last time he's holding me like this. And I'm not ready to let go.*

Silent tears soaked into his shirt as I felt him breathe, deep and slow.

"Hey, my heart," he says gently, trying to break the tension. "What kind of start is this?" His voice is light, vulnerable.

"You seem so... composed," I say.

Adrian pulls back slightly, just enough to look down at me. His voice is steady—almost too steady. "I struggle with the emotional part. It's just how I am."

He strokes my hair. "I usually stay calm, no matter what I feel inside."

Hot tears stream down my face. My mascara runs, and Adrian reaches up, thumbs sweeping gently across my wet cheeks. "Let's wash this away and get you clean."

He leads me to the bathroom and undresses me slowly, with a tenderness that makes my heart ache. "Please don't cry, babe," he murmurs, pressing a soft kiss to my cheek. "You're breaking my heart."

Once I'm bare before him, vulnerable in every sense, Adrian sheds his own clothes and steps into the shower with me. The water pours around us like a curtain, shielding us from everything else. He washes me carefully, like I might fall apart in his hands. The steam curls around us, and I feel both weightless and heavy—barely able to stand as my emotions drag me down.

"Let me get you out of here," Adrian says, soft and steady. "I'll dry you off and we'll move to the living room, okay?"

I can't speak, but I nod weakly. He wraps me in a towel and carries me out, laying me down carefully as if I'm something rare, something breakable. "I'll be right back," he says, brushing a kiss across my forehead. "Just going to rinse off."

He steps back into the bathroom and turns on our favorite playlist. Lou Reed's voice floats in through the door—*Perfect Day*. We've played that song so many times. It captures exactly what this is: beautiful, aching, fleeting:

> "Just a perfect day
> You made me forget myself
> I thought I was someone else
> **Someone good...**"

Ten minutes pass.

Too long.

I sit up, uneasy, the steam still curling out from the bathroom. I walk toward it and find him still under the showerhead, head bowed, tears falling silently.

**My heart.**

"Hey, sweetheart," I say.

"Come out of there."

He doesn't protest. I step in, take his hand, and wrap a towel around him. His body is trembling.

We try to settle on the couch, but it's a struggle to even get there. When we finally make it, we collapse together. "Wow. I didn't expect I'd crumble like that," he murmurs. He pauses and looks at me, eyes glassy. "I think I really need to go now, love."

My heart skips a beat—then starts pounding, wild and erratic. *I can't breathe.*

A sob tears its way up before I can choke it back, and then I'm crying again—messy, unstoppable tears streaming down my face. "Please, don't go just yet." The words rip out of me, more raw and desperate than intended. I remain still, curled into his chest like I'm trying to stay there forever.

I thought I was ready for this. I told myself I could handle it. But now that it's actually happening—now that he's really leaving—old memories suddenly rush in, brutal and uninvited.

I see it all like it's right in front of me—vivid and painful...

... I'm eight again. Tiny. Trembling.

Tears flood my face, just like now. My throat burns.

My beloved father's figure shrinks in the rearview mirror as my mom drives away, silent and cold. The car pulls further and further from the curb. No goodbye. No explanation.

Just me. Abandoned. Alone. In hell with my mom...

"Your entire body is shaking," Adrian says, wrapping me in a warm hug.

"This is much harder than expected," I whisper.

Adrian doesn't know the whole story. I never told him about the moment of separation from my father. About how it shaped me. Haunted me. Now isn't the time—not with all this already between us. But he feels he can't just leave me now. I can see it in his eyes. He knows.

He leans back and lifts my chin. "My heart, look at me."

I try to focus, eyes heavy and stinging.

"We're going to play a little game, okay?" he says gently.

"Okay," I whisper.

"We're pretending I'm not really leaving. I'm just going on vacation. And I'll be back."

"I think I can handle that," I lie.

"Just breathe," he says. "In and out. Look into my eyes." He smiles, warm and heartbreaking. "Nothing bad's going to happen. You stay right here, and I'll be back soon, alright?"

"Alright."

"Do you think you can do this?" he asks, brushing the hair from my face.

"Yes." But it sounds hollow.

He walks towards his bag.

I'm trying to play along. But when I see him lift the bag, something inside me freezes. "Wait, I can't do it," I whisper.

He stops. Looks back. Softens. "I'm just going on vacation," he says again. "And I'll call you right after I leave. Two minutes. I promise."

My chest loosens a little. I nod, barely.

He leans down and kisses me—slow, lingering. "I'll see you soon." And then, he walks out, and the door clicks shut behind him.

The silence that follows is deafening.

A minute later, my phone buzzes.

I grab it like a lifeline.

"Hey, my heart. How are you?" he says.

"Hey. I'm alright. And you?" My voice is shaky.

"Sophie, it's paradise here. The beach is stunning. I'm sipping a cocktail, thinking of you. But why are you still awake? It must be late."

"It is."

"Let me put you to bed, sweetheart. Grab your laptop, make some tea, and get under the covers. I'll stay on the phone while you watch something."

"Okay," I say. I follow his lead, settle into my blankets, my tea in hand. "What should we watch?" I ask.

"*FRIENDS?* We both love it. I don't even need to see it—I've watched every episode a hundred times. I'll just listen."

I press play. Curl up. The room softens around me.

"I'll stay right here," he promises. "Until you fall asleep."

And he does. We chuckle for three hours.

And finally, I drift off.

The next morning, he's already gone. Left New York. I check my phone, and there's a message:

**Adrian:** Thank you, my heart. Thank you for everything. I'll call when I arrive.

A photo follows—Adrian at the airport, eyes red from crying.

**Adrian:** You are strong. I know you can do this. Love, Adrian.

*

The entire morning, I felt hollow. A mere shell of who I used to be.

A couple of hours later, Adrian landed in Paris. He sent photos from his first day—standing in front of the Eiffel Tower, his face lit with excitement for his new life ahead.

***I won't be part of that future.*** My heart ached.

It didn't feel right. It didn't feel like something that was supposed to end. Not after everything we'd shared. Not after those last weeks—or that heartbreaking goodbye.

The images of my father's departure surfacing like that? That had never happened before.

I'd carried my fear of abandonment quietly, folded into the edges of every relationship. But no one had cracked me open like Adrian. He'd gotten in. Deep.

And yet, he didn't know.

He had no idea those memories had come flooding back. No clue just how intense our last night had been for me. He didn't know how much like **home** he felt to me—for those images to resurface like that.

A home I never had, always longed for, and lost with my father.

*

In those first few days, Adrian and I spoke a few times. I clung to the memory of our last night and realized it had shifted something—the goodbye had shown how much we meant to each other. And part of me hoped that, once my absence set in, he'd feel it too—and know. Know that it wasn't meant to end like this, the way I did.

But that moment never came.

Slowly, the shift began. His messages got shorter. The gaps between replies stretched. And even before he said anything, I knew. He was settling in and making room for his new life. Maybe even for someone new.

That had always been him, hadn't it? Able to compartmentalize. To move through intimacy without letting it consume him. To separate touch from love, distraction from meaning. So, it was likely he'd be dating soon, if only to feel happy without me for a while.

Even thinking of it made me feel sick.

I wasn't wired like that. No way I could be dating again soon—and I realized: I didn't want to. I didn't want someone new or a cleaner version of this. I wanted **us**—flawed, untimely, and real. I wanted the complicated truth, not the easier exit. I wanted to see if we could actually make it work.

So finally, after a week—lunch time in New York and evening in Paris—I picked up the phone, my fingers trembling and shot him a message:

**Me:** Can we talk?

My phone buzzed immediately, and before I could even process it, his face filled my screen—Parisian buildings glowing behind him in the night.

"Hey, what's up?" he said casually, as if nothing had changed. "Just stepped out of a restaurant. On my way home now. If you want, we can talk."

I sank onto my couch, pillow on my lap. "Is it ok if we jump right into it, spare the small talk?" I asked.

"Sure, what's on your mind?" he said.

I hesitated, my fingers nervously picking at the edges of my pillow. "This isn't easy for me, but I have to do it." My throat felt tight, my chest heavy.

"Okay," he said.

Silence stretched between us, thick and unbearable.

I swallowed hard.

"Just say it," he urged, his voice softer now.

"No matter what it is, I'll be fine. I promise."

"Alright, look," I said, my voice steady but my pulse hammering.

"I know everything is overwhelming for you right now—moving to Paris, flipping your whole life upside down, ending things with your girlfriend, and then... us." I took a breath.

"And I've been okay with things being uncertain this whole time because that's what I wanted then. I **wanted** to enjoy whatever we had as long as it lasted, without stressing too much over what it meant.

But now, if I'm being true to myself, things have changed, and I can't just keep quiet about it. Or I don't want to."

I paused.

"This separation has been really fucking hard for me, Adrian. I realized how much I care about us. And it honestly feels too soon to just throw it all away."

Silence.

"I guess, I'm wondering what it would be like if we tried to figure this out together. You said yourself that this might be too great to just let it end after all."

I held my breath, waiting.

"I never said that," he replied.

"Yes, you did. At *SPOT ON*. In the bathroom."

"Look, you know how I feel about you," Adrian reassured me, his voice warm, but distant. "But nothing's really changed for me. I still need time for myself. I've never truly been single—not since I was a teenager. And I need to figure out who I am on my own before I can commit to anyone... especially if it's as serious as it got with us.

With you, there is no middle ground. I can feel it in my bones. This isn't random dating. This is about the long-term future, a family—and that's a lot. Too much for now. It's just the wrong time for me."

I felt the punch in my gut before I could even process his words.

He paused, then added, "I might feel differently in a few weeks. But I need space—to settle in, process, figure out what I actually want. Can't we just... give it time?"

I paused. Long enough to feel the sting and push through it. *No, Sophie. No. Don't do that to yourself.*

I exhaled, steady now. "I can't do that," I said, my voice even. "I understand what you're saying. But I can't put my life on hold, waiting for you to make a decision. If we cut ties now, I'll move on."

He nodded, absorbing my words, but there was no change in his expression. No panic. No regret. Just quiet understanding.

"Can we at least stay in touch? I still want us to," he said. "Though, I need to be honest—it probably wouldn't be like before. I need to focus on my life here."

He probably wasn't fully conscious of it, but I was afraid I knew exactly what it meant. He wanted freedom—room to explore whatever, or whoever, came next. And at the same time, he wasn't ready to fully let go of me. He wanted to keep me close enough to soften the loss. A gentle exit. A smooth transition.

A cold, sudden clarity washed over me. I had spent too much time and energy learning to value myself to ignore what was happening now. Sacrificing my own needs, waiting in some undefined limbo, hoping he'd come around—it wouldn't lead anywhere. It would only keep me stuck.

I wasn't going to be the woman pining for someone who had already walked away.

So I made the choice for both of us. "I'm sorry, Adrian," I said, my voice quiet but firm. "I can't do that."

His expression flickered—just for a second. "Are you sure?" His voice was softer now.

"Yes," I exhaled. "I'm sure. Let's go no contact for at least six weeks. After that... we'll see if there's anything left to say."

A beat of silence. "Okay. If that's what you need, I have to accept it." He hesitated. "Just... know you can always call me."

I closed my eyes for a moment, absorbing the weight of it. I nodded. "Okay, take care." Then, without another word, I ended the call.

The silence that followed was suffocating. My stomach clenched, my fingers still curled around the phone like I could somehow take it all back. But I didn't. I just sat there, the finality settling in like a hole in my chest.

It was the right call. But it hurt like hell.

CHALLENGE 17

# Starting Over

The following week was one of the toughest I had ever faced in my life.

I made a crucial decision from the start: I wouldn't cling to hope. *'If he could walk away like this, he doesn't deserve me,'* I told myself, again and again.

But no matter how hard I tried, every day felt like an endless stretch of gray. I could barely muster the energy to get out of bed, with each day blending into the next, empty and dark.

Walking outside felt like a burden.

I remembered how Adrian and I used to transform strolls into adventures, but now, the thought of venturing out alone only deepened the ache of his absence. Cooking had become a hollow ritual; meals tasted bland and lifeless without him preparing them lovingly in the kitchen. Even when I tried to distract myself with a movie, the laughter we had shared echoed in my mind, amplifying the silence surrounding me.

But the ache wasn't just about Adrian. I began to feel alone in my life as a single woman in my late 30s.

I'd spent the last decade building my career, mostly uninterested in dating, laser-focused on my goals. And now, I had no core group of girlfriends to share this moment with. No late-night calls, no commiserating over heartbreaks. Just me—still the solo fighter.

Sure, I could always reach out to Rani and Eliyah. They loved me, and in an emergency, they'd drop everything. But Rani had Rhea to think about and wasn't interested in dating these days, while Eliyah had his rotating list of partners. So, understandably, neither of my friends had the bandwidth for ongoing relationship drama. Everyone had their own lives, and I wouldn't be a burden.

Perhaps this was just a natural part of growing older. In my twenties, friendships felt like lifelines. Back then, no one had life figured out, so we weathered the chaos together—crying on each other's couches, eating ice cream straight from the tub, distracting ourselves until the worst passed.

But by our thirties, things shift. Careers take off. Families form. We settle into long-term relationships. And suddenly, there's this quiet expectation that by now you should have someone—a partner, a home, a plan. If life throws you emotional turbulence, surely you have someone to catch you.

I didn't.

And ironically, my lamp's functional prototype was under reconstruction—just when I could've used a mood lift.

I wasn't going to drown in self-pity, though. I never had, and I wasn't about to start now. What I needed was a healthy distraction—something to fill the days, something I could control.

So, I defaulted to my oldest coping mechanism: work.

I buried myself in the design phase, sketching out new ideas for the lamp's shape, line after line. It didn't fill me with joy like usual, but it was progress. And that was all that mattered for now.

But by the second week, even that felt empty.

I pushed through work during the day, telling myself, *Sophie, you're not going to let things slide just because you're heartbroken.*

But by evening, I was a full cliché—lying on my bed, binging TV shows, drinking Prosecco, gummy worms, and chocolate wrappers scattered everywhere, and tears quietly running down my face.

And then something unexpected happened.

One night, I landed on an episode of *Indian Matchmaking*. A woman—thirty-eight, successful, self-assured—spoke about her decision to freeze her eggs, expanding her options instead of rushing into a relationship out of panic.

I blinked at the screen.

*Wait. That's an option—I thought that only makes sense until the age of thirty-five?*

With chocolate in one hand and my phone in the other, I started searching, and somehow—whether by fate or sheer algorithmic coincidence—I landed an appointment at one of the top fertility clinics in New York for the very next morning.

It felt like a sign.

*

The next day, I made my way to the clinic, and it felt right—as if I were taking back my power.

On the subway, station after station blurred past as I sat motionless, staring out the window.

It was strange.

Before Adrian, motherhood had been abstract—something theoretical, distant, not quite real. Whenever the topic came up, it was always because someone else had brought it into the conversation. Like so many women my age, I'd fielded endless, unsolicited questions: "Why don't you have kids yet?"

"Haven't you thought about starting a family?"

Even strangers felt entitled to weigh in—as if my body and timeline were a public domain, and I somehow owed society an explanation for not reproducing. It always baffled me. More than once, I'd wanted to snap: "Wake up—it's 2024. Women don't exist just to have babies."

But this? This was different.

It wasn't about pressure. Motherhood wasn't just an external expectation anymore. It had become something I **wanted**. And all because of Adrian.

I thought back to that first conversation about our families —the way his eyes lit up when he talked about his childhood and what it had stirred in me then. For the first time, I'd let myself imagine it. A family. A future I'd never allowed myself to picture before, one that shifted everything I thought I wanted. And even though Adrian was gone, that desire wasn't.

*Thanks for that, Adrian,* I thought bitterly. *I was fine before you.*

As I stepped into the waiting room of the fertility clinic, my stomach tightened. The sterile smell, the quiet hum of the receptionist typing—it all felt surreal. My mind fought against the thought of having children with someone else one day. The idea of a future without Adrian in it felt unnatural, like trying to rewrite a story I wasn't ready to finish.

A nurse called my name, and soon I was seated in Dr. Kane's office. She looked around my age, with a warm energy that immediately put me at ease. "You did the right thing coming in," she said, glancing over my intake form, eyes pausing on the note I'd written about why I was here. "A lot of women wait until their late forties—by then, it can get complicated. You're still at a great age."

"I am?"

"Yes. If you're considering social egg freezing, we typically recommend starting before the age of thirty-five. But really, it's about probabilities. Some women have strong fertility well into their forties; others face challenges at twenty-five. It's unpredictable."

She looked up and smiled. "How about we start with some tests?"

I nodded. "Sure."

A few minutes later, I was in the exam chair. Dr. Kane's expression brightened as she moved the ultrasound wand. "From what I'm seeing, you have a lot of viable eggs. That's excellent."

"Oh, really?"

She nodded. "I'd like to run some blood tests to get a clearer picture of your options. Sound good?" Before I could answer, she was already leading me to a nurse for the blood draw. "Come back tomorrow morning for the results," she said. "We're quick."

*

"Everything looks great," Dr. Kane said, scanning the data on her screen the next day. "Your hormone levels and lab values are all in range, and the count of your remaining eggs is off the charts. You're in the highest range possible for women your age."

A beat of silence stretched between us before she tilted her head. "Are you thinking of having a child with a partner?"

I almost laughed. *A partner?*

Let's be real—I had neither a partner nor a plan. Kids weren't even on the horizon. For a moment, I considered telling her the truth: *No, Dr. Kane, this entire appointment was brought to you by Prosecco, chocolate, and a late-night binge of Indian Matchmaking. I have no idea why I'm here.*

But I didn't.

Instead, I straightened, inhaling slowly. "I wasn't planning anything specific yet," I admitted. "My relationship just ended, and honestly, I don't know what the future holds. I just want to keep my options open. So, I guess I'm considering social freezing."

She nodded, decisive. "It's better to take action now than regret it later. With your numbers, one cycle might be all you need. I recommend starting soon to get the best results."

She slid a stack of brochures across the desk. "And something else to consider—you don't need a partner to have a child. More women are opting to do it on their own, and a growing support network is available for single mothers. If that's something you ever want to explore, I can connect you with resources."

I took the brochures but didn't bother looking at them. "Thanks," I said, though I already knew it wasn't for me. I had never envisioned myself as just a mother. If I were to start a family, I would want it to be with a partner by my side.

As I stepped out of her office, the air felt sharper and clearer. The test results brought relief, but it was more than that.

For the first time in weeks, I felt a sense of direction.

I was reclaiming my life without Adrian.

This was mine to shape.

My future. My call.

*

By week six, I was functioning—not healed, but moving again.

I was in the studio, sketching, when my phone buzzed.

**Adrian.** An audio message.

I didn't need to check the date. I knew it was April 10th—the first day after our six-week no-contact phase.

My pulse jumped.

I hesitated for a second, then pressed play.

"Hi, Sophie." His voice was soft, weighted with emotions—sadness, hesitation, maybe longing. "I just wanted to check in. Maybe we can talk?"

A knot twisted in my chest.

I sat frozen, phone in hand, the sound of his voice still hanging in the air.

It had taken me weeks to reclaim a sense of calm and stitch myself back into a solid person. Talking now felt like pressing my fingers on a bruise that wasn't done healing.

I closed my eyes. Inhaled. Exhaled.

Then typed my reply.

**Me:** Yes, we can. Let's talk in two weeks, though. I have a lot on my plate at the moment

His response came quickly.

**Adrian:** Okay

I swallowed hard.

I knew Adrian—when he wanted something, patience was never his strong suit. Maybe he **should** wait. Maybe he deserved to.

But more than anything, I needed to protect what little ground I had reclaimed—no guilt, no regret. Just pride in making myself the priority again.

*

Two more weeks have passed.

I sit curled on the couch, hands wrapped tightly around a cup of tea like it might anchor me. My laptop waits in front of me, its screen glowing.

In a couple of minutes, I see Adrian again.

**Now.**

His name flashes. My pulse spikes.

I answer.

His face fills the screen—soft Parisian afternoon light behind him, rooftops glowing gold.

"Wow," I say, blinking. "Is that your office?"

He nods, adjusting slightly in his chair. "Yeah. I blocked off this hour so we wouldn't get interrupted. People here actually believe in work-life balance."

"How's life there?" I ask.

He smiles, eyes briefly lighting up. "It's... amazing. The impact I can achieve with my work here is insane. The team's inspiring. Food's great. But..." His voice falters.

A long pause stretches between us.

I can feel my chest rising and falling faster and faster.

"I've been thinking about you a lot, Sophie." He looks away for a beat. "I'm surrounded by all this beauty, doing what I love—but it just... feels like less without you. Some of my new friends threw me a birthday party here two weeks ago, and I've never felt less like celebrating. It felt wrong without you by my side."

He looks back at me. "Sophie, I keep wondering if I made a mistake. If we should've given it a real shot. Maybe we deserve that."

My heart skips, stalls.

I slowly set my tea down—the porcelain clinks faintly against the table. "Where was all of that two months ago?" I ask. "Why did you let us end so easily? I honestly struggle to understand why we didn't just give it at least a try."

He exhales. "I was overwhelmed, fresh out of a long-term relationship. I couldn't tell if what I felt was real or if I was just projecting. And it scared me—how good it was with you. It felt too good to be true. That kind of happiness… it felt unreal, unsustainable.

But now I realize I just can't forget you…"

He pauses, voice thickening. "… I've never felt joy like that, Sophie. Not with anyone. Not with my girlfriend, not with family. No one." A tear slides down his cheek. He wipes it away quickly.

*He's crying?*

I swallow hard. "It's nice to hear that what we had meant this much to you. But I'm afraid I'm in a different place now. I told you I wouldn't be waiting around—and I didn't. I moved on."

"You feel so distant, Sophie." His gaze drops.

"Do you still have feelings for me?"

I take a moment.

"Yes. I still have feelings for you," I finally say.

"But I need to protect myself. The last two months have been tough for me, too, you know."

He meets my gaze, unwavering. "I'm so sorry to hear that, Sophie. Please, just visit me in Paris for a week. I'll make it up to you."

"To do what?"

"To enjoy some time together. Get a sense of how it feels when we're in Paris together. See where it goes."

"No," I say quickly. "I'm not just coming for a week like that."

"Are you sure?"

"Look, you weren't ready to commit before, and from what I hear, that hasn't really changed, has it?" I ask.

"I just want to spend time with you. Why do we need a label?" Adrian replies.

"If I were ever to consider giving us another chance at this point, it would have to be for a committed relationship. Nothing less," I say, my voice firm.

"It feels premature. You build the relationship first—then you name it," he states.

I take a breath. "I probably would've jumped at a one-week visit eight weeks ago, but time didn't freeze while you were gone, Adrian. Things have changed—**I** have changed.

The stakes are higher now, and I can't just go to Paris for a few days, have an incredible time, and come back feeling heartbroken again. I'm no longer interested in having just another 'most amazing week of my life.' We've done that."

He stays silent.

"And we **have** built this relationship," I continue. "For six months—or five, if we leave out the weeks of no contact. It may have been intense and imperfect, but it was real."

"You're probably right," Adrian says softly.

I shake my head slowly. "I don't even know if I'd be open to giving this another shot," I say, my voice calm but firm. "But what I do know is this—I'm not going to risk falling in love all over again, or even consider moving to Paris, if you're not sure you're ready for a real relationship. If commitment is still a question mark for you, then we are exactly where we were two months ago."

"Okay. That's fair. And this isn't me making a final offer, Sophie. This was just me saying how I feel for now. Now that I know where you stand, I'll make you a real one, I promise. Just let me think about it for a bit.

Can I call you back tomorrow?"

I hesitate.

“So you can make me an offer—just like that?” I asked, slightly skeptical.

“Yes. Just give me one day.”

“Okay,” I nod. “I guess one day is fine. But this is your last shot.”

*

Every minute of the next twenty-four hours feels like a tug-of-war—between keeping my feet on the ground and getting swept away by what my heart wants.

The sudden shift, the whiplash of it all, is hard to process.

*What if he really was offering me a commitment?*

*Would I even consider it?*

***Finally.***

He calls.

I look at him. Trying to read his expression.

“I’m not sure,” he finally says, voice low.

“I’m so sorry, Sophie. I want to give you what you want. And I really don’t want to lose you. But I just... can’t commit. Not right now. I need more time.”

He hesitates, then adds, “I think it’d be great if you came to Paris. We could spend some time together, see how it feels. I thought about coming to New York, but... I guess the point is to see what it’s like to be together here, in Paris. So it wouldn’t make much sense.”

A pause. “I’m sorry. I know it’s not what you were hoping for. But right now... this is all I can offer.”

*Is he for real?*

*Wow, I’m feeling so stupid for giving him another chance right now.*

“Look, Adrian,” I say, my voice even, “If you can’t make that step at the moment, that’s your choice. But I want to be with someone who’s excited to be with me, not someone who needs months to make a decision. For me, that’s it. I’m sorry too, but I can’t keep doing this to myself.”

I can see the panic in his eyes. "Just give me a bit more time. A week, maybe," he pleads.

My heart hurts seeing him like that.

*Don't let him get to you again, Sophie.*

I channel all the energy I've got left into making it through the end of this call. Going through with this. Somehow. "I won't debate this again," I say. "I told you: Right now, I'm all or nothing. That's not going to change. If you can't meet me there, that's okay, but we have to end this now. And I need to cut contact for good. Otherwise, it'll just keep hurting."

A beat. "Anything you want to say before I hang up?"

"I don't know," he says, looking lost.

"Okay... then I'll go first."

I take a deep breath, steadying myself.

I want my words to come from warmth, not anger.

*This feels unreal.*

"So... This is so weird," I shake my head.

He just looks at me, waiting.

My entire body goes numb. "Okay," I fiddle with my hands, then finally look up. "Thank you for the last months, Adrian. I mean it. I want you to know that as long as it lasted, I was honestly the happiest I've ever been in a relationship by far." My throat tightens.

"I'm truly grateful we met, and I don't regret anything. I had a really, really beautiful time. And I wish you the best in Paris."

I look at him one last time.

Tears spill down his face. "I can't say anything," he whispers, barely holding himself together.

"Are you sure?" I ask, gently.

"Yes," he chokes out. "I can't."

"Then I have to hang up."

"No, **please**—give me a little more time," he pleads, his voice cracking. "I know you need clarity. And I respect that. I just need a little more space to think. Sophie, let's not end it like that."

My chest clenches. "Adrian," I say, my voice rising. "Do you have any idea how hard it is for me to do this right now, do the right thing—again? And you're making it **so** much harder. Can't you see I can't do this anymore?"

My whole body starts to tremble—subtle at first, then full-on shaking.

My voice breaks. "I've held it together for weeks; I'm out of energy."

All the strength I'd clung to—the careful decisions, the mental gymnastics to stay grounded, the quiet discipline of keeping my heart open while protecting it—now fractures in an instant.

It all crumbles.

I get off the couch, walk straight to the bathroom, and shut the door. The lock clicks, and that tiny sound feels like a dam breaking.

I slide to the floor, my back against cold tile, knees pulled in. And then

**—I break.**

The sobs come hard and fast, ripping through me, raw and unstoppable. My chest tightens, my throat burns, and still, I can't stop. My whole body shakes like it's trying to empty itself of everything I've been holding in.

In the distance, I hear his voice shout, "Fuuuck!" It feels far away, like it belongs to someone else's life.

Everything in me is quiet now. Not calm—just emptied.

Maybe fifteen minutes pass. Maybe more.

Eventually, I peel myself off the floor, limbs heavy, like I'm moving through wet sand.

I make my way back to the living room, each step a small act of defiance against the weight in my chest.

Adrian is still there, frozen on the screen. His face is tight with concern. "I'm so sorry," he says, barely above a whisper. "I didn't... I didn't understand how hard this has been for you."

I shake my head slowly, unable to summon words big enough

for the ache. “I can’t talk right now,” I whisper. “I need to hang up.”

“Can I send you one last message tomorrow?” he asks. “Just one. **Please.** Let me say what I need to say. After that, you can block me forever.”

“I don’t know yet. I need to hang up now, sorry,” I say, and close the laptop.

I drag myself to bed, numb and spent.

I turn off my phone too and fall asleep almost immediately.

When I wake the next morning, the first thing I see—still in bed—is his message.

> **Adrian:** I don’t want to lose you. I know you’re my person, Sophie—no doubt about that. I’m in hell right now, and I’d do anything to keep you in my life. For you, I’ll get over my fear and commit to a relationship

CHALLENGE 18

# In or Out?

> **Adrian:** Please just listen to my voice message. If you still want to cut ties for good, I'll respect that. I'll leave you alone and won't ask you for another chance ever again. I promise

My heart flutters—tight and uncertain.

I get up, grab my coat, and step out onto the balcony. The March sun catches me off guard—brighter than expected, warm on my face.

My hands tremble as I pull out my phone.

I take a breath.

Then I hit play.

> "Sophie, my heart..."
>
> "This must be the eighth time I'm trying to record this.
>
> Thank you for giving me this shot. I know I've already had many—and I know how much I hurt you. I hate that I did. You've always seemed so strong, so graceful, and I honestly didn't realize just how hard these last weeks were for you until you broke down during our call. That shattered me. That was never what I wanted. I'm so sorry, Sophie. For all of it."

He pauses.

> I know I want you. I do. More than anything. You are the most incredible person I've ever met.

I've never been this happy in my life, and I'd be crazy to let you go. I can see it all—a future, a family—with you. I want that. I want us. I want to be in a committed relationship with you. To build a beautiful life together.

And I wanted to say all of that yesterday—but I froze. I was scared. Scared I'd make a decision I wasn't ready for and end up hurting you more. But then I realized: I don't want my fears to dictate my decisions. And once I pushed past them, everything became clear.

I told you that part of what scared me was how fast and intense everything happened between us—at such an emotional and transitional time in my life. And I'm starting to understand that, yes, I actually struggle with trusting myself, and with making decisions that affect others. And honestly, I think it started with Perry. After he died, I became the oldest sibling. I had to hold it all together, take care of everyone else. It was too much. And maybe some part of me still fears getting it wrong—making a decision that hurts someone I love.

That's not an excuse. But I hope it helps you understand.

And please—don't let that put you off. I know I sound like a mess. But I'm not. Not when it counts. Once I'm in, I'm the most loyal person in the world. I show up. I won't question us all over and over again. I'll do whatever it takes to make you happy. What trips me up isn't the idea of being in a committed relationship. It's the moment before the leap—because I care too much, not too little. Because hurting someone like you... It would wreck me.

You mean everything to me, Sophie.

And I need you to know this: I'm not just falling in

love with you anymore. I'm **in love** with you. Fully, deeply, irreversibly. Not just infatuated—though, I'm crazy about you, kind of obsessed even. But it's more than that. This is a kind of love I have never felt before. The kind that changes everything.

And I think it can last because we are so fucking compatible in so many ways. The way we walk through life, enjoy the little things, and support each other to follow our dreams.

You are an exceptionally strong woman, but you've also been struggling with a lot in your past. I want you to know it's not too much for me. You're not too much. I can hold you, Sophie. I know I can.

Please don't let this go just yet. Don't walk away from something that could be extraordinary just because we stumbled on the way in. I know I should have said all of this sooner—but I needed time to get here, honestly. And I'm here now.

Everyone has a past. I know you have yours. And I've been fighting mine. But I've done the work. I've arrived.

And I hope I'm not too late."

A picture followed: Their family house in Italy is perched on a cliff overlooking the shimmering blue ocean. The blooming gardens overflow with fragrant flowers and lush greenery like a scene straight out of a romantic movie.

Then more text messages:

**Adrian:** By the way, this is our family house in Italy. Every year, we go there to celebrate and gather with the whole family—thirty to fifty people.

**Adrian:** I hope this doesn't sound too cheesy—or like I'm getting ahead of myself—but for once I'm too emotional to hold back right now. I had a dream last night. And it felt **so** real. We were in the garden, playing with our kids, and we were just so fucking happy.

**Adrian:** I talked to my family yesterday, and the way we spoke about you... It already felt like you were part of us.

**Adrian:** They'd welcome you with open arms, Sophie.

I've stopped breathing.

Warm tears roll down my cheeks.

My heart burns.

I stare into the blue sky, watching the clouds pass by slowly.

*I want that.* ***All of that.***

*Don't be too quick, though, Sophie.*

I start typing.

**Me:** Hi Adrian. Thanks for your message.

**Me:** I'm not going to respond to it in full right now—I can't. I'll get back to you as soon as I can, okay?

**Me:** Please don't read anything into the pause, though. I just really need a bit of rest and clarity first. It's been a lot. A rollercoaster, honestly

**Me:** But there's one thing I do need to say right away: Yesterday, I was completely drained—and still, you kept pleading and pushing my boundaries. That really hurt. The entire situation felt toxic to me at that moment. I felt trapped, like you were holding on so tightly that you couldn't see how much I was struggling. It felt like it had become all about your needs, with very little space for mine

**Adrian:** I totally get that. And I'm really sorry, Sophie

**Adrian:** That wasn't okay, and I can see that clearly now. It's not how I ever want to make you feel. You know me—I'm usually an extremely empathic person. Yesterday was just... something else. It felt like life-or-death in the moment, and I completely shut down

**Adrian:** That doesn't excuse it, I know. But I just want you to understand it wasn't the real me. It was fear and panic taking over. That won't be who I am moving forward. I never want to be someone who causes you harm like that.

**Me:** Okay, I'll get back to you :)

**Adrian:** Heart emoji

*

"If you ask me, you should cut him some slack. He's only twenty-nine—in the prime of his life. He's got a lot coming at him, and honestly? He's truly done the work. What he's doing, especially for a guy his age, takes guts," Eliyah's voice cut through the low hum of conversation around us at the BABES bar.

Rani nodded, picking at a bowl of wasabi peas. "And look at the growth he's gone through in such a short time. He's not just talking about feelings anymore—he's talking real commitment. A future. Maybe even a family."

Eliyah leaned in slightly, elbows on the golden bar top. "If I were in his shoes, I might have freaked out, too. And Sophie—some people only realize what they're ready for when they're on the brink of losing it. If you walk away now, you might always wonder—what if?"

Rani turned to me, her gaze steady. "And come on, he's apparently been acting out of his own history. You, of all people, know what that feels like. Didn't people walk away from you for how you reacted to fear when you were younger?"

I nod slowly, the weight of her words sinking in. She's not wrong.

"You know, I've always been a fan of Adrian. I love him. Everyone at SPARKS does. But we don't know him as well as you do. And I don't want to influence you too much," Rani added.

"Of course. I know that," I say, running my finger along the condensation ring from my glass.

The bartender walks past in a princess costume. They give me a wink, and I try to smile, but it doesn't quite land.

I stare into my drink, watching the last ice cube melt. "What about the other doubts? Like the ones I had because of his friend? Before it all came crashing down?"

"What do you mean? All of his friends praised him endlessly," Rani wondered.

Eliyah tilts his head. "You mean those comments from Mike? The guy who was three drinks in and barely made sense?"

I shrug. "Yeah. I guess I did say that."

Rani reaches across the table, resting a hand lightly over mine for a second. Her bracelets clink against the wood. "Then don't let one sloppy night dictate something this big. But it's your choice, Sophie. The only voice you should be listening to is yours."

I swirl the drink, watching the liquid spiral, as I try to gather my thoughts into something coherent. "The truth is, this whole situation wrecked me emotionally. I've been stuck in this high-stakes loop, trying to make the right choices, trying to protect myself while staying open—and now, at this point, I think my system just... gave up."

I pause, throat tightening.

"The deeper I search for clarity, the more lost I feel. It's like my intuition's gone quiet. It feels like my body literally shut down. My heart's pulling one way, my gut warns caution, though I'm not sure why—and I'm just frozen in between. Exhausted."

Eliyah exhales, long and low. "That's not a sign to push yourself harder, you know."

"I know," I whisper.

The princess sets down a fresh napkin without being asked. I give them another faint smile.

"So **how do I make the right choice?**" I murmur. "What do you do when neither side feels entirely safe, and all you want is to stop feeling like you might be breaking your own heart no matter what you pick?"

No one answers right away.

The music shifts.

Someone across the bar clinks a glass too hard.

Rani finally says, "Maybe it's not about the **right** choice. Who even knows what that is, honestly? Maybe it's just about the **next honest one**. You always talk about not wanting regrets. About wanting to listen to your own voice and be fully yourself. Maybe ask yourself: would you regret it more not giving this a shot, or giving it a shot?"

"That's hard to know in advance, isn't it?" I say, the corner of my mouth twitching. "I don't exactly know what our relationship would even look like. That's kind of the whole point."

Rani studies me for a moment, then says, "I know someone who might help—an incredible mind-body coach—her name's Lina. I can reach out to her for you. If your body's shutting down, if your intuition's gone quiet... maybe it's time to get some help tuning back in."

I pause, then shrug. "Sure. Why not?"

Not because I was convinced it would help, but because I was out of options. And I couldn't keep circling the same questions anymore.

*

*Next day*

It was just past ten when I stood in front of Lina's door, jaw tight, fingers cold despite the sun. My stomach felt like a fist. I didn't quite know what I was doing here—only that I couldn't keep spiraling.

The door opened before I knocked. Lina—mid-fifties, soft red curls, warm eyes—offered a calm nod that made something in my chest loosen, just slightly. She stepped aside, and I followed her in.

Her space was all white, wood, and air. Quiet. Like it could hold everything I couldn't anymore. She sat across from me, one leg tucked under the other, her voice low. "Why don't you tell me what brought you here?"

I hesitated. "It's... messy," I said, staring down at my hands. Then I told her about the crash with Adrian, the choices that felt impossible, the exhaustion I couldn't shake.

She listened in silence, then stood. "Let's try something. Just an experiment. Are you up for it?"

I nodded, already rising to my feet.

"As Rani probably mentioned—I work through the body," she said. "When the mind gets loud, the body's often clearer. So don't overthink it. Just follow my lead and allow yourself to express whatever comes to mind. You can stop anytime." Lina gestured toward the center of the room, and I moved there, the floor cool beneath my feet. She dimmed the light. The air was cool against my skin."Close your eyes," she said softly. "Where do you feel this stuck choice?"

I breathe in. "My chest and my throat. Both are tight."

She guides me through small, fluid movements—shoulders, ribs, and neck. It feels awkward at first, but then something gives. The tightness softens, like a knot slowly unraveling.

"Now think of Adrian," she says.

"Do you want closeness?" she asks. "Or distance?"

My eyes are still closed. "Closeness. I want to feel him near," I whisper.

She steps closer, fingers resting gently on my shoulders. "Stay with that. Forget him for a second. Forget everyone. Just tune into that longing. Does it feel like a reaction or a truth—something your body knows?"

Tears well up before I can answer. I press my palm to my chest. "It feels... right," I say. "And real. Like I'm finally being honest."

Lina gives a soft nod. "Want to hear my take?"

I open my eyes and nod.

"I can't speak to who Adrian is. But from what you've told me —and I'm trusting my gut here—it doesn't sound fake. It sounds like someone who is still figuring out how to love while being afraid to mess it up. That's not rare."

She pauses.

"I'm not saying stay or go. That's your call. And you know Rani trusts me, but I'm not a therapist, doctor, or anything official. I've just been working with people's nervous systems and bodies for over thirty years. And from experience, I can only urge you: make sure your decision doesn't come from fear. Soften first. Because fear wears a hundred faces—logic, boundaries, even strength."

My throat clenches.

"And if you soften, breathe, and it still feels wrong—that's clarity. But if the tightness stems from old defense patterns, mistrust, trauma, or a need to stay in control... be cautious. That's not clarity. That's armor. If that's what's driving you, maybe it's time to finally let it go and start building trust. Only then can you create the life you want—instead of running from it."

I sink to the floor, knees giving out.

The tears hit fast, raw, and silent.

I stay there for a long moment, letting everything spill—grief, confusion, some unnamed weight I've carried for years.

I've spent most of my life in protection mode—scanning for red flags, pulling away before anyone could hurt me. I was good at it. Too good. I built walls and called them strength.

But perhaps Adrian's hesitation isn't a warning sign or avoidance. Maybe it truly **is** fear, just like mine.

Maybe we're both terrified of being hurt either by opening up or by losing something that matters too much.

**Maybe** we are more alike than we realized.

For the first time, I allow that to be true. And to my own surprise, it doesn't collapse me.

It calms me.

Warmth spreads where resistance had been.

Not certainty—but space.

Space, finally, to choose.

And it's a **YES**.

*

I rush out of Lina's studio, heart racing.

The street is bright, too bright. My fingers tremble as I pull out my phone and hit record. "Hey, Adrian," I say, breath catching. "Can we talk?"

He calls back immediately. "I'm just running out of my office—give me a sec." I hear footsteps pounding pavement. Then, a breathless: "Okay. Tell me."

I steady myself. "I'm not promising forever. All of this happened quite fast now. We still need to talk—about the practical things, the real-life stuff. See whether this can actually work. And I need a slower pace for a while... but—"

"I love that 'but'!" he blurts out.

I smile—deep breath. "I'm willing to see where this goes."

"Oh my god, Sophie!" His voice explodes with joy. "This is amazing. Are you coming to Paris? I'll buy your ticket right now."

I hesitate."I can't next week," I say. "I have... a small operation."

"What operation?"

"While we were apart, I saw a doctor at a fertility clinic," I say. "She told me I'm in the highest possible range for women my age—egg reserve-wise. So... I decided to freeze my eggs. It's a two-step process. The first part starts next week. After that, I'll need to stay here and focus on work. It'll be a couple of weeks before I can come."

Silence.

"Adrian?"

"I'm here," he says, his voice unsteady.

"What's going on over there?"

"Sorry," he exhales. "I think it's amazing you're doing this, just in case. You know how much I want a family—the sooner the better. I know it's too early to talk about that now. But hearing that we potentially could have one together just made me more emotional than I already was."

"Really?" I smile, the tension softening. "Okay, enough crying for a while, yeah?"

He laughs through it. "You got it."

A beat. Then: "Couldn't you come sooner, Sophie?" he asks. "I won't push you, obviously. Please, definitely do what's best for you. But... we've worked **so** hard to get here. It feels odd to wait now. Can't you come before the operation? I'll make sure to take excellent care of you to be in your best possible state for your surgery."

I blink. "What? Coming over for just a few days, like... now? You'd still be back in time. Wait a second—Yes, there are flights tomorrow."

My mind spins—appointments, deadlines, hormone shots, flight logistics, my body.

It's too much, too fast.

Again.

"Wait—I need to think," I say, pulse pounding.

"I'll call you back."

I hang up and stand frozen in the sun-drenched street, cars humming past. I close my eyes.

Everything is screaming: 'Not again. Don't rush.'

But I picture his face. His voice. The way it would feel when I finally let myself soften in his arms. And in that stillness, something inside me says: It's a little much, but you'll figure it out. You only live once. Just go.

I pick up the phone.

"I'm in."

CHALLENGE 19

# Paris

When Rani and Eliyah came over for a quick farewell toast, their excitement filled the room.

"Oh my god, girl," Rani said, pulling me into a tight hug and kissing my cheek. "I'm so proud of you. You're really stepping out of your comfort zone."

"And it's kind of epic," Eliyah grinned, raising his glass. "The way he just bought you a ticket? Gentleman move of the year."

I sank into the armchair, tucking my legs under me, still a little dazed. "It feels surreal, though. Two days ago, I thought we were over for good... now I'm twenty-four hours away from being in his arms, in an actual committed relationship. In Paris."

"Yep," Rani smirks. "Very surreal. But also, kind of perfect."

"I'm so jealous," Eliyah chimed in, swirling his drink with theatrical flair, then softening. "But like, the happy-for-you kind. Mostly."

I laughed, shaking my head. "I'll bring you your favorite macarons."

He gasped, hand to heart. "Then I'm officially not jealous anymore. Only radiant with joy."

Rani leans in, eyebrows raised. "But seriously. What does this mean now? Are you moving to Paris or what?"

"We haven't talked about that yet," I say, reaching for my glass. "Would've been way too soon. One step at a time."

She nods slowly. "And what about practicalities—like, are you going to be monogamous or open?"

I exhale through a small laugh. "He's always said monogamy's what he wants—with me. I've told him I might be open to other options eventually, but I couldn't promise anything. We still need to talk about that, too."

Eliyah raises an eyebrow. "Would you really give up New York for him?"

"Look, I don't know yet, okay?" I say.

"The baseline is that we both want to be in this relationship and make it work. If there's a way, we'll find it. I just didn't let myself think about the big stuff before... not until I knew where we stood. Now that I do... We'll figure it out."

I glance between them, a smile tugging at my lips. "Right now, I'm just really excited to see Adrian again—and to be in Paris for the first time."

*

*A day later*

> **Adrian:** I can't believe you're almost here. I'm so excited to see you, Sophie. I'm so sorry I won't be there when you arrive. I'm stuck—stupid traffic. But a driver will pick you up and carry your bags. I'll turn around and head home right now too

I step into the airport hall. "Over here, Mademoiselle," the driver calls out, waving politely.

The moment I slip into the car, I start to realize—***I'm in Paris.***

It's technically spring, but the current weather in the city makes it feel like early summer. Warm pavement, thick air filled with the scent of freshly baked bread, caramelized sugar, and cigarette smoke. The light has that soft gold tint I've only ever seen in French films.

Outside the window, the city flickers by: colorful flower stalls, tiny cafés and bistros, elegantly dressed people strolling around. It's alive, messy, and beautiful.

"We've arrived, Mademoiselle," the driver says, as he steps out and grabs my luggage. "Follow me—I'll show you the way."

My heart jumps as I walk toward the building, its weathered stone and lacy balconies making it look like something out of a Paris postcard.

We climb a grand old staircase, each step echoing. Red carpet. Iron railings. Wide antique windows let in sheets of sun. He stops at a tall door, turns the key, and smiles.

"Voilà. Enjoy your stay."

I push the door open slowly. And stop.

I let out a small, surprised sound—somewhere between a laugh and a gasp.

**Flowers.** Everywhere.

Peonies, tulips, roses, and wild blooms I don't recognize. Vases on every surface, petals spilling gently. The scent wraps around me—sweet, heady, alive.

I wander deeper inside. The apartment is light and open, with high ceilings, cream walls, and worn wooden floors. Through the windows, the Eiffel Tower glows like it's been waiting for me. It's not just beautiful—it's stunning. And it feels much more grown-up than his apartment in New York.

I take a quick shower to shake off the travel fog. Cool water runs down my back as I hear the front door creak open.

My breath catches.

Then a knock on the bathroom door. "Hey, you," Adrian calls. "Everything okay in there?"

"I'll be out in a sec." I slip into my dress and open the door, steam curling out around me.

My heart pounds faster as I see him. He sits on the couch, tie loosened, suit jacket tossed over the backrest. The skyline sprawls behind him like a painting. It's not just his apartment. It's **him** who looks more grown-up.

He looks up. "Oh my god. Sophie. **Finally**," he says.

My feet hesitate for a second. Then I step forward, heart beating. Faster. And faster.

I stop right in front of him and look into his warm eyes.

He pulls me in—slow but certain—and wraps his arms around me.

I don't move at first. I just stand there, stiff, taking in the feel of him, the heat of his chest against mine, his scent, intoxicating to my senses, rushes back to me.

And then, the second my body rests against his, something in me lets go. My forehead drops to his shoulder. My arms wrap back around him.

All the tension—the months of spiraling thoughts, of second-guessing, of holding back—dissolves.

I breathe him in. Familiar. Grounding.

Everything in me eases, and a quiet certainty rises.

*This is real.*

*This is mine.*

*And it feels right.*

His arms loosen just a little, his hands trailing up my back. And then—his lips find mine. ***Soft, so soft.***

Now, his hands grip mine tightly, grounding me.

He kisses my neck.

His lips trail lower, gliding over my collarbone towards my stomach.

With one fluid movement, he slips off my dress and lays me down on the couch. He kisses every inch of me, worshipping every curve and detail of my body, as if he wants to reassure himself I'm really here. He returns to my lips, capturing them in a kiss so intense, so filled with love and hunger, I feel like I'm floating.

Then, his mouth traces down my legs and disappears between my thighs. ***Warm, so warm.***

"Adrian," I whisper, "I missed you **so** fucking much."

He pulls off his shirt and trousers in one swift motion. His underwear follows, and then he's above me, pressing against me, his body impossibly heated.

He enters me in one deep, unrelenting push, and I cry out, the sound swallowed by his lips as he kisses me again—fierce, consuming, his entire being pouring into every thrust.

I'm lost.

In him.

In us.

**His body is my body.**

Blurred in one.

Feelings. Just feelings.

**Love. Everywhere.**

We come...

Then—**Release.**

We sink into the couch and look at each other.

Breathless. Smiling. Happy.

"Come here," he says. I rest my head on his chest. His hands stroke my hair and we just lay there for a while in silence.

*This wasn't just sex.*

*It felt more profound. Primal and sacred all at once.*

*It was epic.*

*And it felt like coming home.*

*

The next morning, I woke with a jolt of disbelief—I was in Paris.

A grin spread across my face as I remembered: Adrian had asked me to stop by his office today, meet his team, and see where he worked.

The alarm hadn't gone off yet. He was still asleep, one arm heavy around me. I carefully slid out from under him, lifted his arm gently, and stepped out of bed. The wooden floor was cool against my feet. I walked over and pulled back the curtains.

Golden sunlight spilled into the room. Outside, the Seine shimmered under the morning sky, and the Eiffel Tower rose in the distance, framed between rooftops.

I stood there for a moment, taking it in. Suddenly, behind me, I felt Adrian stir. Then his familiar warmth wrapped around my waist, his lips brushing the side of my neck. "Good morning," he murmured, still half-asleep. "Thought you could sneak away?" he said with a grin, his hands slipping under my silk top, warm against my skin.

Just then, the alarm cut through the quiet like a siren. Adrian groaned, resting his forehead on my shoulder. "Seriously? Now?"

I laughed, turning toward him. "We have places to be."

He sighed. "How am I supposed to make it through a day at the office knowing you're wandering around Paris without me?" He kissed me—soft, unhurried—then pulled back reluctantly.

We got dressed slowly, stealing glances and small touches, neither of us quite ready to leave the cocoon of the morning.

Finally, we stepped out into the street, the sunlight like a warm wrap around our shoulders. As we walked, he tugged at his tie and looked over at me.

"You know," he said, "we could take the ferry instead of the Metro. Cross the Seine by boat. Could be a nice start to the day."

"Oh, I'd love that," I said.

*Could it get more romantic than that?*

We walked hand in hand toward the dock. The city was just waking up—cobblestones still damp from the morning clean, chairs clinking outside cafés, someone tuning a violin in the distance.

Passing a shop window, I caught our reflection. "We look like we've been together forever," I said, amused. "Honestly, it feels like I'm walking my husband to work."

Adrian laughed. "Did you pack my lunch box, darling?"

I smirked. "Right next to your multivitamins."

He chuckled, but then he stopped, mid-step.

Something shifted in his expression.

He turned to face me fully, brushing a loose strand of hair from my face.

"My heart," he said, quiet and certain. "You know what, as crazy as it sounds—I wouldn't even mind. I'm **insanely**, **madly**, **irreversibly** in love with you."

Then he kissed me.

And just as I was about to disappear into him—*ding!*—A sharp bell rang out behind us. "That's our ferry," Adrian said, blinking. "We've got to run." He grabbed my hand, and we sprinted toward the dock, laughing.

The boat rocked gently on the water as we climbed aboard and found a spot on the open deck. The breeze tossed our hair as the skyline drifted by.

Once we docked again, we walked the last few minutes to Adrian's office, tucked along the Seine. Old stone buildings, flowered balconies, sunlight catching on iron railings—everything felt light, like the beginning of a dream.

And for once, I didn't feel the need to make sense of it.

It was all clear.

As we neared his building—the one I'd only ever seen over video calls—Adrian glanced at me and said, casually but with that unmistakable glint, "I told everyone my partner's coming to visit. They are so excited to meet you, Sophie."

"Really?" A smile spread across my face.

I loved how natural that sounded, how certain he'd become once he made his choice.

But when we finally arrived, his office was empty.

He blinked at the quiet hallway, then turned to me with a soft shrug. "How about a coffee in the park instead? I asked my boss for a slow morning—we've got time. I can introduce you to my team later."

We grabbed two coffees from a little corner café and made our way down to the riverside park. It opened wide before us—green space stretched along the Seine, a breeze teasing the water into soft waves. It looked like something from a film, too perfect to be real.

I pulled a packable blanket from my bag—the kind that folds into its own pouch. A New York habit: never assume there'll be a clean seat. We spread it on the grass, a little off the main path, and settled in.

The park was crowded—most people rushed by, heads down, focused on their next destination, coffee in hand, dogs tugging at their leads. But our little patch of grass felt like a hidden pocket of calm, almost untouched—just enough shade to be cool, just enough sun to feel kissed.

Two days ago, we were ending things.

And now?

We were here.

Just like that.

It felt like the city had paused just for us.

And somehow, even here—on a blanket in a public park in Paris—it was like we were the only two people in the world.

Adrian leans in, brushing his lips against mine. A soft, slow kiss. "It's so nice here," he murmurs. "Just look at the way the light hits the water." His fingers graze the back of my calf, light as a brushstroke. And just like that, the rest of the world slips away again.

His right hand moves slowly, tracing a path upward, deliberate but unhurried. His eyes stay fixed on mine—steady, searching. He doesn't say a word, and he doesn't need to. I know exactly where this is going.

He watches me closely, reading every breath, every shift in my expression. The silence between us is more arousing than words could ever be. Every inch of me feels alive, like I'm being studied and remembered all at once.

My breath hitches.

He stops for a second, just looks at me. Calm. Composed.

My chest rises and falls more quickly now.

Then, his fingers slip beneath the hem of my skirt. His hand feels warm against my skin, sending shivers through my body.

The sun's heat and the sudden closeness make my pulse race.

Adrian's fingers move further, inch by inch, tracing my thighs. He stops for a second, and his eyes pierce mine, waiting, watching, letting the tension build.

Around our little corner, a safe distance away, the faint sound of passersby fills the background, but all I can focus on is him —his presence, his touch.

His hand slides between my thighs, underneath my barely-there thong. He lets the elastic snap back gently, creating a soft noise. Then, he strokes the outside of the fabric before slipping his fingers beneath it and inside me.

I let out a soft gasp as his fingers move back and forth, slow and gentle.

**Bzzz...**

The spell breaks for a second by the buzz of Adrian's phone.

He glances at it, a playful smile spreading across his face. "My colleagues are coming down here now," he says, his tone charged with mischief. "They'll be here in three minutes. You'd better hurry."

He continues to move his fingers inside me with precision.

**Heat.**

"Oh, I see them now. Probably two more minutes," he smiles.

My pulse races.

He waves to them in the distance while his other hand never stops its rhythm.

Then, he leans in and kisses me deeply.

The intensity of it sends me over the edge

—My release hits like a crashing wave.

Adrian swallows my moan as he holds me close.

And just as quickly as it started, he pulls his hand away, wiping it discreetly with a handkerchief.

His colleagues arrive just seconds later, and casual chatter snaps us out of our privacy.

My mind is still spinning, my body trembling, heat clinging to my skin. I fight to steady myself. But somehow, I manage.

I look at Adrian.

The contrast between us is both amusing and mildly infuriating. He appears to be completely relaxed. Steady. Like nothing even happened.

*

That afternoon, I wandered the streets of Paris alone, immediately attuned to the city's heartbeat. Elegant buildings framed the boulevards, and cafés buzzed with conversation and the clink of glasses. The streets pulsed with life—chicly dressed Parisians moving with purpose, each face its own story. I found myself swept up in the rhythm of it all.

Later, I picked Adrian up, and as we walked toward his apartment, someone stopped us. "Bonjour and welcome, Sophie. I'm Mark, a friend of Adrian's." He kissed me on both cheeks. "It's wonderful to meet you finally. Bring her to our next dinner, Adrian," he added with a bright smile, already hurrying off. "I've got to run, but it was lovely meeting you. Enjoy Paris."

I shot a confused glance at Adrian. "He's part of my friend group here," Adrian explained. "We meet every weekend, trying out different restaurants in the city. I told him about you after last week's dinner—he must've put two and two together."

"Did you tell **everyone** in Paris that I was coming?" I asked, laughing.

"Pretty much, to be honest," Adrian said, flashing a big, warm smile. "Why shouldn't I?"

He pulled me closer, our eyes locking. "I'm head over heels in love with you. I could shout it from the rooftops. Should I?"

He looked around theatrically. "Wait, I think there's one up there," he said, turning toward the steps of a nearby building.

I caught his arm."Please don't, I beg you."

He grinned. "Okay. For you, I won't."

Hours later, we were tangled together in Adrian's bed.

"You know what? I really like us in Paris," I said.

"Me too," he smiled.

*

The next few days felt like we'd slipped into our own little movie.

We wandered through hidden alleys with ice cream in hand, got lost in Parisian boutiques and in each other, spent nights tucked away in candlelit jazz bars, and shared secrets over croissant breakfasts that somehow stretched on until noon, our legs tangled beneath café tables.

On our last morning together, while we had breakfast, Adrian's phone buzzed with a video call. "Sophie, this is Brian—my father," he said, a spark of excitement in his eyes. "Is it okay if you're in the picture?"

"Sure," I said, trying to steady the flutter in my chest as he accepted the call.

"Hi, it's so lovely to meet you, Sophie," his father greeted, his voice warm.

Nerves and eagerness mixed in my throat. "Hey, Mr. De Luca. How are you?" I managed.

"I'm well. How are you two?" he asked.

"We're having a great time," Adrian said with a grin.

"Good to hear. I just wanted to say hello," his father replied, smiling into the screen. "Adrian told me how everything feels more special with you. We can't wait to meet you, Sophie. Welcome to the family. Maybe you'll come visit for Christmas?"

A voice in the background. "Sorry, gotta run now—apparently I'm urgently needed in the kitchen." He gave a cheerful wave, and the call ended.

I blinked, still processing. "Wow. Your father is planning way ahead," I said, laughing softly.

"Why shouldn't he?" Adrian shot back, his eyes locked on mine. "Did you want to be somewhere else?" His brow lifted.

Before I could answer, he pulled me into his arms. "Well, you can't be," he murmured. "I won't let you." Then he loosened his hold just enough to look me in the eyes. "Seriously—what **are** your plans for Christmas?"

"None," I said. "Same as most years. No family. No tree. No celebration."

"Well, you **do** have a family now," he said, his voice gentler, more deliberate. "Christmas with my family is magic. And this year we all meet at the house in Italy. Fifty people, maybe more. A full week of food, wine, and chaos—games, singing, ridiculous traditions. You'll love it."

My heart softened. He had talked about me with his family and invited me into his life. This wasn't impulsive or heat-of-the-moment affection.

This was a choice.

He had **chosen** me.

"Sophie," Adrian suddenly says, a distinct shift in his tone —more serious now.

I meet his eyes.

They're steady, full of warmth, and something unguarded.

"I'm so fucking happy with you," he says. "Do you want to move in... live in Paris with me?"

My heart skips.

The room goes quiet.

Even the sounds outside—faint clatter from the street, a bird chirping somewhere—fade.

Adrian glances around, almost sheepishly. "Okay, I don't have flowers here... they're all still in the living room. So it's just my proposal for now."

I laugh, breath catching. "I don't need flowers. I'm not the typical in-need-of-flowers girl anyway. I mean, I love them. They are beautiful, and the gesture itself makes me happy for a second. But eventually they all die, and that's just sad."

He smiles. "And I'm not the typical flower-giving guy."

My eyebrow arches. "Not the typical flower guy? That was a **whole lot** of flowers for someone who doesn't normally give flowers."

He shrugs, a grin spreading across his face. "They were at the bar. I followed my instinct, and you looked happy. So... it kind of stuck and became a thing."

"Well," I say, nudging his knee with mine, "glad we got that cleared up."

He turns back to the breakfast table, hands fidgeting just slightly as if the moment caught up to him again. "Okay then. I guess it's just me. No flowers. What do you say?"

I look at him.

*The man who once ran is now asking me to stay.*

A pause.

My heart flutters.

Then I nod.

And just like that, he releases his breath in a quiet rush. "**Really?**"

"Yes," I say, a grin stretching across my face.

"Oh my god, Sophie." His face breaks open, unguarded and glowing. "Come here." He pulls me into him, arms wrapping tight around my waist as he kisses me deeply—like he's sealing a promise.

When we finally break apart, his fingers brush a strand of hair from my cheek. "Are you sure you want to leave New York?"

I shrug lightly, settling back into the crook of his arm. "I always knew I wanted to live abroad someday at least for a while. And I love Paris. Yes, it'll be hard leaving Rhea, Rani, and Eliyah. But I can't stay just for them. I have to live my own life."

I shift onto my elbow, watching his face. "I can work from anywhere. I'll keep my studio in New York as a showroom and start something here. It might even be an advantage.

The only thing is—I need to be ready for that investment round in a few months, but I don't even need to be in NY for that."

He nods like he's already thought about it. "I'll help with that too," he says. "With your brilliant lights and your vision, people will **throw** money at you. And until then, don't worry about finances. I've got you."

I tilt my head, one eyebrow raised. "What about the visa?"

He hesitates for half a beat, then gives me a sheepish smile. "Well... if we want this to be long-term, we might have to get married after a few months. And we should also chat about kids very soon because... Well, you're thirty-eight and egg freezing can help, but it doesn't stop time entirely, am I right?"

"Right..." I let out a groan, dropping my face into my hands. "Oh god. Are we actually being insane?"

He laughs, cupping my jaw and tilting my face up so our eyes meet again. "Maybe. But I'm all in for insane—if it means I get to keep you in my life, Sophie. When can you come?"

I smile, a little breathless. "I still need to go through the egg-freezing process and tie up a few things. So... two, maybe three months. August, if all goes well."

"August," he repeats, nodding—like he's sealing it into his chest.

"Okay."

A pause. His eyes on mine. He smiles.

"I'll count the days."

I run my fingers along the curve of his collarbone. "There's one more thing."

He leans back slightly, curious.

"I told you I've never been in an open relationship. And while

I might be open to exploring it one day... not now. Not in the beginning. I need something solid first. Trust. A foundation. I'm talking months—maybe a year. Maybe longer."

"And I told you I'm fine with that. I just need to know there is an openness to talk about options, when it's time."

"Yes, but..." I study him. "You've been in open relationships before. I think it's clear now that we... feel a bit differently about it."

"Are you calling me a player?" he grins.

I laugh. "You said it, not me."

His eyebrow lifts. "Continue."

I exhale. "Look. You can separate sex from emotion—easily. You've told me you've had hookups with friends, colleagues, and all sorts of situations without boundaries.

I'm not judging. Honestly. Everyone should do what makes them happy."

"But..." he prompts.

"But I have zero experience with that. I've always said I wanted to try an open relationship at some point, to see if it could work for me. But if I'm being honest, I don't know if I could actually handle it. It sounds good in theory. But in practice? I guess what I'm saying is I can't promise you anything."

Adrian doesn't flinch. "That's fine. We don't need to rush any of that. What would it look like for you—if we ever did go there?"

"Clear lines," I say.

"Fixed boundaries. No emotional gray zones. Perhaps a one-time thing with someone we don't know, without exchanging numbers. But no dating. No friends. Definitely no exes. And **not** while we're still figuring us out."

He nods.

"That makes perfect sense. I want that too—a solid foundation, clear boundaries, and only one-time things. I've made mistakes before by letting things blur too much. It distracted me from the primary relationship. I'm not doing that again."

He pauses.

"One thing, though. My friendships mean a lot to me. I've always had close connections with men and women. They're platonic, but... those relationships are important. Would that be an issue?"

I trace the rim of my glass. "For me, it's about clarity. If it's a platonic friendship—someone where there's never been anything, or never will be—then of course, no problem. If you kissed someone when you were drunk in a club ten years ago, nothing else ever happened, and now she's just a friend? Also fine. That's history."

He watches me—quiet, present.

"Even catching up with an ex once in a while isn't a dealbreaker. But the lines must be clear. I don't do well with gray zones. That murky in-between space... that's where trust erodes. Where things get messy... Ambiguity makes everything harder than it needs to be. I've seen it too often. I can't do that. And I don't **want** to do that. It's just not healthy for me."

I pause, steadying my breath. "So... if we ever try something non-monogamous, it has to be from a place of total clarity. No confusion. No hidden feelings or secrets."

Adrian nods slowly, absorbing every word.

His fingers find mine, lacing his through them with quiet certainty. "I get it," he says. "And I respect that. I'll always be transparent with you, and I'm okay with everything you said, that's what I want too."

He leans forward, resting his forehead gently against mine. "Sophie," he murmurs, "you're the first person I've ever **wanted** to build something real with. Openness with other people is just a fun plus, and we do it only if it makes sense for both of us. The most important thing is that we choose each other again and again."

"Okay, then... I think we can give this a real shot," I whisper.

"We can," he says.

I brush a kiss against his jaw.

"Now all we have to do is survive the first long-distance period, forget about the potential marriage for a visa, build our careers, navigate the social freezing process, decide if and when we want kids, and maybe open up our relationship someday without it imploding."

He laughs, full-bodied and warm, tugging me onto his lap. "That's all? Piece of cake."

He looks into my eyes. "At the beginning, it's just a couple of months in New York and then in Paris. We take it step-by-step. I'll be fine. And Sophie, it'll be worth it," he pulls me close.

And in that moment—wrapped in his arms, the city just beyond the glass, our future still vague but finally possible—I believe him. I believe **us**.

It may be complicated. It may be chaotic. But it's real. And it's ours.

*

Our goodbye that evening wasn't dramatic—no sweeping declarations or last-minute rush. We just held each other for a long time at the station. Not because we were afraid to part, but because we didn't need to say anything more. We both knew this wasn't an ending. It was a pause.

On the plane, the cabin noise blurred into a distant hum. My body sank into the seat.

For once: No spinning thoughts. No edge of panic. Just a strange kind of calm. For the first time in months, I wasn't waiting for the other shoe to drop. Paris was waiting. But this time, I wasn't chasing or bracing. I was just... moving toward something that felt right.

***Peace. Finally.***

I thought.

CHALLENGE 20

# Give and Take

The nurse handed me a gown and some pills. The room buzzed with low sounds—machines, footsteps, voices behind curtains.

I'd only had one night at home. I was exhausted. But it had been worth it.

As they wheeled me toward the OR, the ceiling lights rushed past above me. Panic stirred in my chest, but so did something steadier: hope.

*Focus on that, Sophie.*

A potential future. A family.

This may be the first step.

A couple of hours later, I woke up in recovery, my body heavy and my head spinning. The air smelled of antiseptic and cold coffee. I spotted a small sign taped to the railing:

**Do not get up alone.**

I pressed the call button.

A nurse came and checked the monitor. She helped me up, guiding me toward the restroom. I made it halfway before my knees buckled. "I think I—" I started, but my vision was already graying out. She caught me.

"Is this normal?" I asked, my voice shaking.

"It can happen," she said gently. "The doctor said you'll need to stay a few days. Four, maybe five."

I looked down: three small incisions, bleeding. Panic flickered. "I planned for two days. Why suddenly so long? Did something go wrong?"

She placed a hand on my arm. "Wait for the doctor—he'll explain everything. But as you know, we just removed a cyst today. Many women must undergo this as a preparatory step before the actual procedure. And it won't affect the egg-freezing process you're starting next month."

Later, Adrian called.

"I have to stay in the hospital a bit longer than expected. Not sure why yet, but I think I'm okay. The doctor's coming by later to explain," I told him.

Our call lasted only a couple of minutes.

He didn't ask much.

Sounded somewhat distracted. Distant even.

When I hung up, the quiet in the room expanded.

*Maybe it's just the meds. Or the exhaustion. Don't go there now.*

A couple of hours later, the doctor came by and confirmed what I had already guessed: the surgery had been more complicated than expected. I'd lost a lot of blood.

I'd be fine, but I needed to be monitored and rest.

The following days blurred—naps in strange angles, the slow shuffle to the bathroom, a body that didn't feel quite mine.

Eliyah, Rani, and Rhea visited with a lemon cake and a gigantic paper flower Rhea had made for me.

But Adrian? Just one scattered text in five days.

He had my favorite sweets delivered one afternoon. It was a nice gesture. Thoughtful, even. But what was missing was **him**. His warmth. His presence. A voice that said: "I'm here. I care. You're not alone in this."

By the time I was discharged on May 17th, he still hadn't really asked me anything. Not about the doctor, not about my pain levels, he didn't even know I was leaving the hospital today.

I sat on the edge of the hospital bed, the white plastic bag of meds beside me, my duffel slumped on the floor.

I rechecked my phone—no message from Adrian. By now, his silence had a texture—cold and unfamiliar.

Outside, the car horn barked. Inside, my throat tightened.

I told myself not to spiral.

But my body already was.

*This isn't what love feels like*, I thought.

*Not when it counts.*

And still—I couldn't quite believe it. Just a week ago, it had felt like everything was changing, like it was all going to be fine. Great even. Now, I was feeling more alone than I had in a long time.

I didn't need sweets or flowers.

I didn't need romance or grand gestures.

I just wanted to feel like I mattered to him.

And right now, I wasn't sure I did.

*

Back at home, as I rest in bed, a message from Adrian finally comes through:

> **Adrian:** Sophie, heart. I hope you're doing better
>
> **Adrian:** I'm so, so sorry I haven't been in touch more
>
> **Adrian:** A lot's been happening here. I didn't want to worry you while you were at the hospital, so I didn't say anything —which felt weird
>
> **Adrian:** But... I had a lot on my plate at work. And then—my ex came to Paris. I tried my best to manage everything

I switch to video.

His face flickers onto my screen. He runs a hand through his hair and avoids my gaze for a second.

I blink. "Wait—what? She came to Paris?"

He exhales. "Yeah. She just... showed up. Booked a flight and rang my doorbell."

My face stiffens. "Why?"

"She's... not over it. She said she thought I just needed space. That I'd come to my senses eventually, but then she heard from a mutual friend that I'm seeing someone new—and she freaked out."

I lean back against my pillows, eyes fixed on the screen, trying to read his expression. "Didn't you say you told her about me months ago?"

"I did," he says, rubbing his forehead. "But I told her we were dating as friends, nothing serious."

***That** word again.*

My eyes narrow. "So until now... she thought we were **just friends**?"

Adrian hesitates. "We were already separated at the time. It was complicated. I didn't want to hurt her, Sophie."

"Still," I say, my voice tightening. "That's not how you handle it. You could have said you didn't want to talk about it instead of letting her believe something that wasn't true."

He sighs. "It wasn't technically lying. We hadn't defined ourselves as a couple at the time. We didn't even know what we were."

I don't answer right away.

Adrian watches me carefully.

"Let's not fight about this now, you're exhausted," he says gently. "I'm meeting her again this afternoon—for the last time. She wants to say goodbye properly. I'll call you after."

"She's still there?" I ask.

"It's her last day. Then she'll be gone, I promise. I'll call you right after, okay?"

"Is she staying at your place?"

"Of course not, Sophie. Nothing happened or will happen. Please don't worry about that part at all. She's staying in a hotel.

We will meet at my place because she's crying nonstop, and going outside is out of the question. But I'll send her back to the hotel for the night. I know this is a bit messy, but it's for closure. We'll be free afterward, I promise. I just want to give her the answers and time she deserves. She's really hurting, Sophie."

I stare at the screen, the silence between us stretching too wide. My eyes scan his face, trying to feel something steady in it—some trace of the Adrian I'd felt so sure about just days ago.

I don't.

Then, I nod slowly, but the knot in my chest doesn't ease. "Okay," I say. "Let me know how it goes."

"I will," he promises. "I'll message you once she's gone. Tell me: Anything else you need, Sophie?"

*Don't spend the night with your ex.*

*Be there for me emotionally.*

*Be the partner you promised me to be.*

I don't say any of that. I don't have the energy. And I feel for Kate.

"No."

Then he gives me a half-smile, one that doesn't quite reach his eyes. "Okay, I love you." And the call ends.

I let the phone fall to my chest. My heart sinks.

I'm still sore, still healing, still bleeding—and the person I love is across an ocean, spending the night with his ex.

But that isn't even what hurts the most.

It isn't only that he's with her.

It's that he **isn't with me**.

After all we'd been through, I'd expected more.

More clarity, more steadiness, more care.

Instead, there's chaos—another emotional rollercoaster.

**Again.**

*

When I wake up the next day—late morning in Paris—there's still no message from Adrian.

*Didn't he say he'd text me once she was gone?*

*Why is he doing this to me?*

Finally, around 8 p.m. in New York, he calls. "Hi, Sophie. I'm so sorry it took so long," he begins. "It's been... a lot. I was with Kate until six in the morning. It was draining. I wanted to rest a bit before reaching out. I know that must've been hard on you. Thank you for being patient."

"Look," I say, keeping my voice even. "I get that it can get complicated. But until 6 a.m.? You met in the afternoon. That's a long time to talk."

I pause. "Adrian, I feel like I always have to be the one who's understanding. Always the one making space."

"I know. It's just... since we met, everything's been happening at once," he says, his voice tired. "But that's not who I am, Sophie. Normally, I'm steady. Calm. No chaos at all."

"Well. I just spent a week in the hospital. I had surgery—it didn't go well. And you haven't even asked how I'm doing since our first call. No matter what's been going on in your life, you should've shown up. You should've made me a priority. Or at least one of them. I know I would've."

He sighs. "Yeah. You're right. I'm really sorry you feel unsupported. That's the last thing I ever wanted."

He pauses, looks down for a second before meeting my eyes again. "I'm usually the most caring person in the room—you know that, right? I just... I suck at juggling things. Especially when emotions are involved, you and I—we'd just gone through so much lately. And when Kate showed up like that, full of pain and drama—it threw me off completely. You have no idea how intense it's been here."

"And about that—" I say, "if you need to talk to get closure, fine. But there have to be boundaries. Are more conversations planned?"

"No," he responds immediately. "Absolutely not. She asked if we'd get back together. I told her that's not happening. I don't think there'll be much contact from now on. No regular check-ins or anything."

I exhale—a flicker of relief. "Okay then," I say. "Can I finally lean back now, or is there something else I should know? Any other exes planning surprise appearances?"

Adrian hesitates. "I guess not."

He glances away. "Let's not get into it now. You're still recovering. We'll talk about it when you're stronger, okay?"

I sit up straighter. "What does **that** mean?"

"Look... It's probably nothing, but if we're putting everything out there—maybe I should mention it...
I dated a few women in Paris while we were on that break."

My chest tightens.

"One of them is Aurélie. It's over now, but... she's still in my life."

"So, you **were** dating...
Was it serious with Aurélie?" I ask.

"We had a few nights together. I ended it, though. I didn't want anything real with her."

"But she did?"

He shrugs. "Maybe. Probably. I don't know.

Anyway, we're just friends now. Honestly, she's probably one of my closest ones here."

"So you see her often."

He nods. "She runs a coffee and design shop near my office. Everyone goes there. She's part of the circle. I see her a couple of times a week. I've never believed in cutting people off after something physical, Sophie. It feels artificial and unnecessary."

I try to keep my voice steady. "How many times did you sleep together?"

"A couple."

I exhale. "This doesn't feel right, Adrian," I say. "This was just a few weeks ago—while I'm in New York, missing you, hurting.

And you didn't just have sex—she wanted more. None of that is platonic. We've talked about this. I don't do well with gray zones like that."

"This isn't fair, Sophie," he says, his voice rising. "You said you don't deal well with gray zones, yes. But this isn't one. It's purely platonic. Nothing else is happening anymore. If I wanted to be with her, I would. But I ended it. She's part of my life, my world here. I don't want to lose that for no reason."

I take a deep breath. "Okay. Let's stop right here. I'm tired —from surgery, from everything. I can't keep having these conversations."

"I don't want you to suffer. If you want me to cut contact, I will," he says quietly. "If that's what you insist on, I'll do it. But Sophie, it doesn't feel right. It goes against my beliefs. I'm telling you—there's no gray zone here. I don't think it's a real problem, to be honest. It's about trust. You should trust me."

Silence.

I see it in his face: resistance.

I feel trapped.

Adrian wasn't going to be okay with cutting contact. That much was clear. And if I asked him to do it now, we'd be starting on the wrong foot for sure—I could feel it in my bones.

I couldn't afford to keep wondering or solving anything, either—not in the state I was in. My body was drained. My mind scattered. Even the idea of another unresolved tension made my chest ache. I needed clarity. **Now.** Even if I had to create it myself.

"I don't believe in telling people what to do," I say. "I can tell you how I feel, but everyone has to make choices on their own. And compromises—they only work if they come from a place of willingness, not resentment."

A pause.

"You know what? Okay," I say, my voice flat. "I don't have the strength to argue. For now, I'll try to be okay with it. Let's see how it goes."

"Alright," Adrian says, the relief in his voice almost immediate—until it isn't. He pauses. "Wait... you're not **actually** okay with this, are you?"

"No," I say quietly. "Of course I'm not. But I don't think you'd be either, if you had to cut contact. One of us has to give in and be willing to really try. And it sounds like it's not going to be you today. So I'll do it. If it doesn't work, we'll deal with that later. But right now, I just need rest."

"Okay. Whatever you think is best," he says. "And yes, just rest now, Sophie."

"Just one thing I need to know," I add quietly. "Is it just her? Or are there other flings you're still in contact with? Because honestly—if there's more, I don't think I can do this. If I'm going to try to be okay with this... it has to be just her. I need a clean slate. We need to agree on that."

"It is," he assures me. "Just her. I have dated other women in New York. But I don't need to stay in touch with them or any other women I slept with. And I won't. I just might catch up with my ex once or twice a year, maybe a quick call—but that's it."

"That's fine."

"Okay. Otherwise, **clean slate**. I promise."

I hesitate. "Okay. Clean slate. I can trust you're being honest with me, right?" I ask.

He doesn't react. A pause. Too long.

"Wow," I say. "You can't even agree to that?"

"If we agree on something, just like we did now, you can trust my words. But no one's honest about everything all the time," he replies. "I'll be honest about what matters to **us**. I won't lie about that. But I won't share every detail of my life either."

I understand. But it still lands wrong. It sounds like a loophole.

"I don't know what it is you want to hear, but I can promise you one thing, Sophie: I'll be loyal," he adds. "I'm not going anywhere. Once I commit, I commit. I'm not looking for anything else. I'm here with you, Sophie, trying my best. I love you."

It's not the answer I want. But for now, I need to save my strength—Not for us. For me. And for my upcoming egg-freezing process.

After we hang up, I just sit there—numb. The fears I've managed to quiet for days come rushing back, sharp and loud.

Every time I start to feel safe with him, every time we patch one thing, something else unravels. I'm always fighting—for us, for myself, just to keep going.

But he says he's still figuring himself out. He **is** younger. He **was** in an open relationship with almost no boundaries. And yes—he's just overcome a major fear and taken a real step toward commitment. That counts for something.

So I tell myself it's just a rocky start. Something we'll move through once I get to Paris. That all of this—the tension, the mess—is just because of the distance. And once we're in the same place again, we'll find our way back to the version of us that felt easy. That felt right.

But deep down, where my body still aches and my heart feels scraped thin, I wonder:

*What if loving him will always cost more than I have to give?*

*

The next few days were a mess of ups and downs.

I wasn't the controlling type. And I did trust Adrian not to cross physical lines with Aurélie. But staying close to someone he'd just slept with—and calling it friendship—sat wrong in my gut.

Flat in bed, I kept spiraling. Were they together now? Sharing something intimate? Strengthening their bond while I lay alone in New York, trying to keep it together?

I grew up without safety. My boundaries were crossed constantly. So learning to set them—especially in relationships—wasn't a preference. It was survival.

And on that front, Adrian and I spoke different languages.

I was trying **really hard** to learn his. Telling myself, *'Be positive, Sophie. This may be your chance to grow, to trust through discomfort. Perhaps all you need is to loosen up and come out stronger.'*

But the days that followed were brutal.

I clearly wasn't okay.

I couldn't sleep, my head was fogged over, and I lost over ten pounds—not from discipline, but because my system was shutting down. A nice visual side effect, possibly. But I didn't feel strong. I felt hollowed out.

And Adrian wasn't helping at all.

Aurélie kept constantly creeping back into our conversations. He told me about their daily encounters. Their fitness classes, inside jokes, and lunch breaks.

One afternoon, he was with her, and when I tried to reach him, his phone was off—something that had never happened before. He always charged it overnight, without fail. Nevertheless, he insisted he'd just run out of battery, and I needed to trust him.

Another day, he said casually, "Aurélie wanted my advice on something personal today—a really intimate topic. She was hurting, and I had a long chat with her. I hope that was fine."

I blinked. "Adrian, I don't know what to say or what that even means. What do you want to hear? It's not my job to sign off on everything. You know where I stand. I need to trust that **you** know what's okay."

Then, a couple of days later, came the question that tipped me over: "Would it be okay if I went furniture shopping with Aurélie?—I wanted to pick new furniture for you, for our apartment. I don't think I trust my taste enough, and as a design shop owner, she's an expert."

I stared at him. "Are you for real? Of course it's not okay."

"Relax," he said. "It was just a **harmless question**. You're making a big deal out of nothing."

"Adrian, I have an eye for design too, you know. And there is a line. You need to tell her that's a boundary. That's **our** space to create."

But deep down, I knew—it wasn't about her. It was about **him**. The choices he kept making. Him being oblivious to what was okay for me and what wasn't.

And the more I stretched and bent to make it work, the more doubts kicked in. *Was this really worth it? Should I be suffering like this for a relationship?* It felt absurd.

I started to wonder whether I had made a mistake. *Should I have drawn a firmer line?* But the moment I tried to find clarity, one question split into five. Five into twenty. Every option felt wrong. I was paralyzed—spinning, unable to see straight.

What scared me most was that I no longer recognized myself. Sure, I overthought things sometimes. But I wasn't usually stuck like this.

For months, I'd been sharp, clear—aligned in my thoughts, beliefs, and actions. But ever since our last breakup, that alignment had been slipping. Each new decision I made only blurred it more.

Right now, I had no idea what I was doing—only that I felt completely lost.

*

I curled into the corner of Rani's couch, knees tucked up, a blanket draped loosely over my legs.

I was still sore, still slightly nauseous from the meds. But I couldn't stay in bed another day. Another twenty-four hours spiraling alone, and I'd lose it.

It was time to get moving again—maybe get an outside perspective and do something light. Something that reminded me of who I was outside all this mess. So Rani insisted I come over. We'd do one of Rhea's and my favorite things: make paper flowers. She was still taking her afternoon nap in the next room.

Rani handed me a cup of herbal tea before sinking into the armchair beside me. The house smelled of cardamom, chamomile, and something that had been baked earlier that morning. Across from us, Eliyah sat cross-legged on the floor.

"Sweetheart, it sounds like you're dealing with decision fatigue," Rani said gently. "That foggy kind of exhaustion that can hit after you've had to make too many hard choices in a row. At some point, it wears you down and makes it feel impossible to decide anything—or even see things clearly."

"Yeah," I murmured. "Behavioral science 101. Until now, I only knew the term. But now I actually **feel** it."

"Sophie." Eliyah leaned forward, resting his elbows on his knees. "Maybe you've got to approach this strategically. I know this is hard, but try to let it go, just for now. Pick your battles wisely. Let him feel like he's winning this one—save your energy for something bigger. He's already committed to you. Don't back him into a corner. That'll just make him hold tighter to what he thinks he's losing."

"But I get why you're upset, love," he added. "You know me—I believe in shared intimacy, transparency, open setups. But this furniture-shopping thing? In your relationship context? Ridiculous."

"You know, I just keep wondering whether anyone can actually believe this is okay?" I said, taking a sip of my tea. "I mean... can he really be **that** naive?"

"**Yes**," Eliyah said, nodding without hesitation. "He's young. He's used to freedom. He might genuinely not understand how it feels on your side."

I stared at the mug in my hands. "The thing is: the way he keeps bringing her up—it doesn't make sense at all, but... it almost feels like he's trying to torture me..."

"He probably thinks he's just being honest," Rani said gently. "Trying to show you how transparent he is, how normal all of this is. I'm sure, even if it seems strange to you, his intention is to make this work."

"Well, it isn't working," I said. "But at least he's promised to keep his distance from Aurélie and not bring her up now while I have hormone therapy starting in a couple of days. It's already so much on my body and mind—I don't want to put myself through additional stress there."

"You come from different emotional worlds," Eliyah added. "For you, boundaries are safety. For him, they might feel like a trap. The question is: can you meet somewhere in the middle or not? But not now, Sophie. You're too depleted. Don't risk everything because of a random woman who probably means nothing at all. Wait until you're back in Paris. Let it settle first."

A soft creak echoed from down the hall. Tiny footsteps padded toward us. A moment later, Rhea appeared, blinking sleep from her eyes, her curls wild and flattened on one side. "Sophie?" she mumbled.

"Hey, my love," I said, reaching out my arms. Rhea climbed into my lap, curling up against my chest. "I think someone's ready to make flowers," I smiled.

Rhea yawned. "Are we doing roses or the big poppy ones?"

I shifted forward, trying to hide how much effort it took. "Your choice."

Rhea's eyes lit up. "Poppies, then."

And just like that, the conversation faded into the soft rustle of paper, the sharp sound of blunt scissors, and the comforting rhythm of creating something with our hands. A small, quiet kind of peace. Exactly what I needed.

And the best part: those paper flowers would turn out exactly as expected—we'd done them about a million times.

*They'd stay beautiful.*

*They'd never wilt.*

*And they'd never leave.*

"Here!" Rhea said, her little feet pattering across the floor, curls bouncing with each step. She held out a tiny crumpled pink flower with both hands.

"Oh, sweetheart," I said, bending down to meet her eyes. "It's such a tiny one. And so lovely."

She rocked proudly on her heels, then leaned in close, whispering like it was a secret, "It's a lucky flower, for Paris."

I smiled, gently closing her hand around mine as I took it.

I hoped I didn't need it.

But deep down, I was afraid I did.

CHALLENGE 21

# Did He Just–?

"Let me help you with that," Rani said, taking one of the heavier suitcases and rolling it smoothly through the airport doors.

The automatic glass panels parted with a whoosh, the cool air hitting my face. The terminal buzzed with motion—echoes of rolling wheels, intercom announcements, soft footsteps on tile.

"Thanks for bringing me," I said, shifting the strap of my carry-on higher on my shoulder. "It's really sweet of you."

"I don't even know when I'll see my girl again," Rani said, giving me a sideways smile. "Maybe Paris is so damn romantic you won't want to come back at all. So, **of course**, I had to bring you."

I gave her a quick look, half-laughing, but I felt the sting in my throat. I glanced ahead, avoiding her eyes for a second.

"How are you feeling right now?" she asked gently.

"I'm not sure," I admitted. "Excited, definitely. I can't wait to see Adrian again—finally be with him, really live the life we imagined. I do believe that things can fall back into place once we are together. But… the last weeks haven't been easy on me. On us.

And this also feels like a test. Like I'm walking into something with a clock ticking over my head."

"Right," Rani nodded.

"I mean, we've got three months to figure everything out —whether we want to get married, whether we want kids. Let's be honest, that's a bit wild. Especially after all the tension lately."

"Yeah," she said softly, resting her hand on my shoulder for a moment. "It is a lot. But remember that you don't have to figure everything out at once. Just go there. Have fun. Live. See where it leads."

I nodded, but something inside me clenched. Like my body was holding onto too many emotions at once—doubt, hope, exhaustion—pulling me in different directions.

She nudged me lightly, a playful glint in her eyes. "And hey, I know age and time are still on your mind—but you can breathe now, at least a little. I mean, come on. Twenty eggs in one cycle, girl?—That's off the charts. You can relax a bit."

She grinned, bumping her shoulder into mine. "And you are officially the egg queen."

I couldn't help but laugh. Some of the weight lifted off my chest, just for a moment.

"How did the investment go, by the way?" she asked.

"The entire fund got canceled." I shook my head. "It's bothering me a bit, if I'm honest. I'm not in the best place financially right now."

"Adrian said not to worry, right?"

"True, but I hate relying on anyone. I want to be 100 percent independent. Always have. I just need to land that next round I'm preparing for in two months. No matter what."

"You'll get there, Sophie. You always do. And he offered to help in the meantime if needed. Let him. You're taking a lot of risk on your end, so it's just fair if he chips in."

"I guess."

We reached the security check-in.

"So... here it is," I said.

Rani opened her arms, and I fell into them. She hugged me tightly, her voice warm in my ear. "Enjoy your adventure, Sophie. I hope it's everything you dreamed of. And if it's not—I'll visit anyway. You're not getting rid of me."

"You better," I whispered, trying to swallow the lump in my throat.

She pulled back slightly and grinned. "**Bold move moment**, right?"

"**Bold move moment**," I echoed, and smiled.

"This is the part where Eliyah would start making dramatic sounds—snapping his fingers and singing until I disappeared behind the gate," Rani said.

"Yes, definitely!"

"He'd probably pretend to faint, too." Rani burst out laughing, her curls falling into her face.

Then her face turned more serious. "We're so excited for you, girl. But we're going to miss you, you know."

I squeezed her hand. "I'm going to miss you, too."

She took my hands in hers. "Just make sure to get Eliyah his macarons or you'll have a problem," she joked.

Rani brushed a strand of hair from my face. "And if things get messy—call me. I'm here for you. No matter what."

*

The moment I land in Paris, my heart stutters in my chest.

The airport doors slide open, and my pulse races.

I scan the crowd, eyes flicking over strangers, searching and holding my breath.

And then—**I see him.**

He's there. Waiting.

Standing tall and as handsome as ever. He's smiling in that way I know too well. Like I'm the only person in the world. The only one who matters.

My legs move before my brain catches up.

I step toward him, and he's already walking toward me.

**Slow motion.**

My heart is beating faster.

**Louder.**

The airport noise, the people around us. It all fades away.

When we reach each other, he pulls me in and kisses me—fast, firm, like he needs the contact to believe I'm real. He wraps his arms around me and kisses my neck. "I missed you so fucking much, Sophie," he murmurs, his breath warm against my skin.

We drop my bags at his place, and barely talk.

Just hands brushing. Hearts bumping. Glances held too long.

Then we're outside again, swallowed by the Paris air. Sunlight stretches across the late afternoon, wrapping the city in gold. We walk, fingers laced. The heat of his palm against mine feels steadying and familiar.

I lean into him slightly as we stroll past little cafés—coffee cups clinking, laughter floating through open windows. The smell of espresso and buttered pastries follows us down narrow streets.

Everything looks more vivid than usual. Like Paris itself is pulling me into a hopeful dream. Making up for all the things I've gone through to get here.

We spend the whole afternoon wandering, never too far from each other's orbit.

Crepes. Little kisses. Big smiles.

We stop often, like we don't want time to keep moving.

It all feels so easy. So light.

**He** feels light—and I do too.

"Hey," he says, pointing to a café window. "What about a strawberry tart? Supposed to be the best in the city." He gets one to go, and we share it as we keep on walking.

Then we reach a bridge.

The Seine sparkles beneath us, the Eiffel Tower rising in the distance like something out of a movie.

He stops.

Turns.

Eyes locked.

"I'm so glad you're finally here, Sophie," he says, voice low, and smiling. "Everything will fall into place now. I can feel it. Welcome to Paris."

I look at him.

He seems lit from within. His face glows—warm, open, balanced. He looks like a man who's arrived—a man who knows what he wants. Certain. Calm. As if he's landed exactly where he's meant to be.

Then it hits me.

I've **never** seen him **this** happy before.

He leans in.

His lips find mine—slow, full, anchoring.

A kiss that pulls me apart and puts me back together.

A kiss that says, *We belong together.*

And just like that, **my body lets go**.

Everything in me eases. The ache in my chest dissolves.

My shoulders drop. My ribs expand. My throat loosens.

I hadn't realized just how tightly I'd been wound until now.

At this moment, all the doubts I've carried melt away.

All that's left is this:

Love.

Joy.

Peace.

And suddenly, all of it—the difficult decisions, the pain, the risks—feels worth it.

Because it led us here.

Together.

In this moment.

On the same page.

Feeling nothing but pure happiness.

And my body finally believes what my heart wanted so badly to for a long time:

*It's okay. You're safe.*

*You have a family now. You're home.*

*

*Next morning*

"Can't you just stay home?" I murmur, still curled under the duvet, lips in a pout.

Adrian's already dressed—black shirt half-buttoned, sleeves rolled. He leans down beside me, fingers threading through my hair with that maddening tenderness that makes me forget every argument we've ever had.

"I wish I could," he says softly, brushing a kiss onto my temple. "But we've got people flying in from the States. Big deal. I have to be there."

I close my eyes and let out a groan, exaggerated but half sincere. He smiles and tucks a strand of hair behind my ear. "I'll keep it as short as I can," he adds, lowering his voice. "And—I got you croissants. From that place. The one you love.

They're in the kitchen."

I blink up at him, already softening. "Well... fine. I guess I can survive until tonight."

He kisses me again—slow and sweet—then pauses with his lips against mine for just a second longer than necessary. "Bye, my heart," he whispers. "Enjoy Paris."

The front door clicks shut a moment later.

As soon as I hear it, I spring up, tug on his hoodie, and pad barefoot into the kitchen. The bag on the counter smells like heaven. There's a little heart drawn on it, and beneath it, just: **Adrian**—My smile arrives before I even realize I'm grinning.

The rest of the day is mine: I wander the streets like a local, weaving through galleries and open markets. I buy fresh tomatoes, basil, and garlic—something simple and comforting—for us.

By the time the front door clicks open again, it's 8 p.m. Footsteps. Keys on the side table. Then arms slide around my waist, and I feel him before I see him. "Hey," he breathes against my neck.

I lean into him without turning. "Hey."

His lips graze my skin, and a shiver rises beneath my shirt. "Do you have any idea how hard it was not seeing you all day?" he murmurs. He turns me gently to face him, his hands still on my waist. Kisses me slow—like we've got nowhere to be but here.

Then he inhales. "You cooked? That smell... please tell me it's pasta."

"It is. And yes, I remembered your addiction," I tease. "I made a lot of it. You can eat as much as you want."

"God, I love you," he grins. "This might be one of the sweetest things anyone's ever said to me."

"I'm glad," I laugh.

"Maybe we should just get married right away," he says—half-joking at first, then suddenly serious. His eyes linger on mine.

Before I can respond, he kisses me again—soft, deliberate—like a period at the end of a sentence he meant more than he admits.

Behind me, the sauce bubbles too loudly, pulling me back. I turn to the stove and stir it. "Almost ready," I say.

"How was your day?" he asks, leaning against the counter beside me.

"Perfect. I just walked and wandered around Paris. Yours?"

He nods, watching me. Then casually: "Great too. I actually ran into Aurélie today. She asked if we wanted to go to a party with her this weekend. Do you want to go together?"

And just like that—something shifts.

My spine goes rigid.

The spoon slips from my hand and clatters into the pot.

Tomato sauce splashes onto the stovetop, bright red against steel.

I stare at it for a beat too long—and freeze.

That old, familiar knot coils tightly in my chest, and all the stress I'd been tucking away comes rushing back in an instant.

I'd spent weeks trying to block her out, pretending she didn't exist. That this wasn't an issue anymore.

I don't turn around—just stare at the bubbling sauce in front of me. "No, Adrian," I say finally. My voice is low and measured. "I don't want to go to a party with her."

"Why are you suddenly so tense?" he frowns. "It was just a harmless question."

There it is again: **just a harmless question.**

He's been using that expression more and more lately—making me feel like I'm overreacting and irrational.

I step away from the stove, walk into the living room, and rub sauce from my fingers with a kitchen towel.

I don't look at him.

"You **know** your relationship with her triggers me," I say calmly. "And I've only just arrived. Can't you at least let me settle first?"

"It was **just** a harmless question," he repeats.

*Why doesn't he hear me?*

*What's so difficult to understand?*

My throat tightens. My brain starts spiraling.

He follows, arms now crossed. "Come on, it's just a party. You're making a big deal out of nothing right now."

My jaw clenches.

I turn to him slowly, pulse loud in my ears.

"No," I say, firmer now. "It's not just a party, Adrian. It's the way you keep her in your life like she's a priority for you.
The way you completely ignore how I feel about this. While I'm sitting there trying not to drown in discomfort. I've made space for this over and over again. I bit my tongue when it got too much, and tried to stay chill and supportive. Why am I always the one who has to bend?

And why do you think that's okay?"

He exhales through his nose, annoyed. "You're being dramatic. She's just a friend."

I stare at him.

My voice sharpens. "You slept with her just a few weeks ago. Now you hang out with her **all the time**, Adrian. And you asked her to help pick furniture for **our** apartment.

Don't you get how fucking inappropriate that is?"

He raises a brow. "She owns a design shop. I thought she'd have good taste. You're blowing this up."

"I work in design too and I have good taste as well, you know," I shoot back, my voice sharp, shaking slightly. "And boundaries. Boundaries, I stretched a lot for you."

I take a breath, the words tumbling out now—too full to hold in. "And not once, not once, have you said, 'Thank you for trying to be okay with this, Sophie. I know this is hard for you.'"

Pressure builds in my chest. "Instead, you act like I'm some irrational mess with trust issues." My voice breaks there, just slightly, but I don't let it stop me. "I'm tired, Adrian. Tired of carrying all the weight and then getting blamed for not doing it well enough. All so you can do whatever you want."

Silence stretches between us. Heavy. Sharp.

My heart hammers against my ribs.

Then, he shakes his head, like I'm speaking a foreign language. "You need to calm down, Sophie. I asked if you wanted to go to a party, not if I could sleep with her again."

That does it.

My whole body tenses like a wire that has been pulled too tight. "You don't listen," I say, barely above a whisper. "I've told you from the beginning—I need boundaries to feel safe. You agreed. You promised. And instead, you constantly **push** me—for someone you barely even know. Shouldn't my well-being matter to you?"

His eyes harden. "What's wrong with you lately, Sophie? This level of reaction? It's not normal."

He pauses.

His voice drops, more restrained now. "Honestly, I'm worried about you. You're so unstable lately. I can't be your therapist. Maybe you should find one. I mean this in the most loving way."

It feels like the air is getting sucked out of the room.

*Did he just—?*

My knees nearly give out. It's like the floor shifts beneath me.

My breath catches, then stops.

***Anger, sadness, helplessness.***

I stagger slightly, grabbing the edge of the couch to steady myself. My stomach twists.

"I can't do this," I say, voice cracking. "Let's stop talking for now. I'm **drained**, Adrian. I'm jet-lagged. I just had surgery. I had hormone therapy. My body's still recovering. And I'm wrecked from this insane emotional relationship rollercoaster, too. I **told you** the doctor urged me to take it really slow and avoid stress for a couple of weeks. I can't do this right now." I sink onto the couch and curl into myself, arms wrapped tight around my legs.

Silent sobs shake through me.

But Adrian doesn't move.

Doesn't come closer.

He just stands by the counter. Distant, like my pain is infectious.

I glance up at him, tears streaming down my face.

"Wow. You're just going to stand there? When I'm falling apart right in front of you? Can't you see I'm drowning?"

But Adrian still doesn't stir. In fact, he takes a half-step back.

Then, he lifts his hands, like he's washing his hands of it all.

"You're obviously not well. That's not my responsibility. You need help. Real help. You're not stable right now."

I wipe my face and take a long breath, pressing my palms against my thighs to stop them from shaking. "Okay, Adrian. You know what, I'll sleep on the couch tonight. You take the bed."

He doesn't argue.

That night, we exist like strangers under the same roof.

Two separate bodies.

Two separate hearts.

One big, echoing silence.

I lie awake, listening to the hum of the fridge. The occasional sound of a car passing below. Sleep doesn't come. Only questions.

Yesterday, it felt like Paris would finally bring us peace.

But all I feel now is destruction.

*

The next morning, Adrian leaves for work without saying a word.

The door clicks shut, and I just lie there—sprawled across the couch like something dropped and forgotten. My limbs feel like they're filled with sand. My skin itches with exhaustion. Even the light filtering through the window feels too loud.

The apartment is still, except for the occasional honk or rumble of traffic drifting in from the street below.

I make a coffee and forget it's there. The cup sits untouched on the table beside me, its surface gone dull and cold. I can't drink it. I can't even sit up properly. All I want is to go back to sleep. The kind that's deep and dreamless.

Around midday, my phone buzzes. A message from Adrian:

**Adrian:** Want to do something fun tonight? Grab dinner?

I stare at the screen. My thumbs hover, heavy. Then I type:

**Me:** Still too tired. I just need a little more time to recover.

No reply.

When he finally comes home that evening, the air has shifted even more.

Gone is the version of Adrian I once knew.

He drops his keys on the counter with a sharp clink—louder than usual, deliberate. His shoulders are stiff, his jaw set.

I'm curled up on the couch under two blankets, clutching a mug of tea. The sky outside is dark now. The only light in the room comes from the lamp beside me. Next to it are some sketches I've been working on throughout the day for my lamp design.

Adrian doesn't come over. Doesn't kiss me. He just stands there in the middle of the room, building himself up like someone ready to issue a verdict.

"Sophie," he says, low and cool. "We need to talk."

I don't even bother to look up fully. "Right now?" My voice scrapes its way out. "I'm... really drained."

"Yes, we need to talk **now**."

I sit up slowly, dragging the blanket from my lap like it weighs twenty-five pounds. My head throbs. The corners of the room blur slightly. "Okay," I say, my voice low.

He doesn't sit.

Just stands there, unmoving.

"This isn't working," he says. "I'm not going to do whatever you want. From now on, things will be different. I'll be friends with whoever I choose."

The words land sharply.

My hands clench around the edges of the blanket.

"There is this other woman I had sex with two times back in New York," he continues, his tone almost too casual now.

His eyes pierce mine, waiting, scanning my face. "I had a short call with her recently. Just to catch up," he says. "She might move to Paris. If she does, I'll see her. She's my friend. No discussion." His delivery seems practiced. Scripted. Like he's worked it over in his head already.

A hot pulse of anger flares under my skin. "Are you serious?" My voice cracks. "You slept with her. Twice. And now she's... your friend too?"

He crosses his arms. Doesn't flinch. "So? She truly **is** my friend."

"All of them?" I snap. "All the women you've slept with are your **friends**—and are they all lining up to come back into your life right now?" I stand, the room suddenly too bright. Too warm. The city outside glows in the window—Paris at golden hour—but it feels distant, like a painting behind glass.

"Adrian, this isn't about me telling you what to do or not to do. This is about decisions we made **together**. We discussed this before I came here. We set boundaries. **You** agreed to them. Right after you had a twenty-four-hour meeting with Kate, you said there were no more surprises. No other ex-flings you are in contact with. That I only had to deal with Aurélie, and we were starting with a clean slate."

I pause, trying to steady my voice. "And now there's another woman you've had sex with in the past, and you are breaking your promise? Just like that? Just because she moves here?"

"You just need to trust me," he says, brushing right past it.

"It's not that hard."

A band seems to tighten around my ribs. "You keep saying that, but how am I supposed to trust someone who keeps blindsiding me? Do you hear how ridiculous that is?"

He shakes his head. "I'm not going to limit myself to whatever **you** think is acceptable. That's not a relationship. **You** need to deal with that. Find a way to be okay with this. Work on yourself."

I blink. Hard.

"And while we're at it," he adds, almost like an afterthought, "we need to revisit our finances. That deal we made? It's not sustainable."

My stomach drops. "**What?** You haven't even done anything to support me financially or otherwise yet!"

"I offered to have your back, just in case, and I meant it," he said. "But I meant it only for the transitional phase. I can't keep doing that on an ongoing or unlimited basis. So we need to chat about how to move forward from here."

"We built our entire setup around certain **agreements**—this apartment, this move," I say, my voice rising. "Now you want to just rewrite everything? Do you even remember any of them?"

He doesn't answer.

My throat goes dry.

I push past him toward the door. "I need air. I need to get out of here."

"You can't just walk out," he says, stepping in front of me. "You're upset. This isn't the time."

"**No**," I say, my voice hard but trembling. "**You** don't get to tell me what I can and can't do." I grab my bag.

My breath's shallow. My body's shaking.

But my legs carry me forward. "**I'm going.**"

I grab my coat and storm out, slamming the door behind me.

I step onto the streets.

Paris at night.

Golden streetlamps. Cool breeze. Cobblestones underfoot. But it all feels unreal. Like I'm drifting through a dream. A life that's not my own. And all of that in Paris—the most romantic city in the world.

How ironic.

*Where to, Sophie?*

*I don't know.*

I just started walking. Keep walking.

My legs move fast, powered by rage and something deeper—grief, maybe.

*Should I just go back to New York?*

*But wouldn't I always wonder if I gave up too quickly?*

*And where would I even go?*

My apartment's unavailable—rented out for the next three months. My furniture's in storage. My life is suspended in midair with no real landing spot anymore.

And then there's the part that stings more than I want to admit: I think about everyone I told I was moving to Paris. At SPARKS. At my building. The farewell hugs. The excitement.

***How embarrassing.***

I'm usually the blunt one. I don't need to be liked or understood by everyone around me. But for once, I care what people would say.

What should I even tell them if I end up going back to New York after just two days?

That Adrian turned into a different person within the first twenty-four hours of my arrival?

That I couldn't handle it?

That I just ran?

Admitting that feels... shameful.

And the worst part?

No one would even understand.

Hell, **I** barely do.

All of this would fall back on me.

I'd be the unstable woman. The girl who moved across the ocean for love and couldn't make it work. The insane one who left Paris after only twenty-four hours, after she`d been planning a future with someone for months.

**Not him.**

Not the broken promises or the blurred boundaries.

**Just me.**

And honestly, I'm in no physical state to make good decisions right now—especially not ones this big.

So maybe it's not just that I care too much about everyone else's opinions.

Maybe it's that... I'm not entirely certain of my own.

And still... the question won't leave me:

*Should I just go?*

Eventually, I stumble into a tiny wine bar on the corner—warm, dim, the kind of place where no one asks questions. It's half full: couples tucked into corners, groups of friends laughing over small plates and clinking glasses.

I slide onto a stool at the bar.

*I shouldn't drink.*

But I do.

One glass. Then two. Then three.

The alcohol hits hard and fast.

I glance around.

I'm alone at the bar, and everyone at the tables is having fun. No one notices the unraveling—too busy enjoying their night.

Adrian's name lights up my phone.

Again.

And again.

I don't answer.

I can't.

*I'm not ready.*

I stare at the candle flickering on the bar for a moment, then slowly reach for my phone. My fingers hover. Then I tap **Eliyah**. He, of all people, would be honest with me. He always is. And he'd told me I could call him any time, and it was afternoon in New York.

"Hey, Sophie love," he answers, light and bright.

"Is this a good time?" I ask.

"Absolutely. I'm just wrapping up work for today. Everything okay?" His voice is like an anchor. And suddenly, I'm crying. Silent, unglamorous tears slide down my cheeks. "No," I whisper. "I don't think so."

"Oh no. What happened, Sophie?" he asks, instantly serious.

"I'm sorry. I didn't plan to start crying right away. I actually just wanted to get your perspective on what's been happening here."

"Stop apologizing immediately, love. Don't be sorry. I'm glad you called. What are friends for? Tell me!"

"I don't even know where to start..." I say, my voice catching in my throat.

"I'm just—**so** lost. Adrian brought Aurélie up again. Out of nowhere. Asked if I wanted to go to a party with her after just twenty-four hours of being here. Like it's no big deal."

I pause.

"And now, apparently, he's still in touch with even more exes. After promising there was no one else. After **all** those conversations where I made it clear what I needed to feel safe and he promised he'd be okay with it."

I swallow hard.

"He took back some of the other things he'd promised me, too. And when I tried to talk about it—**really** talk—he told me I was unstable and irrational and shouldn't make such a big deal out of it. Said I should go see a therapist.

Like I'm the problem.

Like I'm out of my mind for reacting at all." My voice cracks.

"Excuse me?" Eliyah blurted out. "I know you, Sophie. I **see** you. And you are not irrational. If anything, he is being irrational right now. Don't let him tell you otherwise."

"I just got here. I'm exhausted, you know."

"Of course you are. Where are you right now?"

"Not sure. I ran outside. Didn't know where to go. I'm sitting in some bar, alone."

There's a pause.

Then his voice shifts—sharper. "What the fuck. Sophie, this isn't okay. You know I've been very understanding of Adrian for a long time. But you moved your whole life for him. You've gone through a lot. And now he's playing these games?

No. No more excuses. It's his job to make you feel safe and welcome right now. Not to let you wander through the streets of Paris late at night, alone and crying."

I choke out, "Thanks for saying that. You have no idea how much it means to hear it."

He exhales. "I'm sorry, love. But something's really off."

"I know," I whisper.

He pauses. "Do you need anything? A hotel? A flight? What can I do?"

"No. I'm old enough. I need to take care of this myself.

Also: you know that making the wrong choices haunts me. I'll stay until I'm 100 percent certain this isn't worth holding onto. Right now, I don't know that yet. I'm just really confused."

I pause for a second. "And you've done so much already just speaking to me right now. Just telling me you see me. That I'm not irrational. I love you."

"Love you too. But—are you sure you don't want to just leave?"

"Yes, that would be too impulsive.

And please, don't tell Rani, okay? I don't want to worry her."

"Okay, I won't. Just promise me you'll be careful. And call me if you need anything. I'm here for you."

I nod even though he can't see me.

"Are you still there?"

"Yes. I promise."

"Good. Get out of that bar now. Go to a hotel or home. Wherever feels right."

I hang up.

Stare into the empty glass. *Home.*

I wasn't even sure where that was anymore. But a hotel would be costly, and staying somewhere else would likely escalate our fight even more.

So I type

**Me:** Heading back now. See you in a bit.

The walk back feels like moving through a fog. Like I've stepped out of my own body, watching someone else's life.

When I finally open the door, Adrian's waiting. His face is cold. "Where the hell have you been, Sophie? I called you a million times. I was about to call the police."

"The police? Why would you do that? I'm not as irrational as you think, you know. I was at a bar."

"At a **bar**?" he shakes his head.

"Who the fuck do you think you are, Adrian? **You** don't get to tell me what I should or shouldn't be doing!" I say firmly.

"So, drinking was your solution? Wow, Sophie. Just wow. This isn't normal," he says. "You know, I'm actually starting to think you might have an issue with alcohol. Wasn't your mother an alcoholic? You should know better. Be a bit more careful."

My body starts shaking. My knees weaken again.

"Stop it now," I whisper. "I can't fight any longer. And I don't have the energy to argue over your accusations or past flings anymore."

I turn to him. "You know what, Adrian, go see your women. All of them. I don't care right now. I just need to rest."

He doesn't react, just stays in the living room.

I go to the bedroom alone.

It's the second night we sleep apart.

And this time, the silence feels like a point of no return.

*

I wake up with a headache. Just stare at the ceiling for a while —lifeless.

After what must be half a day, I finally manage to pull myself outside for a short walk—just a lap around the block—but it still feels like I'm dragging my body through fog.

Grocery shopping? Too much.

Cooking? Forget it.

Even making the bed feels like climbing a mountain in slow motion. I can't shake the feeling that I'm trapped inside someone else's life.

***I crossed an ocean for this. But nothing here feels like mine.***

By the time I get back home, Adrian is already there, sitting in an armchair, his laptop on his knees. "Sophie," he says. His voice is clipped. Too calm. Too measured. "Can you come over here for a second? We need to talk."

I blink up at him—my stomach knots. "Again?"

He nods.

I curl up on the couch across from him.

He takes a breath. "Yesterday… I saw some serious red flags in you."

My body stiffens.

"I said it already, but I'll say it again. You might need help from a therapist." He seems detached. Too detached. "I know you don't think so, but you don't see yourself. I do. And I love you. I only want the best for you.

You seem emotionally unstable—troubled.

The way you reacted yesterday? It wasn't normal.

Honestly… it seemed kind of crazy.

And the alcohol worried me too. With your family history, you need to be careful."

A numb sadness spreads through me like anesthesia. "I'm not crazy," I say, barely above a whisper.

He doesn't respond.

"I'm struggling, yes. But there's a difference." I sit up a little, grounding myself. "I just froze my eggs. My body's still recovering. My finances are falling apart. And the person I'm supposed to potentially marry in just a couple of months—to get a visa, to build a life—just turned into a complete stranger."

My voice shakes. "I just moved to another country for us. And I did that based on promises. On trust. And you just… changed your mind, like our plans meant nothing."

He doesn't flinch.

My voice catches. "I honestly don't know who you are anymore, or what to believe… How, Adrian?

How can you expect me to just be okay with all of that and not react in any way?"

He sighs like he's been patient. "I just mentioned that a friend might be moving to Paris. I was being transparent with you. Isn't that what you said you wanted? Usually, transparency builds trust, doesn't it? That's how it works for normal people. And that's what I'm worried about. You don't see things clearly right now. Why are you twisting everything?"

I lift my eyes to him. "You call it transparency, Adrian, when you're really crossing boundaries. Breaking agreements. Then calling me crazy for reacting like a human being."

He folds his arms and exhales sharply, shaking his head like he's exhausted by me. "I don't know how to explain this to you anymore."

"What exactly made me crazy, Adrian?

That I didn't scream at you?

That I walked out instead of lashing out?

That I needed space to breathe?"

There's a beat. Then he says it: "It was the look in your eyes. The way you stormed out. You looked... off. Like, really off. I'm just being honest. You didn't seem like yourself. Kind of crazy —out of your mind."

My breath catches. "**The look in my eyes**," I repeat. "You're diagnosing me from **the look in my eyes**?"

"I'm just watching out for you, Sophie. Just trying to be honest. I mean... no judgment here. I get it. You did have a troubled childhood, and you told me you went to therapy once."

"Now, you use my family history against me and shame me for having gone through therapy?"

"I'm just trying to take care of you, Sophie."

I take a deep breath. "Adrian... none of this makes sense," my voice shakes. "**What on earth is going on with you?**"

I press my palms into my thighs, grounding myself, holding back the tears.

He stares at the floor.

"Wait a second—Could it be that this is just too much for **you**?

Are you maybe sabotaging us? Is this your fear kicking in again?"

My voice softens but doesn't break. "The moment I arrived, Adrian, you were glowing. You were **so** fucking happy. I don't think I've ever seen you like that. Did that scare you? Are you pulling back now, trying to destroy everything out of panic again?

Because right after you were deliriously happy when I arrived, you suddenly switched into **this**."

Silence.

"I don't know," he says.

"Possibly... I'm not sure."

"Can we stop with that bullshit?" I ask. "**Please.** I need air. I need peace for once. This—whatever this spiral is—it's not leading anywhere. And I'm **drained**."

I search his face for softness. Some signal that he's still with me. "You asked me to come here. You said you loved me, and we'd do this together. So, can we at least give it a real shot before we burn it all down? Can you please just give me some time to recover from jet lag and the recent surgery and get settled in without constant tension?"

He hesitates.

Then, finally, quietly: "Okay. Let's give it a try."

I want to believe him. But the way he says it...

He feels a million miles away.

*Will he ever come back, or will things only get worse from here?*

CHALLENGE 22

# Limbo

We'd made it to some kind of fragile agreement—but something had undeniably shifted.

It felt like an abrupt gear shift. Like we'd suddenly dropped into an entirely different universe. One that felt cold, empty, and forced.

Adrian had changed into another person.

Or maybe he hadn't.

Maybe I was just seeing him more clearly now.

And he was obviously seeing me in a different light, too.

In the days that followed, he started looking at me like I was a stranger—someone who didn't quite match what he'd signed up for.

His eyes, once warm and full of praise, now scanned for flaws. Suddenly, everything I did seemed wrong: the food I ordered, the way I laughed at something on TV, and how I interacted with his friends. Even the way I moved too slowly during our runs—like my exhaustion was a personal insult. I mean, *how could I dare be tired if he wanted to run fast?*

He was still **trying**, at least outwardly. But barely.

And it hurt—so much—to watch him withdraw like that. To see the joy on his face flicker out during dinner, to feel his body stiffen when I got closer to him.

I could feel him pulling away, inch by inch, as if just **being** myself was somehow disappointing to him. As if he'd started measuring me against a standard I didn't even know existed.

And he continued painting me as the irrational one. Sometimes he'd say things he **knew** would hurt me, then act like I was being dramatic for reacting at all. Other times, it was more insidious—subtle comments about being "worried about my mental state," emphasizing that he just wanted to take care of me, when it clearly felt like the opposite.

The worst part was knowing that I hadn't really changed. I was tired, yes. But still me.

**He** had become someone else. **He** had shifted his expectations.

But when I tried to bring it up—gently, carefully—he'd scoff, roll his eyes. "Why would I be disappointed in you?" he'd say. "You're imagining problems again."

And I realized how it started messing with my head. How slowly but surely, I began to doubt myself, even if just for a second: *Am I maybe* ***really*** *just imagining all of it?*

But then, somewhere deep inside, another voice rose—the one who still knew: this wasn't just in my head. I felt it in my gut. The quiet, invisible erosion was real. And it wasn't coming from me.

The ground beneath us was cracking because of **him**.

And right now, I was the only one trying to keep it from falling apart.

*

*A couple of weeks later*

It was a warm summer weekend in late August.

Morning sunlight filtered softly through the curtains, illuminating my workspace in our living room. Documents, notes, and diagrams sprawled across the desk in organized chaos. I sat hunched over my laptop, eyes tired and blurry, rereading my investment proposal for what felt like the hundredth time.

This was **my shot**—if it went through, financial stability would be one less worry for the next few years. But my mind felt fractured, drained by everything that had happened during the last weeks and months.

Adrian and I'd been trying our best, but we were still in limbo. And the sharp, confident version of me—the Sophie from before

Paris—felt worryingly far away now, replaced by someone uncertain, anxious, and full of doubt.

Adrian had been out all afternoon. I'd asked him to give me space this weekend—I needed to focus; this presentation really mattered. So, he went off with some of his new friends to an event—some experimental, meditative mind travel.

When he finally returns, he drifts into the living room slowly, eyes glazed, movements heavy, as if gravity pulls harder on him than usual.

I glance up from my screen. "How was it?" I ask.

He stares past me, settling onto the couch opposite my desk. "Hard to explain," he says distantly, eyes focused somewhere beyond the room.

"But everything feels... **reset**. Like every decision from the past months has been wiped away. There's no solid ground anymore, just questions. I'm honestly rethinking **every choice** I've made. It's all erased."

A chill runs down my spine.

I straighten in my chair, tension tightening my shoulders.

"**Every decision got erased?**" I repeat slowly. "What exactly does that mean, Adrian?"

He shrugs, his gaze finally meeting mine with unsettling calmness. "Just what I said. It's all **erased**. It's like seeing everything with fresh eyes—no attachments, no history."

*He knows.*

He knows exactly how deep that fear runs—how the wrong choices have haunted me for years. We've talked about it over and over. I told him I've been trying to make the right ones, especially since we met. And lately it's only gotten worse—more loaded, and consuming. Every decision feels life-or-death now, and he's watching me carry that weight alone.

"Look," I say carefully, my voice edged with nervousness, "I don't want to pressure you, but that kind of comment, without context, really freaks me out. We've been struggling, but I think things have been better over the last few weeks. So, what does this mean for us now?"

His eyes harden, and a flicker of irritation cuts across his face like a shadow. "You're making this into something bigger than it is, Sophie. As always, interpreting things negatively and creating problems that aren't there. Who says this is even about us or you?"

He doesn't wait for a reply. Instead, he rises slowly, almost theatrically, his gaze never leaving mine. Something in his expression shifts—something colder, sharper.

His mouth curls into a faint smirk, but there's no warmth in it. Then he pierces me with his eyes and starts singing. Deliberate and measured:

"Sometimes I feel I've got to
Run away, I've got to
Get away from the pain
**You** drive into the heart of me..."

He turns away, walks into the kitchen, and starts washing the dishes while singing—his voice growing louder, carrying back to me with deliberate clarity:

"The love we share
Seems to go nowhere
And I've lost my light
For I toss and turn, I can't sleep at night

Once I **ran to you**
Now I'll **run from you**
This **tainted love you've given**
I give you all a boy could give you

Take my tears, and that's not nearly all
**Tainted love** (oh-oh, oh-oh)..."

My stomach knots.

I want to ask him *why*?

*What does that mean?*

*What do you want from me?*

But I don't. He'd never give me an honest explanation, and I won't give him the satisfaction. So, I just stare at my screen, vision blurring with unshed tears, the mocking melody wrapping around me like a chokehold.

That night, sleep eludes me.

I toss restlessly, an abstract anxiety clawing at my chest.

I check the time. *Three in the morning?*

I turn around, and my eyes land on his.

Adrian lies there. Eyes open and awake. Just staring at me.

I jolt. "**Oh my god**, you scared me just now. You're awake?"

Without missing a beat, he sings the song from earlier, in a deep voice: "**For I toss and turn, I can't sleep at night...**"

My eyes widen.

Then suddenly, he breaks into laughter—one of those unexpected, uncontrollable fits that start as a chuckle and grow into something louder, unfiltered.

His chest shakes beneath the covers, and his hand clutches the pillow like he needs it to catch his breath. "You should've seen the look on your face, Sophie."

My pulse races. "Wow. Really? You're being so fucking creepy right now, Adrian."

I just turn around, wait until he calms down, and try to sleep again.

*

When morning finally breaks, I move slowly. Each motion feels like wading through thick, resistant water.

I dress in silence, trying to find a rhythm, something grounding in the ordinary.

Adrian appears out of nowhere, already half-dressed, jacket slung over one shoulder. He doesn't sit, doesn't slow down. Just leans in and presses a quick kiss to my forehead, like I'm fragile. Like I might shatter.

His eyes skim over me with that familiar mix of pity and reassurance.

***I hate that look.***

I feel like a sick rescue pet from a shelter.

"Just... try not to get your hopes up too much, okay?" he says softly. "It's a big investment. Many people are trying to get in. And... you've been kind of behind with your work lately."

I nod faintly, but I feel it—a sharp, quiet sting deep in my chest. I don't say anything, though. I can't.

He hovers for a second, like he might take it back. But he doesn't. He just turns and walks out, the door clicking shut behind him with painful finality.

Of course, the interview is a disaster.

I freeze halfway through the first question. My words tangle. My brain goes blank, and when I finally manage to speak, I talk way too fast.

Nothing I say sounds like me.

Everything I say feels like an apology in disguise.

I can hear it in the interviewer's voice—the shift, the disappointment.

When it's finally over, I sit for a minute in the silence, barely breathing. Then I close my laptop and fold into myself, the shame flooding in fast. *Really? That was a weak performance, Sophie. Why? You can do so much better.*

By the time Adrian comes home, I'm already wrapped in a blanket on the couch, the TV playing silently in front of me, just to drown out the noise in my head.

He walks in like nothing happened.

Drops his keys. Slips off his jacket. Not a word.

He glances over, pausing for a beat—but doesn't ask. Doesn't come closer. Just disappears into the kitchen like the day didn't hold anything meaningful at all.

The silence between us fills every corner of the room. But I'm too numb to even care.

*

*Next morning*

Morning light spills across the tile, golden and gentle, like the city's trying to be kind to me. Paris murmurs softly through the open window—footsteps on cobblestones, the low groan of a delivery truck, someone humming nearby. The apartment smells like espresso and laundry detergent.

Inside, everything feels muted. Like I'm moving underwater. My body feels scraped out, like someone hollowed me with a dull knife.

I haven't slept. Not really.

Another restless night. One of many, recently.

This time, the memory of the interview clung to me like smoke—The words I'd fumbled, the way my voice had caught at the wrong moment. I'd replayed it over and over in the dark, trying to rewrite it in my head. But there was no fixing it now.

We get up to make breakfast.

I'm still in Adrian's oversized sweater, curled at the kitchen table like I'm trying to hold myself. My hands wrap around a mug of coffee, though I'd stopped drinking a while ago. It's cold now, bitter.

The half-eaten breakfast between us looks like we left in the middle of something. Bread crusts. Soft butter. Grapes, he rinsed and slid across the table without saying a word. Next to me is my iPad.

I'm taking notes.

Adrian gets up and leans against the counter, scrolling absently on his phone. His expression is unreadable. Not tense exactly, but... distant. Detached. Like he's already left the room but forgot to take his body with him.

He finally glances up. "Are you working on the investment proposal again? I thought that fell through?"

"Yeah, probably, I don't know yet," I murmur, nudging my laptop slightly—as if it might back me up. "Just trying to clean it up a bit. I know the interview didn't go great, but..." I pause, swallowing. "I heard from someone on the inside that I was actually one of the top three candidates. They've reached out to me a few times, encouraged me to apply. So... I still believe in my idea. I just hope it doesn't look **that** bad."

I try to sound neutral. Confident. Calm.

I don't want him to hear the desperation underneath.

He tosses a grape into his mouth and chews slowly. Then—too casually—he says, "It's funny. If you didn't keep telling me how smart and creative you are, I wouldn't even know."

I freeze.

"**What?**"

He shrugs, already turning away. "I'm **joking**, Sophie. Relax. You know jokes, right?"

But it's not funny. Not even a little.

I say nothing. Just stare down at the coffee I can't bring myself to drink, wondering when we started mistaking cruelty for closeness.

When he stopped being the one who believed in me.

Who praised my work.

Who stood by me.

And even worse—when I stopped expecting him to.

Adrian picks up a grape and walks over to me, his expression softening, voice slipping into that teasing tone he uses when he wants to press reset. "Here," he says, holding the grape to my lips like a peace offering.

I lean in to take it, lips parting, but just as my teeth are about to catch it, he pulls it back with a grin. "Try again," he says, mocking me with his singsong tone.

I blink, caught off guard, unsure whether to laugh or pull away. I go in again, and this time he moves the grape side to side.

I start feeling like I'm a toddler being coaxed into a game I didn't agree to. "Adrian..." I murmur, forcing a laugh that feels more like an exhale than anything close to joy. "Come on, this isn't fun anymore."

He chuckles, clearly entertained. "You almost had it that time. Go again."

By the third try, something about it feels off.

*Am I supposed to laugh or feel humiliated right now?*

I sit back, letting my lips fall into a flat line.

"You need to trust me, Sophie. Try again."

I don't move.

"You look so serious right now," he says, overemphasizing a pout, mocking my expression like it's cute, like his words and behavior are harmless.

"Come on, let's go out. Do something fun. You deserve a break after all that interview stuff. What do you want to do?" His voice gets a little too loud, too suddenly—like he's trying to overwrite the moment.

I hesitate, still catching up to the pivot.

The shift in tone is dizzying—too quick, too polished. Like someone changing masks mid-scene.

"Maybe just... go for a walk?" I suggest. "Palais Royal?"

"You got it," he says with a grin, snapping back into his charming self. "Haven't done that in a while."

He pauses. "But you need to take the grape. Trust me. I can see how stressed you are. I would never pull it away again." I look at him skeptically, then take the grape. "See?" he grins.

About an hour later, we walk through the park near Palais Royal. He holds my hand as we stroll through the tree-lined paths. Points out dogs with strange gaits. Makes lazy jokes about the tourists crowding the benches. The sun filters down in gold slices between the branches, warm on our shoulders.

I glance at him.

*No bad surprises? No hidden agendas or attacks?*

*Be careful, Sophie. You never know.*

We stop for coffee near the fountain and sit on a bench facing the water. A kid nearby throws a crumbled granola bar at a group of ducks while his mother scrolls on her phone, oblivious.

Adrian leans back, legs stretched out, coffee cup balanced on his knee, squinting into the light. "This feels good," he says.

And it does.

Sort of.

*

*Late September*

The air inside the little organic market on Rue des Martyrs smelled like fresh bread, citrus, and a hint of lavender soap. Wooden crates held artfully arranged vegetables, and soft jazz drifted from a speaker. A toddler in corduroy pants clutched a baguette like a stuffed animal while his mother debated yogurt brands.

Adrian pushed the woven shopping basket along, one hand tucked into his coat pocket. I trailed beside him, running my fingers along the edge of a display of local cheeses. "So," he said casually, glancing at a bundle of fresh basil, "what do you want for dinner tonight?"

I looked up. "Maybe a roasted veggie salad? Or sweet potato gnocchi with sage—like the one we did last week?"

"Mmm," he murmured, already picking up a jar of organic ricotta. "I was thinking pasta with smoked ricotta."

I blinked. "But... why do you ask if you won't even consider my suggestions?"

He shrugged, his tone still light but with that now familiar weight underneath. "Because I want things to go my way right now."

The conversation was clearly over.

He turned to admire the fresh pasta in the refrigerated section while I stood there, waiting.

A few aisles later, we arrived at the fruit section.

I stopped at the crate of Juliette apples—the ones I'd been pointing out for weeks now. Beautiful, pale red with flecks of gold, like watercolor brushed onto their skin.

I reached for one. "Let's finally try these," I said, cradling the apple in my palm.

Adrian leaned in, his breath brushing my temple.

"Don't," he said, resting a hand on mine. "We already had those. Two weeks ago."

I furrowed my brow. "No, we didn't."

He smiled softly, affectionately, like I was a forgetful child. "Yes, we did, Sophie-heart," he said, stroking a strand of hair behind my ear, fingers lingering. "I'm sure of it. You probably just don't remember. Let's take something else today, okay?" His voice was low, soothing. But the tenderness in it felt... slightly performative.

*We hadn't tried them.* I was sure of it. I remembered every apple we **had** tried because I'd been waiting for this exact one. I'd told him about it three times.

"Really?" I asked, studying his face. "I could've sworn we didn't."

He gave a noncommittal shrug, reaching for a bunch of dark purple grapes.

Then I turned back to the apples, hesitated briefly, and placed two gently into the basket. "Well, since I can't remember," I said evenly, "we might as well try them again."

"Sure," he replied, scanning the wine shelf. "Whatever you want, Sophie." He smiled as he said it, but his tone was light, too light—like a line rehearsed.

I glanced back at the apples resting at the top of our basket.

They looked almost too perfect there—like they belonged to someone else's grocery trip.

Someone who had made a different kind of home in this city.

*

The call came late in the morning, just as I stepped out of a little boulangerie in the 3rd arrondissement. I had a lukewarm espresso in one hand, a croissant I didn't even want in the other.

My phone buzzed with the US country code, and my stomach tightened before I even picked up. I already knew.

"Hi, is this Sophie?"

"Yes," I said, tucking the croissant under my arm.

"This is Jenna from the Designers Investment Fund in New York. I wanted to thank you again for your application and for taking the time to interview with us. We really love your work—but I'm sorry to say you weren't selected for the final round this year."

I stood frozen on the sidewalk, blinking into the pale Parisian light. "Right," I said, trying to keep my voice steady. "Okay."

She continued gently, "It was a very competitive process. But please know your ideas stood out. We genuinely hope you'll apply again when the next cycle opens—in a year."

"Thank you," I managed. I shoved my phone into my coat pocket, tossed my empty espresso cup in the nearest bin, and just stood there for a moment.

The sounds of Paris carried on like nothing had happened—bikes zipping by, the hiss of a coffee machine from inside the café, someone laughing a few steps away.

I started walking. No destination—just movement. Past shuttered boutiques, tiny bookstores, cafés where couples sipped vin chaud beneath heat lamps keeping them warm.

I moved like a ghost through a city I was supposed to be building a life in.

I knew the interview had gone badly. Yet, I hated that I wasn't even surprised. I hated that feeling of expected disappointment in myself.

*Where is the Sophie who could win anyone over, light up a room with her conviction, infect people with her enthusiasm, and make the impossible feel inevitable?* I could only hope she was still inside me somewhere.

By early evening, I ended up leaning against a stone railing near Pont Marie, watching the Seine catch the fading light in streaks of silver and smoke.

My phone buzzed.

**Adrian.**

I hesitated, then picked up. "Hey," I said quietly.

"Hey! What are you up to?"

"Not much. I didn't make the investment round." I paused. "Didn't you say you'd help, and know investors that would throw money at my brilliant idea—maybe you know of other options?"

"Not for the state you're in, Sophie. I mean, that fund you just applied for—they know what they're doing. You probably just need to improve your idea. Be better."

I stared at the water, stunned. "Wow. You know what, Adrian—never mind," I snapped. "Maybe I should just fly back to New York. At least there are people there who still believe in me."

I hung up. Let out a long breath. That felt... necessary.

A minute later, he called again.

"Hey, mon cœur." His voice had softened. "Are you thinking about leaving? Seriously? Don't. I'm sorry. Where are you right now?"

"Pont Marie. Just standing here. Looking at the river."

"I'm coming to get you."

"You don't have to—"

"I want to. Just send me your location." Then gently: "Do you have your blanket with you?"

"Always."

Twenty minutes later, his car pulled up.

He stepped out without a word and opened his arms.

I walked straight into them, let myself be held.

My face pressed into the familiar wool of his coat.

"You okay?" he asked, fingers brushing through my hair.

"No," I said honestly.

He didn't try to fix it. Just kissed the top of my head and opened the passenger door.

We drove in silence.

Paris flickered past in warm pools of streetlight, bakery windows still glowing, the quiet hush of early nightfall. Then he turned down a narrow side street I didn't recognize, parked near a hidden stone staircase. He took my hand and led me down to a tucked-away stretch of the Seine—quiet, removed, almost cinematic.

Adrian spread out my blanket on a stone ledge like it was a ritual. From his canvas bag, he unpacked a bottle of red wine, two glasses, and a crumpled pack of my favorite sour gummies.

He smiled softly, pouring the wine. "To you," he said, offering me a glass. "The smartest, cutest, and funniest woman I know."

The look he gave me was full of love and tenderness—it reminded me of the Adrian I once knew.

*Had it all been just a bad dream?*

*Had I gotten it all wrong?*

*Were we finally back to who we once were?*

I clinked my glass against his, my lips barely holding a smile. We sat there on the blanket, knees touching, sipping wine, and passing sugar between us like kids.

I didn't feel fixed. But for the first time in days, I didn't feel like I was falling either.

Later that night, back at the apartment, I opened the drawer in the hallway to toss in my keys—and paused.

*Our grocery receipts.*

I pulled out the stack and flipped through them. Granny Smith. Red Delicious. Braeburn...

Not a single Juliette.

*I knew it! We'd never bought them before.*

*

*October*

I walk along the Seine, coffee in hand, watching the water ripple under the pale autumn light.

I sit down on a bench.

For the first time in years, I feel the urge to write.

Not for work. Not for clarity. Just for me.

I probably haven't done this since I was fifteen, when I was stuck at home, no one to talk to, pouring everything into my notebooks like they could carry what I couldn't.

This moment feels eerily similar.

I reach into my bag, pull out the flower-covered booklet I brought in New York. Some of the petals on the cover remind me of the ones Rhea always used to press into my palm.

*Rhea.*

Just the thought of her warms something in my chest.

I uncap my pen. Take a breath.

And start.

> Adrian and I've kept cycling through ups and downs for weeks now.
>
> He invents problems out of nowhere, and I constantly defend myself against his accusations.
>
> One day, he told me, "I don't think you're a family person."
>
> As if he knew me better than I knew myself.
>
> He listed qualities I didn't even recognize—complained I was antisocial, unwilling to compromise, hard to integrate into his life here, and that none of that was surprising with my family history. He said he was worried it would never work with someone like me, but he'd be willing to try because he loved me so

much, and he knew none of this was my fault; it was just due to my upbringing.

Another day, he claimed he was worried I had a drinking problem. Again. "Literally every person with an alcohol issue denies it, Sophie," he told me. "You of all people should know."

Then he circled back, yet again, to our most heated topic—non-monogamy. Said I'd lied. That I'd never be open to it. That I never was.

Even though I'd told him more than once, "It depends on the context. I just need a setup with clear boundaries. I've always been honest about that."

But he didn't listen. He never does.

Everything is filtered through his lens.

He builds entire narratives out of random assumptions and projections. And somehow, his version of me becomes more real to him than anything I say.

Whatever I do, whatever I say, and however I try to say it—it's wrong. So, most of the time, I don't even argue with him anymore. I sometimes even agree or apologize, not really knowing why or for what. Just for the sake of harmony. Just so that we can move on already.

I'm barely holding it together. My creativity is gone, I'm stuck with my business, I'm running out of money, and I'm alone with all of it.

Each time I try to build something of my own here —to make a friend, go to an event to network, take a step toward independence—there's a reason I shouldn't.

He needs me for something.

There's dinner. A conversation. A surprise.

Always just convincing enough to make me cancel.

Always something that makes it feel like **I'm** the one being selfish if I push back.

And I never know what to expect next. Adrian swings—warm, then cold. Affectionate, then aloof.

Praising, then subtly tearing me down.

I keep trying to get my footing, but the ground keeps shifting beneath me.

I'm not sure whether it's him, me, or both of us. But it feels like he's building a world around me that I can't make sense of. Slowly, quietly.

A world that is isolating. Confusing. And all about him. Like I don't quite exist in it.

What scares me most is that I don't feel like myself anymore.

This doesn't feel like **my** life.

But at the same time, I can't even imagine another one.

So where does that leave me?

I feel like a walking contradiction.

I ask myself, 'What's left? What do I even have without him?'

And the moment I do, shame floods in.

Shame that I've lost control.

That I've lost myself.

That I actually believe the only thing I have is some guy who doesn't even treat me right.

Shame that I'm not telling anyone.

That I'm thirty-eight and still here, asking these questions.

I should have it together by now. **Shouldn't I?**

In the first few weeks, I'd already wondered if, maybe, I should just leave.

But I was afraid to make the wrong choice. And then Adrian would do something sweet. Or I'd remember the way we were. So I held on to what my heart wanted.

And I'd convince myself 'This is just a rough patch. It'll pass.'

Now, two months in, I'm not even sure I could leave —Even if I wanted to.

I'm too depleted.

Too confused to make a clear decision.

I used to think, 'Just recover first, Sophie. Then you'll know what to do. Don't make a hasty decision you'll regret later.'

But I don't seem to be recovering with time. On the contrary.

It started probably two weeks ago.

My body began sending signals—subtle at first, then impossible to ignore.

My mind started fogging over. Now, when I walk, I sometimes suddenly feel like I'm swaying on a boat that won't stop rocking.

I have headaches. Dizziness. No appetite. Insomnia.

And this strange, bone-deep cold that no blanket can fix.

I feel emotionally starved—untethered from any sense of safety or warmth.

Every step with Adrian feels like walking on eggshells. I'm doing everything I can to hold the relationship together—not even sure why—terrified that if I drop the ball, even for a second, it will all fall apart. Like my life depends on it.

**Why do I do this to myself?**

Maybe it's because, despite everything—**still** —there's this inexplicable bond.

Something that logic can't touch.

Something that feels like home. Like family.

Adrian, once upon a time, **really** saw me. He was strong enough to hold me in a way no one ever had before.

Deep down, I'm afraid this won't end well.

Maybe I already know—it's unraveling.

But I can't forget the magic from the beginning.

That feeling of **belonging**—to someone, somewhere.

Of not having to perform, or shrink, or explain.

Just being **more** of myself—and being loved for it.

Desired for it. Praised for it.

The way he looked at me, like I was the only person on the planet.

In a world where everyone feels replaceable, I was **chosen**. Unmistakably.

All the noise in my head went quiet. Because I **knew** we belonged.

Like magnets. We could take on the world—together.

So yes, I'm still holding on.

To hope.

To memory.

To the version of us that felt like home.

Like everything I ever missed.

And I'm not ready to give that up.

Not yet.

**I can't.**

*

*A couple of days later*

Adrian turned the lights off. We both lay there in the dark. "Do you think it's weird we're not having sex?" he suddenly asked. "I mean, it's the **one** thing that always worked between us."

"Yeah," I admitted. "It's definitely different. But not necessarily a problem. I mean, it's just been a week. I figured you might be more stressed or something. Are **you** okay?"

He shrugged. "Yeah, I'm just really busy with work right now."

I knew it couldn't be just that. But I didn't want to make it worse by overreacting, so I kept quiet, hoping we'd naturally find our way back.

But the time was never right to bring it up again, and his affection didn't return. Then one night, as we cleaned up after dinner, he opened another drawer and pulled out a medium-sized black box I hadn't seen before.

"What's that?" I asked.

"Just sex toys," he said, casually opening the box, revealing around a dozen colorful objects. "Ones I used to use—with other women."

I blinked. "You're kidding."

He didn't look up. "I don't see the problem. They're just toys. I kept them in case we want to have fun with them at some point. Don't make such a big deal out of it."

I stood frozen by the sink, a plate in my hand. "I will **not** let you use toys on me, or put something inside me that has been inside another woman before," I said, my voice firmer than I intended.

"We'll see about that," he said lightly. "I might just use them one day. Maybe you won't even notice it."

"Why would you even say that?" I asked, feeling something twist in my stomach. "Why do you push my boundaries like this, Adrian? Can't you see how uncomfortable this makes me?"

He looked at me and smiled. "Relax. It was just a joke."

But it wasn't. It never was.

Then came the dream.

He'd told me before that he could control his dreams—steer them, even shape them using a technique called lucid dreaming. That night, I woke to him shifting beside me, whispering something, his breath warm against my neck.

In the morning, I asked, "Did you dream?"

He grinned. "I did. A sex dream. About a strange woman."

There was a gleam of mischief in his eyes, but it didn't land the way he wanted. It just sat in my chest like a stone. If he could control his dreams, it meant this wasn't random. It wasn't even subconscious. It was a choice, made while lying right next to me.

I didn't feel exactly betrayed—that would feel kind of ridiculous, since it'd just been a dream—I just felt... hollow, like I was like watching someone play a game I wasn't part of.

I didn't know how to bring it up without sounding irrationally jealous or petty. What could I say: *You don't want to sleep with me, but then you fuck other women in your sleep, while lying next to me?* That sounded crazy, even to me. So, I said nothing.

I just tucked it away with all the other moments that didn't feel right, stored in the back of my mind.

Meanwhile, I noticed Adrian started looking at other women when we were out—long, lingering stares that made my skin prickle.

He also spoke more about Aurélie and other exes who were still in his life. And he casually mentioned open relationships, like he was setting the stage. "I think I might want to be in an open relationship again someday, and I wonder if we'll get to that point soon," he said once, as if warning me not to get too comfortable with our monogamous setup.

I couldn't quite put my finger on it—but I felt like I was constantly in silent competition. With exes. With fantasies. With the idea of freedom he'd once had. As if our relationship, as if monogamy was a cage, and I was the one holding the key, keeping him trapped.

Slowly and steadily, the anxieties grew, and the pressure built. Then, eventually, came the thought I couldn't shake: *What if I just gave him what he wants?*

All our fights had started with him feeling cornered—because of Aurélie. Could it be that all he needed was openness?

Could it solve everything if I managed to open myself to the idea? Maybe it would ease the pressure.

Maybe, if he had the space to explore, he'd stop pulling away from me. Perhaps it would save us.

*'If he knows he has that freedom,' I told myself, 'maybe he won't even need it.'*

*Are you being insane for even thinking this right now, Sophie?*

*Maybe. Probably.*

*But what other option is there? Nothing else has fixed us.*

Yes, it was a gamble. A last attempt. A desperate one. But it would bring us clarity—either we'd finally make our relationship work or end it altogether.

I wasn't sure whether this was openness or a quiet form of giving up.

*Was I being brave or foolish?*

Maybe both.

CHALLENGE 23

# You've Never Been <u>This</u> Woman Before

It was a gray, chilly October afternoon in Paris when I called Rani.

I had just picked up a coffee from my favorite little café on Rue Saint-Paul—one of those quiet corners of the Marais where the tables spill out onto the narrow sidewalk and people linger for hours, smoking, talking low, watching the world move past.

I sat down at one of the corner tables, clutching the warm cup between both hands like it could steady me.

The metal chair scraped loudly against the stone pavement as I pulled it in.

I tucked one foot beneath me, glanced up at the cloudy sky, and hit call.

She picked up almost instantly. "Hey girl," she said, her voice warm. "How's Paris?"

"Still beautiful. Still gray. How are you? Is this a good time to talk?" I asked, trying to sound lighter than I felt.

"Yes. I'm good! Actually, great," she said brightly. "Rhea and I just made a fort out of every blanket we own. But, we miss you, girl."

Just then, I heard a tiny set of footsteps and a loud, dramatic voice in the background. "SOPHIE! WILL YOU COME VISIT US AGAIN SOON?" Rhea yelled, stretching the word *soon* like it was part of a musical.

My heart squeezed. I smiled, staring down at the pale swirl in my coffee. "Yes, sweetheart. It won't be long."

"Alright, baby, go play for a bit," Rani murmured off to the side. Then, back to me, her voice soft but sharp with intuition:

"What's up, girl? I can hear it in your voice. Something's going on."

I hesitate. "I'm okay."

Then, more honestly: "Actually... I don't know if I'm okay."

"Talk to me," Rani says.

I lean back in the chair, watching a cyclist glide through the slick morning light. "It's Adrian. And the open relationship conversation—again."

A pause. Not silence. Just space.

"I thought you shelved that," she says. "Wanted to focus on other stuff."

"So did I." I exhale. "But it's circling in my head. Again, and again. Before Adrian, I was genuinely curious to try it someday, remember?"

"Yeah, you liked the idea of freedom. Exploration. Control. You just never knew if it was something you could **actually** live with."

"Right. But now... It's like Adrian's giving me no choice. No matter what he said in the beginning, he's obviously made for it. He radiates it. And I keep asking myself: if I know that but am not sure if I want or can do it—why am I still here trying to build a relationship with him?"

"You know why," she says gently.

I run a finger around the rim of my coffee cup. "I mean, we know plenty of people who thrive in open relationships—look at Eliyah—and that's great. Good for them. Truly.

But we also know other cases, right? We have a couple of girlfriends who initially said they were okay with it, but then they weren't. Because it wasn't really okay—it was fear.

Fear of losing someone. And I just... I'm starting to wonder if I'm doing the same."

"Yeah," she says. "I get that. And look, I'm all for people doing whatever works for them, too. You know that.

"But I'm also a feminist. And when open relationships become the default in cities like New York—and women are going along with them just to keep their partners from leaving—that's not freedom. That's pressure. Wrapped in shiny packaging, with a fake freedom label.

It's patriarchy all over again, just sold in a new way. You should be able to choose what you really want, not what you are supposed to want to fit the mold of a modern woman!"

"But Rani, the thing is that I honestly don't even know what it is I want at this point. I don't know if I'm scared because it's new, because it's bad timing, or because it's genuinely wrong for me.

What if I just need to push past the discomfort?" I wonder.

"That's fair," she says. "But trust your body, too. What happens when you picture him with someone else?"

I don't even hesitate. "My stomach caves in."

"There's your answer, babe. You can't build something solid if one person's just swallowing discomfort to keep the peace."

I press a hand to my chest. "I love him. A part of me just wants to see him happy."

"I know," she says. "And that's **exactly** what makes this so hard. But love doesn't mean reshaping yourself until you disappear."

"I know. I **know** that," I whisper. "It actually feels **awful** hearing you remind me of that. *Like, **really**, Sophie? Do you really need to be reminded of that?* ***God!***"

A pause.

"I'm just scared, Rani. In a very irrational, existential, all-consuming way. Scared that if I say no without trying, I'll regret it. That I didn't give it everything I had."

I swallow hard.

"I don't usually struggle like this. You know me.
I normally know what I want. I'm decisive. Grounded.
But right now? I feel pathetic. I'm so fucking tired.

Tired of trying to say the right thing. Do the right thing. **Be** the right thing.

I don't even know what's mine anymore. What I want. What's real."

Rani is quiet for a beat. Then her voice softens. "Sophie. You're not pathetic. You're just exhausted. And apparently trying really hard to stay true to yourself while someone keeps tugging the floor out from under you."

She exhales. "Here's what I'll say:

If you say no, yeah—it might all fall apart.

But if you say yes, and you're not really okay with it?

An important piece of you might start to go quiet.

And you might notice it too late."

**Silence.**

My throat closes up.

I listen to the café noise around me: metal spoons clinking, a baby fussing, a man adjusting his coat.

"Choose the risk you can live with," she says.

"The one that lets you stay closest to yourself.

And no matter what—try, walk away, pause—I'm here. Always."

*

That night, as Adrian and I settled into bed, I took a deep breath and pushed past the tightness in my chest.

"If you want to explore something with someone else," I said, steadying my voice, "let's talk about it. I think I could handle it. Or at least—I'm open to trying."

He turned to me, surprised. "Really?"

"Yes," I nodded. "I guess this is a make-or-break point for us. Maybe the only way to really know how I feel is to experience it."

"Are you sure?"

"I'm not sure it will work, I'm just sure I want to give it a try. **But** if we go there, it must be within the boundaries we agreed upon. No friends or people we see regularly. Only strangers. No repetitions. And it can't be a habit. It needs to be rare—no stretching of those boundaries. No discussion. That's all I can give.

And before the first time—when you feel like you want to give it a go—you'd have to let me know beforehand, so that I'm prepared."

Adrian's expression softened. He reached for my hand, his thumb brushing over my knuckles. "I see how much you're trying, Sophie. That you'd even consider this means a lot to me. Honestly, I don't want to be with anyone else right now. But knowing we can talk about it—it changes things. Maybe it will all fall into place now."

For the first time in what felt like weeks, the air between us felt easier. The tension in his body eased. I felt it in the way his shoulders dropped, how he pulled me a little closer.

The next few days were calm—strangely calm.

It felt like we'd found a rhythm again, like maybe we'd turned a corner.

*

*The following weekend*

We're in the car, headed to a luxurious seaside getaway with some of Adrian's friends—way out of my budget. But he'd begged me to come. "They're expecting you, Sophie. It'll look terrible if you back out now," he'd said. Then, quieter: "And I don't want to stay alone in my room. I'd be **sooo** sad," he added with wide eyes, much like a puppy trying to manipulate its owner.

So, I finally gave in.

It's a two-hour drive.

The low hum of a Beatles song spills from the car speakers, familiar and oddly melancholy.

I crack the window slightly, letting in a rush of cold air.

Then, out of nowhere: "Hey Sophie," Adrian says, way too casually. "Since you're more open to new experiences now... what about sleeping with friends? Wouldn't it be fun to have some friends in our circle to be more intimate with from time to time?"

My stomach drops. My hands clench in my lap. "**No**," I say sharply. I've already told you. That's not okay for me. Not right now, at least."

He tightens his grip on the wheel and flashes me a glance, like he wants to read my face. "Fine. But what about me sleeping with women and **then** becoming friends after? There are studies, you know—it can actually be a great way to build trust."

I stare at him, trying to keep my voice from cracking. "**Wooow.** Are you serious right now? Did you hear anything I've said? **Ever?**"

He shrugs. It's sharp. Dismissive. "I'm just saying—we could create something that actually works for **us**. Why cling to outdated conventions, now that you're finally open to exploring?"

"Because what you're describing doesn't work for **us**. It works for **you**." I feel my voice rising, try to breathe through it. "You're not listening, Adrian. Are you even aware that I'm in this relationship too?"

I pause, staring at the road ahead as the coastline starts to flicker into view. "Can we just have **one** weekend of peace? You begged me to come. And I just agreed to something you've really wanted for a long time. Why bring this up now? Why create the next conflict right away?"

He sighs loudly, dramatically. "It was just a **suggestion**, Sophie. A car chat. You're making it into a thing."

But I knew it wasn't just a suggestion. It was him stretching my boundaries without even flinching, **over and over again**.

I thought if I gave him what he wanted, maybe things would calm down. But it was obvious: If we'd stay together, Adrian would always keep pushing my limits, and I'd never find peace with him. *Would I really be willing to put up with that?*

At the hotel, Adrian disappeared into the group within minutes. Laughing, drinking, blending in with the ease of someone who always assumes he belongs.

I watched from the edges—his girlfriend in theory, but not in reality. He didn't introduce me. He didn't seek me out. I was just *there*. So, I decided to introduce myself. I walked over and joined his group of friends.

"Hi, I'm—"

"This is Sophie, my girlfriend," Adrian cut in.

"Right, didn't you just move here from New York?" someone asked.

"Yes, she did," Adrian answered again, quick and smooth.

"Wow," a woman said, raising an eyebrow. "Let her answer for herself, dude."

I flushed.

She was right. And the fact that a **stranger** realized something was wrong within a minute made it so much worse.

I hadn't even clocked it myself. Not in real time. Not until she did.

"No drink? Let's get you one, girl," she added, steering me gently toward the bar. "I'm Charlie, by the way." Then, after a pause, "Are you okay? You look a bit... I don't know. Did what I said bother you? I can be a little blunt."

I laugh. "Don't worry. All my friends are like that. No, it's just... he doesn't usually do that. I guess he's just really excited for me to meet everyone."

"Got it," she said, not entirely convinced.

And just like that, I'd lied.

To protect him.

To protect myself.

To make the moment a little less humiliating.

*What's happening to you, Sophie?*

*You've been through shit in past relationships—but you've never been **this** woman.*

The quiet one in the background. The one smoothing over weird moments so no one feels uncomfortable. The one covering for someone who's slowly chipping away at her voice.

Later, in the dim hotel room, I gently touch Adrian's shoulder. He flinches like I'd burned him. "You've been obsessed with sex lately, Sophie. Just... drop it."

I blink. My heart stings. "Can we talk? I thought we'd spend time together this weekend. **You** wanted me to come. I said yes —despite how expensive this is for me—because I thought it mattered **to you**. And now I feel like I don't even exist. There are six of us here. You haven't said a single word to me in **eight hours**."

He doesn't look at me. His voice is flat, distant. "I'm just socializing, making new friends. I just moved here and don't know many people yet. It's not always all about you, Sophie. End of discussion."

He flips off the lights and turns his back to me.

I stay still, staring into the dark.

*I'm always too much—and never enough.*

*My discomfort, inconvenient.*

*My voice, too loud.*

*My needs, a burden.*

*And my love?*

*Something he only appreciates if it looks exactly the way he wants it to.*

*Is this it?*

*If I stay, is this how it's going to be... forever?*

*

The next morning at breakfast, sunlight streamed through the hotel's tall windows, spilling across crisp white linens and clinking silverware. The dining area was warm, relaxed—too perfect, almost.

Adrian had said he was here to socialize—and so was I, now. I wasn't going to spend the rest of the weekend sulking over being sidelined. If he could enjoy himself, so could I.

I'd laugh with his friends, lean into the conversation, let myself have a little fun. I'd stop waiting to be seen by him and start showing up for myself instead.

Everyone was easy, open, and curious. We shared bits of stories while passing around baskets of pastries and bowls of fruit. For a moment, I let myself soften into it. I was actually having fun for once.

Across from me, Adrian stirred his coffee slowly, eyes tracking me like a storm brewing behind glass.

Then suddenly

—"Sophie, babe," he said, his voice overly bright, cutting through the conversation. He reached across the table with exaggerated cheer, plopping a pastry onto my plate. "Look! I saved your favorite."

I blinked at him, then smiled politely. "Thanks," I said, keeping my tone even before turning back to the person beside me. But I could feel his eyes still on me and a few minutes later, his foot nudged mine under the table. Then again. I looked up.

"Hey," he said, tilting his head, grinning in that too-big, too-obvious way. "Don't forget about **me** over here. Thought we were supposed to be together." His voice was playful, but sharp underneath—like a joke with something sour stuck to the edges.

"We are," I said gently. "I'm just... talking."

He let out a loud, theatrical sigh, flopping back in his chair. "Alright, fine. I guess I'll just talk to myself."

The table went quiet for a beat too long.

Then someone chuckled, trying to smooth it over.

I kept eating, trying to pretend my stomach hadn't just flipped.

After breakfast, as I stepped into the hotel lobby, he caught me by the arm. His smile was gone. "You're ignoring me," he said, voice clipped. "What are you trying to do—punish me?"

I stared at him, stunned. "Adrian. You can't keep swinging from distant to clingy and expect me to match your rhythm like it's normal. I'm doing my best here."

He scoffed. "You're being fake. What's up with all that performative friendliness—laughing too loud, flirting with everyone? You're not having fun. You're just trying to provoke me."

I felt the blood drain from my face. "I'm trying, Adrian," I said, barely above a whisper. "I'm **really** trying so hard to make this work."

But he just shook his head, like I'd failed a test I didn't know I was taking, and walked away.

I stood there in the middle of the lobby, sunlight pouring in through glass doors, people drifting past us with beach bags and sunglasses.

I felt entirely out of place in my own skin.

Everything I did was wrong. And no matter how many times I adjusted, it was never the right setting.

For a moment, I considered walking out—grabbing my bag, finding a train. But I didn't.

The weight of that decision—what it would mean, what I'd have to admit—was too much for now, too much for a rushed decision and the state I was in.

That night, while Adrian stayed downstairs laughing with the others, I slipped quietly into bed. I wasn't angry—just tired. In need of silence. A pause from the chaos.

I was about to fall asleep when the door opened.

**Adrian.**

He walks toward me—fast, determined. Then he leans in.

And without saying a word, for the first time in two weeks, he kisses me.

Intentionally. Lovingly.

It catches me off guard.

It feels strange. Sudden.

But his lips—his lips feel familiar.

For just a second, I remember.

All the good times.

The softness. The warmth. The version of us that used to feel like home.

My entire body longs for him. So badly, it hurts.

It wants to forget everything that happened.

Make it a bad dream that's over now.

Make all the good things return.

"You want me?" he whispers into my ear.

I nod.

Adrian doesn't hesitate.

He slides my top and thong off and immediately slips a finger inside me, deep.

My body **screams** for more.

But then—just as suddenly as he started it—he pulls back.

He stands up, walks to the door, and just leaves the room.

No turning back. No hesitation. No explanation.

"Adrian. **What the fuck?**" I shout after him, my voice sharp with disbelief.

"Are you serious right now?"

The door stays closed. Silence swells in its place.

My words echo into the emptiness he left behind.

I sit up, pulling the blanket over my naked body, chilled. Exposed. *What the hell was that?*

*Why would he come in, turn me on like that—and then walk out?*

A cold shower washes over my spine. And clarity sets in.

Right then and there, I know with absolute certainty:

This isn't just a rough patch.

It isn't miscommunication or mismatched needs.

It isn't about other women, or what I was willing to give—or not give.

**It isn't about me at all.**

This is about him.

Something is deeply, fundamentally wrong **with him**.

I thought this was love—but it's control.

I understand it now: the way he just reeled me in, only to abandon me again, couldn't be fear or confusion. It's a game.

It's deliberate. Evil.

And it hurts like hell.

After that night, I barely spoke to him. Not during breakfast.

Not on the ride back to Paris.

I didn't have the words anymore.

And I wasn't sure he deserved them anyway.

*

The Parisian city lights shimmer across the damp pavement.

The night air clings crisp against my skin as we walk in silence, our footsteps echoing faintly on the slick stones.

My legs are numb, my heart is heavy and every step takes effort. I have to push myself to keep on going. All the while, I don't even know why I keep walking or where we are headed at all.

Then Adrian breaks the silence. "Can we talk about the weekend?"

I glance over at him. "Okay."

"I've been thinking," he says, his voice low, steady, too controlled. "I'm concerned about something. I think you might be... sexually obsessed. Maybe also obsessed with domination over others. I think it plays a major role in your life. And I don't think it's appropriate."

I stop walking.

The world blurs for a second.

"**What?**" I say, my voice barely above a whisper.

"What are you even talking about?"

He turns to face me, hands in his coat pockets, posture relaxed—unnervingly so.

His eyes scan me like he's diagnosing something broken.

"At the hotel," he says. "One of my friends made that comment, you know, about how you have this magical power of influencing people with your presence, with your words.

The way you smiled, laughed—it felt... sexually charged. You leaned into it. It made me uncomfortable."

My stomach drops.

"That was a dumb **joke**," I say.

"And **he** brought that energy. I literally laughed it off. Also, on the way over to the coast, you told me you wanted to **fuck** your friends. But if a guy makes slightly sexually charged comments about me—that's crossing a line?

Wow, Adrian. I don't even know what to say."

Adrian's face doesn't move—stone still, his calm is icy, his voice like cut glass. "That's something entirely different, Sophie," he says evenly. "I want an open relationship like an adult. I just want to enjoy exploring my sexuality with different people. But I'm not sexually obsessed like you are. I don't use sex to manipulate or push others."

My pulse races.

*I'm so damn furious right now.*

"For instance, what about all the fantasies you told me about? There were... a lot of them. I've never had a girlfriend who talked about sex that much. You think about it constantly."

I take a step back, the breath punched from my lungs.

A cold weight settles inside me. "**We** enjoyed having a lot of sex—**both of us**. And you never complained about it once. On the contrary, you wanted to have sex with me, like **all the time**. And you **asked** me to tell you my fantasies. You wanted all the details. You said no judgment. You said that was intimacy and that I could trust you."

"I know what I said," he replies flatly. "But it became too much. You've been pushing me to sleep with you lately, even when I didn't want to. Even when I was exhausted."

"That is **not** true," I say, my voice breaking.

"You started the conversation, and I just asked if everything was okay. I **checked in**. That's not pressure, Adrian. That's being in a relationship."

But he keeps going. Calmly. Methodically.

Pulling scattered moments out of context like beads from a broken necklace—Citing looks, jokes, gestures, words from months ago.

As if he's building a case.

As if I'm on trial.

I'm speechless.

Numb.

Then,

I stare at him—really look—and something inside me goes still. Whatever softness, whatever safety or love I thought we had...

It's gone.

I can't even find the shape of it anymore.

It's like someone ripped the rose-colored glasses from my face in one violent motion.

And now I can finally see him. **Really** see him.

In his true shades.

**Very** dark ones.

A cold shock floods my body.

I still can't take my eyes off him. It's like watching a car crash in slow motion.

I don't recognize this man.

Nothing about him feels familiar. Or lovable.

His eyes are hollow.

His body moves like a stranger's.

Even his face—it's vacant. Empty.

Like the face I know has been erased.

And then

—Something clicks.

A slow, sharp realization settles in my chest.

Heavy.

Undeniable.

He's not **lying**. He's not performing.

He **believes** it.

This story he's been weaving in his head—he thinks it's real. That I'm not just a flawed partner, but a manipulative, sex-obsessed aggressor.

That my sexuality is control, my openness is seduction.

He's rewritten our intimacy as a threat. And in his version, **he's the one** being hunted. **He's** the victim.

This is him. The real him. Slipping into variations of reality, he's constructing himself. And maybe that's the most terrifying part of all.

We keep walking.

He keeps talking, but I stop listening.

And eventually, his narration becomes background noise, drowned out by my own inner voice.

Because right now, my instincts are screaming at me louder than ever, reaching, filling, shaking every cell in my body—a sharp voice inside me, clear and unrelenting:

***RUN. RUN NOW.***

I take a small step back. Then another. The cool air rushes into my lungs like relief.

And in that moment, I know it isn't just about leaving the conversation.

It's finally about leaving **him**.

CHALLENGE 24

# You Can Do It, Sophie

I sat on a bench by the Seine, fingers wrapped tightly around a paper cup of coffee gone lukewarm.

After everything Adrian had said yesterday evening—all those twisted accusations he attacked me with—I'd just gone silent.

I didn't speak another word the entire evening. Not angry. Not defensive. Just... done. Like my body had realized there was no more fixing. No more trying to explain.

Just the sudden weight of the truth, landing hard:

There was no coming back from this.

This morning, Adrian left for work without saying goodbye. Neither of us had reached out. No communication at all. And I'd decided I needed fresh air.

The wind tugged at my coat, and across the water, the boats drifted by like they always had—slow, indifferent.

Around me, Parisians moved with purpose, scarves tucked neatly, heels clicking against the cobblestones.

*Sophie, is this really happening?*

It felt like just yesterday when I'd pictured a life here. A future. Building something real—a relationship, a career, maybe a family. A home with someone I could be fully myself with.

Now, I was saying goodbye to all of it.

It felt unreal. And a part of me was still clinging to irrational hope. Like maybe if I just waited a little longer, things would soften and change course. I'd wake up and realize it had only been a bad dream.

But it wasn't. I knew that now.

My time in Paris—this version of my life, the dream of Adrian and me—it was over. **My heart ached.**

I knew what I had to do. I **had** to leave him. And I would.

But a part of me froze at the thought. Adrian wouldn't see this coming. Not really. And that scared me—not just because of what he'd say, but because I didn't know who I was dealing with anymore.

Would he try to stop me?

Would he beg, shout, twist things again?

Would he continue to abuse me verbally, or even worse?

My phone buzzes.

**Rani.**

I'd texted her earlier to call me when she had time. I know she'd be surprised. So far, I hadn't told her about all the things that were going on with Adrian, aside from our discussions about potentially opening our relationship.

I take a deep breath and pick up my phone. "Hey, girl. What's going on?"

"Hey Rani," I whisper. "You have no idea how great it is to hear your voice right now." My voice snaps on the last syllable. Then I spill everything—Adrian's behavior, the accusations, the way he pushed my boundaries, called me crazy and obsessive, and how something in me finally understood who he really was.

A pause.

Silence stretches.

"Oh god, Sophie," Rani finally says. Her voice is laced with quiet outrage. "This is awful."

Another pause.

"Why didn't you tell me sooner? I wish you had! I'm here for you, Sophie—always. You know that, right?"

I nod slowly, throat tight. "I know. I think I was just... overwhelmed. Maybe I didn't want to make it more real by saying it out loud. Maybe I didn't want to worry you. Or maybe I felt too ashamed, too scrambled in my own head to even know where to begin."

"This **fucking** asshole," she suddenly bursts out. "I'm going to kill him. How can he do that to you? **You**, of all people." Rani's voice quivers, equal parts fury and heartbreak.

"And then he walks around acting like some kind of saint—this 'humanist' who helps vulnerable families, women in need? Didn't he also lure you in when you first met by telling you he was this free-minded spirit who allows women to explore their sexuality without judgment?"

"Yes."

"What a **fucking** hypocrite. Puhh... I'm getting seriously furious over here." She catches her breath. "But this isn't about me. It's about **you**. Sophie, my love... I'm just so sorry this happened. I wish I were there with you right now. What can I do? Tell me."

My body starts warming up. "It honestly feels so good just to hear your voice. To talk to someone who loves me. Just tell me what you think."

"Well ... you see what this is, right? The way you've described it. I don't use the word lightly, but the pattern sounds... incredibly narcissistic."

"I know," I breathe. "I mean, obviously, I'm not qualified to diagnose anyone, so who knows. But yeah—that's what I've been thinking. Full-on narcissist, or at least traits that lean hard in that direction. And you know... It's not the first time I've dealt with something like this."

My voice is thinning. "It's just that with him... it caught me off guard. I didn't see it coming. Not like this, at least. I had doubts, sure, but I figured he behaved the way he did, mostly due to baggage from his past. Plus, all the signs appeared totally different this time. He was subtle. Way quieter. Way less obvious than the ones I dealt with before."

I pause.

"I just don't understand. Why is this happening to me **again**?

I've been **so** careful.

Is this my fault somehow? Should I have seen it sooner?"

"**No**," Rani cuts in instantly.

"Don't do that to yourself. Don't turn this inward. This isn't on you, Soph. I've watched you try so hard to protect yourself, to choose differently this time. You set boundaries, you checked your instincts, you **tried**. Really hard. It's not your fault he's been hiding behind a polished mask like a fucking king. We all bought it. I mean, I **defended** that man, for god's sake. I thought he was just wounded, trying to do better."

She stops for a second. "When you told me about your gut feeling, I should've listened harder. I should've taken it more seriously. Instead, I told you, you should step out of your comfort zone and overcome your fear. I'm so sorry, love."

"Hey," I say softly. "How could you have known? Don't do that to yourself either. I love you."

"Look. You know I'm no expert," she says, "but when you texted me, you had some kind of emergency, I spoke to Lina, just in case. She knows a therapist in Paris—Michelle. Lina swears by her. She says if it's urgent, Michelle can probably fit you in today. Maybe it's a good idea to talk to her before you confront Adrian with anything. Better to be careful."

"Yes, that'd be great. Thanks, Rani."

"I'll text her right now." Rani's voice softens. "Promise me you'll go see her before speaking with him. Don't tip Adrian off either. If he senses you're pulling away—"

"I know," I cut in. "I'll stay quiet before I make plans and talk to him."

After I hang up, deep sadness hits me like a wave. I feel strange—like I'm watching myself inside the classic story of "the abused woman." The woman who's been taken apart. Not loudly, not in any obvious way. Slowly, subtly, and quietly. Worn down, cornered, and afraid. Afraid to end it, afraid of what might happen in that moment. Afraid of someone I once trusted. Someone I once loved.

It's still hard to accept how far things have shifted. How it all crept in without me noticing what was really going on.

But in the middle of that grief, there's also a strange sense of gratefulness—for the toxic heartbreaks before Adrian, that in their own brutal way disillusioned me, and at least allow me to see clearly now.

It's never been exactly like this. They always hide in a new shell. But now that it's all unraveling, it's still enough to recognize the pattern. To understand the mechanics behind it. To see what's happening right now—and have the strength to end it. Maybe not early enough. But at least not too late.

Because I know from experience: when someone with narcissistic traits flips—from love-bombing and idealizing you to slowly breaking you down, devaluing, and discarding—there's no way back.

There never is. I learned that the hard way.

From that point on, it only gets worse and it's all downhill.

And in a weird way, that makes it easier. Because I know now with absolute certainty: **those good times I'm holding onto will never truly return.** He'll never look at me the same way again.

If I stay now, I'll vanish.

No excuses, no other possible outcome.

And I'm not going to allow him—or anyone else—to do that to me ever again.

So I have to leave.

**Now.**

While there's still some part of me intact.

While I still remember the sweetness we had—before it gets too twisted, too buried under everything else.

Before I forget who I was before him. Who I worked so hard to become.

As sad as it is, it's, for once, without a doubt, the only right choice to make.

*

*A couple of hours later*

I'm in Michelle's office.

It's tucked inside a beautiful Parisian building—the kind with creaky floors and high ceilings that smell faintly of wood and time.

The space feels warm and oddly safe—coral-painted walls, hanging baskets overflowing with plants, a riot of colorful furniture that somehow doesn't clash but comforts.

I sink a little deeper into the brown leather couch beneath me, the material soft but slightly cold against my skin. My shoulders curve inward, as if folding around to protect something fragile inside me.

Michelle—chic and effortlessly elegant, mid-50s, with a gentle but grounded air—sits in a velvet armchair across from me. Her flowery silk blouse blends into the jungle of tall exotic plants behind her, as if she's part of the room itself.

"First of all, Sophie, thank you for being open with me," Michelle says. "I'm just so sorry this happened to you," she says, her voice soft but assured. "Unfortunately, it's all too common. You're **not** alone in this."

I clasp my hands together in my lap, gripping them tighter than necessary. Everything inside me feels oddly frozen—like I'm here, but hovering just slightly outside my own body.

I nod once, but my throat is too tight to speak yet. "What kills me," I finally manage, my voice breaking at the edges, "is that this time I went in with open eyes. I tried so hard to see things clearly and figure out whether he was being real. But I still failed to recognize what was happening."

Michelle tilts her head slightly, folding her hands. "Sophie. **Nothing** is wrong with you.

Even therapists can fall for people like that. And there are **many** very skilled people out there, hiding in plain sight—they literally surround us. Especially in urban and high-achieving environments."

For a second, I want to argue back, to point to every missed sign, every moment I didn't leave, although my gut told me otherwise, but all I do is let my shoulders drop a fraction. Just that small shift feels like letting go of a hundred pounds.

She pauses, then continues gently, "It could, however, be that you're a bit more used to those kinds of behaviors than many other people. Is it maybe something you grew up with? Something you were surrounded by and became used to?"

A shiver runs through me. "Yes... my mom—she's been diagnosed with many things... I'm not sure she was a full-on narcissist, but... she had zero empathy. She was extremely self-absorbed, pushed me around, and manipulated and gaslighted me all the time."

Michelle doesn't interrupt. She nods once, patiently, encouraging me to go on. "And your dad, if I may ask?" she says, her voice softer now.

I exhale through my nose, eyes darting to a spot on the floor. "I loved him more than anything. In my mind, he's a hero. I know... I idealize him **way** too much, but... out of those two, he seemed like the much better choice.

The one person to hold onto.

My light in the dark.

Sure, he was moody too, but I didn't see him that often, to be honest. And he disappeared when I was eight."

My voice grows quieter. "Before that, the few times he was home—when he wasn't traveling for work—he was just this hilarious, out of this world charming, fun person.

**Everyone** loved him. All the ladies were charmed by him. All my friends wanted a dad like him. With him, we were still respected in our neighborhood. After he left... we became social outcasts. Because of how my mom behaved."

I pause, twisting a ring on my finger. "And now that I think about it... my aunt sometimes called him a narcissist, but I figured she just said that out of anger because he'd left.

I was way too little to even know what that meant. And I loved him way too much to look at him that way, anyway."

Michelle offers me a warm, steady smile. "Okay. So maybe you are a bit more prone to finding partners like that. But it's not your fault, and it doesn't have to always be like that."

She leans in slightly, her tone firmer, more deliberate. "Sophie, you did everything you could. You navigated this situation as well as anyone could have. It's not on you! And you're here now, right?"

Something in my chest loosens.

Tears start rolling down my cheeks.

I wipe at them quickly.

"Thanks," I exhale. "It feels really good to hear that.

"So, Adrian—am I dealing with what I think I'm dealing with?" I ask.

Michelle's voice stays calm. "You mentioned the term already when you talked about your parents. I can't diagnose your partner from a distance, of course. But from what you've shared, yes—he shows strong narcissistic traits.

And maybe even more importantly, you're showing signs of narcissistic abuse. That's what you need to focus on now—rebuilding your trust in yourself. Ending the triangulation. Respecting your boundaries. Believing your reality. And letting go of the blame that was never yours to carry."

"What's triangulation?"

"It's a technique to get and intensify supply from multiple sources," Michelle says. "Narcissists sometimes subtly pull in other people who desire them—exes, flings, 'friends'—to keep you uncertain, off-balance, and making you feel like you're competing with other women for his attention. It's a way to provoke jealousy and stay in control while making you feel like you're overreacting."

I think of Aurélie and his other exes.

How deliberate it all seemed.

And how ridiculous I'd felt for feeling that way.

"They thrive on attention from many," she adds. "No matter how much you give, it's never enough. And when you push back? They gaslight you—say you're insecure, too sensitive, imagining things. But it's all part of the dynamic. It becomes extremely dangerous when a person like that is in an open relationship. It can be used as a very effective tool for destruction."

*So, it had never been about me.*

*And it had never been about sexual freedom or creating a relationship that fit both of us. It was just about getting validation from multiple sources—and making me doubt myself.*

I take a deep breath. "Wow. I'm not even sure how to move on from here," I say. "Obviously, things weren't as they seemed at all. How do I even begin to get over that?"

Michelle leans forward slightly. "Find more ways to break up the magic spell you felt in the beginning. Sometimes it helps to understand what you are to them—how they perceive you.

"See, at the core of narcissistic people is a fragile sense of self. They rely on others to feel whole—what I just called 'narcissistic supply.' It's not about loving the person, but needing what they bring."

I nod slowly. "Adrian always said he wasn't creative, artsy, and didn't have access to his feelings, like his brother Perry did. Perry died when he was young. He said his family praised those traits, and he saw those things in me."

Michelle gives a soft, knowing smile. "Right. Partners of narcissists usually fill a void, supply them with something. But it's important to understand that narcissists don't see or love you fully—they don't see you as a person, they idealize what you represent, what they want you to be, until it turns into fear or resentment. Then comes the devaluation."

I swallow. "Could it be that he genuinely believes the stories he's telling himself about me?"

"He might," Michelle says. "That's the thing. It's not always calculated. His version of reality might feel as real to him as this moment, sitting on my couch, feels to you. Whatever they construct, no matter how absurd it is, can become their reality.

They are not interested in truth, only what benefits them. And they can't tolerate facing their flaws, so they externalize them, push them onto you. Projection. Deflection.

It's about survival for them—but it can destroy you."

"So... did he **want** to hurt me?" I ask, barely above a whisper.

"That depends on the person. Some do, some don't. But it's not always the goal," she says gently. "Either way, when protecting himself means breaking you down, he'll do it because he can't face himself. His needs are **always** his priority."

I look down at my hands. It makes sense. Heartbreaking sense.

Michelle glances at her watch. "Sophie, I'm really sorry, but I have another client waiting. I wanted to see you at least briefly today, but we'll have to continue this another time, if that's what you want. You can text me, okay?"

"Sure," I say.

She pauses, then adds, "One last thing—don't tell him you think he's a narcissist.
He'll twist it or worse, and you'll walk away doubting yourself.
Just protect your peace."

*

It's only 3 p.m.—Adrian won't be home yet.

I go back to my bench by the Seine, the one that's slowly becoming mine. My place to think.

I sit there, elbows on knees, head in my hands.

*How do you end this, Sophie?*

It feels surreal to be afraid of Adrian. But it feels even more naive not to be. *Should I pack my things in secret? Just leave?*

My whole body tenses.

The idea of staying and being dragged into another toxic cycle makes my heart beat faster. I feel incredibly fragile right now. Like I'm the most vulnerable version of myself.

Without even thinking, I grab my phone and start searching for flights. My mind quietly packs a suitcase. I rehearse the escape. Step-by-step. Silent. Safe.

But then something stops me.

*Wait. No. Sophie.*

*You could do that, yes. But wouldn't it make all of this even more surreal? Even more traumatizing and weird?*

For a moment, I just sit there, watching the boats drift past —calm, indifferent—while my own pulse hammers in my ears.

Then, slowly, I lift my phone.

My hands are shaking.

*How do you end something without telling the whole story—just enough to protect yourself?*

I type.

> **Me:** Hi Adrian. What we have feels like it's coming to an end. We view relationships fundamentally differently—how we communicate, how we hold space for each other. I need something that feels equal, kind. A partner who asks questions, instead of throwing accusations

I pause. The screen blurs for a second. I blink it away.

> **Me:** I'm not feeling well. And I no longer see a future for us. I can't imagine building a family like this. There are things I'll always be grateful for, but I need to end this. Now.

His reply comes fast.

**Adrian:** I can't believe you're doing this. Are you sure? Is your decision firm?

**Me:** It is.

**Adrian:** Can we meet at the apartment, please? Let's not do this over text.

I hesitate a second. *It's going to be okay, Sophie.*

**Me:** Okay.

As I walk toward the apartment, memories crowd in.

The first trip to Paris. How alive I felt. How I believed this was the start of everything. The way we laughed—so sure the world belonged to us.

Now I'm returning to the same space, but everything's changed. He's no longer my partner. Just someone I need to say goodbye to.

I unlock the door. Inside, it's too quiet.

Then I hear it: the muffled sound of water.

I find him in the bathroom, shoulders hunched, silent tears mixing with the steam.

My anger falters. "Come out," I say gently. "Let me dry you off."

He steps out of the shower, shivering.

I wrap a towel around him like he once did for me when we said our goodbyes in New York. The roles reversed.

"I'm sorry," he says, eyes downcast. "I shouldn't have treated you like that." But there's something flat in his voice. Like he's repeating a line. Like, even now, he's not sure what he's apologizing for.

"What if we just... start over?" he asks.
"Forget this happened.
I can be better, I promise."
I shake my head.
"That won't work."
He pleads. "Just stay a little longer.
Let's talk. Let's figure this out.
You're the love of my life, Sophie.
Do you have any idea how much I love you?"

*Don't let him get to you...*

"Okay," I whisper.
"Let's get you to the couch now."
He reaches for me like a child.
"Come with me."
"I'm here," I say, running a hand through his damp hair.
"I'll come."
We lie on the couch, curled around each other.
His tears are warm against my skin.
"You feel like home," he says.
"With you, I was once the best version of myself.
The happiest version."

Maybe it's stupid. But I believe him.

"Yet now here we are. Both at our worst," I say.
His body shakes slightly.

For a moment, I let myself feel it.

The deep, complicated love I still carry.
The part of him that wanted to be better.
Who tried, in his way.
Who wanted to be a good man. A good partner.
Who truly loved me, in the only way he could love.

Grief settles in my chest like stone. Not just for what I've lost, but for him—for the man he almost became, but couldn't.

The man I once loved. The man I have to let go of—because he never really existed.

And that's a very specific kind of pain.
Hard to name.
Impossible to explain.

*

*Next day*

We're sitting on the bed. Not close—just... parallel.

Adrian's just come home from work, the weight of everything sitting heavily between us. He begged for one last talk before I head back to New York the next day.

He exhales, eyes down. "I talked to Gabriel about some stuff. And I get now that I behaved like I had the moral high ground when we talked about open relationships," he says slowly.

"And to be honest... I still feel that way." He glances up, almost apologetic. "That's the part that bothers me."

His face is drawn, like he's trying to show sincerity. "I understand, in theory, that it's not okay to feel superior in a conversation like that," he adds.

"I just don't **feel** it."

I stare at him.

My mouth wants to move, to say something—anything—but nothing comes.

He looks at me then, wide-eyed and searching, like I hold some answer he's desperate for. **"What's wrong with me?"** he whispers.

I don't know. Is this reflection? Or just another manipulation in disguise?

I can't tell anymore.

And even if it's genuine

—It doesn't matter.

I'm done.

We're done.

But then, right on cue, he pivots. "Maybe we should just forget everything," he says suddenly, voice tight with urgency. "Maybe we should just... have kids. We were so fucking happy, Sophie. I love you." His voice cracks a little, but I can feel it—it's not clarity. It's panic. Desperation, not love.

And when that doesn't work—when I stay silent, stay still, don't give him what he wants—he flips.

The energy shifts. I feel it in my spine. He starts pacing, voice getting sharper. "I need to figure out how to tell our story," he mutters. "What this breakup sounds like. What's the version that makes sense?"

I blink. "What are you talking about? Who cares how it **sounds**? We broke up. That's it. This isn't a press release."

But to him, it is. It always has been.

A narrative to control. A version to spin.

And just like that, the story shifts again

—And I become the villain.

He sighs like a saint. "You know I told my friends about your trust issues already. And you do have some very uncommon traits," he says. "I really tried to accommodate them. I did my absolute best."

Then the final blow. "I spoke to my family too today," he says. "And they understood. They got the essence of your behavior immediately."

I narrow my eyes. "What does that even mean? What did you **say** to them?"

He shrugs, casually. "Oh... a lot of things. I don't even remember. But they saw it clearly. They get how you operate."

And just like that, the story was his again. Curated, self-serving, sealed tight.

The truth erased.

Me, rewritten.

But it didn't matter any longer.

Because he didn't own my reality anymore.

*

*Next day*

The day of my departure arrives—but not like I imagined.

My noon flight gets delayed to the evening, so I find myself lingering in the apartment longer than planned. Alone.

Adrian left this morning for work, as we'd agreed. Quietly. No goodbye. Just the soft thud of the front door and silence ever since.

I feel numb, almost robotic.

It takes all the energy I've got left to stay on course now.

*You can do it, Sophie.*

I move through the apartment slowly, almost ritualistically—folding the last of my clothes, wiping down the kitchen counter, taking one final look out the window at the Eiffel Tower framed in gray sky. The air feels too still and grief clings to everything like dust.

I pass our big mirror. And stop.

*Who is that?* **Me?**

I stare. Frozen.

A year and a half ago, I remember seeing my reflection before I walked on stage—stiff, composed, polished—right before I had a panic attack and quit my job.

Powerful Sophie. The one who stayed in control and never asked for too much. The one who didn't even allow herself to look for love.

Now I look... hollow. Disoriented. And then

—This expression on my face. **No.**

My breath catches.

*I look a bit like my mother.*

A wave of panic rushes through me.

*Did I become her?*

*Falling for the wrong man and losing myself, again and again.*

*Is this what it was like for her?*

My whole body starts to shake.

I drop to the floor, tears streaming down my face.

Then, after a couple of minutes, slowly—slowly—I get up again, weirdly composed now.

*No, Sophie. You're **not** her.*

You opened your heart. You took the risk. And when the truth became clear, ***you walked away***.

***You broke the pattern. You broke it.***

I settle down on the couch and rest.

Around noon, I suddenly hear the lock turn. My stomach twists.

When the door creaks open, I immediately sit straight up.

A woman steps in—dark coat, expressive brown eyes. Probably in her mid-twenties.

She looks startled, pauses in the entryway. "Hi," she says cautiously. "I'm April. Adrian's sister. Sophie, you're still here?"

I blink and nod. "Hi," I manage.

We've only seen each other once on a video call. She looks younger in person. Softer. Unsure.

"I'm visiting for a couple of days. I thought you were gone already," she says, stepping in. "I didn't mean to intrude. Sorry."

"My flight got delayed," I say quietly, still holding a pillow in my hand.

She hesitates for a beat, then walks over and pulls me into a hug. Tight. Warm. "I'm really sorry," she says, her voice low against my shoulder.

"For everything."

I close my eyes. Let myself feel it. "Thank you," I whisper.

*Don't cry again, Sophie.*

We pull apart, and I look into her friendly face. "You know what. I'm actually sad I won't be part of your family. Adrian always spoke so warmly about all of you."

Her brows lift.

A small, almost bitter smile.

"He did?"

I nod. "Said you were close. Loving. Like a real team."

She exhales, stepping back a little, folding her arms. "Interesting that he sees it that way."

"Why?" I ask.

She looks away for a moment, then back at me.

Her voice is steady now, but something flickers behind her eyes—anger, maybe. Or pain.

Or both.

"Because our family... it may look perfect from the outside. But it's really not," she says. "Sure, we're close. But not in a healthy way. Like, not at all.

Everyone has their role. And Adrian's always been the one blamed for everything. The one who wasn't Perry. Never enough. He carried a lot."

I just stare at her, the truth settling slowly into my body like fog.

She takes my hands in hers. "I promise you—you're not missing out on anything, Sophie," she adds gently.

"Really. You're not."

She pauses a moment, then lets my hands go.

"But for what it's worth... I think he truly loved you.

I've never seen him like that before.

He was the happiest version of himself he's ever been."

Tears prick behind my eyes, but I don't let them fall.

I just nod.

"I'll let you finish packing, and I'll come back later." She gives me a faint smile, touches my arm once more, and then she leaves—quietly as she came.

After she's gone, I stand there for a long time, just watching the door.

Then, I pick up a piece of paper and write Adrian a goodbye message:

Adrian,

I believe you did the best you could. We both did.
It's all going to be alright, Adrian. I promise.
It'll just be a bit dark in the beginning.

Heart,
—Sophie

Hours later, I climb into my Uber, watching the city blur past the window—every café, every park, every crosswalk carrying some memory. The ride turns into a quiet, aching goodbye.

At the airport, I move like a ghost through the crowds, the noise and movement oddly soothing.

When I finally board and settle into my seat, I close my eyes. Sleep comes fast—a mercy.

And when I wake up, I'm already back in New York.

CHALLENGE 25

# Delicate Pink Blossoms, Bright Green Leaves

As I step off the plane in New York, everything feels strange. I move through the airport in a haze, like I've landed in a world that is no longer mine. ***My body's here, but my heart is still in Paris.***

My apartment is still rented out, but Eliyah's away for a month and left me his keys.

By the time I reach his place, I'm barely holding it together. The key turns in the lock, and when I step inside, relief floods me.

*I'm alone.*

*Safe.*

*The chaos is behind me.*

I look around.

Everything is tidy and quiet. Eliyah's even stocked the fridge and left folded towels by the bed.

I drop my bag and just stand there, overcome with gratitude. It's the first time in months I feel truly cared for.

But within minutes, the exhaustion hits—bone-deep and consuming. I sink into the bed and then, I sleep for days. My appetite vanishes. I drift through the apartment in a fog, untethered, like I'm watching my life from outside my body. Even breathing feels like an effort.

My heart's broken, yes—but it's more than that.

I feel wrecked. Dizzy. Disconnected. Constantly spiraling, constantly questioning what was real and what wasn't, trying to make sense of what happened to find peace.

Michelle checks in by phone. "You're in post-traumatic stress," she says gently. "Your nervous system has been overwhelmed. Gaslighting, emotional chaos, too many contradictions at once

—eventually your body shuts down to protect you. Do you have people to talk to?"

"Yes. My friends Rani and Eliyah check in regularly, and I love them for it—but I can tell they don't fully get it."

"That's common," Michelle says gently. "As sad as it is, you can't always count on the people around you to understand what you're going through. Some people just haven't been there yet. Others can't handle how dark some relationships really get. And some are stuck in their own difficult situations and don't want to admit it—so they pull away.

Either way, they might be trying their best and still not be able to show up for you the way you need right now."

It's true. Rani and Eliyah think I'm grieving a heartbreak—a lost future. But it's so much more than that.

I'm grieving someone who may have never even existed.

The person I loved most in this world.

The one I could finally imagine building a family with.

The man who made me feel more alive, more myself, than anyone ever had.

That man disappeared in Paris.

And what was left... was a stranger.

It's a kind of heartbreak that's impossible to explain —like losing someone who died, only to realize they were never really alive to begin with.

*

There's one final step I know I have to take.

I know Adrian might try to come back someday and catch me in a moment of weakness. So I write myself a letter—a quiet reminder for the days I'll miss him, and the nights I'll forget why I left.

Then I open our chat.

**Me:** I'm blocking you now, Adrian. That's the only way forward for me. I wish you all the best

He's coming online.

Two blue hooks—that means he's seen it.

My pulse starts to race.

He's typing.

I block him—before the reply even lands.

*That's it.*

*You chose closure over emotional roulette.*

*You can be proud of yourself, Sophie.*

My heart aches. But I know I did the right thing.

I take a deep breath and text Michelle.

**Me:** Hi Michelle, this is my last message I think... It might sound naive, but... do you think he ever really loved me?

**Michelle:** Maybe he did. In the only way he could. If he truly is a narcissist, he can't stay connected to love without distortion.

**Michelle:** Maybe he loved what you gave him. Or how loving you made him feel.

**Michelle:** But Sophie, he can't love you as you are. Not fully. Not when he can't even accept the flawed parts of himself. If you are in a relationship with a narcissist, you need to shrink emotionally in order for peace to exist.

**Michelle:** So maybe the better question isn't whether he loved you. It's: How do you want to be loved?

**Michelle:** Do you want to be loved wholly? Messily, imperfectly, but truly —by someone who stays when it's hard, sees all of you, and chooses you still, not despite but because of it?

**Michelle:** Because that kind of love exists. You just have to leave the wrong kind behind to find it.

*

*Two weeks later*

Where are my earrings?

I rummage through my bags, distracted—until my fingers brush something familiar. There it is. The little paper flower Rhea made for me before my trip to Paris.

Delicate pink blossoms. Bright green leaves.

Still perfect and unchanged.

I hold it in my palm, remembering why I love them so much.

*Paper flowers stay beautiful.*

*They don't wilt.*

*And they never leave.*

*Just like you didn't, Sophie,* I think.

*You made it.*

You didn't disappear.

You're still here. You stayed true to yourself.

And then, a wave moves through me. Landing deep and sudden.

***I'm still me. I'm still Sophie.***

I didn't lose myself.

I didn't abandon myself.
I was just out of sight for a while.

I start to cry.

Soft, steady tears spill down my cheeks. Warm and slow. Then, land on the little paper flower in my hand.

My chest expands—slowly, calmly.

***Breathe in.***
***Breathe out.***

And in that quiet, something opens.

There's space again.
To create. To be. To thrive.
And it belongs to no one but me.

I stretch my arms up toward the ceiling. Then I do a full-body shake to get rid of all the tension, emotion and sadness.

I wipe the tears away, grab my phone, scroll to Rani's name, and hit call.

"Hey. I was thinking of you two," I say. "I'm holding Rhea's tiny goodbye flower in my hand right now."

"Oh wow," Rani says. "She's never stopped making those since you showed her how, you know. One whole corner of her room is overflowing. What's the plan—any idea what to do with them?"

I smile, the warmth rising in my chest. "Actually, yes. Can I borrow Rhea for the afternoon? You too, if you want."

"Sure," she says. "We were going for a walk anyway."

I head over right away—fast, light. My body starts feeling like mine again.

We pack all the flowers into the car. "Okay, Rhea," I say. "Want to play a game?"

She nods, curls bouncing.

"You know how my job was to help people feel less alone?"

She nods again, eyes wide.

"Well, once I created a day where we gave small gifts to strangers who looked a little sad or lonely, without telling them why. Just to be kind. To make them smile. Want to try that?"

"Yes!" she squeals.

And so we do.

We walk around the city, handing out tiny paper blossoms to strangers. All of them smile, and some of them even start crying.

And somewhere in the middle of it all, I remember who I am.

Who I still want to be.

Someone who brings light.

26

# Just Me

*Nine months later*

I stand in front of the mirror, and what I see is me. Finally.

No forced power-boss.

No heartbroken wreck.

**Just me.**

I'm back on track. Maybe more than ever.

I'm leading a research project now, helping singles navigate modern dating through behavioral design. When I pitched the idea to Aiysha—who runs a cutting-edge research institute—she didn't even blink.

"This is exactly the kind of work the world needs," she said. "And with your background and personal connection to the topic, you're the perfect person to lead it."

My mood lights? Flying off the shelves.

A huge investor backed me 100 percent, and I hired someone to run operations so I could focus on new things.

And in those first months—when I wasn't ready to be fully in the world—I sat down and wrote it all down: the pain, the love, the unraveling. *Love, Sex & the Narcissist.*

I didn't expect much. I just needed to make sense of it.

But then, the book exploded. Readers saw themselves in it. They went on the journey with me.

And just like that, the thing that almost broke me became the very thing that connected me—deeply—to others.

To readers who'd known that kind of heartbreak.

Who'd had to be brave like me.

Who'd fought to find their way back to themselves.

Maybe this wasn't just a story about Adrian and me.

Maybe it was about falling in love—with a new path, a new purpose, and people across the world who shared pieces of the same pain.

Right around the time the first royalty check landed, I met someone new. He was sweet. Funny. Smart. The chemistry? Undeniable.

And this time, my gut and my mind agree: he's different. Still, I'm in no rush. I stay grounded, present. I watch and listen. I know now—complete trust in others is a fantasy. And trusting my gut when I'm in doubt isn't paranoid. It's wise.

I won't listen to other people's voices over mine anymore. My well-being is my own responsibility. It's not anyone else's job to steer my relationship or protect my peace. That's on me.

We've been sold fairytales—rom-coms, perfect weddings, kids on cue. But look around: most people I know are overwhelmed, stretched thin, or quietly lonely inside their partnerships.

True connection—the kind that's real, raw, nourishing—is the exception, not the rule. And even when it looks perfect, it often isn't.

I finally get it now:

I don't need the guy to be perfect on paper.

I don't need to be perfect either.

I need someone who sees me and stays.

And when I don't have that, I damn well better be that person for myself.

How do I remember Adrian?

It took months to unpack the anger, the grief, the unraveling. But now, I feel gratitude.

Yes, I still long for a family. Yes, time is moving forward. But no—I don't regret a thing.

Why? Because I made conscious choices at every step of the way. And I own them.

I **chose** to love boldly.

To explore freedom.

To picture what a family could look like.

To soak up laughter, sex, play, and adventure.

Even if some of it turned out to be an illusion, even if it broke me, at that time, it was real to me. It mattered.

And I figured, in the end, the most important question is:

**Do we value ourselves enough to leave what hurts us?**

Because nothing is more soul-crushing than betraying ourselves. If we ignore our own needs and who we truly are, others will too.

Life is way too short to shrink.

To self-abandon.

To dim our light to make someone else feel bigger.

Yes, there will be pain.

Yes, there will be hard choices.

But if we stay true to our values, our gut—we can build something real.

And being single a bit longer?

Changing our plans?

That's not failure.

That's wisdom.

Do you remember the number one regret of the dying?

> "I wish I had lived a life being true to myself—not the life others expected of me."

Just think about it: How heartbreaking would it be to disappear from your own life?

Please don't do that. You'd be missed.

So.

**What's your choice?**

Printed in Dunstable, United Kingdom

80002261R00211